MUSIC:

A Comprehensive Introduction

Steven Porter, Ph.D.

Dir. of Music, City Schools of Binghamton, N.Y.

A Complete Music Appreciation Course

MUSIC:
A COMPREHENSIVE INTRODUCTION
by Steven Porter

Library of Congress Cataloguing-in-Publication Data
Porter, Steven, 1943-
    Music: a Comprehensive Introduction
    Includes index.
    1. Music appreciation. I. Title.
MT6.P843M9 1986   780   85-16847
ISBN 0-935016-81-3

First Edition

Cover Design and Illustrations by:

Lucille Baron

Typesetting, music engraving and layouts by:
Excelsior Typographers and Engravers, Unltd.
(Division of Excelsior Music Publishing Co.)

Published by:
Excelsior Music Publishing Co.
15 West 44th St., New York, N.Y. 10036

Distributed to the book trade by:
Scientific and Technical Book Service, Ltd.
50 West 23rd St., New York, N.Y. 10010

Distributed to the music trade by:
Theodore Presser Co., Bryn Mawr, Pa. 19010

This book is dedicated to

my Mother and Father

who first introduced me

to the world of music.

CONTENTS

PART I
The Fundamentals of Sound

PART II
The Fundamentals of Music

PART III
Listening and History

PREFACE

This book is designed to address most if not all the questions a beginning student might have about music. It is organized in five parts.

Part I deals with music as a sound, as a topic in the larger world of the science of acoustics.

Part II discusses the fundamentals of music as a craft. It introduces the basics of musical notation and describes how music is built from its components of melody, rhythm, harmony, and counterpoint.

Part III deals with music as an art. It provides a technique for listening with greater enjoyment, and it traces the history of music from the earliest primitive cultures of man to the present day.

Part IV provides an opportunity to make music. It introduces the five instrumental families - string, wind, percussion, keyboard, voice - and then gives the rudiments of performance for guitar, recorder (tonette), drums, piano, and singing.

Finally, Part V discusses the uses of music in modern society. It describes the many careers which require a knowledge of music and the many ways music interacts with contemporary life.

The order in which the material is presented is important since an understanding of Parts III, IV, and V depends on an understanding of Parts I and II. However, the amount of time spent on each part is really up to the reader. If one wishes to devote the majority of his time to listening, he can de-emphasize Parts I, II, IV, and V and concentrate on Part III. If one wishes to do more performing, he may spend most of his time with Part IV. It all depends on the individual (or his teacher if he is using this book in a classroom situation).

Whatever approach is taken, the writing style of the book is informal and designed to help the reader through a personal excursion of one of mankind's most enduring creations. It is my hope that this book enriches the reader's life and provides the basis for many days and years of fulfillment.

Steven Porter

VI

PART I

THE FUNDAMENTALS OF SOUND

CHAPTER ONE

MUSIC AS A SOUND

What Is a Sound?

Sound can be understood as the interaction of four things: energy, an object to which the energy is applied, an environment, and a receiver. The energy activates an object causing it to vibrate. The vibrations are conducted through an environment until they are collected and interpreted by a receiver of some kind.

Ingredient	Interaction
Energy	Activates an object
Object	Vibrates in an environment
Environment	Conducts vibrations to a receiver
Receiver	Collects and interprets vibrations

Let's consider a simple example: a teacher talking to you in a classroom. The energy is the muscle and breath power which the teacher uses to speak; the vibrating object is the teacher's vocal chords; the environment is the air in the classroom; and you - your hearing mechanism and brain - are the receiver.

The teacher begins to talk, breathes and applies muscle and air pressure to the vocal chords of the throat. The vocal chords vibrate sending the vibrations through the teacher's mouth where they are shaped by the teacher's lips and tongue. They continue to travel on into the air of the classroom until they reach you. Your outer ear collects them and channels them through your hearing system and into your brain where finally they are interpreted as recognizable sounds.

Ingredient	Interaction
Air and muscle power	Cause vocal chords to vibrate
Vocal chords	Vibrate causing air to vibrate
Air	Transports vibrations to ear/brain mechanism
Ear/brain	Collects and interprets vibrations

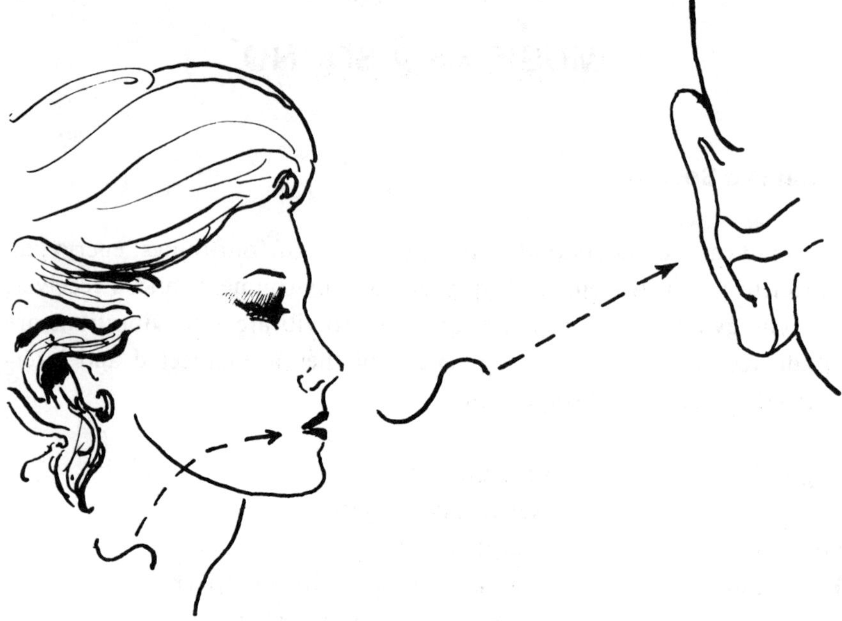

This is a rather simple illustration. Things can get much more complex. Take listening to a news broadcast on your car radio, for example. Here the sound begins in the broadcast studio. The broadcaster applies energy to his or her vocal chords which in turn vibrate causing the vibrations to travel into the air of the studio. But once there they cannot go directly to you. Rather they are collected by a microphone which is but the first part of a complex electrical system. This system converts the vibrations to electronic impulses and beams them out to the environment of the earth's atmosphere. They then travel at incredible speeds to the antenna of your car which is but the first part of a complex receiving system. This system gradually reconverts the impulses to vibrations which travel through your radio speakers into the air inside your car. The air conducts the vibrations to your ear and brain, and once again you recognize them as sounds.

Things can get even more complex than this: transmissions from astronauts in outer space, for example, which you hear - and see - on your television sets. But no matter how complicated things get, they must always involve at least one source of energy, one vibrating object, one environment, and one receiver. For our purposes here, that's all we really need to know.

What should happen if any of our four ingredients is missing or malfunctioning? We would not have a sound. If there were no energy or the energy were not applied, it would be as silent as a piano with no one to play it. If there were energy but nothing to vibrate, again there would be no sound. It would be as if the pianist were to move his fingers through the air instead of onto the keys. If there were no environment, there would be nothing to carry the vibrations to where they could be heard. Outer space provides this condition. A piano struck on the surface of the moon would seem silent to an onlooker because the atmosphere of the moon is practically a vacuum, incapable of transporting the vibrations of the piano strings to anyone who might happen to be there. Finally, if energy did activate an object in an environment capable of conducting the vibrations and there was no receiver - no person, no animal, no microphone - then all you would have would be vibrations. In the living world of human beings, vibrations aren't sounds until they are collected and interpreted by our senses or by machines which take the place of our senses.

A Closer Look at the Ingredients of Sound.

Energy. Sounds can have many sources of energy, anything from human power to electric power to the wind rustling the leaves of a tree. When energy is applied to an object, the object begins its vibrations in the direction from which the energy has come.

Object. Objects vibrate better when they are fixed in place at one or both ends. Before energy is applied to them, they are said to be at rest or in a state of equilibrium. After the energy is applied, they will vibrate until the energy is expended and they once more return to a condition of equilibrium.

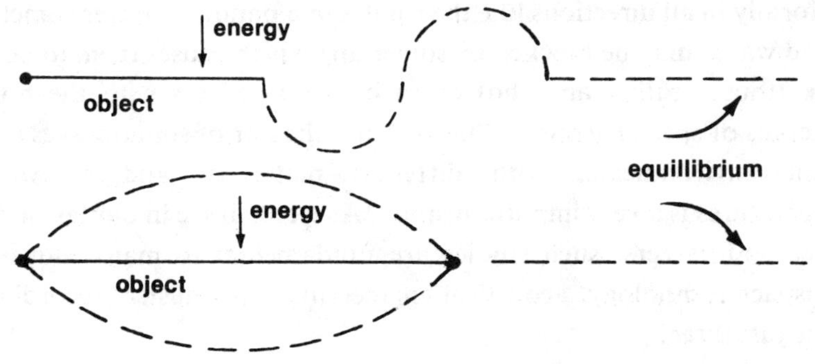

Environment. Environments are really collections of molecules which become displaced when an object moves through them. Just as a still pond develops ripples when a stone is thrown into it, an environment builds up waves of molecules as an object within it starts to vibrate. The peaks of these pressure waves are called areas of condensation; the valleys, areas of rarifaction.

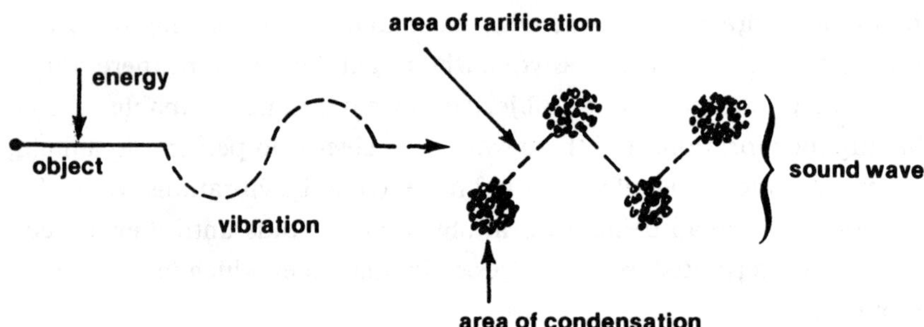

Sound waves ripple through the air at approximately 1,100 feet per second (750 miles per hour). However, the denser the air (that is, the more molecules per unit of air), the faster the sound will travel. Because air is denser at sea level than at high altitudes, sound will travel faster at sea level. In fact, the denser any environment, the better it will conduct sound. For example, sound travels faster in water than air; faster in metal than water; and as we have noted, because a vacuum has no molecules at all, sound can't travel at all in the environment of interplanetary space.

When a vibrating object creates a sound wave, the wave will travel uniformly in all directions like the ripples in a pond. However sometimes sound waves may be blocked by something which causes them to bounce back (thus creating an echo) or to be absorbed (as with the porous materials of special acoustical tiles). The behavior of sound waves in different environments, with different materials, and at varying temperatures is a very important study. As we shall see in our last unit on music and careers, such studies are fundamental to many industries: aerospace technology, acoustical engineering, and musical recording to name just three.

Receiver. Whatever microphones or other mechanical equipment intervene between us and the source of the sounds we hear, our primary receptor is our ear/brain system. Very simply stated, our outer and middle ear structures collect vibrations from the air and channel them through the ear drum (tympanum) and a network of bones (the hammer, anvil, and stirrup bones) to hairs (cilia) located in a fluid-filled chamber of the inner ear (the cochlea). As these hair fibers vibrate, they create electrical impulses which are routed through the auditory nerves to the cerebral cortex of the brain. There, in a process we do not yet fully understand, the impulses are interpreted as sounds with many definite characteristics.

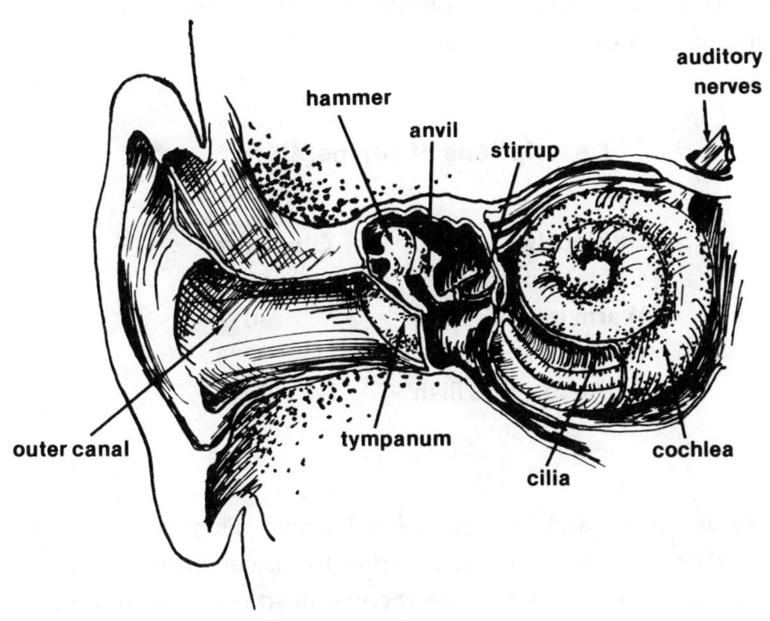

The most important characteristics of sound which our brain distinguishes are volume, pitch, and quality. By volume we mean how loud or soft a sound is. By pitch we mean how high or low it is. By quality we mean its general nature or origin. Is it a musical sound or a non-musical one (a flute or a freight train)? Was it made by a living thing or an object (a voice or a passing car)?

Our brains can distinguish the special characteristics of sounds because of the way in which those characteristics are created. To understand how our brains do this, we need to take a closer look at the different characteristics of volume, pitch, and quality.

Volume, Pitch and Quality.

Before we look closer at the three most dominant characteristics of a sound, we need to say a word about the way human beings describe the characteristics of anything. We tend to talk in two descriptive ways: subjective and objective. Subjective descriptions usually show how we feel about things. Objective descriptions usually show how we measure them regardless of personal reaction. Consider the following table which deals not with sound but with temperature.

Descriptions of Temperature

Subjective	Objective
Cold to an Eskimo	-60° F
Warm to an Eskimo	30° F
Cold to a Brazilian	30° F
Warm to a Brazilian	100° F

The words "cold" and "warm" are subjective. They mean different things to different people. They are relative to the conditions and expectations of those who use them. The thermal degrees we use to describe temperature have an unchanging meaning to us. "30° F" is the same in Alaska as it is in Brazil. Whichever place experiences that temperature, the measurement "30° F" will describe it accurately.

In the world of sound we also have two descriptive languages. Subjective characteristics are called "psychoacoustical properties." Objective characteristics are called "physical properties." The terms "volume, pitch, and quality" are all psychoacoustical. In the ensuing pages we will describe what they stand for in terms of physical measurement. The table below provides a beginning.

Properties of Sound

Psychoacoustical   **Physical**

Psychoacoustical	Physical
Volume	Amplitude of vibration
Pitch	Frequency of vibration
Quality	Overtone production

Amplitude. Amplitude is a measure of the arc of vibration from the plane of equilibrium.

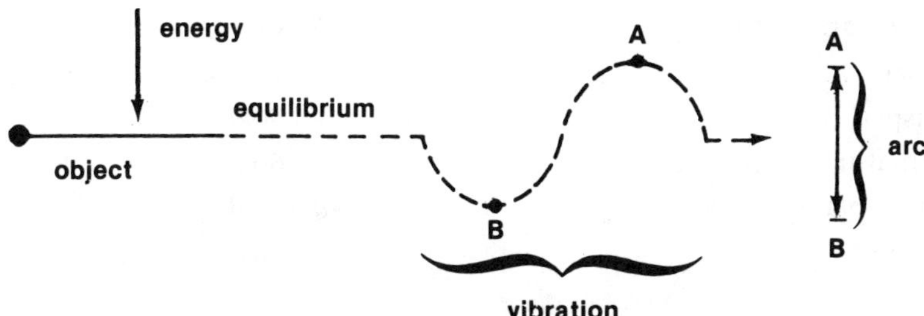

Using the illustration above, the distance from point A to point B is the arc of the vibrating object. The greater the amount of energy applied to the object, the greater its arc will be. The greater the arc, the more intense the pressure wave. The more intense the wave, the louder the music.

Large wave - small wave.

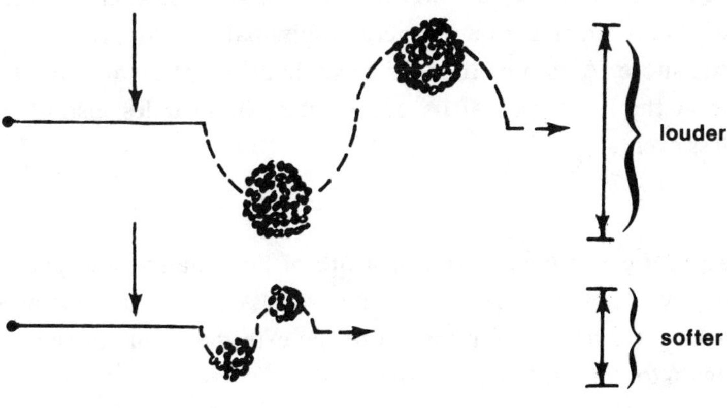

Amplitude is measured in units called bels and decibels (1/10 of a bel). It is important to understand when using these measurements that they represent geometric relationships, not arithmetic ones. In other words, 2 bels is not twice as loud as 1 bel; it is ten times as loud. Three bels is 100 times as loud as 1 bel; 4 bels, 1000 times as loud; and so on. The table below will give you a psychoacoustical and physical reference for the loudness/amplitude dimension of a sound.

Loudness/Amplitude

Psychoacoustical	Physical	
Silence	0 db	(decibels)
Whispering at 3 feet	30 db	
Normal speaking voice	60 db	
Loudly playing orchestra	90-100 db	
Threshold of pain	120-130 db	

It is also important to remember that sound is a product of energy and amplitude a measure of that energy. If the amplitude is great enough, the sound can have destructive power. Just as waves on a beach become more dangerous the larger they get, sound waves also become dangerous when they pass the 130 db level. At that level and beyond, sounds can cause deafness, break objects, and render great harm.

The further one is from the source of the sound, the less the energy is felt. Again, the destructive power of a wave is greatest where it swells and crashes. Many yards distant its energy is dissipated, and it rolls harmlessly to the shore. A clap of thunder or sonic boom of an airplane is most intense at the local spot of its occurrence. Many miles distant, it is a harmless event.

Frequency. Frequency is a measure of how many times per second an object vibrates through a complete cycle. A cycle is defined as a motion from the plane of equilibrium to the extreme points of the arc and back again to the equilibrium plane.

The greater the frequency - that is, the more cycles per second the object vibrates - the higher the pitch.

Frequency is measured either in Hertz units (Hz) or simply in "cycles per second" (cps) - they mean the same thing. As a general rule, human beings can distinguish sounds as low as 16 Hz and as high as 16,000 Hz, though there are other members of the animal kingdom who outstrip us neatly. Dogs, for example, can detect sounds vibrating at frequencies well beyond 16,000 Hz. Below is a pitch/frequency reference table.

Pitch/Frequency

Psychoacoustical	Physical
Range of a piano	about 25-3200 Hz
Woman's singing range	about 220-880 Hz
Man's singing range	about 110-300 Hz
Tuning note of an orchestra	440 Hz
Human hearing range	about 16-16,000 Hz

Overtones. As it turns out, when an object vibrates, it does so both as a whole and in sections. How can an object move in two ways at once? It is very common. Consider the earth which rotates on an axis as it revolves around the sun; or a runner who pumps his arms like a piston as he accelerates his legs around a track.

We already know that vibrations produce sounds, so by deduction we reason that an object vibrating in more than one way produces more than one sound. The sound produced by the vibration of the whole object is called the fundamental sound. Each sound produced by the vibration of part of the object is called a partial or overtone. The diagram below will help to illustrate:

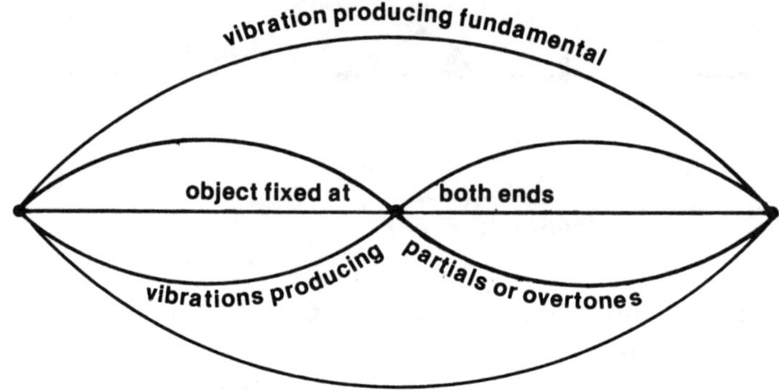

On this diagram, the black dots occurring where the vibrations seem to touch the object are called nodes. In a musical sound, the nodes occur at exact fraction points of the object: the 1/2, 1/3, 1/4 points etc. This means that the frequencies of musical overtones are exact multiples of the fundamental: twice as much, three times as much, four times as much etc. (see below).

Musical overtones.

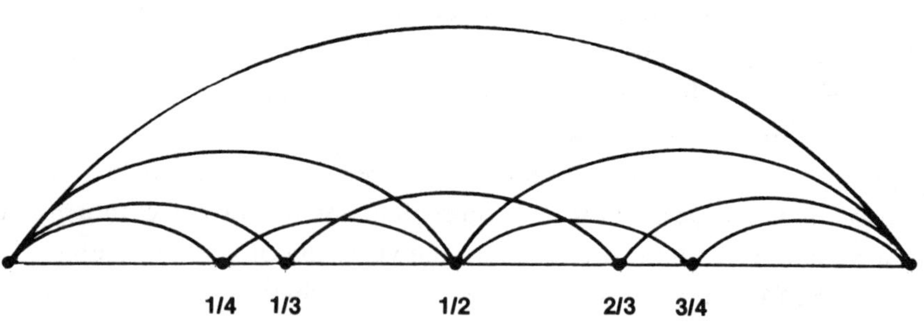

Non-musical sounds produce overtones which are not exact frequency multiples of the fundamental. Their nodes do not occur at the exact fraction points of the object (see below).

Non-musical overtones.

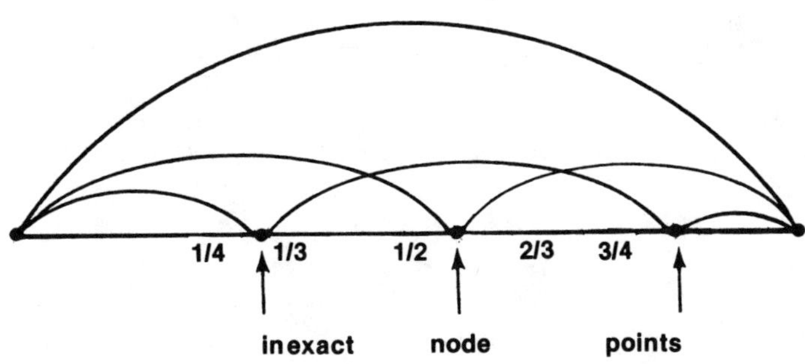

Musical overtones are higher and softer than their fundamentals because their frequencies are greater and their amplitudes are less.

What causes the difference between one set of overtones and another is the difference in the size, shape, and materials of one object from the size, shape, and materials of another object. A violin is quite different from a freight train. It is considerably smaller in size, not at all the same shape, and made of completely different materials. For these reasons, violins and freight trains produce different ovetones. This difference between the overtones is perceived by the human brain as a difference in the quality of the sound.

A musical sound produces a whole pattern of overtones known as the overtone series. Below is an example of the overtone series produced by the note "C" vibrating at 65 Hz. (For the purpose of reading the overtone series below, you should know that musical tones are notated on a staff of lines and named for the letters A, B, C, D, E, F, and G of the alphabet.)

Overtone series.

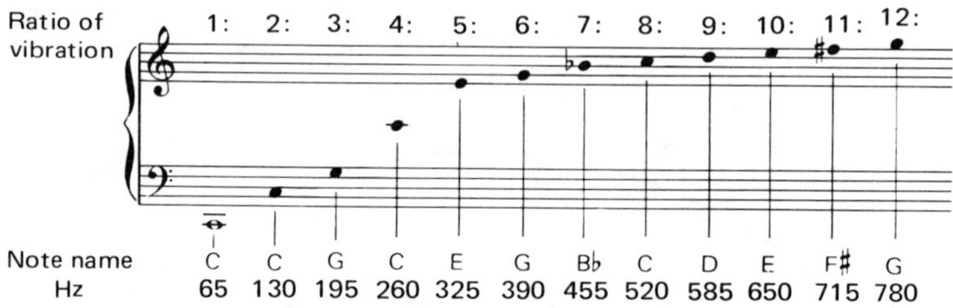

What this chart means is that a piano string (or any object producing musical overtones) which vibrates at 65 Hz will produce the fundamental C. The vibration of half the string will produce the C at 130 Hz. The vibration of one-third of the string will produce G (195 Hz); one-fourth, C (260 Hz); one-fifth, E (325 Hz); and so on up to the twelfth note in the series.

Human beings can't hear each separate overtone, just as when we blend two colors (say yellow and blue to make green) we can't see the component colors. We see only the result of our blending, and in sounds we hear only the composite effect of the fundamental and its overtones. But the overtones are there, and to the extent the overtones of one series differ in strength and number from the overtones of another series, the quality of the sounds involved will be different.

Our violin and freight train produce radically different overtone series because they are radically different in size, shape, and materials. But a violin and a bass fiddle are not so different. They will sound much more alike because they are similar in size, shape, and materials and thus produce overtones of similar strength and numbers. They will not be exact because violins and basses are not exact physical matches, but they will be much more like each other than unlike each other in quality.

Intervals and Tuning.

Intervals. An interval is the distance between any two pitches. Intervals are calculated by the ratio between their frequencies and named according to the number of letters of the musical alphabet they employ. Using the overtone chart above, take the distance between C-65 Hz and C-130 Hz. This interval is called an octave. It requires using up eight letters of the alphabet (CDEFGABC) in naming its pitches, and its pitches vibrate in the ratio of 1:2 (65 Hz:130 Hz).

In the next part of this text, we will deal again with intervals in some detail. For now, it is necessary only to consider a few intervals: octaves, fifths, thirds, and seconds.

We have already defined an octave - an interval using eight letters in its spelling whose members vibrate in the ratio 1:2. Let's consider the others. The distance from the 2nd note in our series (C-130 Hz) to the 3rd note (G-195 Hz) is a fifth. It uses up five letters in the naming (CDEFG), and its members vibrate in the ratio 2:3 (130 Hz:195 Hz). The distance from the 4th note of the series (C-260 Hz) to the 5th note (E-325 Hz) is a third. It uses up three letters in the naming (CDE), and its members vibrate in the ratio 4:5. The definition of these intervals is condensed in the table below.

Basic Intervals

Name of interval	Number of letters required in naming	Frequency ratio
octave	8	1:2
fifth	5	2:3
third	3	4:5

Any two pitches using 8 letters in their spelling and vibrating in the ratio of 1:2 is an octave. *Any* two pitches using 5 letters in their spelling while vibrating in a 2:3 ratio is a fifth. For example, the distance between G-390 Hz and D-585 Hz is a fifth. The frequency ratio (390:585) can be reduced to 2:3, and five letters (GABCD) must be used up in naming its pitches. The overtone series below is marked to show the octaves, fifths, and thirds.

Intervals.

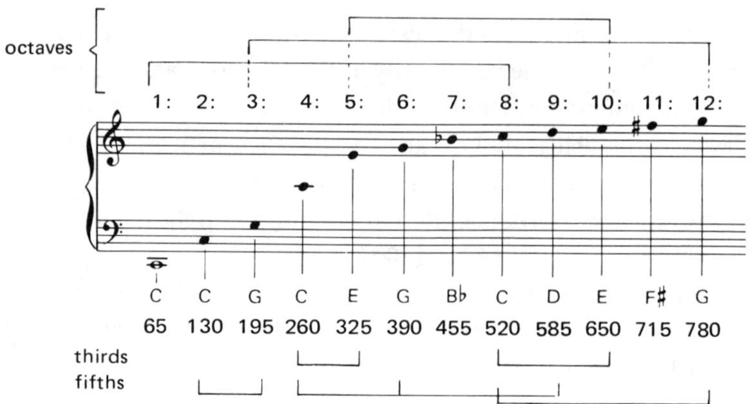

Tuning. Defining octaves and fifths is relatively easy. Defining seconds is not as easy. That is because nature has thrown us something of a curve. There is more than one way to calculate the interval of a second, and that presents some pretty monumental problems.

A second is an interval which uses up two letters of the musical alphabet in its spelling (for example, C to D or D to E), but it is impossible to say exactly what its ratio of vibration is. In our overtone series above, the second C-D has a ratio of 8:9 while the second D-E has a ratio of 9:10. To make matters worse, it is possible to calculate any second so that it comes out either 8:9 or 9:10 - and is correct in both cases.

Consider what that would mean if it were to apply to intervals of physical rather than musical distance. You have two points, X and Y, and you wish to know how far apart they are. You measure the distance with a ruler - a perfectly accurate ruler - and you get 12 inches. You measure again with another perfectly accurate ruler and you get 13 inches. Which is correct, and how would you know, and if you could not determine which was correct, how could you ever measure anything? How could you ever draw a diagram, or build a house, or even space the lines of a football field?

Well, that is the dilemma of the interval of a second, and if you are wondering how it can be, consider the example below. Let us calculate the distance from C to D using our knowledge of octaves, fifths, and thirds. To do this, we must use the simple fractions which represent the measurements we need. The table below provides them.

Interval Calculations

Upward	Downward
8 ↑ = 2/1	8 ↓ = 1/2
5 ↑ = 3/2	5 ↓ = 2/3
3 ↑ = 5/4	3 ↓ = 4/5

Briefly, what this table means is that if we wish to know the frequency of the note one octave above "X", we multiply "X" by 2/1. The frequency of the note an octave below "X" is "X" multiplied by 1/2. A fifth above "X" is "X" multiplied by 3/2, and so on.

In the case of the interval C to D, two possible measurements can be taken. In the first we go from C up two octaves, up another third, down a fifth, down another fifth, then down an octave. (See below).

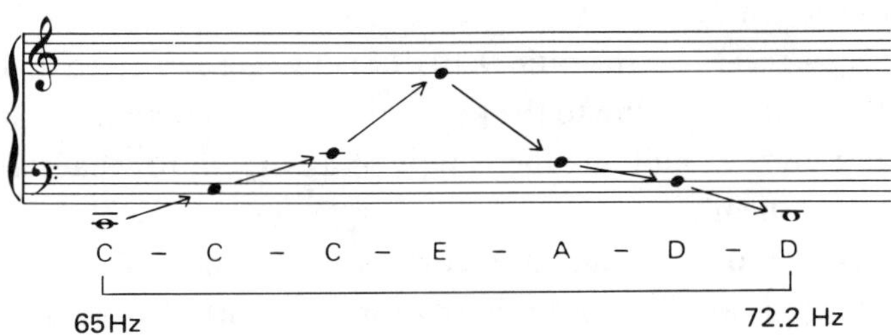

Using this means of going from C (65 Hz) to D, we calculate the frequency of D by multiplying 65 Hz by 2/1, 2/1, 5/4, 2/3, 2/3, and 1/2 successively.

$$65/1 \times 2/1 \times 2/1 \times 5/4 \times 2/3 \times 2/3 \times 1/2 \; =$$

$$65/1 \times 80/72 = 65/1 \times 10/9 = 72.2 \text{ Hz}$$

In this calculation the interval of a second from C to D is figured as the ratio 9:10. If C = 65 Hz, then D must be 72.2 Hz.

Now consider taking another route from C (65 Hz) to D. Suppose in another calculation we go from C up two fifths, then down an octave. (See below).

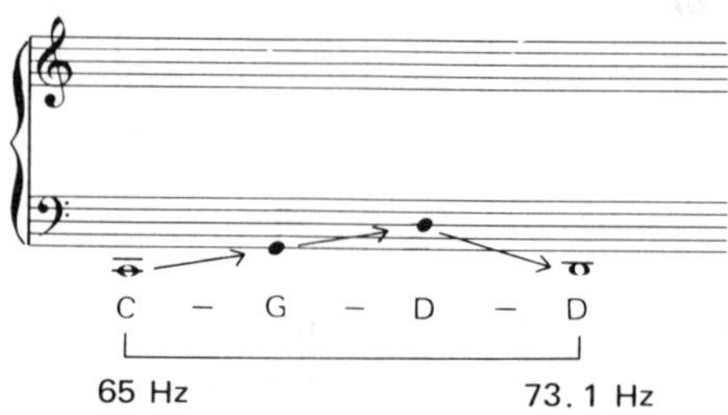

Here we calculate the frequency of D by multiplying C (65 Hz) by 3/2, 3/2, and 1/2 successively.

$$65/1 \times 3/2 \times 3/2 \times 1/2 = 65/1 \times 9/8 = 73.1 \text{ Hz}$$

In this calculation, we determine the ratio from C to D as 8:9, and D has a frequency of 73.1 Hz.

Which is correct? Is it the ratio 9:10 or 8:9? Is D to be fixed at 72.2 Hz or 73.1 Hz? And even more to the point, if we were tuning the D string of a piano or guitar, or building the D pipe of an organ, to what frequency would we tune them?

The dilemma of calculating seconds is not the only one nature presents. There is an even more thorny problem with fifths and octaves. If you were to place your finger on the lowest note of a piano and count up seven octaves, then start on the same low note and count up twelve fifths, you'd get to the same upper note. On a piano, 7 octaves equals 12 fifths.

Mathematically that means $(2/1)^7$ (going up seven octaves) should equal $(3/2)^{12}$ (going up twelve fifths). Unfortunately, the math doesn't work out.

$$(2/1)^7 = 128 \quad \text{and} \quad (3/2)^{12} = 129 \ 3057/4096$$

If the lowest note on which you start has a frequency of 1 Hz, the upper note could be tuned to either 128 Hz or 129.75 Hz. Again, which is correct?

People have been wrestling with these problems since the days of Ancient Greece when the philosopher Pythagoras expressed them in mathematical terms. At various times they adopted different solutions, but none was really workable. If octaves and fifths were tuned to mathematical perfection, thirds and seconds sounded out of tune. If thirds and seconds were tuned to perfection, octaves and fifths sounded wrong. Finally, in the early 1700's a workable solution was reached.

The octave would remain in the perfect mathematical ratio of 1:2. Moreover, it would be divided into twelve absolutely equal intervals called "half steps" or "semitones" (just as a foot is divided into twelve equal inches). Each half step would be calculated using the figure $\sqrt[12]{2}$, an expression which when multiplyed by itself twelve times yields the number 2. ($\sqrt[12]{2}$, is approximately 1.05946).

The system was called "equal temperament" or "equal tuning," and it has been in use since its inception. With equal temperament, fifths are not quite the 2:3 ratio Mother Nature provides; thirds not quite 4:5. But the adjustments are slight, and we can't really notice them. It is as if we have all squeezed into a shoe size just a little smaller than perfect. The misfit is not enough to hurt us, and over the years, our feet get used to it.

Sound as an Event.

When a musical tone is produced, the human ear and brain perceive its pitch, volume, and quality, but actually, more is happening that we don't hear. If we could listen to a sound "in slow motion," so to speak, we would find that it has quite a complex life.

To begin with, most musical sounds do not start at their perceived level. Rather, they swoop up to that level from lower amplitudes and frequencies. This phenomenon is called the "initial attack" of a sound.

Initial attacks often shoot past the desired levels in a kind of over-enthusiastic burst of energy. The sound must then drop slightly to the desired level. This drop is called the "initial decay."

The sound, now holding where it is supposed to be, is sustained for however long it is supposed to last. This phase is known as its "steady state."

Finally, in returning to silence, the sound does not abruptly drop to zero amplitude and zero frequency. Rather it decays slowly like a watch gradually running down. This is known as its "final decay."

The life of a sound from initial attack to final decay - including all its overtones which have attacks and decays of their own - is called the "sound envelope." The illustration below provides a visualization of an envelope.

Sound envelope.

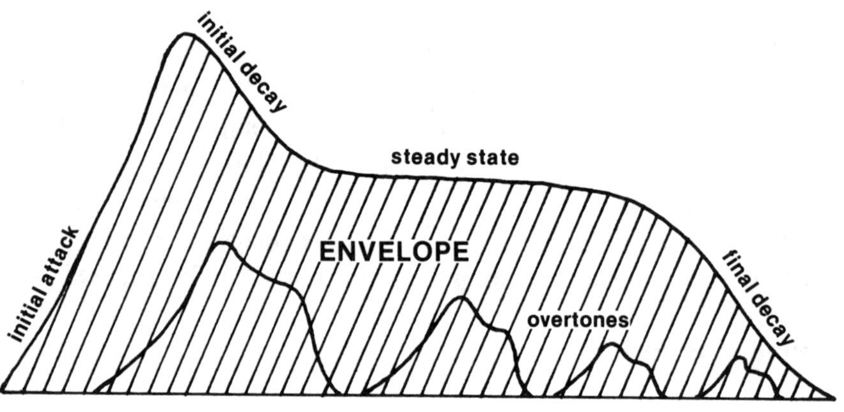

Modern electronic sound synthesizers can control many of the characteristics of the envelope. They can eliminate all the overtones, for example, creating a sound whose visual picture looks like the sine wave of a trigonometry problem. They can eliminate certain overtones creating "sawtooth," "square," or "triangle" waves. They can shorten or lengthen attack times and decay times. They can bounce sound waves off objects to create echoes or allow sounds to continue after their energy sources have ceased (reverberation). They can add non-musical overtones to a sound, alter its volume, reduce it to utter silence. Synthesizers can even feed sounds into a computer so that they are manipulated at incredible speeds with incredible effects.

The science of sound (acoustics) is behind many facets of modern engineering, recording, communications, even medicine. But for now, you need understand only the basic characteristics of sound in general and musical sound in particular. With that knowledge, you are ready to see how musical sounds are put together to create music itself.

Further Reading.

1. Articles on "Acoustics," "Tuning," and "Intervals" in the **Harvard Dictionary of Music,** 2nd ed. Willi Apel, ed. (Cambridge, Mass.: Belknap, 1973).

2. Article on "Acoustics" in **Grove's Dictionary of Music and Musicians,** 5th ed. Eric Blom, ed. (New York: St. Martin's Press, 1970).

3. **Acoustics.** Alexander Wood (New York: Dover, 1966).

4. **Music, Sound, and Sensation.** Fritz Winckel (New York: Dover, 1967).

5. **Science and Music.** Sir James Jeans (New York: Dover, 1968).

6. **Sound and Hearing.** Charles Gramet (London: Abelard-Schuman, 1965).

PART II

THE FUNDAMENTALS OF MUSIC

CHAPTER TWO:

NOTATING AND READING MUSIC

Naming the Notes.

We have already learned that musical pitches, or notes as they are called, are named for the letters ABCDEF and G of the alphabet. Actually, the letter is only one part of a note's name. The other part is known as the "accidental" label.

An accidental is a symbol which is applied to a letter to help identify a musical note more precisely, just as we have a last name (or family name) applied to our first name to identify us more precisely. The musical accidentals and their symbols are written below.

Accidentals

Name	Symbol
Sharp	♯
Double sharp	𝄪
Flat	♭
Double flat	♭♭
Natural	♮

There are seven possible letter names and five possible accidental labels per letter, making 35 (7 x 5) possible note names in all (A♯ , A𝄪 , A♭ , A♭♭, A♮ ; B♯ , B𝄪 , B♭ , B♭♭, etc.) Often, you may see a letter name without any accidental label attached to it (A or B etc.). This is simply a shorthand way of saying A♮ or B♮ . In music, no accidental label equals the accidental "natural" (♮).

At this point you may be wondering why, if there are only twelve possible pitches within any octave, there are thirty-five possible pitch names. That is because all pitches have more than one name, depending on how they function in the music. That is not such a strange concept.

We have many titles for people - beyond their given names - depending on how they function. This is especially true in naming royalty. "Elizabeth Tudor, Queen of England," is an example. Queen Elizabeth I was known not only by first name and family name but by title as well, a title which implied her function in the governmental structure of Britain.

The same pitch might be called D♯ or E♭ or F♭♭, depending on how it is used in the music. How this occurs will become clearer as we explore the principles of musical notation and music theory, so let us turn our attention to those subjects.

Writing the Notes.

The Staff. Pitches are notated by placing open or closed dots (noteheads) on a five-line arrangement called a staff (see below).

The modern staff took centuries to evolve, as we shall discover later in this text when we look at the history of music. Today it is universally used and accepted.

Clef Signs. Simply having five lines on which to place musical notes is not enough for effective notation. There must be something that lets the reader know the letter name for which each staff line and staff space stands. Fortunately, there is. It is called a "clef sign," and there are seven such signs, four of which are used commonly in modern notation (see below).

Treble clef places the note G on the second line of the staff by curling its "tail" around that line. For this reason, it is often called the "G clef." Moreover, the second-line G which the clef indicates is not any G.

It is the one which occurs just above the middle of a piano keyboard, the G which vibrates at 390 Hz. Once the clef fixes this G, all the other lines and spaces of the staff can be named. For every line or space one ascends, a letter is used going forward in the alphabet (G-A-B-C,etc.). For every line or space one descends, a letter is used going backward in the alphabet (G-F-E-D,etc.). (See below.)

Bass clef places the note F on the fourth line of the staff - the F just below the middle of the piano keyboard (the one which vibrates at about 167 Hz). In doing this, it gives a different letter pattern to the staff (see below).

Why would anyone want to use more than one clef, more than one staff letter pattern? Because music is performed by people and instruments of such great variety. A flute or woman's voice produces notes which are high in the frequency range. For them, a clef like treble clef is needed if the notes are to be written conveniently on the staff. A bassoon or a man's voice will produce notes of a much lower frequency. For these sounds the bass clef allows convenient notation.

The other clefs (alto, tenor, soprano etc.) are convenient for notating the registers or ranges for which they were named. Alto clef conveniently places the notes of the lower woman's range (the alto range); tenor clef conveniently places the upper male (or tenor) notes etc.

In modern musical notation, treble and bass clef are by far the most frequently used. Alto clef is used chiefly by people who play the viola. Tenor clef is sometimes used by trombonists and cellists. Soprano, mezzo soprano, and baritone clefs are hardly used at all.

Leger Lines. Despite the fact that by using different clef signs notes can be conveniently kept on the staff, there are times when the music requires very high or very low pitches which the staff cannot accommodate. To notate these pitches, we extend the range of the staff by adding lines to it. We call these lines "leger lines," and they can be placed above or below the staff (see below).

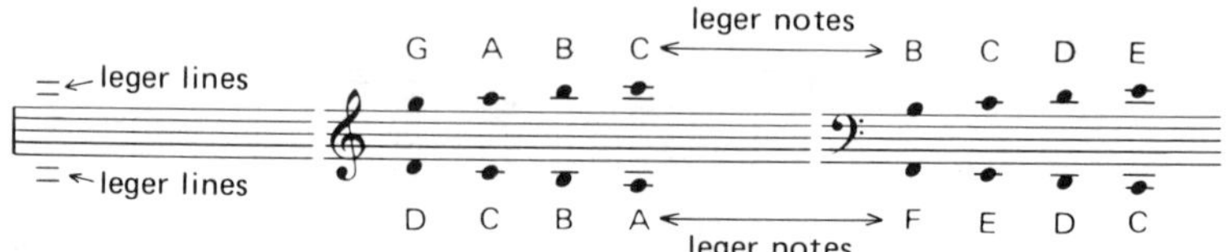

The Octave Sign. Occasionally, notes are so high or so low that leger lines alone are insufficient for convenient notation. At these times a dotted line - sometimes called an "octava sign" - is placed above or below the group of notes involved. If placed above the notes, the sign means "play these pitches an octave higher than written;" if placed below, "play an octave lower." The example below shows the use of the octava sign and how much easier it is to read than the leger lines it replaces.

Sometimes an entire part is performed an octave above or below where it is written. The tenor voice part in a chorus, for example, is written in treble clef but sung an octave lower. The piccolo part of instrumental music is written in treble clef but sounds an octave higher. For such cases, instead of using leger lines which would be far too cumbersome or octava signs which would have to stretch over the entire composition, an octava sign is indicated above (or below) the clef at the beginning of each staff. This means "play all the notes an octave above (or below) where they are written" (see below).

The Great Staff. Modern composers use a combination of treble and bass clef braced together to notate a tremendous amount of music. Piano music, vocal music, even some instrumental music can all be written easily in this way. The arrangement is called the "Great Staff" or "Grand Staff," and it can be learned most easily in association with the piano keyboard (see below).

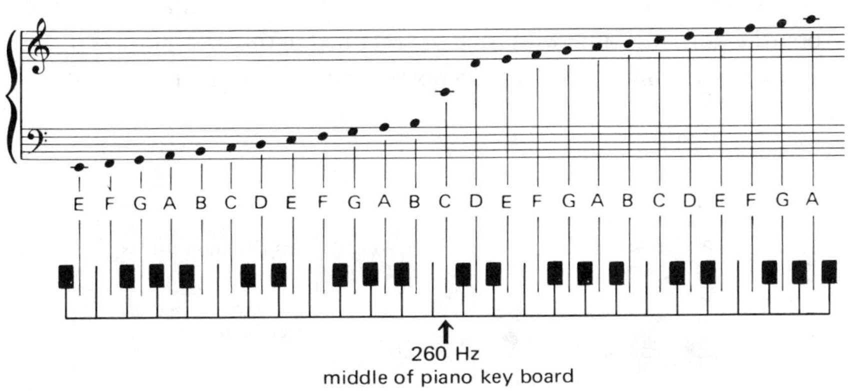

Just as leger lines and octava signs are possible with any single staff, they are possible on the Great Staff, giving it expanded capability (see below).

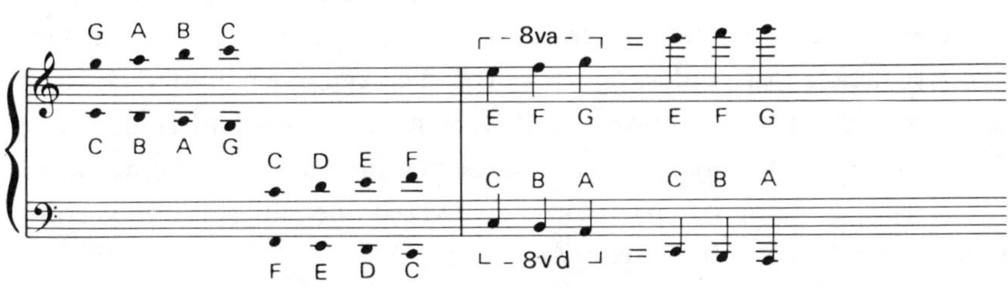

Accidentals can be placed on the Great Staff in front of the notes to which they apply. Each one has a very specific meaning in reading the notes. The table below explains.

Accidentals

Symbol   **Meaning**

♯ . . . . Raises the pitch one half-step

× . . . . Raises the pitch two half steps

♭ . . . . Lowers the pitch one half-step

♭♭ . . . . Lowers the pitch two half-steps

♮ . . . . Cancels any of the above

The table becomes more understandable if we visualize the piano keyboard again, this time with each note named in the several ways it can be named. (Remember, there are 35 possible names for the 12 steps of the octave.)

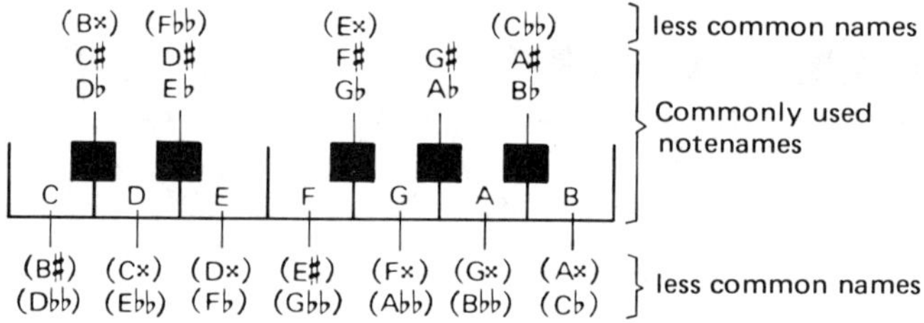

Of the twelve notes in a piano octave, seven are white (that is, the piano keys corresponding to them are white in color) while five are black. Each note can be known by several names, some more commonly used than others. The white key "C," for example, can also be called "B♯" or "D♭♭." It is this point which illustrates the meaning of the accidentals. B♯ means "one half-step above B." The key one half-step above B on the keyboard is also known as C. D♭♭ means "two half-steps below D," also the C key. Similarly, the black key just above C can be called C♯ (C raised one half-step) or D♭ (D lowered one half-step). Less commonly it is called B× (B raised two half-steps).

The relationship between the notes on the staff and the corresponding keys of the piano keyboard is illustrated below.

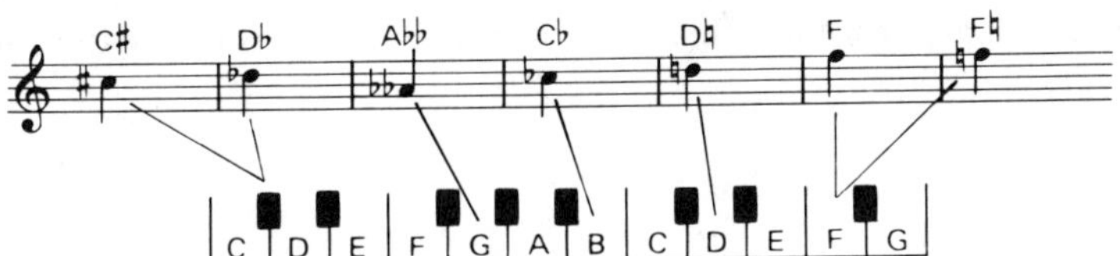

(Notice that when writing on the staff, the accidental precedes the note, whereas it follows the note when writing letter names. Notice also that a note with no accidental is the same as that note with a ♮ sign - as in the F and F♮ at the right of the illustration.)

Enharmonic Equivalents. Pitches which have the same sound but different spellings (for instance, C# and Db) are called "enharmonic equivalents." They are no less usual in music than similar equivalents in language, and they have much the same purpose. Consider for a moment the words "bear"and "bare." They sound alike but are spelled differently, and they are spelled differently because they have different meanings. C# and Db sound alike but are spelled differently because in the context of the music they will mean different things and function in different ways. As we learn more about intervals, scales, chords and their many interactions, this concept will be illustrated more completely.

The Components of a Written Note.

A musical note can be drawn with three component parts: a head, a stem, and a flag or beam. All notes have heads; some, heads and stems; some, all three parts.

Note Heads. Note heads are the dots placed on the staff to indicate pitch, but they can also indicate the duration of the pitch. The note head may be darkened in - indicating a shorter sound - or left open - indicating a longer sound (see below).

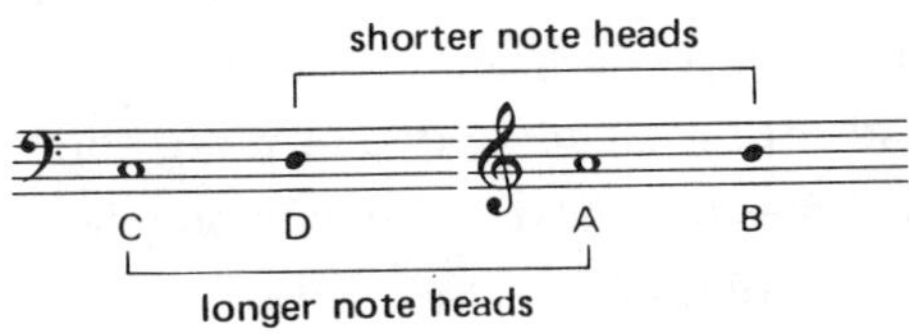

Stems. Stems are straight lines drawn either upward or downward from the note head. They have two functions: (1) to indicate a note of shorter duration than a note having just a head and (2) to differentiate one musical part from another if two parts happen to be written on the same staff.

In the illustration above, notice that upward stems are drawn on the right side of the note head while downward stems occur on the left. In modern notation that is the correct procedure. The pattern at the far right of the illustration shows the stemming of the two simultaneous parts. When note heads are stacked one on top of another, they are meant to be played together. In the case above, one part will play C-D-E as the other plays A-B-C. The stemming makes it easy for each performer to follow his part.

Generally, when the note which is to receive a stem is on or above the center line of the staff, it is stemmed downward (unless it is part of a double group like the case above). If the note is below the center line, the stem goes upward. In this way, stems usually point inward toward the center of the staff, keeping the space between staves more clear for ease of reading.

Flags and Beams. A flag is a short line drawn outward from the end of the stem back toward the note head. It indicates a note of shorter duration than one with just a head and stem. A beam is a straight line connecting the ends of the stems of two or more notes. It, too, indicates shorter duration. Notes may have more than one flag or beam. The more they have, the shorter they are.

Notice that flags are always drawn to the right of the stem. In modern notation, that is the proper position. Notice, too, that beaming a group of notes together causes the reader to consider the group as a unit to be read as a single concept rather than a series of separate notes. Often beaming can facilitate reading in this way, the patterns of the eye aiding the understanding of the mind.

Relative Note Values.

We have seen that the components of a note indicate both the pitch and duration of musical sounds. Pitches are indicated precisely by the placement of the note head on the staff. Duration is indicated precisely through a hierarchy of note values.

There are six commonly used note values, and they relate to each other exactly as mathematical fractions do. A "whole note" equals two "half notes," a half note equals two "quarter notes," and so on. The table below illustrates.

Note Values

Note shape	Note name		Relative value
o	Whole note	=	2
	Half Note	=	2
	Quarter note	=	2
	Eighth note	=	2
	Sixteenth note	=	2
	Thirty-second note	=	2

Theoretically, one can add more and more flags to a note to create sixty-fourth notes, one hundred twenty-eight notes, and so on. However, these values are so rare as to seldom if ever be used. For our purposes here, the ♬ (32nd note) will be our smallest value.

Remembering that notes can be stemmed up or down and grouped by beams, below are the same six values written with variations of stemming and beaming.

Note Values

Note name	Writing variations
Whole note	𝅝 No variations possible
Half note	𝅗𝅥 or 𝆏
Quarter note	𝅘𝅥 or 𝆏
Eighth note	𝅘𝅥𝅮, 𝆏, 𝅘𝅥𝅮𝅘𝅥𝅮, ♫, 𝅘𝅥𝅮𝅘𝅥𝅮𝅘𝅥𝅮
Sixteenth note	𝅘𝅥𝅯, 𝆏, 𝅘𝅥𝅯𝅘𝅥𝅯, ♫, 𝅘𝅥𝅯𝅘𝅥𝅯𝅘𝅥𝅯
Thirty-second note	𝅘𝅥𝅰, 𝆏, 𝅘𝅥𝅰𝅘𝅥𝅰, ♫, 𝅘𝅥𝅰𝅘𝅥𝅰𝅘𝅥𝅰

Remember, too, that these note values are not indications of actual time. A whole note does not automatically mean that the sound it represents will last one second or two seconds or a minute or an hour. Note values can only tell us the duration of a sound relative to other sounds. In other words, if our whole note actually does last for one second, then a half note (in the same piece of music) will last one half of a second, a quarter note will last one quarter of a second and so on. Change the duration of the whole note to, say, two seconds, and the duration of every other note value must change accordingly.

It is the combining of note values in a piece of music which produces the specific rhythm of the sound. We will discuss rhythm in much greater detail later on, but for now, you can get the idea of how note values produce rhythms by thinking of a nursery rhyme you know (see below).

Three blind mice. Three blind mice. See how they run. See how they run.

The words "three blind mice" have a rhythm which we might describe as "short-short-long." That rhythm is represented musically by the note values "quarter-quarter-half" (𝅘𝅥 𝅘𝅥 𝅗𝅥). Next, the quarter, eighth, and half note values are combined as above (𝅘𝅥 ♫ 𝅗𝅥) to produce the rhythm which accompanies the words "see how they run." By combining note values in similar ways, any conceivable rhythmic pattern can be represented, read, and ultimately performed.

Dots, Double Dots, and Ties.

Dots, double dots, and ties are three symbols which can be attached to any note value in order to lengthen the duration of the note. Each works in its own particular way.

Dots. A dot is a small symbol resembling the period found at the end of a sentence. It is placed to the right of a note head and increases the duration of the note by one half its original value. Thinking of notes as if they were money for a moment might make this clear. A "dotted dollar" would be equal to one dollar plus fifty cents (half the dollar) for a total of $1.50. A "dotted half dollar" would equal 75¢ (50¢ + 25¢ = 75¢). The table below gives the values of the most frequently encountered dotted note values.

Dotted Notes

Note		Equivalent value
𝅗𝅥·	=	2 ♩ plus 1 ♩ or 3 ♩
𝅗𝅥.	=	3 ♩
♩.	=	3 ♪
♪.	=	3 𝅘𝅥𝅯
𝅘𝅥𝅯.	=	3 𝅘𝅥𝅰

Double Dots. A double dot is a symbol resembling two periods placed side by side to the right of the note head. Double dots lengthen the note by three quarters of its original value. Again, the money analogy may help. A "double dotted dollar" would equal one dollar plus three quarters ($1.00 + 75¢) for a total of $1.75. The table below provides the most commonly found double dotted notes.

Double Dotted Notes

Note		Equivalent value
𝅗𝅥··	=	4 ♩ plus 3 ♩ or 7 ♩
𝅗𝅥..	=	7 ♪
♩..	=	7 𝅘𝅥𝅯
♪..	=	7 𝅘𝅥𝅰

Ties. A ties is a curved line extending from one note head to the head of another note of the same pitch. The tie elongates the value of the first note by the value of the second. (see below).

In reading music, ties should not be confused with "slur marks" which are also curved lines. A slur mark (or "phrase mark," as it is sometimes called) is a line which curves over a group of notes which are to be performed as an unbroken unit. When a singer sees a slur mark it means, "sing these notes without taking a breath." When a pianist sees a slur it means, "play this without lifting your hand from the keys so that the group is an unbroken sound series." Slurs are an umbrella covering many different pitches. They have no effect on the duration of the notes to which they apply. Ties *must* connect note heads of the *same* pitch, and they serve to add the durational values together. The music below provides an example of a slur and a tie within a slurred group.

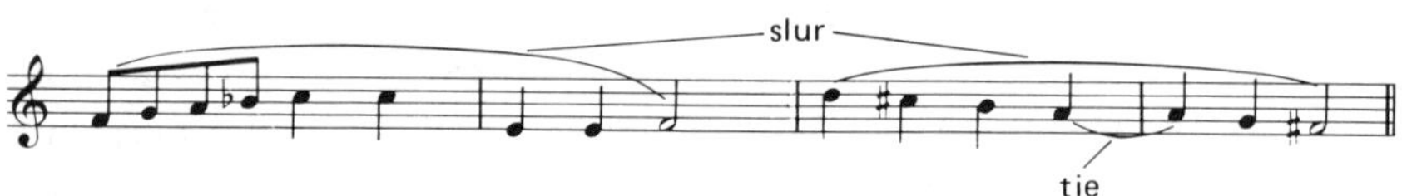

Rests.

Music involves more than sounds. It also involves the space between the sounds, silence. In fact, if you are inclined toward definitions, this is not a bad one: music is the organization of sound and silence in time.

Just as there are symbols for sounds in music (notes), there are symbols for silences. They are called "rests." Rests have specific durational values in exactly the same way notes do. The table below provides them.

Rests

Symbol	Name	Note value equivalent
▬	Whole rest	o
▬	Half rest	♩
𝄽	Quarter rest	♩
𝄾	Eighth rest	♪
𝄿	Sixteenth rest	♬
𝅀	Thirty-second rest	♬

Just as notes can be dotted and double dotted, rests can be dotted and double dotted. Again, the table below illustrates.

Rest Values

Rests		Dotted rests		Double dotted rests	
▬	= o	▬.	= o.	▬..	= o..
▬	= ♩	▬.	= ♩.	▬..	= ♩..
𝄽	= ♩	𝄽.	= ♩.	𝄽..	= ♩..
𝄾	= ♪	𝄾.	= ♪.	𝄾..	= ♪..
𝄿	= ♬	𝄿.	= ♬.	𝄿..	= ♬..
𝅀	= ♬	𝅀.	= ♬.	𝅀..	= ♬..

Note Value Tables.

The following tables summarize much of the information above in a somewhat more convenient form. The first table provides the most commonly found note values; the second (read like a matrix) illustrates the relationship between note values. For example, if you wish to know how to symbolize 3 quarter notes, read across the "3 row" and down the " ♩ column" to the place where they meet (♩.).

Common Note Values		
Basic value	**Dotted value**	**Double dotted value**
𝅝	𝅝· = 3 𝅗𝅥	𝅝·· = 7 𝅘𝅥
𝅗𝅥	𝅗𝅥· = 3 𝅘𝅥	𝅗𝅥·· = 7 𝅘𝅥𝅮
𝅘𝅥	𝅘𝅥· = 3 𝅘𝅥𝅮	𝅘𝅥·· = 7 𝅘𝅥𝅯
𝅘𝅥𝅮	𝅘𝅥𝅮· = 3 𝅘𝅥𝅯	𝅘𝅥𝅮·· = 7 𝅘𝅥𝅰
𝅘𝅥𝅯	𝅘𝅥𝅯· = 3 𝅘𝅥𝅰	
𝅘𝅥𝅰		

Matrix of Relative Values

		𝅝	𝅗𝅥	𝅘𝅥	𝅘𝅥𝅮	𝅘𝅥𝅯	𝅘𝅥𝅰
1		𝅝	𝅗𝅥	𝅘𝅥	𝅘𝅥𝅮	𝅘𝅥𝅯	𝅘𝅥𝅰
2			𝅝	𝅗𝅥	𝅘𝅥	𝅘𝅥𝅮	𝅘𝅥𝅯
3			𝅝·	𝅗𝅥·	𝅘𝅥·	𝅘𝅥𝅮·	𝅘𝅥𝅯·
4				𝅝	𝅗𝅥	𝅘𝅥	𝅘𝅥𝅮
5				𝅝＿𝅗𝅥	𝅗𝅥＿𝅘𝅥𝅮	𝅘𝅥＿𝅘𝅥𝅯	𝅘𝅥𝅮＿𝅘𝅥𝅰
6				𝅝·	𝅗𝅥·	𝅘𝅥·	𝅘𝅥𝅮·
7				𝅝··	𝅗𝅥··	𝅘𝅥··	𝅘𝅥𝅮··

Measures and Bar Lines.

In the notation of music, units of time are marked off by vertical lines drawn across the staff. These lines are called "bar lines." The distances between bar lines are called "measures" (see below).

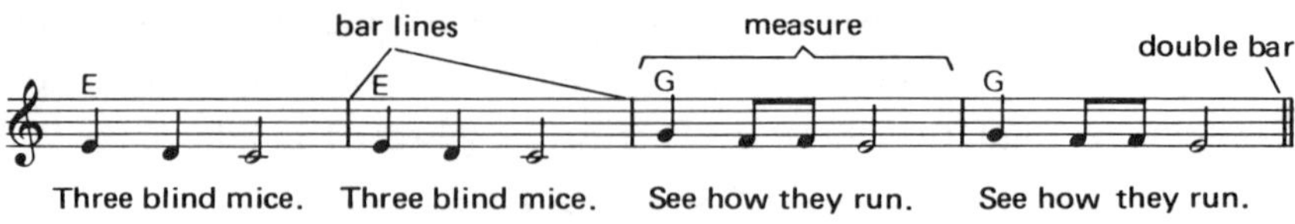

Bar lines and measures are a convenient way of indicating where the stresses or accents of the music belong. The primary stress occurs on the note which immediately follows the bar line. In the example above, the words, "Three," "Three," "See," and "See" receive the primary accents when the nursery rhyme is sung. The notes which correspond to those words (E, E, G, and G) received the accents when the tune is played.

The "double bar" at the right of the example is the musical symbol used to designate the end of either the entire composition or a major section of it.

In modern notation, it has become standard practice to indicate a full measure of silence with the whole note rest. Thus, the whole note rest can equal either 4 ♩ or a full measure, whatever the value of that measure (see below).

In Example A, there are 3 ♩ in measure 1. The full measure rest in measure 2 is written as a whole note rest which now stands not for 4 ♩ but 3 ♩ (the value of the first measure). In Example B, the whole note rest stands for 6 ♪. In Example C, it stands for 2 𝅗𝅥 (or 4 ♩) which in this case is both its "normal" meaning and its "full measure" meaning.

The Musical Score.

The full printed work of music is known as a "score." There are piano scores, vocal scores, orchestra scores - whatever the music itself calls for. Reading a score involves many things and can be an extremely complex undertaking if the music itself is complex. The general characteristics of most musical scores are discussed below.

The System. Scores consist of "systems." A system is a series of staves braced together. A piano score will have 2-stave systems because piano music uses the Great Staff. String quartet and chorus music will normally be written in scores which contain 4-stave systems. Music for orchestras often contains systems of many staves because many instruments are playing together. Below are examples of various multi-stave systems.

(PIANO)

(STRING QUARTET)

(ORCHESTRA)

CORIOLAN
Overture

L. van Beethoven, Op. 62

The thing to remember about reading systems is that every staff in a system is being played simultaneously, so the conductor or the person following the score must read them all at the same time. Obviously, the more staves per system, the harder this is to do. In fact, score-reading is something of an art, and musicians can spend many years of training learning how to read scores.

The scores above are for piano, string quartet, and full orchestra. The piano score has 6 2-stave systems; the string quartet score 4 4-stave systems; the orchestra score 1 11-stave system. Thus, in terms of reading, the piano score contains 7 "lines" of music; the string quartet score 4 lines; the orchestra only 1 line.

Notice (on the left margin of the string quartet score) the two heavy, slanted lines. These are often placed in multi-stave scores to help the reader's eye separate one system from another. They are saying, in effect, "follow the first 4-stave system as if it were one line, then drop down to the next system and follow it."

Rehearsal Marks. Because scores are often difficult to read, reference points are frequently placed in the music to help both musician and reader follow along. These references are called "rehearsal marks," and they come in two forms, letters and numbers. The string quartet music above provides an illustration. Just atop the fourth measure of system 1 is a large "A." Lower down, on system 3 is a "B." As the music flows along, these can be used to keep one's place. They also provide convenient spots to begin rehearsing, if during a rehearsal the performers have to stop to correct an error and then start up again. Additional rehearsal marks are given in numerical form below each system. In the example above, the numbers 30, 35, 40, 45, and 50 etc. appear. These refer to the measure number of the music. We can now see that "A" occurs at measure 29 and "B" at measure 48.

Repeat Signs. Music is quite expensive to engrave and print. Therefore anything that can help cut costs is welcome by both manufacturer and consumer alike. When sections of music repeat, rather than writing them out again - which is both time consuming and needlessly expensive - symbols called "repeat signs" are used to indicate exactly what is to be played again.

The most common repeat sign is a double bar with two dots placed next to it. It is followed by another double bar and dot configuration somewhat farther ahead in the music. The instruction to the performer indicated by this pattern is "repeat what lies between the double bars." In the example above, this would mean the following:

    a) Play measures 1-5

    b) Go back to measure 2

    c) Play measures 2-4, then

    d) Skip measure 5 and play measures 6, 7 etc.

The feature of the repeat sign which tells the performer to "skip measure 5" the second time around is the "ending sign." This says, "the first time around, play the first ending (the music beneath the "1"); the second time around, play only the second ending (the music beneath the "2") and go on from there."

In the piano score above, there are similar repeat signs in the second system. In this case, however, there is no repeat sign before the first ending. When that happens, it is understood that the performer is to repeat from the beginning. For the piano music above, the following, then, should be done.

    a) Play m. 1-8 (m. is an abbreviation for "measure")

    b) Go back to the beginning and play m. 1-7

    c) Skip m. 8, play m. 9 and go on from there.

There are other repeat signs also commonly used, many of which use a configuration formed by a slanted line with dots on either side of it. Below are illustrations of how this symbol may be applied to the music.

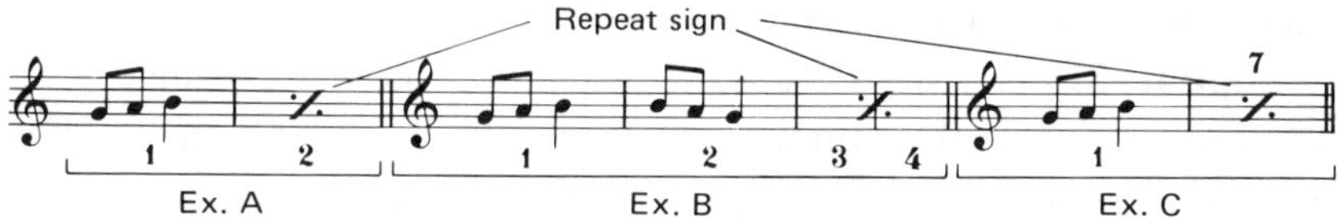

In Example A, the repeat sign means simply, "do in m. 2 what you did in m. 1." In Example B, the repeat sign means "play m. 3-4 in the same way m. 1-2 were played." In Example C, the sign means "repeat m. 1 seven more times."

Finally, very complex repeats may simply be described in combinations of language and symbols. Often the language involved is Italian since Italy was the birthplace of so many musical practices. Below is an example of a complex repeat using language as well as symbol.

To interpret this example, one must know the following:

a) D.C. stands for the Italian words "da capo" which mean "go to the beginning."

b) Segno is Italian for "sign," and it is symbolized by ✖.

c) Coda is Italian for "ending" and it is symbolized here by ⊕.

Armed with this knowledge, the example above can be interpreted as follows:

a) Play m. 1-8

b) Go back to m. 1 and play until the sign ✖ at m. 5, then

c) Skip to the Coda (marked ⊕) at m. 9 and play to the end (m. 12).

Complex repeat instructions like these are not needed for short bits of music, but they can save hours of writing and many dollars of cost when applied to music which may repeat many pages of material. The piano score above, for example, has a D.C. repeat at the very bottom of the page. It refers the performer not back to the top of the page but to music several pages before.

Following a score requires practice and the ability to count measures, often very rapidly. In the case of complex orchestra scores, it also requires a knowledge of where the important musical activity is focused. For example, it is often easier to follow an orchestra score by concentrating on the violin part because, in a good deal of orchestral music, the violins carry the melody, and melody is relatively easy to focus on.

If you plan to learn how to follow scores, you might begin with vocal scores since they have words which will be easier to read than music at the start of your studies. You might also choose music which moves slowly so that you have time to recover if you lose your place. As your skills increase, you can turn to more complex multi-stave systems and faster pieces of music. At the very least, you should learn to read treble and bass clef and learn to follow music on the Great Staff, since those skills will be necessary for the performing you may wish to try in Part IV of this text.

Further Reading.

1. **Scored for listening: a guide to music,** 2nd ed. Guy Alan Bockmon and William J. Starr (New York: Harcourt, Brace, and Jovanovich, 1972).

2. **The sense of music.** Victor Zuckerkandl. (Princeton: Princeton University Press, 1959).

3. **The undertanding of music.** Charles R. Hoffer (Belmont, California: Wadsworth, 1967).

CHAPTER THREE:

THE ELEMENTS OF RHYTHM

The word rhythm has several meanings. In its most general sense, it refers to anything having to do with time or duration of music. In a more specific sense it refers to exact patterns of sound as they unfold in time. Whatever its true definition, the concept of rhythm is dependent upon the concepts of pulse, tempo, pulse division, and meter. It is to them we must first turn our attention.

Pulse, Tempo, Pulse Division, and Meter.

Pulse. Pulse is the uniform, even marking of time. The key word here is uniform. Just as the human pulse is a regular thump-thump-thump of the heart, the pulse of music is a recurrent and even beat against which the various sounds occur. That beat may be an audible, actually- performed part of the music or an underlying ingredient which, like the silent swing of a pendulum, is felt but unheard.

There are three things that can occur to pulses: (1) they can be sped up or slowed down; (2) they can be divided into parts; and (3) they can be organized into groups.

Tempo. Tempo is the speed at which pulses travel. By altering the speed of a musical pulse, the character of the music is changed. A rapid pulse generally indicates more excitement in the music; a slower pulse, more calmness.

Tempos are indicated in two ways, by descriptive words like "fast" or "slow," and by the mathematical measurements of an instrument called a metronome. A metronome is a mechanical device run either by weights and gears or (in more modern times) by electricity. It emits clicks, much like the tick-tock of a clock, but unlike a clock it can be set to click faster or slower. The clicks represent musical pulses which can then be assigned a particular note value.

$\flat$ = 60, for example, is a typical metronome marking. It means that in one minute 60 quarter notes will click off in an even stream of pulses, one $\flat$ per second of time. The marking $\flat$ = 120 means that there will be 120 eighth notes per minute; $\flat$ = 72 that there will be 72 half notes per minute. and so on.

Most composers like to use both words and metronome markings to indicate tempo. Below are some of the more common tempo descriptions. Again, because of the influence of Italy on the history of music, they are in Italian.

Tempo Indications

Term	Meaning	Typical metronome mark
Lento	Very Slow	$\flat$ = 30
Largo	Slow	$\flat$ = 60
Moderato	Moderately paced	$\flat$ = 72
Andante	At a "walking" pace	$\flat$ = 84
Allegro	Fast	$\flat$ = 120
Vivace	Lively	$\flat$ = 132
Presto	Extremely rapid	$\flat.$ = 144
		and beyond

There are three more terms commonly applied to tempos which don't correspond to specific metronome markings. "Accelerando" means "gradually getting faster" (accelerating). "Ritardando" means "gradually getting slower." "Rubato" means traveling with an undefined, imprecise pulse. Rubato tempi are generally quite slow and drawn out.

Pulse Divisions. Pulses can be divided in multiples of 2 or in multiples of 3. Divisions in multiples of 2 are called "simple" pulse divisions. Those in multiples of 3 are called "compound" divisions.

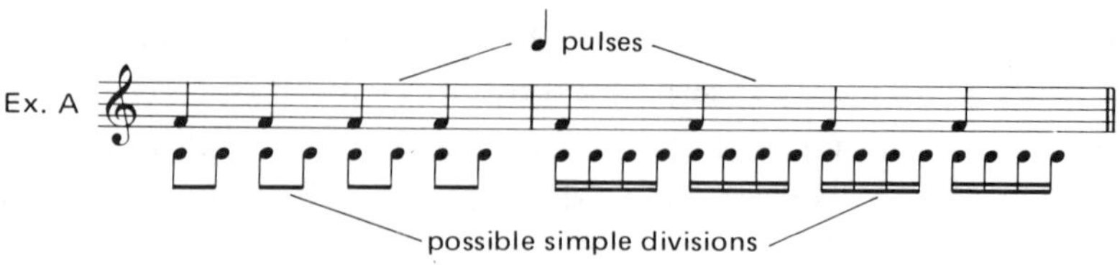

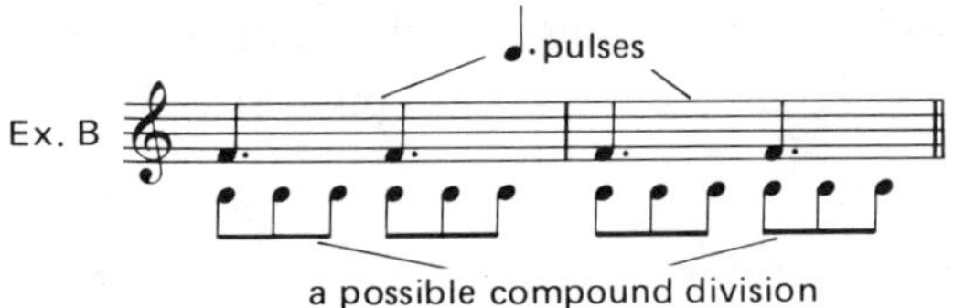

In Example A above, a stream of ♩ pulses is divided first into two, then into four parts per pulse. Each division is simple, conforming to the mathematics of duple division. In Example B, a stream of ♩. pulses is divided into three parts, thus conforming to the mathematics of compound division.

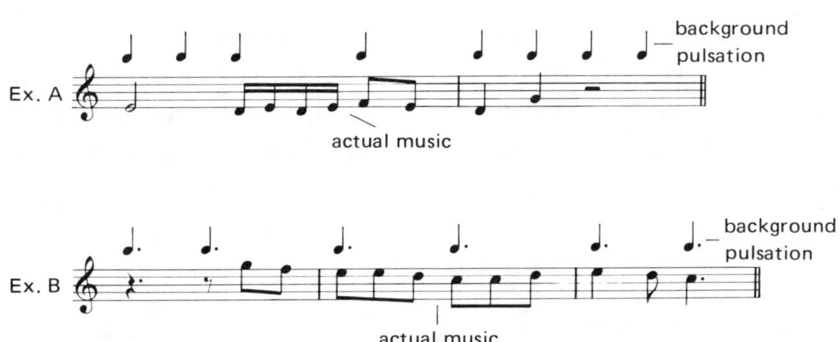

In Example A, the unheard background pulse is that of the quarter note. When it is divided - as it is in the last two beats of the first measure - the division is into 4 ♪ and 2 ♪, both simple divisions. In Example B, the background pulsation is the dotted quarter. When it is divided, the division is either 3 ♪ or the equivalent of 3 ♪ (♩ plus ♪), a compound division.

It is important to be aware that in real music the pulse may not be part of the performed note values. In the first example the pulse coincides with the actual note values only on the last two notes; in the second example, only on the last note. At other times it is camouflaged, so to speak, by other note values. Again, pulses are backgrounds against which the reality of the music unfolds. Sometimes they are articulated by the actual music. Often they are not. They remain in the background only to be felt by the "internal clock" of the listener or performer, only to be revealed by the tapping of a toe or snapping of a finger.

Meter. In addition to dividing pulses, they can be grouped together by accenting or stressing certain numbers of the pulse stream.

Above is a stream of 12 quarter note pulses. No one is more prominent than any other in the stream.

Now an accent mark (>) has been placed above the first, fifth, and ninth pulses, thereby creating a pattern of 4 ♩ to the group. In musical notation, the bar line and measure accomplish the same thing as a regularly recurring accent mark. Thus, the grouping above may be represented:

Of course, with 12 pulses, the grouping could have been done differently.

gives us 4 measures with an accent on every third pulse, for example.

Meters are the grouping of patterns which result from the regular placement of accents or bar lines into the music. Just as there are two families of pulse division (simple and compound), there are two families of metric grouping, duple and triple.

Duple meter is a grouping in which there are multiples of 2 pulses per measure. Triple meter is a grouping in which there are multiples of 3 pulses per measure. Below are two examples which are no doubt familiar.

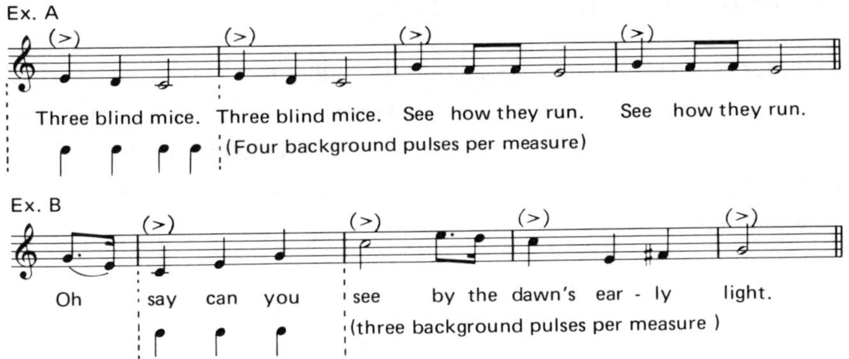

In "Three Blind Mice," the words as well as the music indicate a primary accent after every 4 ♩ pulses. Since 4 is a multiple of 2 (namely 2^2), this is an example of duple meter. In the National Anthem, the words and music indicate a primary accent after every three ♩ pulses, thus creating a triple meter.

There are two additional points to note about the National Anthem example. First, there is a slur mark above the first two pitches. That is because they are sung on only one syllable, the exclamation "Oh." In vocal music, any group of notes sung on only one syllable is slurred together indicating that the group should be performed in one breath. Second, the opening and closing measures appear to contain fewer than the 3 ♩ pulses required by the triple meter. This is true because the music doesn't begin on the first beat of the measure. Rather it has two notes which lead into the first primary accent. Such a lead-in (or "pick- up" as many musicians call it) is referred to as an "anacrusis." Whenever the music begins with an anacrusis, the very last measure is reduced in value so that the anacrusis and final measure equal a regular measure when added together.

In the example above, the anacrusis is ♪. plus ♪ (which equals ♩). The last measure is ♩ (which equals 2 ♩). Together they total the 3 ♩ of the triple meter of all the other measures. The mathematics of Example B are below.

$$\text{Remembering that } \quad ♪\!. = 3 ♪ ;$$
$$♪\!. + ♪ + ♩ =$$
$$3/16 + 1/16 + 1/2 =$$
$$1/4 + 1/2 =$$
$$3/4 \text{ or } 3 ♩$$

Meter Signatures And Their Meaning.

Meter Signatures. A numerical sign called a "meter signature" is placed at the beginning of a musical composition to alert the performer to the metrical characteristics of the music. A meter signature looks something like a fraction without the dividing line. Below are some common examples.

$$\frac{2}{4}, \quad \frac{4}{4}, \quad \frac{3}{4}, \quad \frac{6}{8}$$

The lower number tells the performer what kind of note to count. The upper tells how many of that note value will occur per measure. For example, the first meter signature above indicates that each measure will have 2 ♩ (or the equivalent value, say 4 ♪ or 1 ♩) per measure. The second signature states that there will be 4 ♩ (or the equivalent) per measure; the third that there will be 3 ♩ ; the fourth, 6 ♪ per measure.

Chart of Common Meter Signatures. Meter signatures tell a performer both how pulses will be divided and how they will be grouped. The chart of the common meter signatures below indicates how pulse divisions (simple and compound) and pulse groupings (duple and triple) combine in the various meter signatures.

The combination of pulse divisions and pulse groupings creates four families of meters: (1) simple duple meters, (2) simple triple meters, (3) compound duple meters, and (4) compound triple meters. Using the chart of common meters, we can investigate each family a bit more closely.

Chart of Common Meter Signatures

	Duple meter (2n pulses per m.)			Triple meter (3n pulses per m.)		
Simple division (2n parts per pulse) Pulses are ♪ , ♩ , or ♩	Simple duple meters			Simple triple meters		
	2/4	4/4	2/2	3/4	3/8	3/2
	(2♩)	(4♪)	(2♩)	(3♩)	(3♪)	(3♩)
Compound division (3n parts per pulse) Pulses are ♩. or ♩. .	Compound duple meters			Compound triple meters		
	6/8	12/8	6/4	9/8	9/4	
	(2♩.)	(4♩.)	(2♩.)	(3♩.)	(3♩.)	

Simple Duple Meters. The most common simple duple meters are 2/4, 4/4, and 2/2. 4/4 meter is sometimes symbolized by what looks like a capital C. 2/2 is sometimes symbolized by ₵. These symbols emanate from medieval times, and in Part III of this text we will discuss how and why they originated. For now, it is necessary to know only that they are frequently used today.

2/2 meter is often used in march music, and for that reason it is also called "march time." 2/2 differs from 4/4 not in the total value of the notes in any measure (2 ♩ are equal to 4 ♪) but in the number of pulses one feels per measure. In 2/2, there are 2 pulses (each equal to the ♩); in 4/4, there are 4 (each equal to the ♪). Below are examples of rhythmic patterns in each of the common simple duple meters.

In each case above, there are either 2 or 4 pulses per measure, and when those pulses are divided, they are divided into 2, 4, or 8 parts. Such are the characteristics of simple duple meters.

Simple Triple Meters. These are meters having 3 pulses per measure where each pulse is normally divided into 2, 4, or 8 parts. 3/4, 3/8, and 3/2 are the most frequently found simple triple meters with 3/4 by far the most common. Because 3/4 meter is the signature used in virtually every waltz, it is sometimes called "waltz time." Examples of simple triple patterns are written below.

Compound Duple Meters. Although the common compound duple meters - 6/8, 12/8, and 6/4 - have either 2 or 4 pulses per measure, unlike their simple duple cousins, each compound pulse is normally divided into 3 (not 2, 4, or 8) parts (see below).

(The accent marks are placed in the examples to provide a visual reference for where the pulses occur.)

At this point students often ask why 3/4 meter and 6/8 meter belong to different metric families. After all, 3/4 and 6/8 are mathematically equal. A measure of 3/4 will contain the equivalent of 6 ♪, as will a measure of 6/8. The answer lies not in the total value of the notes but the way in which they are grouped and accented. Consider the illustration below.

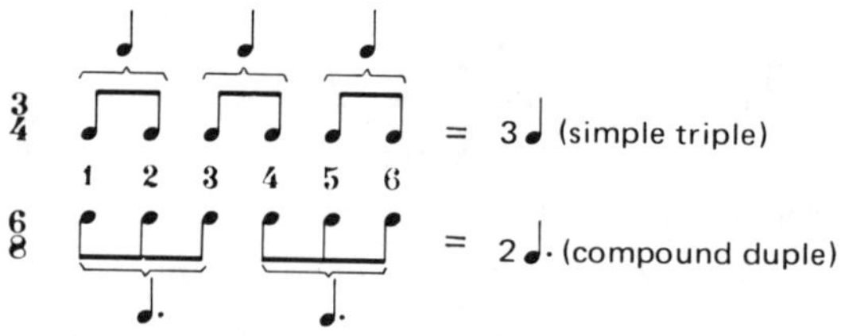

In the 3/4 time, there are 3 pulses per measure, each divided into 2 equal parts. In the 6/8 time there are 2 pulses per measure, each divided into 3 equal parts. Mathematically, both meters have 6 ♪ , but each is quite different from the other.

You can feel the difference if you transform the notation above into words. The word "music" has 2 syllables with an accent on the first. The word "musical" has 3 syllables, also with an accent on the first. But if you say "music, music, music," the feeling of the rhythm is not at all like saying "musical, musical." In total, both phrases have 6 syllables, but one is grouped in simple triple meter, the other in compound duple (see below).

simple triple: mu - sic,   mu - sic,   mu - sic   = $\frac{3}{4}$ (3 ♩ pulses)

compound duple: mu - si - cal,   mu - si - cal   = $\frac{6}{8}$ (2 ♩. pulses)

Compound Triple Meters. The common compound triple meters, 9/8 and 9/4, each have 3 pulses per measure with the pulse divided into 3 equal parts. Below are examples of these metric patterns.

Conducting Patterns.

For the performers of music and the conductors who direct them, there are visual patterns which depict the various metric families and which enable ensembles to play together. The most common patterns are the ones for meters which contain 2, 3, or 4 pulses per measure (see below).

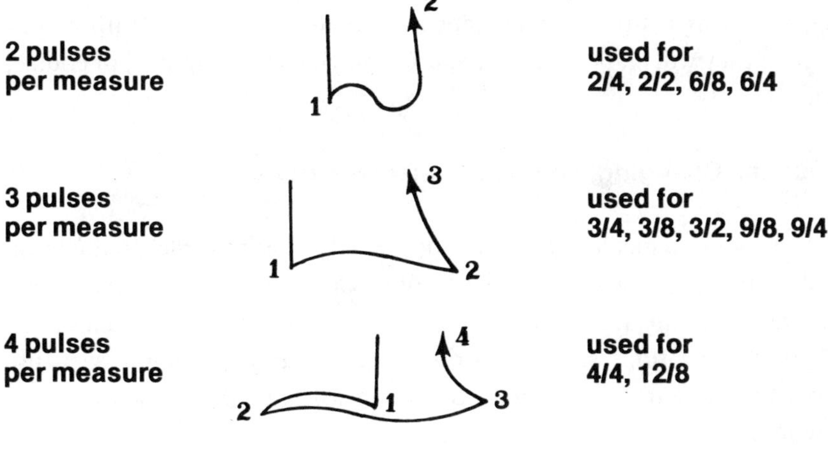

2 pulses per measure — used for 2/4, 2/2, 6/8, 6/4

3 pulses per measure — used for 3/4, 3/8, 3/2, 9/8, 9/4

4 pulses per measure — used for 4/4, 12/8

There are many variations of these basic patterns. The variations depend upon the complexity of the music, its tempo, and the idiosyncracies of the conductor. For example, in a very fast waltz, even though the meter may be 3/4, there may not be time for a conductor to beat three separate motions. Instead, he may simply beat the first beat of every measure (see below).

In 3/4 at a moderate tempo   indicates 3 ♩ .

In 3/4 at a rapid tempo   indicates ♩. (1 measure).

This is frequently referred to as "conducting in one," or using only one motion per measure.

Whatever variations a conductor employs, it must be understood that ensembles of many players need a conductor to mark time with visual hand patterns. If there were no conductor, the "internal clocks" of each performer would differ from his fellow performers, and the result would be chaos. That is because human beings have such a poor sense of time and need something to unify their separate notions of duration. If you ever want proof of this, ask a class of students to clap their hands after just 15 seconds have elapsed - without looking at a clock or watch. You'll get almost as many separate claps as people in the class. With a conductor, they will all be together, and for playing music, that is, of course, crucial.

Unusual, Changing, and Simultaneous Meters.

The common meters above are not the only ones possible. In the twentieth century particularly and to some extent in the fourteenth century as well, unusual meters containing 5, 7, even 10 pulses often occur. Many compositions shift from one meter to another. Some even use more than one meter at a time. Below we will investigate some of these phenomena.

Unusual Meters. By combining pulse groups of 2, 3, and 4, it is possible to come up with meters with strange numbers of pulses in the measure. For example, alternations between 2 ♪ and 3 ♪ can produce a meter of 5 ♪ (see below).

Among the unusual meters, groupings of 5, 7, and 10 are probably the most frequently found. The pattern ♩ ♩. ♩ (2 ♪ + 3 ♪ + 2 ♪ or 7 ♪) is used by the twentieth century Russian composer Serge Prokofiev in his Seventh Piano Sonata. His 7/8 meter looks like this:

In the theme for the television show "Mission Impossible," composer Lalo Schifrin uses a meter of 10/8 grouped 3 ♪ + 3 ♪ + 2 ♪ + 2 ♪ (see below).

Jazz composer Dave Brubeck experiments with all kinds of unusual meters in his album "Time Out." Among them are groupings of 5 (see below)

and a very unusual division of 9 (see below).

(2+2+2+3)

There are almost as many possibilities as there are musical compositions, and the modern composer, performer, and listener must be able to deal with all of them.

Changing Meters. It is also possible to have more than one meter going on at the same time. Pitting 2 against 3 or 3 against 4 are not uncommon occurrences, especially in the music of the fourteenth and twentieth centuries. The example below illustrates the simultaneous use of 3/4 and 6/8.

Syncopation and Hemiola.

Syncopation. Unusual meters are not the only possible variations from the common routines of rhythm. Another variation is the placement of accents where they would not be normally found. This practice is called syncopation.

We have already seen that the dominant stress of any measure is the first pulse of that measure. For this reason, the first pulse is often called the "strong beat" while the less prominent pulses are referred to as "weak beats." Some meters - like 4/4 - have two strong beats, one on the first pulse and another, slightly less strong, later in the measure on the third pulse (because it marks the halfway point of the measure). Below are some examples of strong and weak beats in common meters.

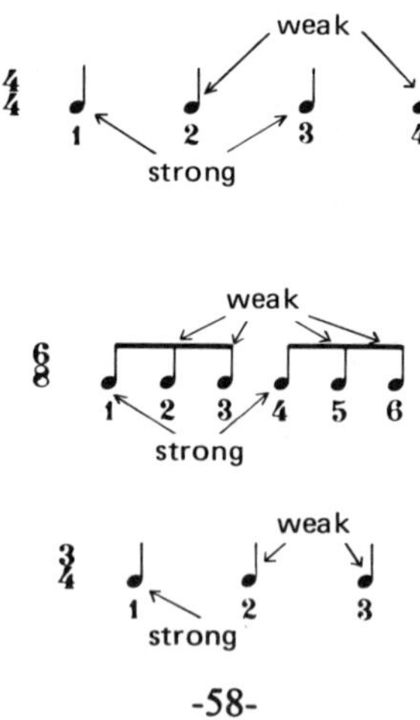

A syncopation places a strong accent where it normally would not occur, either on a weak beat or - more often - between pulses. Consider the example below.

Here the accents in the music do not always coincide with the accents of the background pulse. In fact, they occur between pulses rather than on them, setting up a kind of cross-relationship between what is expected (the pulse) and what is actually heard (the musical syncopation). When the same syncopation is written with tied note values, this cross-relationship becomes even clearer.

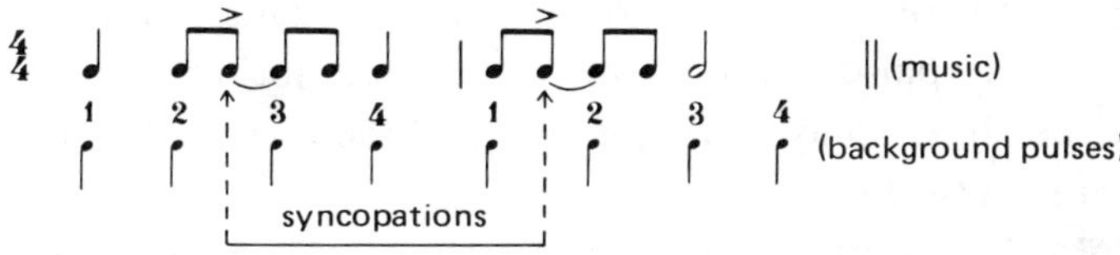

We can now see that the syncopations (usually placed accents) occur on the "second half" of pulses, in between the stresses which are normally expected.

Syncopation provides rhythmic variety and a sense of musical drive and vitality not otherwise possible. They are used in the music of all ages, but to a modern listener they are particularly prominent in popular music, in the world of jazz and rock where a feeling of "aliveness" is so important to the style. It is syncopation which lies at the rhythmic heart of that style.

Hemiola. A hemiola is a form of syncopation in which tied notes can cause the music to appear as if it has slowed down. The pattern below is an example.

Here we are traveling along with three pulses per measure in a normal simple triple meter. Then, by using ♩ values (created both by the ♩ and by a ♪ tied to a ♪), we appear to create a new pattern of 3 ♩ pulses. ♩♩♩ thus elongates to ♩♩♩ (written ♩ ♩♩ ♩), creating the "slowed down" effect.

Hemiolas are encountered in the music of all ages. They were a favorite device of composers during the fourteenth, fifteenth, and sixteenth centuries; they were used by many composers of the eighteenth century; and they are often used today. The example above is taken literally from the Symphony Number 2 of Johannes Brahms, a great composer of the mid and late 1800's whose music we shall encounter in Part III of this text.

Triplets, Duolets, and Other Unusual Pulse Divisions.

We have already seen that pulses are commonly divided into a simple or compound number of parts. While these procedures account for the vast majority of pulse divisions, they do not account for all of them. We conclude our brief study of rhythm with a look at some less frequently encountered pulse divisions.

Triplets. You are traveling along in a normal simple meter - 2/4 or 3/4 or 4/4. Each time your ♩ pulse is divided, it splits into 2 ♪ notes or 4 ♬ in the usual manner of a simple meter. But now suppose, just for the sake of variety, you would like to divide one of your pulses into 3 rather than 2 or 4 parts. This would be possible with a configuration called a "triplet." The triplet becomes a temporary substitution of a division of 3 for a normal division of 2 or 4. The key word here is "temporary" (see below).

The ♩ pulse which is divided into 2 ♪ or 4 ♬ fairly consistently is in one spot divided into 3 ♪ . These 3 do *not* have the value of ♪ + ♪ + ♪ (or ♩. note). Rather, they are "squeezed into" the time normally taken up by the usual 2 ♪ or 4 ♬ divisions of a simple meter. To show that the ♪ triplet is to be given the time value of 2 normal notes, a slur mark with the number 3 is written over them. For a brief, temporary moment ♩ = ♩ . A division of 3 has been substituted for a normal division of 2, each ♪ of the triplet compacted so that the triplet takes up no more time than the 2 normal ♪ .

Duolet. What a triplet is to a simple meter, a duolet (or duplet, as it is also called) is to a compound meter. In compound time, the normal pulse division is 3. A duolet is a temporary substitution of 2 for that normal division of 3 (see below).

Here the pulse is a ♩. note. It is normally divided into ♫ or some equivalent (♩ ♪ , for example). The duolet replaces the ♫ division with two even notes which take up the same amount of time. Again, the slur over the duolet means that it equals the ♩. note pulse, not a ♩ note.

Other Unusual Pulse Divisions. Substituting a triplet for a normal division of 2 and a duolet for a normal division of 3 are not the only substitutions possible. Any number of notes can be squeezed into the duration of a pulse.

The example above shows 5 ♪ substituted in the amount of time normally occupied by 4 ♪ . One might call this figure of 5 ♪ a "quintuplet," but the term is really not used. However, the concept is. In slow tempos especially, it is possible to find normal simple and compound divisions replaced by groupings of 5, 6, 7, 9, 11, or even more notes - all of them occurring within the same amount of time as the regular pulse. Each unusual grouping is written with a slur mark and the number of divisions (5, 6, 7, 9, 11 etc.) being played.

The effect of this kind of substitution is to give the music a measure of variety and rhythmic freedom not possible in any other way. In Part III of this text we shall encounter a great composer of piano music, Frederick Chopin (1810-1849) who used such unusual pulse substitutions to great advantage.

Further Reading.

1. **Principles of rhythm.** Paul Creston. (New York: Franco Columbo, 1964).

2. **Rhythm and tempo.** Curt Sachs. (New York: Norton, 1953).

3. **The rhythm of sound.** E.A. Bryce. (Sydney: McGraw-Hill, 1969).

4. **The rhythmic structure of music.** Grosvenor W. Cooper and Leonard B. Meyer. (Chicago: University of Chicago Press, 1960).

CHAPTER FOUR:

INTERVALS

An interval is two precisely fixed points. In space, we can fix intervals in terms of inches or feet, meters or miles. In time, we can fix intervals in terms of minutes or hours, years or milennia. It is 500 miles from New York to Cleveland; two hours from 4:00 A.M. to 6:00 A.M.

In music, an interval is the distance between any two pitches (that is, any two frequencies). We already know that for most of the music of mankind, the most fundamental interval is the octave. We have defined the octave as an interval such that the ratio of the frequency of its pitches is 2:1. We have also seen that modern musicians have divided the octave into twelve equal increments called "semi-tones" or "half steps" much as a foot is divided into twelve equal units called inches.

Using this knowledge we are now in a position to define all the other intervals. In doing so, we will frequently refer to the piano keyboard for visual reference and clarity. For that reason, one full octave of the keyboard is pictured below with the letter names of each key.

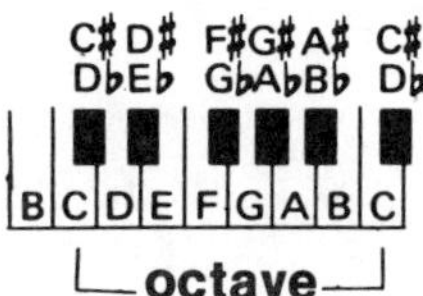

How Intervals Are Defined.

A musical interval is defined by two things: (1) the number of half steps between its pitches and (2) the way in which those pitches are spelled using the letter/accidental system of the musical alphabet.

Counting Half Steps. On the piano keyboard above, a half step is the distance between any two immediately adjacent keys. The distance from C to C♯/D♭ is one half step. From C to D is two half steps (or one whole step). From E to F is one half step. There is no intervening black key between E and F as there is between C and D. Therefore E and F are immediately adjacent while C and D are not.

Precise Spelling. The distance from C to C♯ is exactly the same as the distance from C to D♭ because C♯ and D♭, as we already know, are enharmonic equivalents. However the interval C-C♯ does not have the same name as the interval C-D♭. In sound, they are identical, but in spelling they have different intervallic labels. As it happens, the interval C-C♯ is an "augmented unison" while C-D♭ is a "minor second."

Naming the Intervals.

A Family Name. An interval is named primarily for the number of letters used up in its spelling. If it uses up two letters of the musical alphabet (C-D, E-F, A-B etc.), it is called a "second." If it uses up three letters (C-E, E-G, A-C etc.), it is called a "third." If four letters are required (for example, C-F), the interval is a fourth; five letters (C-G), a fifth; and so on.

The basic intervallic families are given in the table below.

Basic Intervallic Families		
Family name	**Number of letters used**	**Example**
Unison	1	C-C
Second	2	C-D
Third	3	C-E
Fourth	4	C-F
Fifth	5	C-G
Sixth	6	C-A
Seventh	7	C-B
Octave	8	C-C

More Precise Names. Family names are fine for distinguishing general characteristics, but as we know from our own names, we need more than just a last name for precise identification. The same is true with intervallic names. In each family of intervals, there are several types. In the family of seconds, for example, there are four types: (1) major seconds, (2) minor seconds, (3) augmented seconds, and (4) diminished seconds. In the family of fourths, there are three types: (1) perfect fourths, (2) augmented fourths, and (3) diminished fourths.

The thing which places an interval in a certain family is the number of letters it uses in its spelling. The thing which gives an interval its specific name within its family is the number of half steps between its pitches. For example, let us consider the family of fourths. A perfect fourth has 5 half steps between its members (C-F, for instance). An augmented fourth has 6 half steps between its members (C-F♯). A diminished fourth has 4 half steps between its members (C-F♭).

Below are a series of tables which will help us to define precisely every member of every intervallic family.

Complete Table of Intervals								
	Unison	2nd	3rd	4th	5th	6th	7th	Octave
Major		2	4			9	11	
Minor		1	3			8	10	
Augmented	1	3	5	6	8	10	12	13
Diminished	−1	0	2	4	6	7	9	11
Perfect	0			5	7			12

This first table lists all the possible intervals (there are 28 of them) and gives the number of half steps in each. The family name (unison, second, third, etc.) is given across the top of the table. The specific intervallic type (major, minor, augmented, etc.) is listed in the left column. By reading down the family name column and across the interval type row, one can find every interval.

For example, a major sixth is an interval with 9 half steps between its members. A "major octave" is an interval which does not exist. To help illustrate the intervals more clearly, the table below provides an example of every interval between the low C and high C of our piano keyboard octave.

Intervals Above C								
	Unison	2nd	3rd	4th	5th	6th	7th	Octave
Major		C-D	C-E			C-A	C-B	
Minor		C-D♭	C-E♭			C-A♭	C-B♭	
Augmented	C-C♯	C-D♯	C-E♯	C-F♯	C-G♯	C-A♯	C-B♯	C-C♯
Diminished	C-C♭	C-D♭♭	C-E♭♭	C-F♭	C-G♭	C-A♭♭	C-B♭♭	C-C♭
Perfect	C-C			C-F	C-G			C-C

More Precise Definitions. It is now possible to use our knowledge of musical spelling and half steps to define every interval precisely. A perfect unison, for example, is an interval such that there are zero half steps between members which are spelled with the same letter of the musical alphabet. A major sixth is an interval such that there are 9 half steps between members whose spelling uses up 6 letters of the musical alphabet. The table below gives a capsule definition of all 28 intervals along with an example of that interval both above and below the note C.

Table of Intervallic Definitions				
Name of interval	No. of half steps	No. letters used	Example ↑C	Example ↓C
Perfect unison	0	1	C-C	C-C
Augmented unison	1	1	C-C♯	C-C♭
Diminished unison	-1	1	C-C♭	C-C♯
Major second	2	2	C-D	C-B♭
Minor second	1	2	C-D♭	D-B
Augmented second	3	2	C-D♯	C-B♭♭
Diminished second	0	2	C-D♭♭	C-B♯
Major third	4	3	C-E	C-A♭
Minor third	3	3	C-E♭	C-A
Augmented third	5	3	C-E♯	C-A♭♭
Diminished third	2	3	C-E♭♭	C-A♯
Perfect fourth	5	4	C-F	C-G
Augmented fourth	6	4	C-F♯	C-G♭
Diminished fourth	4	4	C-F♭	C-G♯
Perfect fifth	7	5	C-G	C-F
Augmented fifth	8	5	C-G♯	C-F♭
Diminished fifth	6	5	C-G♭	C-F♯
Major sixth	9	6	C-A	C-E♭
Minor sixth	8	6	C-A♭	C-E
Augmented sixth	10	6	C-A♯	C-E♭♭
Diminished sixth	7	6	C-A♭♭	C-E♯
Major seventh	11	7	C-B	C-D♭
Minor seventh	10	7	C-B♭	C-D
Augmented seventh	12	7	C-B♯	C-D♭♭
Diminished seventh	9	7	C-B♭♭	C-D♯
Perfect octave	12	7	C-C	C-C
Augmented octave	13	8	C-C♯	C-C♭
Diminished octave	11	8	C-C♭	C-C♯

You might wish to test your understanding of this table by counting out the half steps for any given interval on the piano keyboard above. For example, to reach the interval a major third below C, the table says "count down 4 half steps and use up 3 letters (C-B-A) in spelling your answer." Counting down 4 half steps gets you to a black note which can be called A♭ or G♯. According to our spelling instructions, A♭ is the correct choice. Had we chosen G♯, we would have spelled a diminished fourth below C. (Remember, if you are figuring intervals *above* a note, count *forward* through the alphabet. If you are figuring *below,* count *backward.*)

Below are five intervals written on the Great Staff. Using your knowledge of notation and intervals, see if you can identify all five.

The answers are: (1) F-A, major third; (2) B♭-E♭, perfect fifth; (3) C♯-G, diminished fifth; (4) F♯-g, major seventh; and (5) E-F, minor second.

Perfect and Imperfect; Augmented and Diminished.

Probably for reasons having to do with difficulties of tuning in the days of the early Christian Church, some musical intervals were considered more "godly" than others. The unison, octave, fourth, and fifth, being easier to tune with mathematical precision, were regarded as "perfect" intervals. The others (seconds, thirds, sixths, and sevenths) were considered "imperfect."

Perfect intervals were used more often; imperfect ones tended to be avoided. As we shall see in our investigation of music history, this gave the music of the first milennium after Christ a very distinctive sound. In any event, the labels "perfect" and "imperfect" persist to this day.

Perfect intervals have three forms: perfect, augmented, and diminished. Imperfect intervals have four forms: major, minor, augmented, and diminished. All of these are reflected in the table above. (The fourth, for example, is a perfect interval; the third, imperfect.)

In general, the terms "augment" and "diminish" mean "to make larger" and "to make smaller," respectively. The augmented form of an interval is an enlargement of its basic form. A diminished interval is a contraction of its basic form.

Since there is only one basic form of perfect intervals (the perfect form), to augment them requires increasing the distance between their members by one half step. This can be done either by raising the top note or lowering the bottom. Consider the perfect fourth from C to F as an example. To augment the perfect fourth C-F, one can raise the F a half step (C-F♯) or lower the C a half step (C♭-F). Either will produce an augmented fourth.

To create the diminished form of a perfect interval, the distance is contracted one half step by moving either the top note down or the bottom one up. For example, a diminished fourth from C-F might be either C-F♭ or C♯-F.

In the case of an imperfect interval, there are two basic forms: major and minor. The augmented form can only be secured from the major form since it is the larger of the two basic forms. The diminished can only be secured from the minor. The third C-E is a major third. If we contract it to C-E♭ we do not get a diminished third but rather a minor third. To get a diminished third, we must contract the minor form. C-E♭♭ is the result. Conversely, we cannot get an augmented third by enlarging the minor form. That will simply give us the major. We must, instead, enlarge the major (in this case, C-E♯).

The augmented and diminished forms of every interval are defined in the tables above. It is important, however, to know how they are figured and why some intervals have three forms while others have four. The concept of "augmented" and "diminished" will arise again in connection with chords. If understood in the realm of intervals, it will be more digestible in the realm of chords.

Finally, it must be remembered that when augmenting or diminishing a basic interval, the letters used to spell the interval must not change. An augmented fourth from C-F is C-F♯, not C-G♭. In sound, C-F♯ and C-G♭ are equal, but in meaning and use, they are quite different.

Enharmonics Revisited.

We have already noted that some musical pitches have the same sound but different letter/accidental spellings (C♯ and D♭, for example). We have also noted that some intervals have the same sound yet are spelled differently (C-F♯ and C-G♭, for example).

The reason for these enharmonic spellings is a difference in function between the two intervals. C-F♯ is an augmented fourth, C-G♭, a diminished fifth. They each contain 6 half steps between their members, but they will in all probability not resolve to the same sound. C-F♯ easily moves to B-G, while C-G♭ goes more easily to D♭-F (see below).

The way in which one interval moves (or resolves) to another is dependent upon many factors. Most of these have to do with principles of harmony which we have not yet investigated. For now it is only necessary to be aware that enharmonic equivalents occur with intervals as well as with single notes. Enharmonics arise whenever two intervals contain the same number of half steps but different letter/accidental spellings. They signify a difference in musical function.

The Concept of Inversion.

The word "inversion" implies the reversal of an order or position. In weather forecasting we speak of a thermal inversion where warm air - which usually rises to the top of the weather system - is trapped close to the ground by cooler air above. An intervallic inversion is a shift in note position. One of the notes of the interval is moved the distance of an octave, thus reversing the order of the pitches. For instance, the third C-E when inverted becomes the sixth E-C (see Example 1 below).

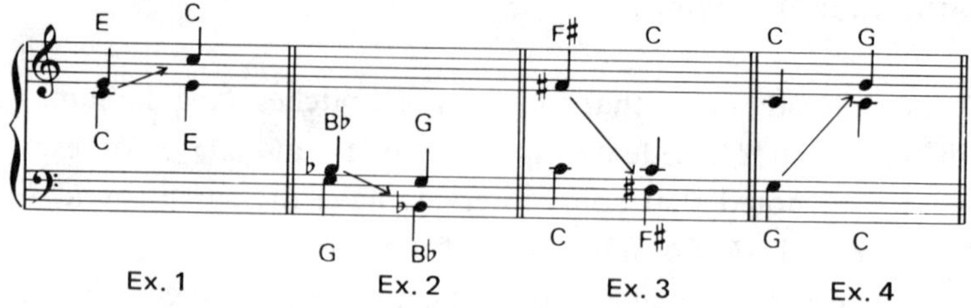

When an interval is inverted, not only its size changes. Its quality is also subject to change. All minor intervals invert to major ones, for example. Below is a table illustrating how to determine every intervallic inversion.

Table of Intervallic Inversions		
Interval size	**Quality**	**Direction**
Unison → Octave	Major → Minor	Up → Down
2nd → 7th	Minor → Major	Down → Up
3rd → 6th	Augmented → Diminished	
4th → 5th	Diminished → Augmented	
5th → 4th	Perfect → Perfect	
6th → 3rd		
7th → 2nd		
Octave → Unison		

The "interval size" column tells us that if we invert a unison, we get an octave; if we invert a second, we get a seventh; thirds invert to sixths; etc. Notice that the total value of the original and its inversion always equals 9 ($1 + 8 = 9$; $2 + 7 = 9$; etc.). This is an easy way to remember the size of inversions. The "quality" column tells us that major intervals invert to minor ones; minors to majors; augmenteds to diminisheds; diminisheds to augmenteds; and perfects remain perfect. The "direction" column tells us that a certain interval below a given pitch will invert to a certain interval above the pitch (and vice versa).

Putting all three columns together, we can see that a minor third above G (B♭) will invert to a major sixth below G (see Ex. 2 above). In Ex. 3 we see that an augmented fourth above C (F♯) will invert to a diminished fifth below C. Finally, in Ex. 4, the interval a perfect fourth above G (C) inverts to a perfect fifth below G.

The principle of inversion is not just a way of manipulating intervals. It is also a way in which composers mold and shape whole sections of melody. Later we shall investigate in some depth the process of inversion when it is applied to an entire composition. For now it is necessary only to understand the general concepts of inversion as they apply to intervals.

Further Reading.

The topic of intervals is covered in many basic music texts and general reference books. A good place to start more detailed reading on intervals is the article entitled "Intervals" in the **Grove's Dictionary of Music** (New York: St. Martin's Press). Another good basic source is the **Harvard Dictionary of Music** (Cambridge, Mass: Belknap). These works are periodically updated, so you should be sure to use the latest editions. Each article will refer you to other articles and provides a bibliography should you wish to read more.

CHAPTER FIVE

SCALES, TONALITY, AND ATONALITY

Notes and the intervals which they may form are not the only building blocks of music. Behind almost every composition is another organizational structure, a kind of skeleton, on which the rest of the music hangs. That structure is called a "scale."

Scales.

A scale is a consecutive series of pitches (usually arranged in whole and half steps) within the confines of an octave. C-D-E-F-G-A-B-C, for example, is a "major" scale within the confines of the octave C-C. Like the genes of a cell, scales determine the character of the music. They provide the predominant notes and intervallic relationships from which the melodies and harmonies of the music are formed.

There are many types of scales. Some are the products of certain geographical regions; some are the products of certain historical eras. Below we shall investigate a few of the more frequently used scales to see how they shape the music we hear.

The Pentatonic Scale. The pentatonic scale is a five-note pattern found extensively in the music of Oriental and native American Indian cultures. One common form of the scale appears below.

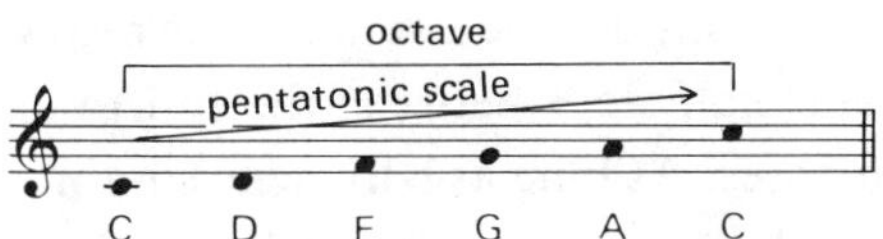

This scale generates a certain melodic flavor, a certain style of intervallic harmony. It is responsible for providing the special character we associate with Chinese or American Indian music. Below is a melody constructed from the notes of the pentatonic scale. The melody appears alone and then with an intervallic accompaniment which is also derived from the scale. As the solo melody and its accompanied version are played, it is easy to hear the influence of the underlying pentatonic pattern.

Pentatonic melody

Melody with intervallic accompaniment

The Modal Scale System. The ancient Greeks used four-note groupings called "tetrachords" to build eight-note scales called "modes." The Greek modes survived the centuries and became the forerunners of a modal system which dominated Western music from the advent of Christianity to around 1600 A.D. At the height of its popularity, the modal system contained several different scales. The four most common ones are written below.

Although the Dorian mode was usually built on the note D, the Phrygian on E, the Lydian on F, and the Mixolydian on G, any mode could be built on any starting note. By preserving the whole step and half step relationships within a given mode, the mode could be moved (or "transposed") easily. Consider the Lydian mode below. In its usual position on F, it contains half steps between the fourth and fifth notes and seventh and eighth notes. As long as half steps continue to occur at those places, the mode can begin on any note. Below, it is transposed to begin on C.

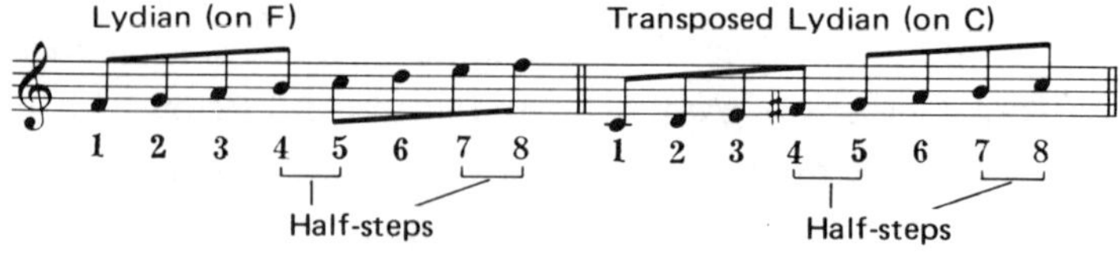

Just as the pentatonic scale gives a specific flavor to the music in which it occurs, modal scales endow modal music with special characteristics. Below is the opening section of a chanson (song) by the French composer Giles Binchois. It was written around 1450 A.D. and utilizes the Lydian mode (onF). The flavor of the mode is readily apparent as the chanson is played.

(The example contains an F ♯ in the bass clef of the second measure. The ♯ was used here to avoid the interval of an augmented fourth which would have occurred between an F ♮ and the B in the treble clef. At the time Binchois was composing music, augmented fourths - and certain other intervals - were scrupulously avoided. Frequently, accidentals were applied to the modes so that undesirable intervals would not occur.)

The Major-Minor System. Toward the end of the Renaissance and into the 17th century, the modes were gradually replaced by the major-minor scale system familiar to us today. This system formed the basis of most of the music we consider "standard" in the listening repertoire; the music of Bach and Beethoven, of Chopin and Verdi; the music of Broadway shows and high school dances. The major-minor system has four scales, one major scale and three forms of the minor scale.

The major scale divides the octave into an 8-note pattern such that there are half steps between notes 3 and 4 and notes 7 and 8. As with the modes, any note can be the first step of a major scale. Below are two major scales, one beginning on C, the other on D.

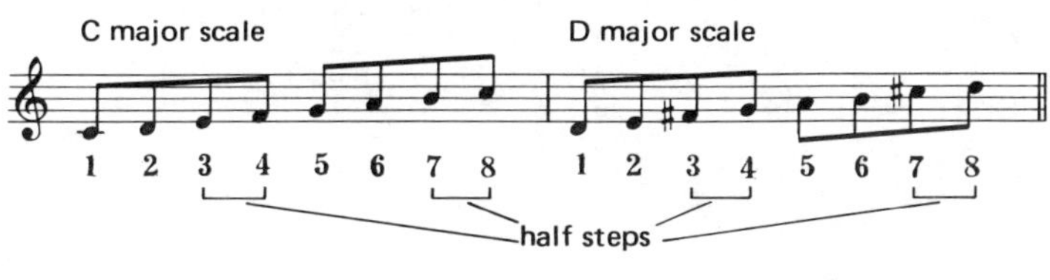

Major scales produce characteristically sounding music. The beginning of "Yankee Doodle" below is a good example. Both its melody and harmonic accompaniment are derived from the major scale starting on C.

The minor scales are all 8-note patterns with a half step between notes 2 and 3. After that, the upper portions of the scales vary.

The "natural" minor scale has half steps between 2 and 3, and 5 and 6. Below is the natural minor scale built on C.

The problem with using the natural minor scale for many composers was the fact that it lacked a half step between notes 7 and 8. In the major scale, because the 7th note lies only a half step (rather than a whole step) below the 8th, it leads much more convincingly to the 8th. In fact, it is called the "leading tone" for exactly that reason. The lack of a leading tone in the natural minor scale thus presented a compositional problem.

The problem was solved by simply raising the 7th note of the natural minor scale so that it would lie a half rather than a whole step below the eighth. It was now more than a 7th note. It was a leading tone, and it could become a part of harmonies which would pull more dramatically to the final note of the scale. The new minor form thus created was called the "harmonic" minor. Below is the harmonic minor scale built on C.

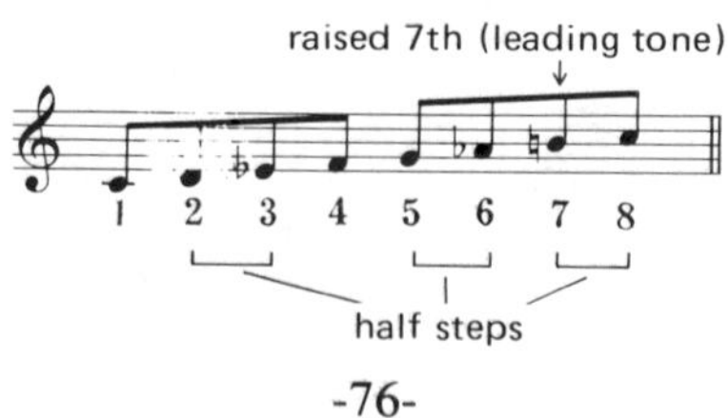

While the harmonic minor solved one problem, it created another. By shortening the interval from 7 to 8, the interval from 6 to 7 was increased. Whereas in the natural minor scale it was a major second, in the harmonic minor it became an augmented second. This was a difficult interval to perform, especially for singers who must rely on their minds rather than the mechanics of an instrument to produce the correct pitch. The new problem was solved with a third and final form of the minor scale. To accommodate a smoother flow of melody, the new "melodic" minor scale would raise both the 6th and 7th steps when going in an upward direction toward the end of the scale. In a downward direction, the leading tone would not be necessary. Consequently, notes 6 and 7 would be restored to their natural position (the position they had occupied in the natural minor scale). The melodic minor scale built on C is written below.

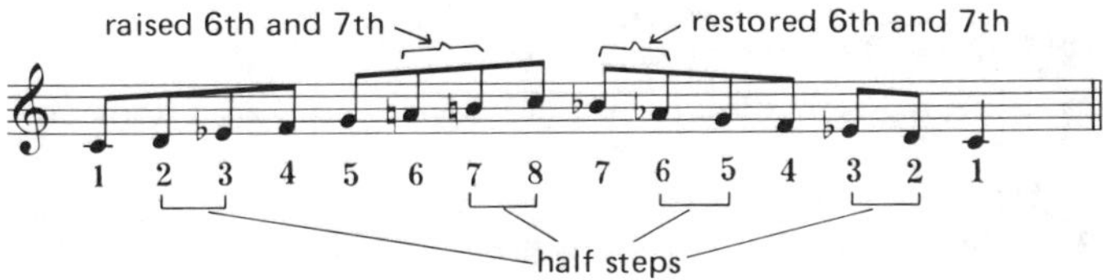

The minor scale system gives a very distinctive flavor to the music which employs it. Below is an example, the opening of the Opus 52 Ballade of Frederick Chopin, written in 1842. It utilizes the tones of the minor scales built on F. The F harmonic minor scale appears below the example. Notice the raised seventh scale step (E♮) in each.

The Whole Tone and Chromatic Scales. In the late 1800's composers began to experiment with scales which altered the sound of the major-minor system. Two such scales were the whole tone scale (built entirely of whole steps) and the chromatic scale (built entirely of half steps).

The whole tone scale divides the octave into six major seconds. For this reason, it has only seven notes from beginning to end. Below is a whole tone scale built on F♯ and an example of music which uses the scale. The music is from a song called "The Cage" by the 20th century American composer Charles Ives.

The chromatic scale uses all twelve half steps within the octave. The example below shows a descending chromatic scale starting on the note C♯ . Below the scale is the opening melody of Claude Debussy's "Prelude to the Afternoon of a Fawn" written in 1889. Notice how the melody begins with the notes of the scale.

Tonality.

The whole step/half step relationships of both the modal and major-minor systems leaves the aural impression that the note upon which the scale is built is the most important tone of the music. It is like one's home: the place from which one departs, to which one returns, from which all other things take their meaning, without which there is a feeling of incompleteness. The starting note of the scales which establish this hierarchy of tones is called the "tonic" note, and any music in which one tone assumes the character of the tonic is called "tonal" music. Tonality, then, is music which employs a tonic and uses scale systems which create the tonic. Let us consider an example.

Above is the familiar melody "Yankee Doodle" written out so that it uses the F major scale. As one plays or sings the song, the note F assumes the character of the tonic. No other note within or outside of the F major scale will give the same degree of stability to the music. F is the tonic; the F major scale creates the hierarchy which supports the tonic; "Yankee Doodle" is an example of tonal music. Moreover, had the melody been written out using the G major scale, then G would be the tonic. In any event, the music would still be tonal in character.

Solmization. The notes of the modal and major-minor scale systems have been given names to designate their position in the tonal hierarchy. The syllables "do, re, mi, fa, sol, la, and ti" stand for the notes of the scale. These syllables were first used in the 9th century A.D. by the monk Guido of Arezzo for a hymn to St. John. It was Guido who devised the technique of naming each tone of the scale, a technique we call "solmization."

There are two variations of the technique of solmization. One is the "fixed do" system; the other, the "moveable do" system. In the fixed do system, "do" is always the note "C" - no matter what scale is involved.

In the moveable do system, "do" is always the first note of the scale, the tonic note. If the music is centered about the F scale, then F is "do;" if it is centered about the D scale, the D is "do;" etc. The moveable do system is far more widely used today simply because it preserves the idea of the tonal hierarchy. "Do" is always the first scale tone; "sol," always the fifth; etc. Below are two scales illustrating the moveable do system.

In addition to the syllable names of solmization, the various tones of the scale have other names which indicate their position relative to the tonic. The chart below lists all these names for easy reference.

Tones of the Scale		
Scale step	**Solmization name**	**Positional name**
1	Do	Tonic
2	Re	Supertonic
3	Mi	Mediant
4	Fa	Sub-dominant
5	Sol	Dominant
6	La	Sub-mediant
7	Ti	Leading tone
8	Do	Tonic

The Concept of Key. Tonal music which uses a given note as the tonic is said to be "in the key of" that note. For example, the melody "Yankee Doodle" above is in the key of F major because it establishes F as its tonic and utilizes the F major scale as its principal organizational structure. Similarly, the Opus 52 Chopin Ballade cited earlier is in the key of F minor because it is constructed around the F minor scale with F as its tonic. Any of the twelve steps of the chromatic scale may serve as a tonic. Therefore, there are twelve possible major and twelve possible minor keys (C major, C minor, D♭ major, C♯ minor, D major, D minor, E♭ major, E♭ minor, etc.)

Key Signatures. We already know that in constructing major and minor scales we must use accidentals (sharps, flats, etc.) to preserve the proper whole step and half step relationships which the scales require. For example, the D major scale below requires us to use an F♯ and C♯ in its construction.

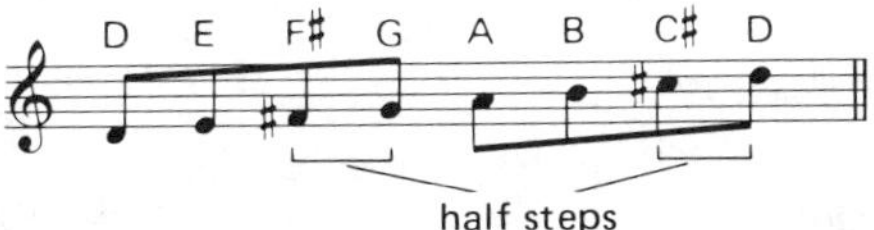

In writing out music which is in the key of D major, however, it is cumbersome to add a sharp to every F or every C each time one appears. Therefore, the sharps are placed after the clef sign at the beginning of each line of music. The performer thus understands that every time an F or C occurs, it is really an F♯ or C♯ which is played. The accidentals placed in this manner at the start of each line are called "key signatures." Below are some examples.

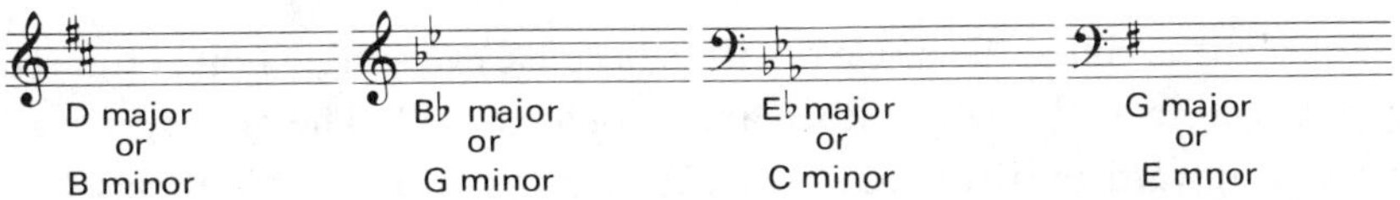

Note that any key signature stands for both a major and a minor key. The D major and B minor scales, for example, both contain two sharps (F♯ and C♯). Therefore, the key signature containing two sharps applies to both.

The Circle of Fifths. The chart below, known as the circle of fifths, is useful in determining the key signatures of all the major and minor keys. One begins reading the chart at "12 o'clock" with the keys of C major and A minor. (On the chart all major keys are indicated by capital letters while minor keys are indicated by lower-case letters.) C major and A minor have a key signature of no sharps and no flats. As one reads clockwise to the right, one encounters all the keys with sharps in their signatures. The "flat keys" occur as one reads counter-clockwise to the left of C major.

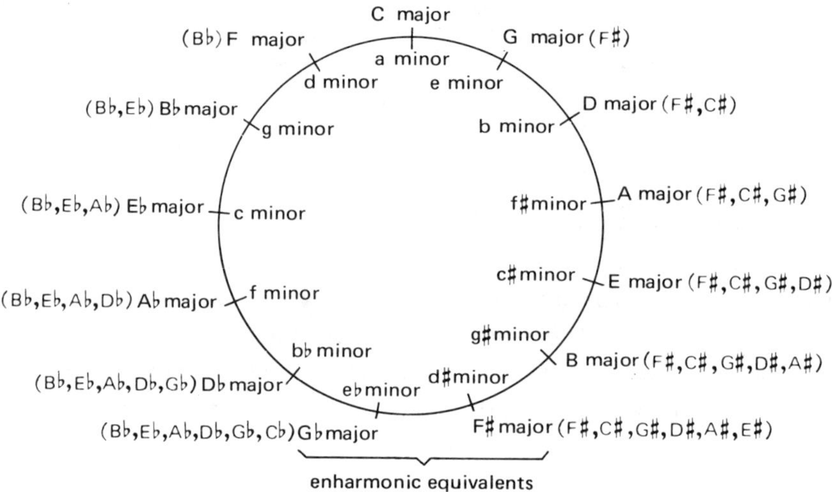

The chart is called the circle of fifths because everything in it is figured by counting perfect fifths either above or below C. The "sharp keys" proceed upward by fifths (C, G, D, A, etc.), as do the ♯'s themselves (F♯, C♯, G♯, etc.). The "flat keys" proceed downward by fifths (C, F, B♭, E♭, etc.), as do the ♭'s themselves (B♭, E♭, A♭, etc.).

The circle of fifths thus tells us at a glance the specific key signature of any major or minor key. The signature of D major, for example, has two sharps (F♯ and C♯). The signature of C minor has three flats (B♭, E♭, and A♭). (Note that the keys of F♯ major and G♭ major, D♯ minor and E♭ minor, are enharmonic equivalents.)

Writing Key Signatures. The sharps and flats of all key signatures are written in a certain order on the staff. The correct placement of the accidentals is indicated below. It may help to use a "V" and an inverted "V" to visualize the placement more clearly.

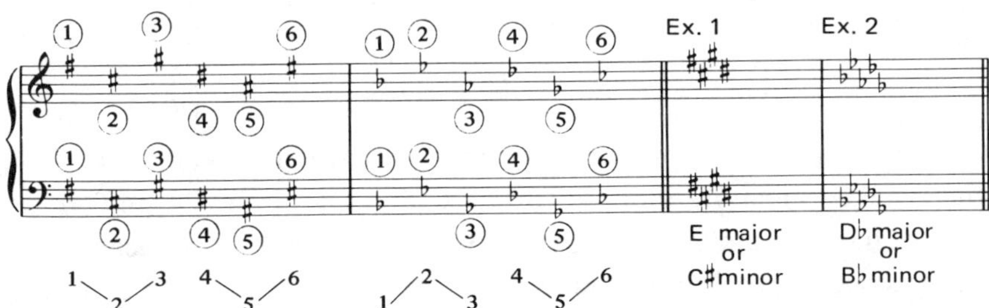

The accidental diagram above has two examples illustrating the use of the placement order. In Example 1, we see the signature of four sharps (the signature of either E major or C♯ minor). The sharps are placed in the positions reserved for accidentals 1, 2, 3, and 4. Example 2 illustrates the proper placement for the five flats in the signatures of D♭ major and B♭ minor.

The Concept of Parallel and Relative Keys. Keys and key signatures allow us to identify two kinds of relationships between the various keys: parallel relationships and relative relationships. Parallel keys are those with the same tonic but different signatures. C major and C minor, D major and D minor, for example, are parallel keys. C major and C minor both have the same tonic (C), but whereas C major has no sharps or flats, C minor has three flats in its signature.

Relative keys are those with the same signatures but different tonics. C major and A minor, F major and D minor, for example, are relative keys. One speaks of C as the "relative major" of A minor, and A as the "relative minor" of C major. In the circle of fifths above, all the relative majors are connected by straight lines to their relative minors. Relative keys always lie a minor third apart (C-a, F-d, G-e, etc.).

Notating "Foreign" Tones. If in the course of a work, a composer wishes to use tones other than those in his key signature, he does so by adding the desired accidental to the note involved. The accidental remains in effect for the duration of one measure after which the notes of the original key signature again apply. The example below illustrates this principle.

In measure 1, both F's are F♯ 's because we are in the key of D major and our key signature indicates that F♯ and C♯ are to be performed unless otherwise indicated. In measure 2, both F's are F♮ 's because a ♮ sign has been affixed to the first note (F). The ♮ remains in effect for the entire measure, thus the second F is also an F♮ . Had we wished the second F of measure 2 to be an F♯ , we would have to add a ♯ in front of it, thus cancelling the preceding ♮ . The F in measure 3 is an F♯ again because we are in a new measure. The ♮ sign of measure 2 no longer applies. The original key signature is again in effect. The B♭ in measure 3 is a tone foreign to the key and scale of D major (D-E-F♯ -G-A-B♮ -C♯ -D). If B♭ is the desired note and one is in D major, the ♭ sign must be added as it is above.

Modulation. Frequently it happens that during the course of a composition, the composer moves from one key to another, usually for the sake of having a greater variety of sound. Such a change in key is called a "modulation." Modulations may be indicated either by using accidentals within the body of the music or by altering the key signature itself. In the example below the modulation from C major to D major is accomplished first with the use of accidentals and then with a change in signature.

Atonality.

Tonal music is by no means the only kind of music. Scales like the whole tone and chromatic scales which divide the octave into equal increments can be used to generate music in which no particular tone seems to emerge as a satisfying musical or emotional center. Such music is generally referred to as "atonal" music, and it has gained great prominence during the 20th century. The fragment below is an example of atonal music. It is based upon a certain arrangement of the twelve notes of the octave called a "tone row." The row appears below the fragment.

Besides atonality of the kind above, with today's sophisicated electronic equipment it is possible to generate not only the traditional twelve semitones of the octave but many other frequencies as well. Digital computers can be wired to sound synthesizers to produce an infinite number of pitches between any two notes a half step apart. Between C and D♭ , for example, there are "quarter tones" and "microtones" that no mere piano can play.

Music utilizing intervals smaller than a semi-tone is called "microtonal" music. Such music is often controversial. Many listeners regard it as unpleasant. They hear it not as microtonal music but rather as "out-of-tune" tonal music. Tastes in music, like tastes in fashion or art or food, are often matters of conditioning. We will return to this aspect of music in a later chapter. For now, you need only be aware that microtonality is a part of the musical world, a part quite distinguishable from the more traditional sounds of tonal organization.

Further Reading.

The musical literature abounds with books and articles on the topics covered in this chapter. As with many other topics, the **Harvard Dictionary** and **Grove's Dictionary** are excellent places to begin supplemental reading. Their articles entitled "scales," "modes," "tonality," and "atonality" will all provide information and further bibliographical references.

Of a more technical nature is the book **Serial Composition and Atonality** (Berkeley: University of California Press, 1962) by the composer George Perle. It should be noted, however, that Perle's is a demanding work, not easily digested by the beginner. One of the best general discussions of scales occurs in Alain Danielou's work entitled **Introduction to the Study of Musical Scales** (1943). The theory and use of modes is treated in some depth by Hugo Riemann in his work **The History of Music Theory.** A translation of Riemann's book by Raymond Haggh has been published by the University of Nebraska Press (Lincoln, Neb.: 1962).

CHAPTER SIX

POLYPHONY: HARMONY AND COUNTERPOINT

Scales and the melodies created from them constitute only one kind of music - "monophonic" or "single-line" music. A melody played alone with no accompaniment can be a beautiful thing, but it hardly represents the majority of the music we hear. Most often our music occurs with tones sounded together. This kind of "multiple-line" music is called "polyphony," and some music historians argue that the development of polyphony in Europe around 900 A.D. was one of the greatest cultural achievements of mankind.

Generally speaking, polyphony has two ways of manifesting itself: harmony and counterpoint. Harmony is the use of sounds conceived as verticalities. A group of notes is played together and followed by another group of notes played together. One verticality after another, the progression of sounds adds a new dimension to the single monophonic line. Counterpoint is the use of lines sounded simultaneously. I sing a melody, and you sing a second melody at the same time. Our polyphony is not the sequence of one simultaneous group of notes followed by another, but rather the interaction of one line with another.

To use the crude analogy of a crossword puzzle, harmony is the "down" and counterpoint the "across." Harmony is a vertically conceived form of polyphony, counterpoint a horizontally conceived one.

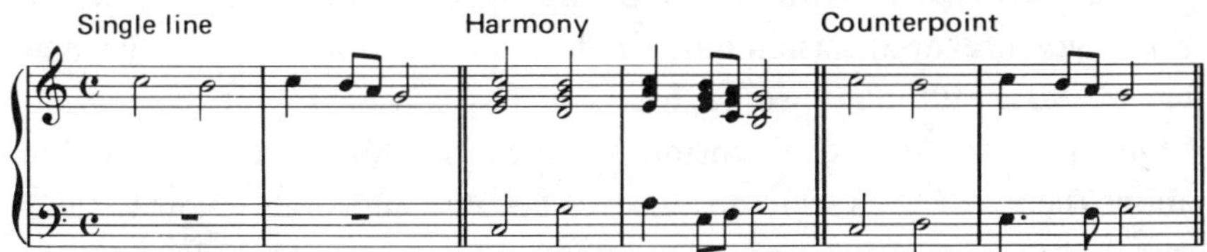

Chords and Harmony.

A chord is any group of three or more tones played simultaneously. (Remember that two simultaneous tones constitute an interval, not a chord.) Over the course of music history there have been many types of chords. Some of the most important are described below.

1. An "8-5-1" chord - used widely in the early middle ages.
2. A "triad" - the most important type of chord in use between c. 1300 A.D. and today.
3. A "chromatic" chord - used more frequently after 1700.
4. A chord built in fourths - used in the 20th century.
5. A "polytriad" - used in the 20th century.
6. A "tone cluster" - used in the 20th century.

As you may have deduced, these chords often derive their names from the intervals with which they are built. The "8-5-1" chord, for example, is constructed with an octave and a fifth above its lowest root note. The "triad" is a three-note chord built in thirds. The "chromatic" chord uses accidentals and a variety of intervals above the root note. The "chord built in fourths" is exactly that, a chord constructed with one perfect fourth piled on top of another. The "polytriad" is a combination of two triads; the "tone cluster," a mass of closely grouped pitches.

Any of these chords can be used to form the polyphonic verticality which supports a melody line and adds dimension to an otherwise monophonic setting. Harmony is the study of how one chord moves to another to form a progression of verticalities.

The Concept of Consonance and Dissonance. Just why certain chords gain favor at certain times in the history of music is largely a matter of taste, although some theorists have argued that the various sonorities have divine or cosmic or even psychological inevitabilities about them. "Triads were destined to become important chords," they say; or "the use of an augmented fourth is the work of the Devil." Such statements are, of course, impossible to prove, and they make the study of harmony difficult and imprecise.

What is clear is that certain sounds seem to dominate the musical styles of certain times just as clothing fashions, trends in art or architecture, movements in literature or politics rise to positions of prominence during various eras. At a certain moment in history, one chord will be more pleasing to the ear just as one style of gown will be more pleasing to the eye.

The two terms most often used to describe the pleasantness or unpleasantness of musical sounds are "consonance" and "dissonance." Generally defined, "consonance" is that which is pleasing, harmonious, and acceptable. "Dissonance" is that which is unpleasant or discordant. Consonances tend to produce feelings of stability, dissonance feelings of instability or tension. From a purely musical (rather than psychological) point of view, consonances are generally those sounds which are native to the chords or scales being used. Dissonances are generally "foreigners." The examples below provide an illustration.

In Example 1 we are in C major. Our idiom is tonal, our scale the major scale, our chords triadic. In Example 2 the added F♯ is foreign to the key, scale, and chords of C major. It thus seems out of place, harsh, strident. In musical terms, the F♯ is a dissonance, the other tones consonances.

All of this is not to say that dissonances are totally avoided. On the contrary, their very pungency gives them power and makes them useful to the musical art. It is just that one must recognize their power and treat them carefully, not unlike the use of spices in cooking. If there were no garlic or cayenne pepper, salt or oregano, foods would be forever bland and uninteresting. However, one must be careful to use spices in places where they are appropriate and in quantities where they enhance rather than destroy the flavor of the dishes to which they are applied. Garlic does not seem to enhance the flavor of ice cream, for instance, and a pound of pepper is just too much for a cup of soup.

In the history of Western music, the different intervals and the chords which employed them were treated variously as consonances or dissonances at different times. Thirds, for example, were viewed as dissonances before approximately 1100 A.D. Then their status began to change so that by 1750 they were the most consonant of intervals. The fourth, a consonance in the early Middle Ages, took on elements of dissonance by 1300 or so, but only in certain special circumstances. The table below provides a useful if greatly simplified historical overview of consonance and dissonance.

Intervals: A Historical Overview					
Type	Before c. 1000	c. 1000-1200	c. 1200-1800	C. 1800-1900	1900 +
Consonant Intervals	Unisons, Octaves, 4ths, 5ths	Unisons, Octaves, 4ths, 5ths	Unisons, Octaves, 3rds, 5ths, 6ths	Unisons, Octaves, 3rds, 5ths, 6ths	
Dissonant Intervals	2nds, 3rds, 6ths, 7ths, Augmented and Diminished	2nds, 7ths, Augmented and Diminished	2nds, 7ths, Augmented and Diminished		
Intervals of Variable Status		3rds, 6ths	4ths	2nds, 4ths, 7ths, Augmented and Diminished	All

Perhaps the most important thing the overview chart provides is the notion that as music progressed toward the 20th century, the distinction between consonance and dissonance became less and less sharp. As we shall see in our historical investigations later in this text, the 20th century became a repository of many musical styles. From rock music to Broadway, the symphony hall to the electronic studio, modern music has so much variety that it is impossible to generalize about consonant and dissonant sounds. In the tunes of a Broadway musical, intervals like seconds and sevenths may be treated as dissonances while in the background music to a horror film they are so acceptable that the word dissonance no longer applies.

For the purposes of this chapter, we will continue our investigation of chords and harmony only with the triad. This will be our course for several reasons. First, triadic harmony accounts for the vast majority of music written between c. 1300 and the present. Second, triadic harmony provides the firmest background for the study of more complex non-triadic music. Finally, in an introductory text such as this, pursuing more complicated topics is inappropriate. Should you become so fascinated with the study of music that you wish to probe deeper into its make-up, you will need more advanced texts and more in-depth teaching than this volume is intended to supply. The suggested reading at the end of this chapter and the harmony courses provided in most colleges and some high schools across the country can easily move you into more advanced musical study.

For the present, our topic will be triadic harmony, harmony in which the unison, octave, fifth, third and sixth are always consonant; the second, seventh and any augmented or diminished interval always dissonant; and the fourth an interval of variable status. Whose music is this? The music of Bach and Beethoven, "My Fair Lady," and the Beatles. In short, most of the music to which you listen.

The Triad. Triads are three-note chords built in major and/or minor thirds above a root note. Because they are constructed in thirds, they are spelled with every other letter of the musical alphabet (see below).

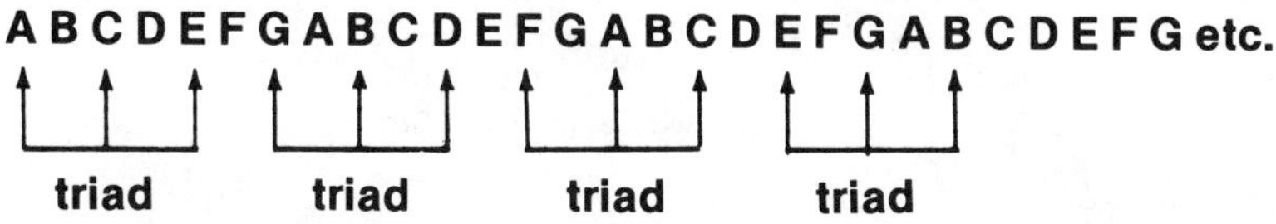

The three notes of a triad are called the root (the note on which the triad is built), the 3rd (the note a major or minor third above the root), and the 5th (the remaining note which always lies a perfect, diminished or augmented fifth above the root). The examples below illustrate the parts of the CEG and ACE triads.

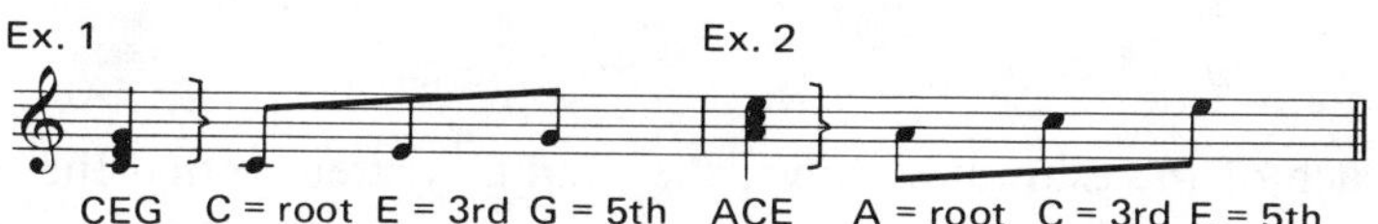

There are four kinds or "qualities" of triads: major, minor, augmented and diminished.

A major triad is constructed with a major third and perfect fifth above the root. The C major triad appears below.

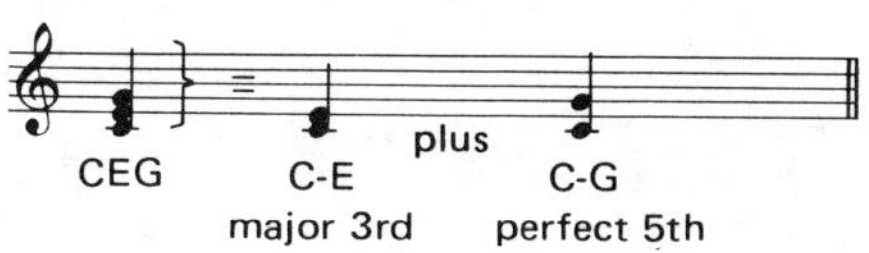

A minor triad is constructed with a minor third and a perfect fifth above the root. The C minor triad appears below.

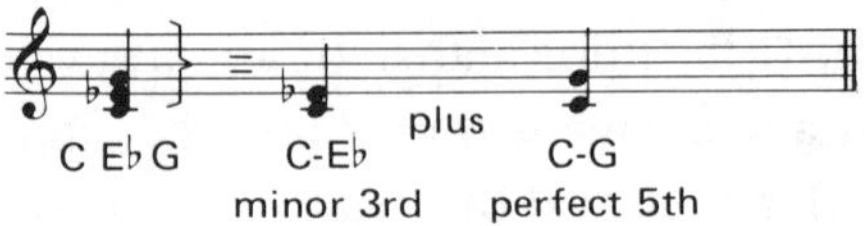

An augmented triad is constructed with a major third and augmented fifth above the root. The C augmented triad appears below.

A diminished triad is constructed with a minor third and diminished fifth above the root. The C diminished triad appears below.

In each of the examples above, the triad is written so that the root is the lowest note. That does not always have to be the case. The position of the notes of the triad can be rearranged so that the 3rd or 5th becomes the lowest note. There are thus three possible positions for any triad: root position where the root is the lowest note; so-called "first inversion" where the 3rd is the lowest note; and "second inversion" where the 5th is the lowest note. The five examples below provide an illustration.

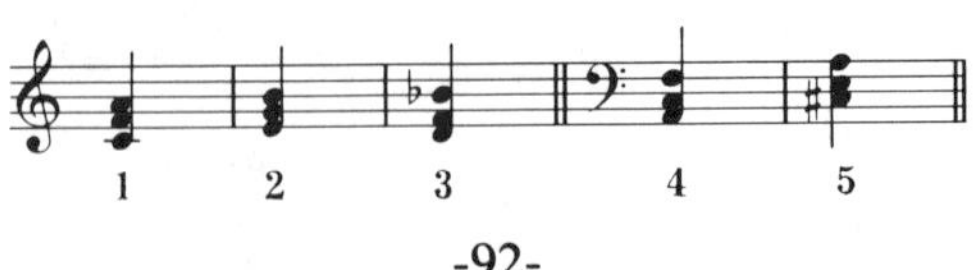

Reading upward from the lowest note of each chord, the five triads are analyzed as follows:

1.   CFA, an F major triad in 2nd inversion.
      (F = root, A = 3rd, C = 5th)

2.   EGB, an E minor triad in root position.
      (E = root, G = 3rd, B = 5th)

3.   DFB♭ , a B♭ major triad in 1st inversion.
      (B♭ = root, D = 3rd, F = 5th)

4.   ACF, an F major triad in 1st inversion.
      (F = root, A = 3rd, C = 5th)

5.   C♯ EA, an A major triad in 1st inversion.
      (A = root, C♯ = 3rd, E = 5th)

The Roman Numeral/Figured Bass System. Any step of the major or minor scale can be the root of a triad. The chords constructed in this way are identified by the Roman numerals I through VII (see below).

Above are the triads generated by the C major scale. The triads of all major scales have the same qualities. They are:

I	=	major	V	=	major
II	=	minor	VI	=	minor
III	=	minor	VII	=	diminished
IV	=	major			

In a minor key, the qualities of the triads are different because of the different nature of the minor scale. Below are the triads of the C minor scale. Note that the harmonic form of the scale is used and that in the III chord, the natural 7th step (B♭) is employed rather than the leading tone (B♮). The use of the natural 7th scale degree in III and the raised 7th degree in V and VII is almost universal in the writing of triadically oriented music.

VI Polyphony: harmony and counterpoint

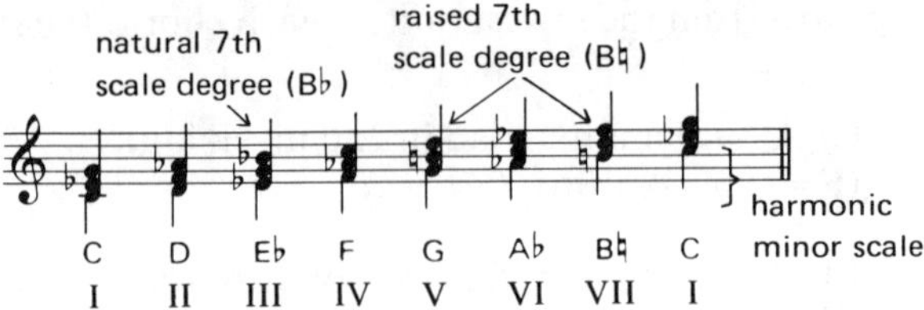

The qualities of the triads of minor scales are:

I	=	minor
II	=	diminished
III	=	major (using the natural 7th scale step)
IV	=	minor
V	=	major (using the raised 7th leading tone)
VI	=	major
VII	=	diminished (using the raised 7th leading tone)

The various positions of triads (root position, 1st inversion, and 2nd inversion) are often indicated by a kind of numerical shorthand called a "figured bass." Figured bass symbols originated around 1600 and, like modern guitar chord symbols, they aided performers in the improvisation of music. The figured bass symbol for root position is 5/3; for 1st inversion, 6/3; and for 2nd inversion, 6/4.

It is easy to see how the figures originated. If a triad is in root position, with the root as its lowest note, the other notes of the triad will lie a fifth and a third (5/3) above the root. If the triad is in 1st inversion with the third as its lowest note, the other notes of the triad will lie a sixth and a third (6/3) above. In 2nd inversion, the fifth is the lowest note with the others a sixth and fourth (6/4) above it. The figure below illustrates with a C major triad.

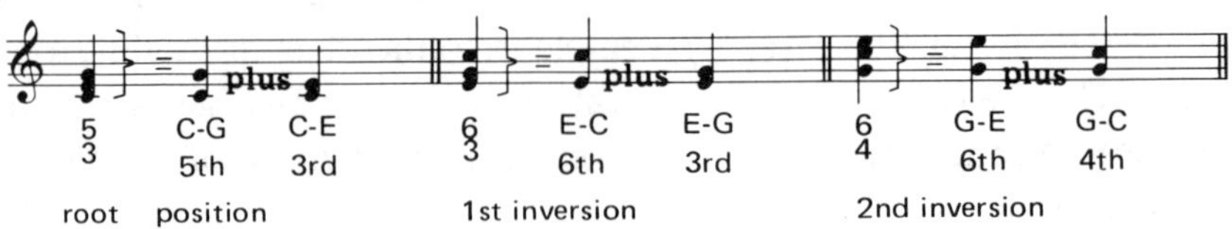

By combining the use of Roman numerals and figured bass symbols it is possible to identify any triad in any key. Below, for example, are the I 6/3 in C minor and the V 6/4 in G major. The examples show both the triads and the scales from which they are generated.

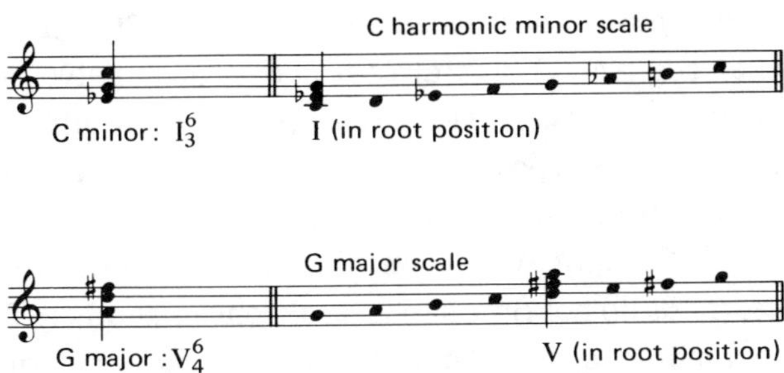

With the Roman numeral/figured bass system, it is also possible to show how the very same chord can function differently in different keys. For example, EGC is a 1st inversion I chord in C major, but it is also a 1st inversion V chord in F major (see below). Its label depends on how it is used.

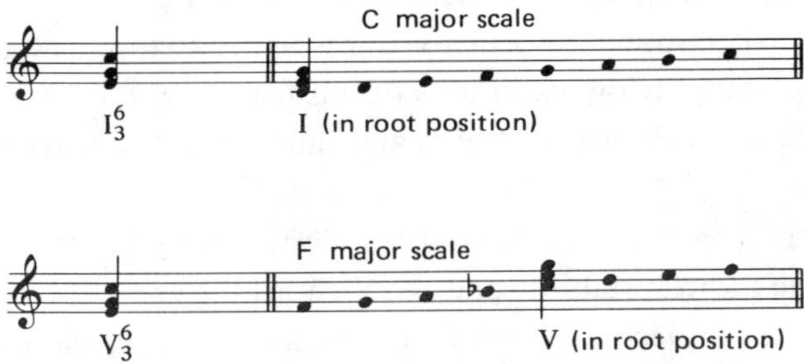

This is not such a strange concept. It occurs in language all the time. In the sentence "Brown is not a primary color," the word "brown" functions as a noun, the subject of the sentence. However, in the sentence "The leaves are brown," the same word "brown" is used as a predicate adjective. Its grammatical label changes according to its literary function even though it is spelled and pronounced exactly the same in both cases. So, too, with the 1st inversion C chord above. It will be spelled the same and sound the same in C major as in F major, but it will move to different chords and take on different meanings in the separate keys. Hence, it will have separate labels in the chord grammar of harmony.

More Complex Chords. As we have already seen, triads are hardly the only chords in the language of music. More complex chords can be built from triads by continuing to add thirds above the root note. So-called 7th chords (like CEGB♮ or CEGB♭), 9th chords (CEGBD), 11th chords, and 13th chords are not only possible, they actually came into prominent use as music approached and entered the 20th century. These and the other complex chords already mentioned (polytriads, chords built in fourths, tone clusters, etc.) are all part of more advanced studies of harmony. For our purposes, we will note their existence but concentrate on the use of triadic harmony.

Harmony: A System of Usage. In the tonal world of major and minor scales, triads do not flow haphazardly one to another. They do not appear in a random order, but rather in sequences determined by a system of predefined usage. The flow of triads is thus to the musical language not unlike the flow of words in the syntax of the written or spoken language. In any sentence, simple or complex, words have an order which is determined by their function. We say, for example, "The dog jumped over the fence," not "Dog the fence the over jumped." True, we might also say, "Over the fence, the dog jumped," but in any proper rearrangement of the sentence there will always be certain rules of syntax which determine the order of our words. So, too, with triadic motion. In the many, many variations of musical flow, there are principles which guide the ordering of chords and thus form a system of harmonic syntax.

The overriding principle behind triadic harmony is that the I chord provides the greatest stability and the V chord the greatest tension. I and V are like the subject and verb of the music sentence, the positive and negative poles of the musical magnet. The I chord (or tonic, as we have seen it called) is the place from which the harmonic action flows and to which it seems emotionally destined to return. The V chord (or dominant) is the sonority which leads most convincingly to the tonic. Everything else in the harmonic scheme takes its meaning from this tonic-dominant relationship.

Harmonic Levels. Because of the polarity between I and V, it is possible to think of triads as existing on three architectonic levels: the tonic level, the dominant level, and a third plane which, for lack of a better term, we shall call the intermediary level.

The tonic level is that which serves as the basis of tonal stability. It is embodied by the I chord but may occasionally be represented by a chord (like the VI) which substitutes for I.

The dominant level is that which serves to draw immediately and convincingly to the tonic. It is embodied by the V chord and occasionally by VII, both of which contain the leading tone that draws the ear toward I.

The intermediary level is the repository for the other triads of the scale: II, III, IV, and VI. It serves as a kind of buffer between tonic and dominant, providing a measure of chordal variety.

Most harmonic chord progressions fall into the pattern tonic-dominant-tonic (t-d-t) or tonic-intermediary-dominant-tonic (t-i-d-t). The most basic harmonic progressions appear below.

$$
\begin{array}{l}
\text{I-V-I (t-d-t)} \\
\left.\begin{array}{l}
\text{I-II-V-I} \\
\text{I-III-V-I} \\
\text{I-IV-V-I} \\
\text{I-VI-V-I}
\end{array}\right\} \text{(t-i-d-t)}
\end{array}
$$

There are, of course, uncounted combinations of chords which form the harmonic progressions of triadic music. The ones above represent only the simplest. Yet even the most complex tend to follow the t-d-t or t-i-d-t structure. Usually, the expansion of a progression occurs on the intermediate level. Consider, for example, the progression which goes I-VI-IV-II-V-I (not uncommon in tonal music). The VI, IV, and II chords are all intermediate sonorities, so the basic underlying structure remains t-i-d-t (see below).

$$
\begin{array}{cccc}
\text{I} & \text{VI-IV-II} & \text{V} & \text{I} \\
t & i & d & t
\end{array}
$$

The Harmonic Pyramid. A kind of chordal flow chart in the shape of a pyramid is useful in presenting a visualization of the harmonic motions of triadic tonality.

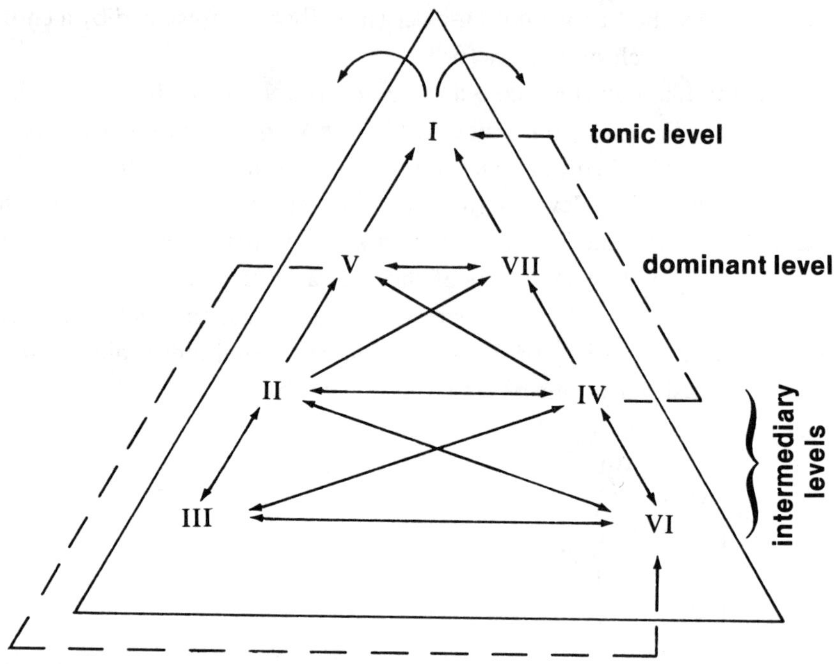

The pyramid indicates that from I, motion can go anywhere, but that after I has been left, motion tends to be (a) among chords of the same architectonic level or (b) upward through the pyramid. For example, a II can move conveniently to any intermediary or dominant level sonority, but not conveniently to I. Thus the pattern I-V-II-I is unlikely, while the pattern I-II-V-I is very likely.

The two dotted lines (V-VI and IV-I) are common exceptions to the t-d-t and t-i-d-t structures we have discussed. V-VI is called a "deceptive cadence;" IV-I, a "plagal cadence." Both are frequently encountered and will be discussed a bit later in this chapter. For now, it may be useful to apply the ideas of the pyramid to an actual piece of music. Let us take the "Yankee Doodle" melody used earlier.

In the harmonization of the Yankee Doodle melody, we see three simple, overlapping progressions: I-V-I, I-V-I, and I-IV-V-I. Each displays the t-d-t or t-i-d-t structure common to the music of triadic tonality.

Cadences. The strong association between I and V in tonal music is powerful enough to create places where the music seems to pause or rest, much as periods create such places for sentence and paragraph structure. In music these places are called cadences.

While the terminology which describes various kinds of cadences is not identical from text to text, the six definitions below are generally accepted and will serve our purposes here.

> Full cadence: a chord progression ending with V-I.
>
> Half cadence: a progression ending on V.
>
> Strong cadence: a cadence ending on a strong beat.
>
> Weak cadence: a cadence ending on a weak beat.
>
> Plagal cadence: a progression ending IV-I.
>
> Deceptive cadence: a progression ending V-VI.

The plagal cadence, which seems to contradict the t-d-t and t-i-d-t structures, is an outgrowth of the modal scale system. Some modes (the Dorian, Phrygian, and Mixolydian, for example) are incapable of generating a major V chord because they lack a leading tone. V-I is thus an impossibility; IV-I becomes a kind of substitute. the plagal cadence is especially common at the end of church hymns. It is the final cadence on which the word "Amen" is sung.

The deceptive cadence is simply a variation of the dominant-tonic pattern. By resolving to VI, the composer introduces an element of surprise which not only spices up the moment, but makes a true V-I cadence later on all the more satisfying. The VI chord is frequently the "deceiving" chord of the pattern, but there are others (some more complex than the triad) which are used as well. In any event, the principle of the cadence is the same: V never reaches the anticipated I chord, going instead to a substitute which only sharpens the listener's appetite for the real thing.

Counterpoint.

If harmony can be said to represent the "down" of the musical crossword puzzle, then counterpoint represents the "across." Where harmony is concerned with vertical chordal sonorities, counterpoint is concerned with horizontal lines. More strictly, the study of counterpoint is the study of line and the interaction of one line with another.

By line (or melody) we mean a succession of tones which has some coherence. Usually the coherence is provided by the architecture of the line (that is, its rise and fall) and by the scalar or harmonic context in which it occurs. In the study of counterpoint we see not only what shape or motion the individual line possesses, but we also see how one line is pitted against others in much the same way the separate threads of a fabric are woven together to produce cloths of varying designs.

Contrapuntal Motions. There are six fundamental motions in counterpoint. They are listed below, and we shall study each in turn.

1. Passing motion
2. Motion in thirds
3. Neighbor motion
4. Embellishing motion
5. Motion within a chord
6. Motion in fifths

A passing motion is simply a scalar pattern (upward or downward) made of whole and/or half steps. The notes of a passing motion are called passing tones. Below is an example of a passing motion first written alone, then with supporting harmony.

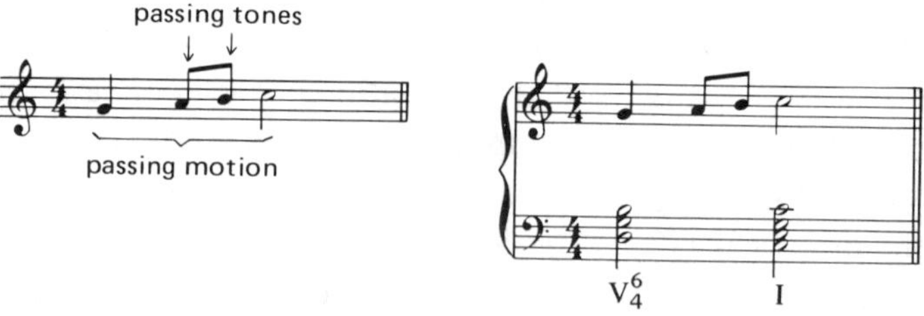

We have a tendency to think that melody (or any linear motion) always occurs as the highest musical part with chords below it. That is not always true, and to demonstrate the variety possible, here is the same passing motion with supporting chords above it.

Motion in thirds is nothing more than passing motion with every other note removed. Once again, this "skipped passing motion" can be found in either the upper or lower musical parts.

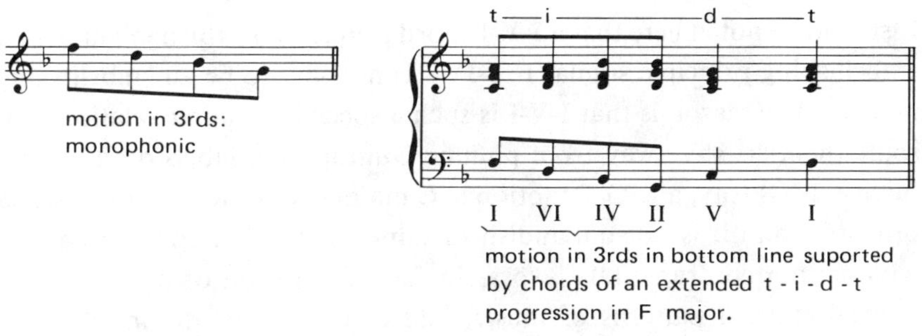

motion in 3rds in bottom line suported by chords of an extended t - i - d - t progression in F major.

Neighbor motion is movement from an original tone to another tone no more than a whole or half step distant, then back to the original tone. The tone between the two original ones is called a "neighbor note." There are "upper neighbor motions" (UN), "lower neighbor motions" (LN), and even "double neighbor motions." The examples below illustrate the principle in both monophonic and polyphonic applications.

VI Polyphony: harmony and counterpoint

Embellishing motions are like neighbor motions but with distances larger than a second between the original tone and the so-called "embellishing tone." The plagal cadence (I-IV-I) uses an embellishing motion. The examples below illustrate.

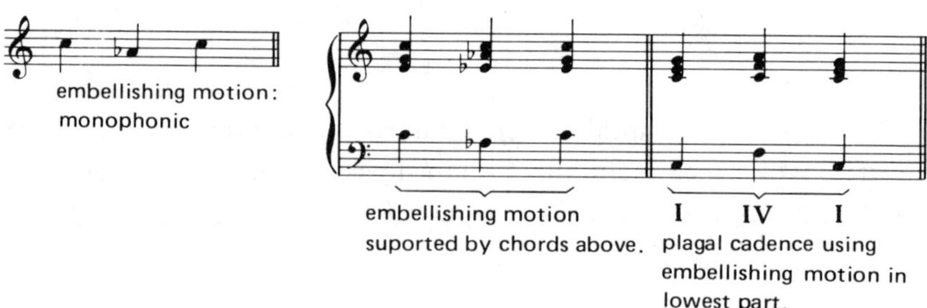

It should be noted here that a I-V-I chord progression which might use an embellishing principle similar to I-IV-I is not said to be an embellishing motion. The reason is that I-V-I is such a special harmonic relationship, some theorists shy away from pinning contrapuntal labels on it. In actuality, I-V-I (say, a C-G-C motion in C major) does use the embellishing principle, and it is not outlandish to think of it as a harmonic pattern with certain contrapuntal flavors. In fact, the fusion of harmony (the vertical chordal patterns of music) and counterpoint (the interlocking linear patterns of music) is at the core of almost all Western polyphony. Seeing the two kinds of motion as a single fusion is often inescapable.

Motion within a chord (or "arpeggiation" as it is also called) is simply movement from one chord tone to another. The example below shows motion within the F major triad.

Motion in fifths is just that, linear movement which utilizes the interval of a fifth. In the example below (taken from the G minor Passacaglia of G.F. Handel) the motion occurs in the bass (lowest) part. Note that in order to keep the notes on the staff, the line moves down a fifth, then up a fourth, then down a fifth, etc. Note, too, that though the line moves in fifths, there is no V-I (G-D) relationship.

The Construction and Manipulation of Line. The contrapuntal motions above do not in and of themselves constitute clear, convincing lines. They are only the horizontal building blocks from which lines may be created. It is the skill with which lines are composed and then used which lies at the heart of counterpoint.

The construction of a good line encompasses many ideas. The line should have a clear sense of beginning and end; it should have a climactic point to help give it shape; it should not contain internal patterns (like undue repetitions or chordal outlines) which take the listener's focus away from the horizontal flow; it should balance the tension of intervallic leaps with the stability of step-wise motion; it should not violate the use of consonance and dissonance called for by the scale or modal system from which it originates. There are many things in the compositional crafting of line for the composer to think about before he commits his ideas to paper.

The study of writing lines and then pitting one against another takes years, and it is not part of the scope of this text to go through a complete counterpoint curriculum. But it is possible here to examine the construction of a good line, a good counterline, and some of the ways lines can be manipulated.

The line above represents a well-crafted example. It begins and ends on the same note and convincingly conveys the flavor of the C major scale from which it is derived. It has a climactic goal (the note A) which gives it an overall architectural rise and fall, yet it is not just an upward or downward scale. There are smaller convolutions which give it a variety of direction and thus a more interesting shape. Leaps are balanced by returning steps so that the tension created by the gap in a leap is relieved when that gap is filled in. There are no repetitions, chordal outlines, or harsh dissonances to break the linear flow.

In the language of counterpoint study, this line is called a "cantus firmus" (Latin for "strong chant"). It is the first thing a student learns to write, and so that the student may concentrate only on line, it is written with no rhythm. The adoption of rhythm to line occurs much later in the formal study of counterpoint.

Having written a good cantus firmus, the next step is to pit an equally well-crafted counterpoint against it. In doing this, another dimension is added to the composition. Not only must the new line make good horizontal sense, it must fit with the first line according to the proper use of consonance and dissonance.

The example above sets a counterpoint below the original cantus. Notice that the counterpoint has all the elements of good craftsmanship the cantus demonstrates, and that when played with the cantus it produces consonances which allow the lines to fit harmoniously into the major/minor scale system of tonality from which they come.

Having constructed a good line and counterline, the composer may then manipulate his lines using any or all of the following compositional techniques:

1. Augmentation	4. Retrograde motion
2. Diminution	5. Retrograde inversion
3. Inversion	6. Imitation

Augmentation is simply the re-working of a line so that it has longer rhythmic values. Below is a line treated in this way.

The greatest compositional craftsmen usually find ways to combine the original line with its augmentation, in this way creating a special kind of unity in their works. The example below is a simple illustration.

Diminution, logically enough, is the re-working of line so that it has shorter rhythmic values. Below is our line in its original form; its diminution; and then in a setting in which the original, the augmentation and the diminution are pitted against each other.

Notice that because the diminution (upper part) is moving so much faster than the original line (middle part), there is much more of it. Similarly, because the augmentation (lower part) is moving more slowly, there is much less of it.

The technique of melodic inversion is based upon the concept of intervallic inversion discussed earlier. Simply described, melodic inversion utilizes a change of linear direction. If the original line goes up, the inversion goes down, and so on. Below are two examples of inversion; the first using intervals, the second, line.

Again, in well-crafted composition, the original line and its inversion are often designed so that they can be played together (see below).

The word ''retrograde'' means ''backward.'' The retrograde of a line is the line played in reverse order. Below is a line, its retrograde, and a combined setting of the two. In the combined version, note that the rhythm of the retrograde is different from that of the original. There are also inner voice parts added to the setting. These changes enable a smoother fit of the two contrapuntal lines.

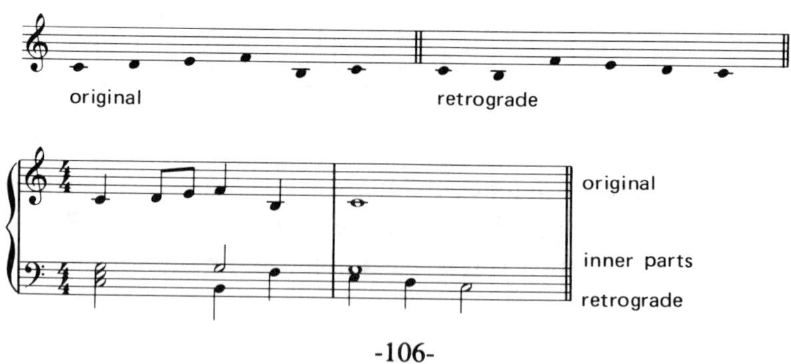

The retrograde inversion of a line is the inverted form played backward. Again, it is possible to write a retrograde inversion so that it can fuse with the original (see below).

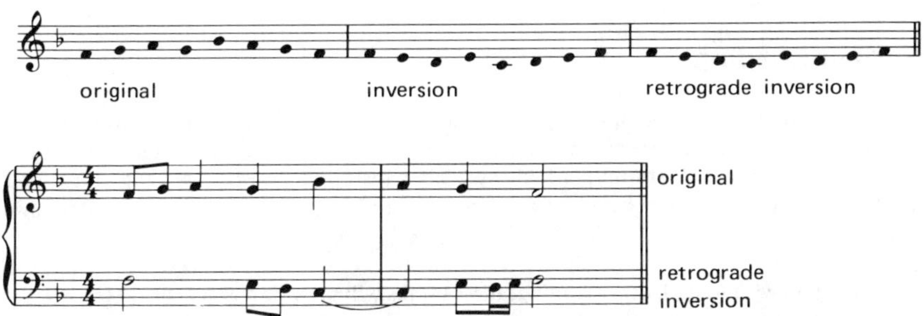

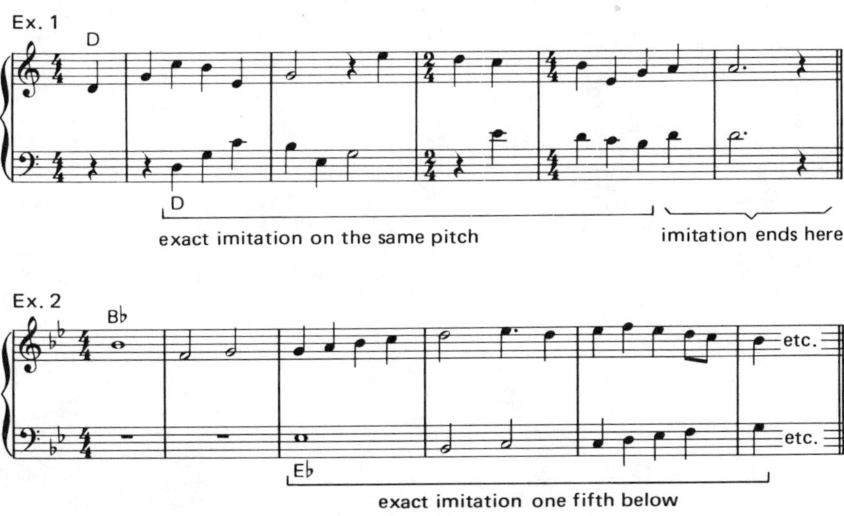

Imitation, the last form of contrapuntal manipulation we shall investigate, is one of the most frequently encountered compositional techniques. Simply stated, it is the mimicking of one line by another, usually while the original line continues on its own way. Such imitations are known by many terms, "canons" or "rounds" being two of the most common. You may, for example, recall the children's rhyme, "Row, Row, Row Your Boat" which is often sung as a round. Below are two illustrations of imitation, the first from a 20th century composition, the second from an early 16th century setting of the "Ave Maria" prayer by the Netherlands composer Josquin des Prez.

Notice that in Example 1 the imitation begins on the same tone (D) in both parts. In Example 2 the original line begins on B♭ while the second line starts on E♭ . Both kinds of imitation are common compositional techniques.

Further Reading.

The information in this chapter represents only a beginning to the study of harmony and counterpoint. There are dozens of texts which treat both subjects in great detail. Two of the more widely used are **Harmony,** 3rd ed. by Walter Piston (New York: Norton, 1962) and **Counterpoint in Composition** by Carl Schachter and Felix Salzer (New York: McGraw-Hill, 1969).

Should you wish to do further reading, these books will provide a good start. However, it must be understood that the study of harmony and counterpoint is very demanding. To master it, textbooks alone are really not sufficient. In addition to the texts, the student should really enroll in formal music theory classes so that the guiding hand of an expert teacher is available.

CHAPTER SEVEN:

CONTOUR AND FORM

The elements of rhythm, harmony, and counterpoint in and of themselves do not provide the architectural shape of a musical work any more than the colors of a painting provide its shape or the materials of a building its overall contour. The structure of music is determined by the way in which small motives of sound combine to make larger forms. Below we will investigate this process.

Common Musical Structures.

The Motif. A motif is a fragment from which larger sections are derived. Probably the most famous example is the opening 4-note motif of Beethoven's Symphony Number 5. This fragment is the acorn from which the entire musical oak is generated.

(see example on following page)

Melody. As we have seen, melody is more than a fragment. It is a coherent, extended thought with a beginning, a climactic goal of motion, and an end which resolves the tensions of tonality and direction. The early Christian hymns codified around 600 A.D. by Pope Gregory I represent to many the purest study of melody. The D minor melody here exemplifies the principles of Gregorian architecture.

SYMPHONY NO.5

L. van Beethoven, Op. 67

Below is another more extended melody, but one showing the same principles of construction. It is from the Andante movement of Mozart's piano sonata K. 545.

The Phrase. In many examples of melody, the overall line is structured in parts, each part ending with a cadence. Such a melodic section is called a phrase, and in a great number of cases, phrases are found in groups of two. This produces the so-called ''antecedent/consequent'' or ''question/answer'' effect. A first phrase is played ending on V, then a second is played cadencing on I, thus completing the musical thought. The example below from the opening of the C major Sonatina of Joseph Haydn is a clear example of consequent/antecedent phrase structure.

Phrase structure is by no means always this regular. Here each phrase is four measures long; each seems to balance the other. However, phrase lengths can vary greatly, and phrases need not combine in the ''question/answer'' grouping we see in this example.

The Musical Period. Several phrases may be grouped together to form a section of music which seems to stand on its own as a coherent unity within the larger whole. Such a section is called a musical period. An example of a musical period is the first 16-measure segment of the Haydn Sonatina above. A second period occurs between measures 16 and 35. The combination of both periods forms yet a larger 35-measure section which seems to possess a unity of its own.

Through-composed Form. When the entirety of a work appears to have only one section or one musical period with no cadences or pauses which mark the clear end of one thought and beginning of another, the composition is said to be through-composed. Through-composed works are generally (though not always) short works designed to be digested by the listener in a brief span. The Little Prelude Number 1 in C major by J.S. Bach (below) is an example of a through-composed work. There is a half cadence at measure 8 and a full cadence at measure 18 which gives the piece a kind of two-period balance within the whole.

LITTLE PRELUDE NO. 1

J.S. Bach

Binary Form. Works which are divided into two clear parts (either by repeat signs or double bars) are said to be in binary form. In general, many dances fall into this category, as does the example below, the Menuet from the C minor French Suite of J.S. Bach.

MENUET
Moderato
p
cresc.
mf
1.
2.
cresc.
f
p

Here, the first and second sections are repeated with melodic hints of the opening recurring in the lower part eight measures before the very end. This kind of thematic restatement at the end of a binary form is quite common. Where the restatement is extensive, the form is called a "rounded binary."

In the analysis of musical forms, letters are used to designate the different sections of a composition. For the Menuet above, the following would be an apt description of the entire form:

$$\|: \quad A \quad :\|: \quad B \quad :\|$$

This would tell us that we were in a 2-part form, each part using different melodic material, each part repeated. If the work were in rounded binary form, the symbol for it might look like this:

$$\|: \quad A \quad :\|: B \ A' :\|$$

Here the second part shows a return to thematic material used in part one. The fact that the material which returns is marked A' rather than A indicates that it is not an exact repeat of the original material. The Gavotte (another dance) from the G major French Suite of J.S. Bach (below) shows the rounded binary form.

GAVOTTE
Allegro
f ben accentuato
5
f
10
p
15
f
mf
20
f

In this example, the thematic material which begins in Part A is really never abandoned. Part B starts with the original motif in inversion (measures 8-9) and ends (measures 20-24) with a repeat of the rhythmic and intervallic elements of the melody.

Ternary Form. Three-part or ternary form can be much more complex than binary form if for no other reason than the fact that many more possibilities exist. Perhaps the most common ternary form is ABA form, an example of which appears below.

25
f
dolce
p
30
fz
cresc.
35
fz
fz
fz
p
pp
cresc.
dolce
40
cresc.
f
45
cresc.
f
ff

Here the opening A section occurs in measures 1-16. The B section, which uses different melodic material, lasts another ten measures. Finally the A section returns with slight variations and a small extension at the very end. Because the return of the A section is somewhat different from its original form, the composition should most properly be labeled ABA'.

An even more common ternary form is the so-called 32-measure song form used by a tremendous number of popular ballads, especially those in the Broadway musical repertoire. A classic example is the traditional Christmas carol, "Deck the Halls with Boughs of Holly."

Here the A section (8 measures) is repeated, followed by an 8-measure B section, and then a final 8-measure A section repeat. The AABA[1] form bears similarities to the rounded binary we saw earlier but is different because both the B and final A section are generally more clearly separated and extended than in the binary.

Another common ternary form is the AAB or so-called bar form used by German singers of the Middle Ages and by the 19th century German opera composer Richard Wagner. An example of the AAB form is the medieval German song "Willekommen Mayenschein" by the 13th century composer Neidhart von Reuenthal.

Neidhart von Reuenthal (13th C.)

Minnelied

Finally, there are ternary forms which can be quite complex. The Minuet-Trio or Scherzo-Trio form is an example. Here the composer combines the binary form of the Minuet (a dance) or Scherzo (a short, rather playful composition) with the Trio (another short, binary work). The minuet (or Scherzo) is played; the Trio is played; then the Minuet returns, forming a large ABA structure, each section of which is in binary form. The analysis looks like this:

The Scherzo-Trio from Beethoven's Piano Sonata Op. 28 in D major is a clear example of the form.

60
65
p
cresc.
sf
70
f
ff
Fine
Trio
p
75
La seconda parte una volta
80

Mozaic Form. The great art of the Byzantine Empire achieved its effects through the integration of hundreds of small ceramic tile squares, each of which, like the separate pieces of a jigsaw puzzle, contained a part of the larger picture. There are some musical forms which are similarly structured. That is, the total architecture is achieved when several sections are strung together.

An example of such a "mozaic form" is the Rondo. Here an A section is presented, then contrasted with a B section, then repeated, then contrasted with a C section, etc. Always the A section returns, and it is this constant returning of A which is the hallmark of the Rondo. There are many varieties of Rondo form. ABACA, ABACABA, and ABACADA are all found in the literature.

The Adagio of Beethoven's Piano Sonata Op. 13 is an example of an ABACA form, somewhat unusual because most rondos tend to be light, fast compositions while this is slow and rather melancholy.

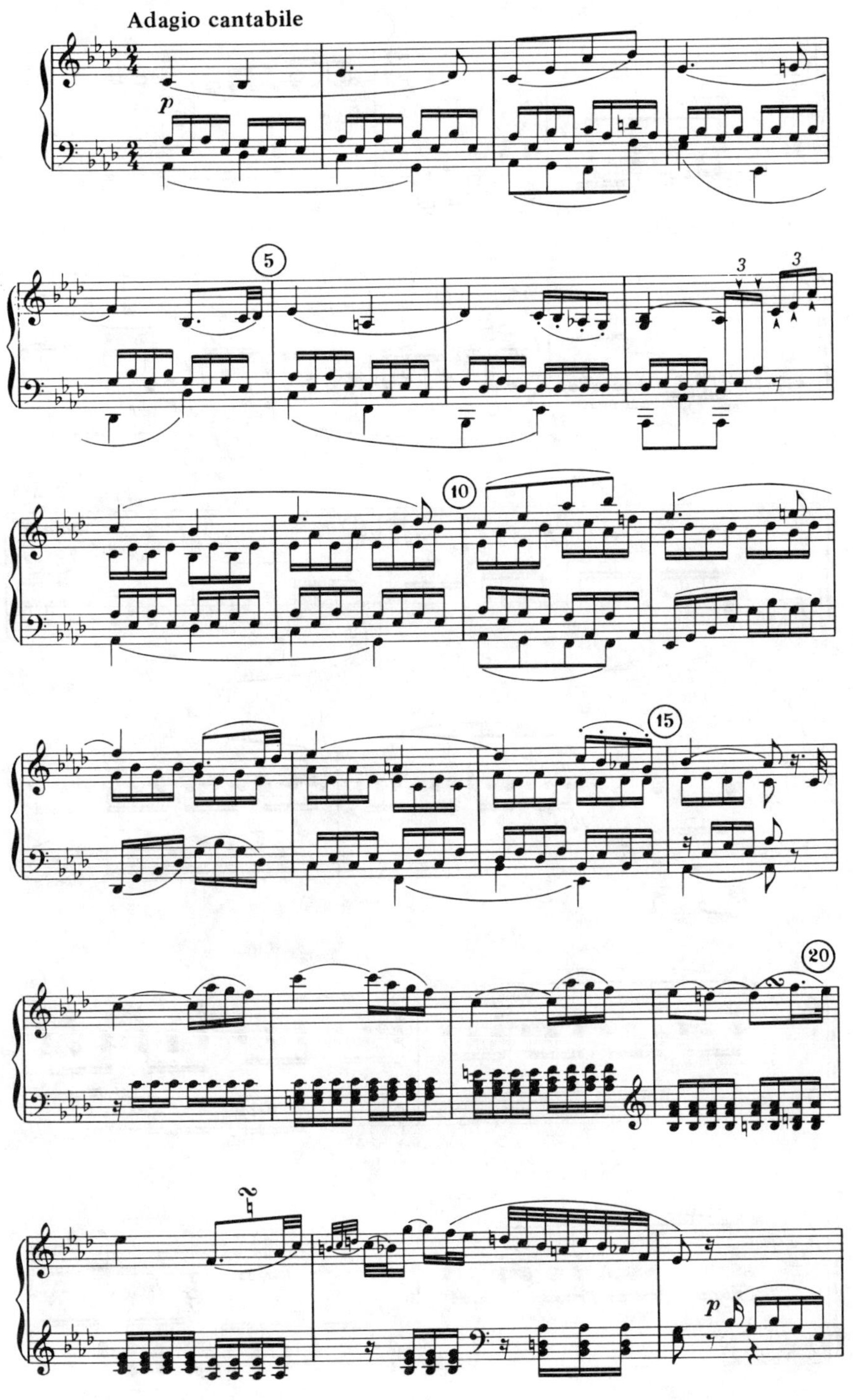
Adagio cantabile
p

25
cresc.
(p)
cresc.
p
30
pp
p
35
pp 3
3
40
cresc.
sf
sf

VII Contour and form

The design of the Adagio breaks down as follows:

A^1 = measures 1-16
B   = measure 17-28
A^2 = measures 29-36
C   = measures 37-50
A^3 = measures 51-73

It is characteristic here - and throughout all of music - that the sections of musical forms frequently contrast one another. This may be done by changes in melodic material, tempo, key, etc. The C section of the Beethoven, for example, changes from A♭ major to A♭ minor, and from duple pulse subdivisions to rapid triplets.

Another commonly found mozaic form is the Theme and Variation form. Here an idea (theme) is presented and then repeated many times, each time with something changed or varied. The number of variations and the degree to which each is different from the others and from the theme itself is entirely up to the composer. It is frequently the case, however, that while other elements change from variation to variation, the length of each section and the harmonic structure underlying it remain constant. That is the case in the example below from the G minor keyboard Passacaglia of G.F. Handel.

PASSACAGLIA

G.F. Handel

In this example, there are fifteen variations of the theme, each more difficult to play, each building up to a musical climax, yet each preserving
the length (4 measures) and structure (a I-II-V-I progression with a motion in fifths between I and II) of the theme. The Passacaglia was an instrumental form of Handel's time (c. 1700) precisely devoted to this idea
of theme and variation.

Yet another clear example of the mozaic form is the theatrical architecture found in the structure of many operas, ballets, and musicals. In the
traditional American musical, for example, there are two acts, each
divided into many scenes (often ten or more). Stage works organized in
such a way are often called "numbers operas" or "numbers musicals"
because one finds his way around such a work by assigning a number to
the various scenes of each act.

Complex Individual Forms. When a composer creates new music,
he may use the forms he knows as models, but there is nothing to prevent
him from being innovative and changing or adapting any design he
wishes for his immediate needs. Thus, there are countless individual
forms of a very complex nature which may contain the structural underpinning of a musical work.

Having said this, however, there is one highly complex form which made a major contribution to the development of musical architecture. It is called the Sonata-allegro form, and it arose during the 1700's, many think as an outgrowth of the rounded binary or **ABA** ternary form.

The Sonata-allegro form is not only a design plan but also implies certain tonal organizations because it is usually found with very carefully prescribed modulations of key which go along with changes of melody. The overall form appears below.

The detailed workings of this general plan are as follows:

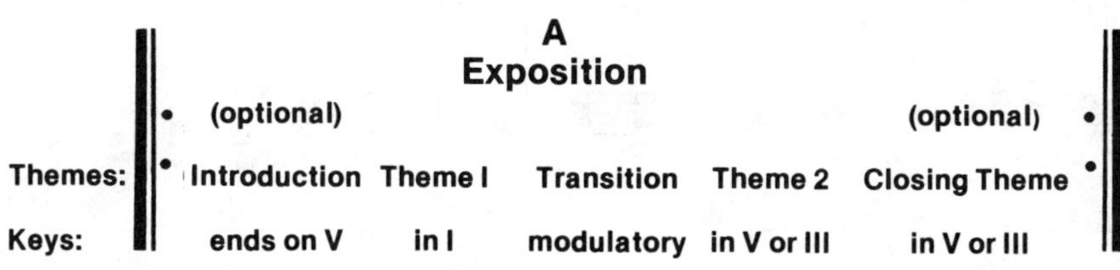

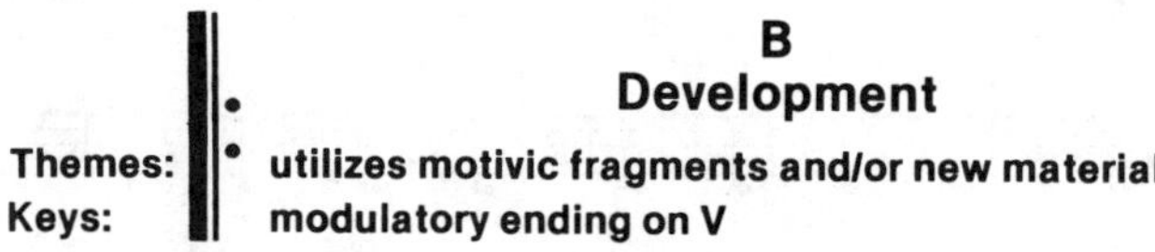

Often, extended musical works are divided into large sections called "movements," much as dramas are divided into acts. The sonata-allegro form is frequently the architecture of an entire movement. The C major Sonatina of Joseph Haydn (which we viewed earlier) uses the sonata-allegro form as the plan for the first of its three movements (see below).

SONATA

Jos. Haydn

Here, the organization breaks down as follows:

Exposition **A**	There is no introduction. (It is optional.) Theme 1 in the tonic key of C (I): m. 1-16 Transition modulating to V of V: m. 16-35 Theme 2 in the key of G (V): m. 36-62 Closing Theme (V): m. 63-67
Development **B**	Previously stated melodic fragments are woven into a series of moulations ending on V: m. 68-103
Recapitulation **A'**	Theme 1 in C major (I): m. 104-111 Transition to Theme 2: m. 111-125 Theme 2 in C major (I): m. 126-151 Closing Theme in C major (I): m. 152-170

Unity in Musical Structure.

Compositions with many sections and many themes are often unified by having one melody grow out of another. Careful analysis of the music of the greatest composers shows that over and over again thematic unity is a conscious and pervasive part of the creative process. There is, perhaps, no composer who exemplified this better than Beethoven.

Above is the opening motif of the first movement of his Symphony Number 5 in C minor which we have seen before. Note the use of the thirds (G-E♭ and F-D) and of the rhythm ♪♪♪ ♩ (short-short-short-long). This first movement is in sonata-allegro form. The second theme of the movement (at m. 63) is:

Note the opening interval of the fourth (B♭ -E♭) followed by an unfold-ed third with a passing motion (D-E♭ -F).

In the second movement of the symphony, Beethoven begins with the following theme:

Notice the opening fourth (E♭ -A♭) followed by the unfolded third (C-B♭ -A♭). Even though the rhythm is different and we are in a new key (A♭ major), the underlying structure in this theme is the same Theme 2 of the first movement. By removing the rhythm and placing both themes in the same key, the similarity is made clearer.

Later in the second movement (m. 22-24) Beethoven uses a second thematic motive (see below).

Notice the unfolded third (A♭ -A♭ -B♭ -C) and the rhythm ♪ ♪ ♪ | ♩ (short-short-short-long). Compare it to the opening theme of movement one. Beethoven is using the technique of inversion and rhythmic repetition to achieve thematic unity (see below).

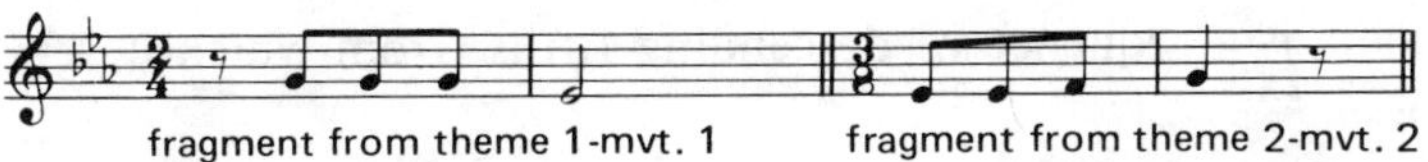

This kind of internal unity occurs many more times throughout the symphony. At measure 19 of the third movement, for example, Beethoven uses the following motif:

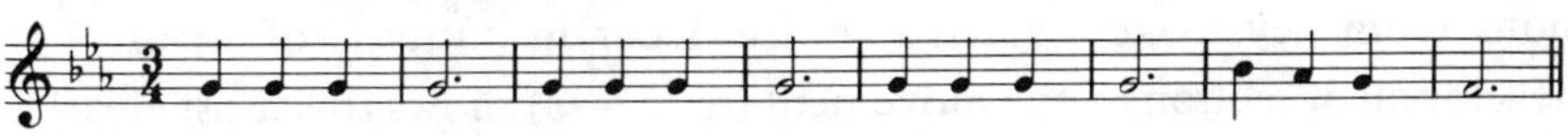

The rhythmic similarity to the opening of the first movement is immediately apparent. Then again at m. 44-45 of the fourth and final movement, the short-short-short-long motif occurs in yet another theme:

These instances of thematic unity are not analytic manufacturings, nor are they isolated examples. They occur over and over again in the works of great craftsmen and serve to bind complex compositions into organic wholes - even though the average listener may be unaware of the techniques involved. The techniques are there; they are felt; they serve to mold the music into unified creations, even when they are intellectually unnoticed. Just as the traveler may appreciate the solid construction of a bridge without the slightest conception of its structural underpinning, the musical audience can "feel" the solidarity of a composition without a specific awareness of thematic unity or formal architecture.

In fact, the unity of thematic material is only one kind of unity practiced by a great composer. There is another, more complex kind of unity - the unity between the momentary motif and the long-range tonal wanderings of a composition. This cohesion between microcosm (small-scale, immediately apparent musical material) and macrocosm (large-scale, overall tonal plan) is far more subtle and harder to detect. But again, in great composers, one sees it over and over. A clear example of the unity of microcosm and macrocosm may be found in the D minor string quartet Opus 76, No. 2 by Joseph Haydn, the so-called "Quinten" quartet.

The first movement of the quartet is in sonata-allegro form. Its opening theme is a sequence of descending fifths (from which it derives its name).

Not only do the opening fifths (A-D and E-A) form the melodic seed from which other melodies are derived, but they also spawn the excursions from key to key which likewise occur in patterns of fifths. The development section of the movement (m. 57-98) shows this most clearly.

70
mf
fz
fz
fz
fz

As we leave the exposition (measure 55) we are in F major (the relative major of the original key of D minor). By measure 98 we are going to be on V (A major), the place one expects to be at the end of a sonata-allegro development. The pertinent thing for our discussion here is that we get from F major to A major by traveling to key centers a fifth apart.

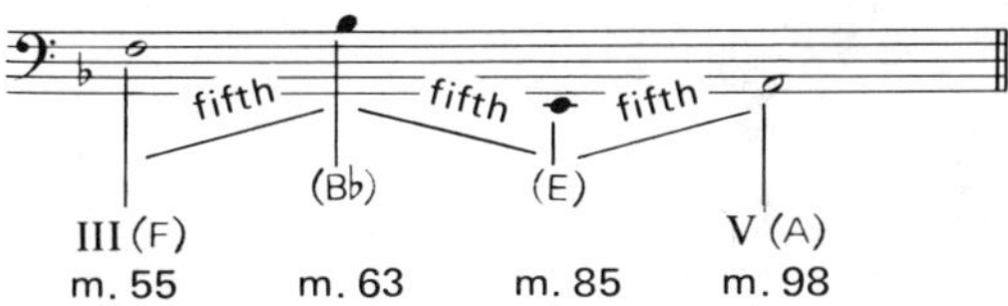

As the scheme above shows, Haydn modulates from F to B♭ (at measure 63), from B♭ to E major (at measure 85), and finally from E major to A (V). In this way, the microcosmic motif of descending fifths utilized in the very opening melody is now expressed as the choice of keys used to expand the larger, macrocosmic ideas of the development.

Further Reading.

The study of musical form, like the study of harmony and counterpoint, is a complex business. It usually requires the aid of an experienced teacher and takes many years to master. However, if you wish to pursue it on your own, it is not an impossible undertaking. The following text should help: **Form in Tonal Music,** by Douglass M. Green (New York: Holt, Rinehart and Winston, 1965).

Perhaps the most important thing to remember, not only as you go on in your individual study, but also as you go on through this text, is that your reading will be sterile and meaningless unless you listen to the music itself. Listening and following along with the musical score is as indispensible to the study of music as seeing is to the study of art.

There are, of course, thousands upon thousands of musical works to hear, dozens of which are mentioned in this textbook alone. It is impractical, probably impossible, for you to purchase the records and scores for all that music. But fortunately you don't have to. Your local libraries, schools and colleges contain all you need to continue and enhance what this book begins. You have but to visit them.

PART III

LISTENING AND HISTORY

CHAPTER EIGHT:

THE FUNDAMENTALS OF LISTENING

Concepts of Time and Emotion.

Music is the organization of sound in time. Being able to perceive time for the listener is no less crucial than being able to perceive space for the viewer. However, if asked to describe even a short composition, most listeners (including those who understand musical form) become tongue-tied. They can't assign a meaning to what they have heard. Rather, they describe a series of events difficult to relate to one another. It is similar to describing a motion picture by recalling only the isolated frames of film. Every note, like every frame, is available for study, but each separate piece of data only takes on its meaning in relation to the movement of the whole. The whole is more than its separate parts.

To understand a film, one must see the picture move and perceive a logic to that motion. In music one must hear the tones move and perceive a logic to that motion. For this, one needs a mechanism to order time through sound.

Perception of Time. In a film, where the mind deals with verbal communication, time is ordered by events. The passage of an hour or two in a theatre makes sense because we can recall a sequence of action which presents a coherent story. Music, however, is non-verbal. There are no literary events to recall, and it would be impossibly complex to recall the details of structure, harmony, and counterpoint - even if one could recognize them (a feat which only the most highly trained musical minds can do). But one can recall the emotional rise and fall of music since it is designed to strike an emotional rather than intellectual response.

With or without formal musical training, almost anyone can respond to the emotional flow of sound. One feels it become more exciting or calmer, more active or more serene. And one can make some sense of the entirety of a musical work by charting the rise and fall of the feelings which that work evokes.

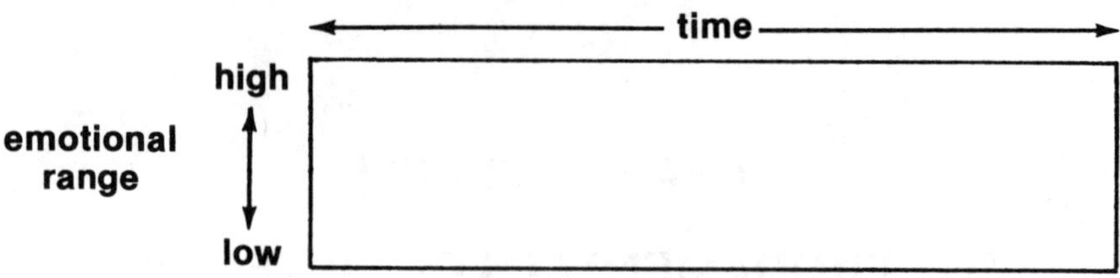

In the rectangle above, we can make a kind of line chart or graph of a musical composition by using an emotional rather than a literary flow of events. This is not quite as easy as it looks because charting one's emotions is not a familiar activity. Many musical compositions do not unfold in neat, identifiable packages. Thus, in using this technique, it is best to listen to a shorter work (around ten minutes or less). In fact, it is advisable to listen more than once before writing anything down so that the passage of time may be more easily grasped. It is also wise to begin with musical compositions which have a clear emotional architecture. One excellent example is the Prelude to Richard Wagner's opera "Tristan und Isolde."

Play the work once or twice, timing it to see roughly what events unfold and approximately where they occur. Now set up your chart with minutes marked off along the time coordinate. Given certain variations between one recorded performance and another, you should find the Tristan Prelude takes about eleven minutes to play. It starts very quietly and builds to a modest emotional peak toward the end of the second minute. Then it settles down again until a bit before the sixth minute. From there it begins to build to a significant peak just after the seven-minute mark and continues to an even higher level around the eight-minute mark. From then on, with a small upward inflection, the composition drops sharply to a low emotional level, finally fading out altogether at the end. Your pictograph should look something like the one below.

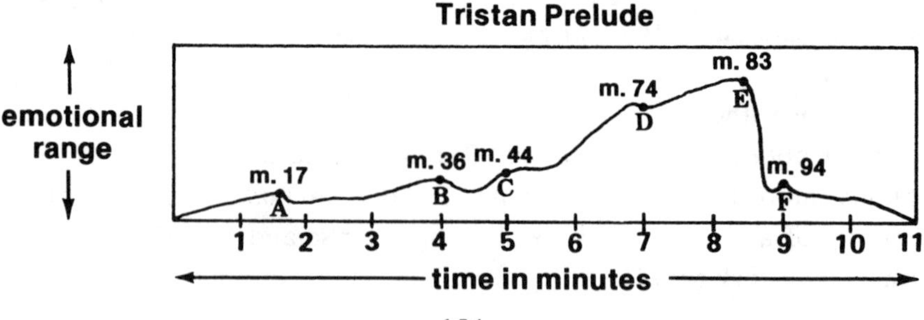

The points of reference in the pictograph (A-F) are accompanied by measure numbers which will serve as guides later on when we listen again with the score in front of us. For now, it is only important that our reference letters - indeed, our whole pictograph - provide us with an overall, very general view of the music. The measure-by-measure details are not represented and, in fact, can really only be understood when one has a view of the whole. It is very much like understanding the plot of the film we talked about earlier. In recalling the events of the action, the smallest details of dialogue only become meaningful when one understands the most significant structural points of the story. Any comment the wolf makes to Little Red Riding Hood, for example, is best seen against the broadest outline of Riding Hood's walk through the forest, the wolf's attempt to eat her, and her rescue by the brave woodsman.

The technique of the pictograph allows us to see at a glance the totality of an architecture which unfolds over an extended period of time. It is thus useful in determining how a composer has organized time and may even begin to account for our emotional response to a work. A chart whose shape is flat and rather motionless (see below) might easily explain

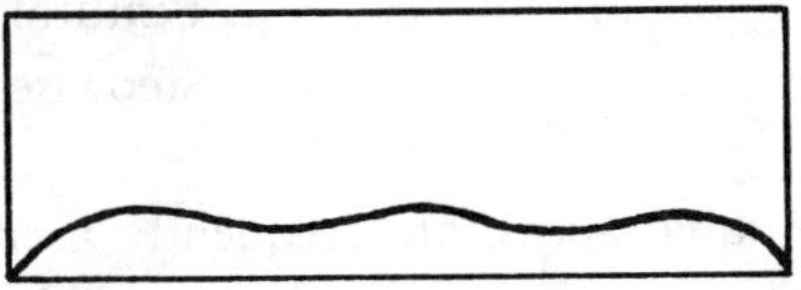

why a given work seems boring or (on the positive side) serene. An active shape (see below) might explain a work which is exciting or (on the

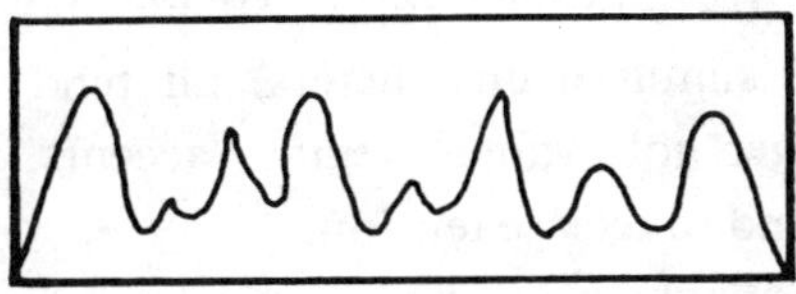

negative side) overdone. But regardless of the subjective opinion we may have of a work whose architecture is revealed in this way, the architectural sketch invites a very important question: why do the peaks and valleys occur where they do?

Principles of Tension and Stability. Almost every kind of natural motion we know has a periodicity to it. There is a tension which is built and then released. There is a calm which is not permanent but gathers a momentum, reaches a point of climax and is restored to start a new cycle. The waves of an ocean, the seasons of the year, the rhythms of the human body, perhaps even the ebb and flow of matter in the universe - perhaps time itself - each illustrate the principle of tension and release. Because this phenomenon is so pervasive in the human experience of living, it affects the way in which humans react to music. When the tension of a composition is built, the emotional graph rises. When it is released, the graph falls.

Tension	Stability
Dominant harmony	Tonic harmony
Increased rhythmic activity	Decreased rhythmic activity
Dissonance	Consonance
Chromaticism and modulation	Diatonicism
Registral extremes	Centralized registers
Dynamic extremes	Centralized dynamics
Textural thickness	Textural thinness
Leaping motions	Stepwise motions

The items in the table above are frequently used by composers to create and release musical tension and thereby sculpt musical emotion. Let us look at each briefly.

In the dominant/tonic scheme, the leading tone, V, and VII chords all create tension. The resolution of V to I (or a substitute in a deceptive cadence) releases tension.

Rhythmic activity (i.e., faster tempos, smaller note values, syncopation, changing and simultaneous meters) all tend to create tension. Slower tempos, longer note values, regular accents, and stable, simple metric patterns all tend to release tension.

Whatever the historical style period, those intervals which are defined as dissonant create tension; those which are defined as consonant release it.

Diatonicism - that is, the use of only the pitches of the scale system of a given tonality - tend to produce a very stable musical environment. Tension is brought into that environment through the use of chromaticism -

that is, the pitches of tonal centers other than the original. A favorite device of many composers is a series of upward modulations to produce greater and greater musical tension. A composition which begins in C major, for example, and modulates systematically to D♭, D♮, E♭, E♮, etc. is bound to create a feeling of excitement.

By register we mean placement on the pitch scale in terms of high or low. Women, for example, usually sing in a higher register than men. Flutes play in a higher register than tubas. As a general rule, tension is created by the extreme registers. Very high and very low pitches tend, like very high or very low temperatures, to create a feeling of uneasiness.

The term dynamics refers to the loudness or softness with which the music is playing. Below is a table of the most common dynamic references.

Term	Meaning	Musical symbol
Pianissimo	Very quiet	*pp*
Piano	Quiet	*p*
Mezzo piano	Moderately quiet	*mp*
Mezzo forte	Moderately loud	*mf*
Forte	Loud	*f*
Fortissimo	Very loud	*ff*
Crescendo	Gradually louder	<
Descrescendo	Gradually quieter	>
Sforzando	Suddenly loud	*sf*
Subito piano	Suddenly quiet	*sp*

Generally speaking, the louder the music, the more the tension; the quieter, the less the tension.

Texture refers to the number of parts sounding at any given time. This is not to be confused with the number of performers. If, for example, we have twenty violinists all playing exactly the same pitch (playing "in unison"), we have only one-part texture.

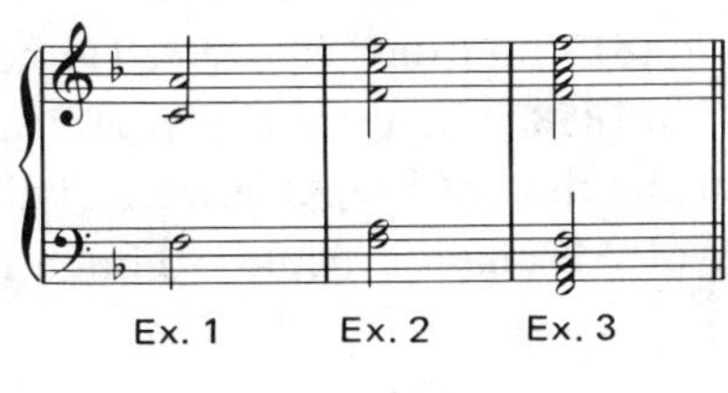

Above we see an F major triad in three textures: thin (Ex. 1), fairly thick (Ex. 2), and very thick (Ex. 3). Generally, the thinner the texture, the calmer the feeling. As the texture thickens and more and more parts are added, the tension increases.

Finally, music may move in seemingly smooth or seemingly disjunct ways. When tones go stepwise to each other, they produce a calmer feeling than when they leap. Similarly, if tones are shortened so that there is a gap between them (a musical effect called "staccato"), they create more tension than when they are connected smoothly ("legato"). Such musical techniques are analogous to the use of dotted versus smooth, solid lines in drawing. Points A and B can be connected in either way, but the broken line tends to disorient the eye and create more spatial tension.

Above is the opening phrase of a well-known song written first with notes moving stepwise in legato fashion, then with disconnected, staccato leaps. When played, the first will evoke a much greater feeling of calm. The second will seem more active, more tense.

Tension and Stability in Practice. Now that some of the more common techniques of creating musical tension have been explained, it will be interesting to return to the score of the Tristan Prelude to see why the peaks and valleys of our graph occurred where they did. We may compare measures 1-6 with measures 80-83, for example, to see how Wagner produces two emotional extremes.

In the opening measures the texture is thin, the ranges centralized, the dynamics soft, the note values long, the intervals predominantly stepwise, the motion legato. All of this is calculated to give a very calm, quiet effect. The only element of tension here is a bit of chromaticism which, as we will see later in our historical study of music, was a pervasive part of both Wagner's style and the century (19th century) in which he lived. (Wagner was born in 1813 and died in 1883. He completed his opera "Tristan und Isolde" in 1858, and it was first performed in Munich, Germany in 1865, just at the time of the American Civil War. Wagner was thus a contemporary of Abraham Lincoln - though their political views were vastly different).

TRISTAN AND ISOLDE
Prelude

Richard Wagner

80
Fl.
Ob.
E.H.
Cl.
B.cl.
Bsn.
a3
ff espress.
in F
Hrn.
in E
espress.
espress.
piu f
Tr. in F
1.
f
Trb.
f
Tuba
Timp.
tr
p cresc.
Vl. I
piu f
Vl. II
piu f
Vla.
piu f
Vlc.
espress.
f
piu f
Bass
piu f
80

Fl.
Ob.
E.H.
Cl.
B.cl.
Bsn.
in F Hrn.
in E
Tr. in F
Trb.
Tuba
Timp.
Vl. I
Vl. II
Vla.
Vlc.
Bass
a3
a2
a2
1.
piu f
piu f
ff
trem.

Now compare the opening to the climactic measures 80-83. The texture couldn't be thicker. Every instrument is playing its own part. The violas (third staff from the bottom at m. 83) are even sounding two notes at a time (a technique called "doublestopping"). The range is enormous. The violins are playing at their highest pitch levels while the bass tuba plays the F several octaves below. All the space in between is filled by one or another instrument. The dynamic marking is FF and has been achieved through an extended crescendo, especially in the tympani part (m. 81-83). While many of the instruments are playing in long note values, the strings have very short notes which ascend rapidly many times from m. 64 onward. There are many leaps in the horn, bassoon, cello, and bass lines. The tonality is highly chromatic and has been modulating almost constantly so that the ear at this point has very little reference to a tonic key of any stability. All of this combines to produce a tremendous amount of musical tension which is not resolved until after m. 83 when the texture thins, the range centralizes, and the dynamics return to P.

Craft versus Opinion in Listening.

The manipulations of harmony and counterpoint, the creation of soundly constructed melodies, the use of the mechanisms of tension and release to create architectural interest, the integration of thematic material and tonal motion to create organic unity - these are all part of the craft of the composer. They are things which the student of music can evaluate and either admire (if well-handled) or criticize (if poorly-handled). However, they do not guarantee the enjoyment of a work. They do not automatically make a work beautiful or well-liked. That is because they do not emanate from the listener himself.

When a listener says, "I like this," it implies an emotional response on his part. That response may or may not be accompanied by an understanding of the music or the craft of the composer. It is simply a personal reaction. The words, "it is good" imply a judgment on the part of the listener, an evaluation of the craft of composition which does not have to be accompanied by an emotional reaction. One hopes that one will develop standards of judgment and personal likes which coincide; that one will like what is well-crafted and not like what is poorly-crafted. However, that doesn't always happen. Nor does it always happen that understanding music guarantees the enjoyment of it. There are plenty of deeply appreciative concert-goers who have never heard of a V chord and don't know anything about retrograde inversions.

Then why study them? Because experience has shown that the more one understands - the more one is exposed to a variety of musical experiences - the more one is able to enjoy what is presented. Studying music makes us more knowledgeable, more appreciative consumers, consumers who will respond more deeply and be less susceptible to a contemporary musical marketplace which at times asks a very high price for a very poor product.

All of this is very much like food. You may not like peppermint ice cream, but the ice cream may be well-made. It is therefore quite possible for you to say, "That is good ice cream, but I don't like it." It is also possible to say, "That ice cream is not well-made, but I like it anyway." One hopes that eventually your taste buds and your mind will get together; that you will like it, in part, *because* it is good. Of course, to do that, you must study what makes for good and bad ice cream. Once armed with that knowledge, you can protect yourself, if you choose, against an unscrupulous manufacturer who will charge you a big buck for a bad dessert. Finally, when you begin your life as an ice cream consumer, you must be willing to taste a lot of flavors. Only then can you find what you like and don't like. And remember, it is necessary for you to discover both extremes so that you do not waste your money. Your knowledge will even allow you to give a strange flavor a second chance after a time and thus cultivate a new taste.

As music students, your task is to accumulate the knowledge that makes you an intelligent consumer and to get to know the flavors in the musical marketplace. In this way you will not only have an understanding of one of humankind's most enduring forms of expression but a better chance of enjoying it as well. You will also have the ability to protect yourself from the purchase of inferior musical products. You will be able to evaluate things on your own without being a slave to the propaganda of a commercial, the overkill of a radio station, or the personal opinions of a newspaper reviewer.

To understand what is available to you, you must travel through the history of music and see its styles, its works, its composers, and its development. That history can be conveniently divided into seven periods:

1. Antiquity (ancient times to the life of Christ)
2. The Early Christian Era and Middle Ages (c. 100-1400 A.D.)
3. The Renaissance (c. 1400-1600 A.D.)
4. The Baroque Era (c. 1600-1750)
5. The Classical Era (c. 1750-1825)
6. The Romantic Era (c. 1825-1900)
7. The Twentieth Century (1900-present)

To this history we now turn.

CHAPTER NINE:

THE MUSIC OF ANTIQUITY

In comparison with modern style periods, not much is known about ancient music. It was not preserved in written form, and those bits of writing or painting which describe it are few and often vague. Perhaps the only clear idea we have of ancient music is what has survived in the present-day cultural rites of African, Indian, Oriental, Middle Eastern, and island societies. And here we see only the modern-day forms of these ancient hand-me-downs, forms which may or may not closely resemble their original ancestors.

The Use of Ancient Music.

We gather that ancient music had three purposes:
- in communication - to gather a tribe or warn of impending danger, as with the jungle drums of Africa or mountain horns of Himalaya.
- in work - to break the monotony of labor or keep a strict working rhythm, as in the singing of field hands or cadences of an oarsman.
- in religious and ceremonial expressions, such as wedding dances or sacrificial rituals.

The Characteristics of Ancient Music.

We surmise from our limited sources that ancient music was rather simple in comparison to the orchestral developments of later times. It was probably:
- monophonic
- sung or played by primitive instruments
- variable in mood according to the event expressed
- not extended in duration

Ancient Musical Instruments.

The instruments of antiquity largely fell into four types: those with strings, those meant to be struck, those activated by human breath, and those activated by water or wind power.

Stringed Instruments. The Psaltery (Hebrew), lyre and kithara (Greek), and harp (Egyptian) were all ancient forerunners of the modern harp. There were also oblong instruments such as the chyn (China) which sat on the floor or across the lap and were plucked like a banjo or guitar.

Percussion Instruments. Cymbals of metal, and of course drums of all kinds, were the principal instruments which were struck. Drums were probably first made of animal skins stretched over hollowed logs. Later, the skins were fitted over frames (as with the Greek tympanon).

Instruments Using Human Breath. The panpipes of Greece were a series of reeds bound together something like a modern harmonica. The Greek aulos was a kind of verically held flute. Many such wind instruments were made of hollow reeds with holes bored in them. By contrast, primitive horns like the Hebrew shofar were made of hollowed animal horns or sea shells.

Wind and Water Powered Instruments. These included things like the hydraulus, an early organ of Greece, and the wind chimes of China and Japan which were hanging collections of shells or metal pottery that produced sounds when blown about by the wind.

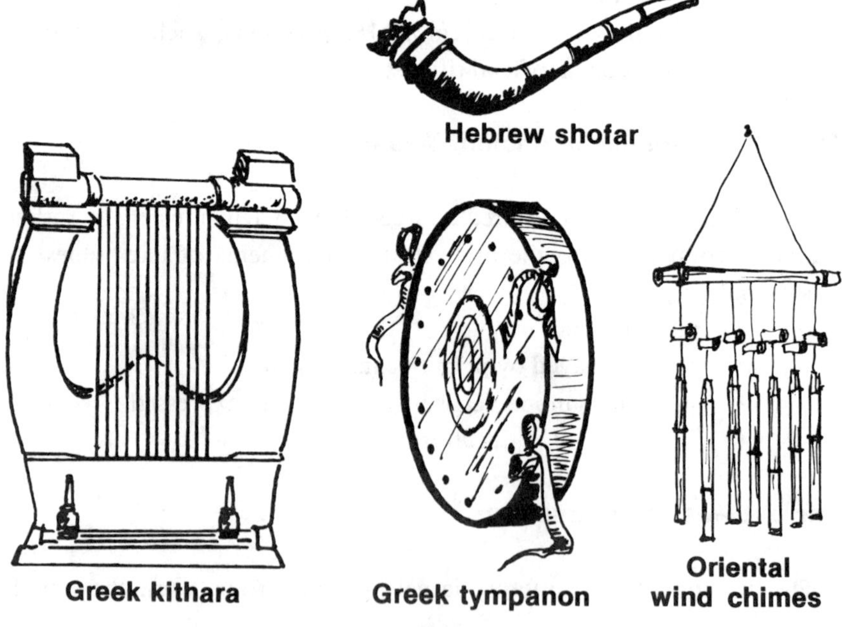

Hebrew shofar

Greek kithara   **Greek tympanon**   **Oriental
wind chimes**

Important Ancient Musical Cultures.

In our necessarily brief excursion through antiquity, we shall look cursorily at Chinese music as representative of the Pacific sphere and at the Mediterranean basin, the forerunner of the European culture which contains the great bulk of our study.

Chinese Music. The music of China can be traced back to 2000 B.C. and beyond. Early Chinese writers like Confucius (500 B.C.) indicated a considerable use of music both for religious and ceremonial purposes. The Chinese employed the pentatonic scale (discussed earlier) which generated their characteristic Oriental melodies. They incorporated it into a sophisticated system of music theory hundreds of years before anything similar appeared in Western cultures.

The ancient Chinese appeared to have orchestral ensembles whose music was apparently conceived linearly. That is, several instruments would play separate lines simultaneously without a predominant concern for their vertical integration (a style known as heterophony). These instruments also apparently used improvisation as a technique, especially as a way of embellishing or decorating a simple melody.

Examples of Chinese music can be found on side 1 of Volume I of "The History of Music in Sound." (HMS, as it is abbreviated, is a ten volume record set with accompanying pamphlets produced by Oxford University Press and RCA Victor Records. It is a fine historical reference to which we will turn often in this chapter.) Particularly interesting are the three ancient melodies which date from the Sonq, Yuan, and Ming dynasties.

Suggested Listening: HMS - Volume 1, Side 1, Band 1

Hebrew Music. Ancient Hebrew music is described many times in the Old Testament, and there are many pictorial references to the music of ancient Egypt. Of the two cultures, however, it is the Hebrew which survived in sound and which cast the greater influence toward modern times. Religious celebration and rituals of state provided the more serious occasions for music, but there are also accounts of singing and dancing on a far more informal basis. The religious music of ancient

Israel was mainly in the form of psalms which could be sung chorally, or by a single voice, or in various combinations. Two enduring forms were the responsorial psalm (solo alternating with chorus) and antiphonal psalm (two alternating choruses).

It is possible, perhaps probable, that early Hebrew psalms were accompanied by stringed harp or reed flutes. In any event, the character and voicing of the psalm remained a lasting influence on the Greek and early Christian cultures. The structure of the early Hebrew psalms can be found in the first volume of HMS with the 8th Psalm of David (c. 1000 B.C.) and Psalm 137. These works are still sung today by Yemenite and Babylonian Jews who preserved the old melodies despite the influences of other cultures.

Suggested Listening: HMS · Volume 1, Side 4, Band 1

In the 8th Psalm, the note pattern above occurs many times. We see an ascent to a repeated tone on which most of the text occurs (in this case, A), the so-called "psalm tone." From this tone melodic inflections are made above and below with an eventual descent to the starting note. It is this melodic structure which came to dominate the chants that became the central music works of early Christendom well beyond the year 1000 A.D.

The structure of ancient Hebrew chant does not seem to have been duplicated in the Muslim prayer of the region, but that is not to say that the melodies of Islamic cultures had no influence on later developments. Some of them, in fact, were products of 8-note modal scales which were similar to those of ancient Greece and early Christendom. It seems logical to assume that a blend of Muslim and Hebraic music found its way into Christian chant no less than the music of ancient Greece. Several examples of Islamic music can be found in the HMS series.

Suggested Listening: HMS · Volume 1, Side 4, Bands 4-11

Ancient Greece. The music of Ancient Greece was extensively described by Terpander (c. 675 B.C.), Aristoxenos (c. 500 B.C.), Plato (c. 400 B.C.), Aristotle (c. 350 B.C.), and Ptolemy (c. 150 A.D.). However, little Greek music survives to this day. From the writings about it, we know that the Greeks employed 4-note scale patterns called tetrachords and that these were combined to form the 8-note modes which were eventually transplanted to early Christian music. We also know that the Greeks employed in their music certain rhythms found in their poetry. The patterns below, known as the rhythmic modes, became the rhythmic basis for all early Christian music.

Greek Rhythmic Modes			
Name	**Poetic symbol**	**Note value**	**Character**
Trochaeus	– U	♩ ♩	long-short
Iambus	U –	♩ ♩	short-long
Dactylus	– U –	♩. ♩ ♩	long-short-long
Anapest	U – –	♩ ♩ ♩.	short-long-long
Spondeus	– –	♩. ♩.	long-long
Tribrachys	U U U	♩ ♩ ♩	short-short-short

It is important to note the triple meter nature of the rhythmic modes. The characteristic of triple meter dominated Western music for centuries. As we shall see it was not until the fourteenth century A.D. that duple meter was acknowledged as an equal rhythmic partner.

In addition to a highly developed theoretical system, the Greeks spoke of music as having certain emotional powers. They divided the emotional effects of music into two camps. The first was said to bear the character of their god, Apollo. Apollonian music was simple, clear in form, objective in spirit, restrained emotionally. The favorite Apollonian instrument was the stringed kithara. The second camp was presided over by Dionysus. Here the music was freer, more expressive, subjective, and emotional. The instrument associated with Dionysian music was the aulos. As we shall see these two Greek viewpoints, the objectively clear and subjectively free, influenced many different developments in Western music.

Suggested Listening: **HMS · Volume 1, Side 4, Bands 2-3**

CHAPTER TEN:

THE EARLY CHRISTIAN ERA AND MIDDLE AGES
(c. 100-1400 A.D.)

Difficult as it is to sum up 1400 years of history, we can safely say that this era was a time of beginnings for European culture. In its early phase, Christianity slowly replaced the power of Rome. In its middle phase, feudalism became the accepted economic and political order. Power was consolidated in the hands of the nobility; fiefdoms grew into nations. By the late Middle Ages, feudalism gave way to a new mercantile spirit. Trade and invention began to open a new era of economic and social order. Cities rose up to become important centers of business and thought, coexisting side by side with the centralized power of kings, nobles, and the Church in Rome. Spiritually, it was a time of religious domination with the Church the central force of European life. Indeed, one of the great moral purposes of life was to devote oneself to pursuits which would culminate in an ascendancy to heaven after death.

Musically, the history of the art was largely bound to the history of the Church. Although there was music of a secular, non-religious nature, the great proportion of music was intended for sacred purposes. Technically, the musical era was also one of beginnings. It developed from an age of one-part, monophonic music to a period of many voiced polyphony. Systems of notation began and were refined. Styles and regions arose to become important influences on the general musical culture. And all of this occurred with the most influential musical form of the time, sacred chant.

Monophonic Music.

Music which has one part (a flute playing alone; a voice singing one line) is called monophonic music. Medieval monophony can be divided into two general categories, sacred chant and secular song, of which chant is by far the more influential.

Sacred Chant. The structure of Hebrew psalms, the modal scales of ancient Greece, the inflections of Islamic prayer all blended into a series of regional melodies which provided the bases of Early Christian chant.

There were four styles of chant which formed the bulk of Early Christian sacred music. They were:

- Gallican chant from the region of what is today modern France
- Mozarabic chant used in Spain and greatly influenced by North African and Moorish culture
- Byzantine chant used in the region of modern-day Turkey and descended from the Semitic cultures
- Ambrosian chant named for St. Ambrose, the Bishop of Milan during the late 4th century A.D.

By the 6th century A.D. Christianity had become a firmly established religious force throughout the Mediterranean and Western Europe. As part of the consolidation and solidification of its growing power, the Christian Church began to unify its practices and traditions - things which, if left to develop in regionally different ways, might fragment and weaken it. The universal language of the Church became Latin (since the hand of Rome has extended throughout all Christendom). A unified body of religious celebration and a unified calendar were issued by Pope Gregory I in the late 6th century. Finally, from Gregory's time through the reigns of Charlemagne and Pope Leo III in the 9th century, the codification of chants began. Rather than being passed on verbally from one generation to another, they were written down and collected in books which are still used today. The general term "Gregorian chant" (after Pope Gregory) has been adopted for the chant of this period.

Musically, besides being monophonic, chants were modal, sung without instrumental accompaniment, and quite free rhythmically (that is, there were no proportional note values, no meters, no bar lines employed in them). The melodies moved mostly by step. Leaps, when they occurred, were small (thirds or fourths, predominantly).

The text of the chants were always in Latin and were, of course, completely religious in nature. The texts and music could coincide in any of three ways: syllabically, neumatically, or melismatically.

- Syllabic: one note for one syllable
- Neumatic: a few notes for each syllable
- Melismatic: many notes for each syllable

Texts were taken from the wording of the Mass or the recitations of prayers said at certain prescribed times of the day. The Mass and Divine Offices (as the prayer sessions were called) were the most important events in medieval worship services.

The Mass is a reenactment of the Last Supper. It is divided into eleven sections, five of which always have the same text (the Ordinary segments) and six of which have texts that vary from day to day according to the Biblical event being celebrated (the Proper segments). For example, during Christmas, the sections of the Ordinary would be as they always are while the sections of the Proper would deal with events such as the birth of Jesus. At Easter, the Ordinary portions would remain the same while the sections of the Proper would speak of things like the crucifixion or the resurrection of Christ. The eleven sections are listed below:

- Proper: Introit, Gradual, Alleluia, Tract, Offertory, and Communion
- Ordinary: Kyrie, Gloria, Credo, Sanctus, and Agnus Dei

Each of the eleven sections had chants associated with it, but, as we shall see, it was the Ordinary of the Mass for which the greatest musical works were written during the Middle Ages and beyond.

The Divine Offices were prayer sessions set for different hours of the day beginning with Matins (before daybreak); continuing with Lauds, Prime, Terce, Sext, and Nones; and ending with Vespers and Compline in the evening. Psalms, prayers, and Biblical quotations were all part of the text of these eight sessions, some texts being particularly associated with some sessions. For example, the Magnificat prayer (''My soul doth magnify the Lord, and my spirit rejoices in God, my Savior,'' etc.) was always chanted at Vespers. During Compline, the votive prayers to the Virgin Mary (the most noted, perhaps, being the Ave Regina) were chanted. Some prayers of the Divine Offices remained constant throughout the year; others changed like the text of the Proper from day to day. For each prayer there were chants which allowed them to be sung rather than spoken.

Fine examples of Gregorian chant can be found in the book *Masterpieces of Music Before 1750* by Carl Parish and John Ohl. The book is accompanied by a three-volume record album set and is commonly abbreviated ''MM.'' We shall refer to it extensively in our historical discussions.

Suggested Listening: MM No. 1. Antiphon and psalm

Around the 9th century A.D. newly composed additions to the old chants began to appear. These were called tropes, and they were either new lines of text or original melodies (or both) interpolated between the words and music of an existing chant. For example, for the Feast of Epiphany (the celebration of the discovery of the baby Jesus by the three wise men who followed their guiding star to Bethlehem), the text of the Alleluia of the Mass was expanded with the words "vidimus stellam ejus in Oriente et venimus cum muneribus adorare Dominum" (we have seen His star in the East and have come with gifts to worship the Lord). These words were accompanied by a newly composed section of chant.

Suggested Listening: MM No. 2. Alleluia trope

Special tropes which had the musical form of aa, bb, cc...n (that is, where each line of the trope was repeated) were called "sequences." The practice of troping chants began in and around the monastic abbey of St. Gall in Switzerland. The two monks most associated with the composition of tropes were Tuotilo (d. 915) and Notker Balbulus (d. 912).

Suggested Listening: MM No. 3. Easter sequence

Secular Monophonic Song. Though sacred monophonic chant dominated the Early Christian era, it was by no means the only kind of monophony. Secular songs dealing with subjects like love, war, nature, and historical occurrences were a significant part of the scene.

Musically, most of these songs were syllabic, metric (predominantly triple meter), modal, and sung in the vernacular of the region in which they were composed. They also tended to exhibit a rather clear formal structure.

Though they existed in England through the works of traveling minstrels and gleemen, it was in France and Germany that the largest body of secular monophony was found. Southern French composers called troubadours flourished from around 1100 to around 1300 A.D. Among them, Bernart de Ventadorn (c. 1127-95) is perhaps the best known. Northern French noblemen, cultured men called trouveres, flourished slightly later. Of these the most famous was Adam de la Halle (c. 1235-85) whose play-with-music, "Jeu de Robin et de Marion" (the story of Robin Hood and Maid Marion), was heralded throughout the region.

Two frequently used forms of the French secular monody which illustrate the clarity of its construction were the virelai (ABCCabAB) and the rondeau (ABaAabAB). (The capital letters here indicate repetitions of both text and music. Lower case letters indicate repetition of music with new text.)

Suggested Listening: MM No. 4. Trouvere virelai

In Germany, secular monophonists were called minnesingers or meistersingers. They flourished from the 12th to the 14th centuries and wrote many of their works in an aab structure known as "bar form." Walther von der Vogelweide (c. 1170-1230), Neithardt von Reuenthal (c. 1180-1240), and Hans Sachs (1494-1576) were among the best known German monophonists.

Suggested Listening: MM No. 5. Neithardt minnelied

Secular monophony also occurred in Italy (the ballata) and Spain (the villancico). Thus, with the songs of France, Germany, and England the art form was one of universal scope in medieval Europe.

The Development of Polyphony.

Music with more than one part is polyphonic (many-voiced) music, and the development of polyphony must be regarded as one of the most important events in the entire history of music - indeed, the entire history of all artistic expression. It occurred well into the Middle Ages, around the 9th century A.D. and coincided with the growing political sophistication of Western Europe which followed the crowning of Charlemagne (800 A.D.). Musically, early polyphony was associated with chant, and it brought to the art a concern not just for line but also for the vertical interaction of one line with another. Like the integration of the horizontal with the vertical words of a crossword puzzle, polyphony added a wholly new and powerful dimension to Western musical sound.

The Principle of Independence in Polyphony. To understand how polyphony developed it is necessary to understand the concept of the independence of line. Lines can be independent of one another in any or all of four ways: pitch, direction, rhythm, and quality of sound.

If two violins are playing the same part, the result will be monophony, but if one of them should play pitches different from the other, the lines of music will begin to show a degree of independence. (See below.)

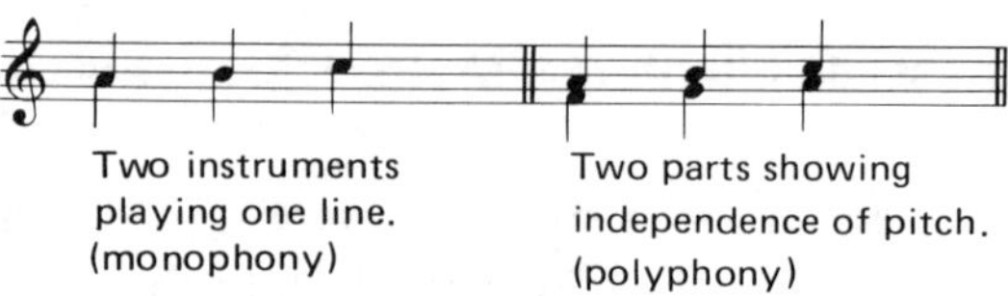

When lines move relative to each other, they can travel in several ways: parallel motion (where both parts move in the same direction at the same intervallic rates), similar motion (where both parts move in the same direction but at different rates), oblique motion (where one part remains stationary while the other moves either up or down), and contrary motion (where one part moves up while the other moves down). (See below.)

Parallel motion shows no directional independence; similar motion a bit more independence; oblique motion still more; and contrary motion the greatest amount of independence.

The lines above all move in quarter notes, but lines need not move at the same rhythmic rate. That is, if one is moving in ♩ , the other need not move in ♩ , but may move in ♪ or ♪ or combinations of different note values. To the extent the note values of one part differ from the note values of another, to that extent the parts are rhythmically independent.

Finally, lines can have different timbres. Timbre refers to the quality or characteristic of a sound. A violin has a different timbre from a trumpet, for example. To the extent one part differs from another in timbre, to that extent it shows greater independence.

The history of polyphony is really the process by which music achieved independence one line from another; independence of pitch, direction, rhythm, and timbre.

Organum. The first type of music to show the principles of independent polyphony was chant composition known as organum. Organum began to appear in 9th century tropes when a second voice traveling in fourths or fifths above or below the chant was added. This second voice had little or no independence of direction (since it merely paralleled the first voice) and absolutely no independence of rhythm. Because of the parallel motion of the two voices, the music was known as parallel organum. (See below.)

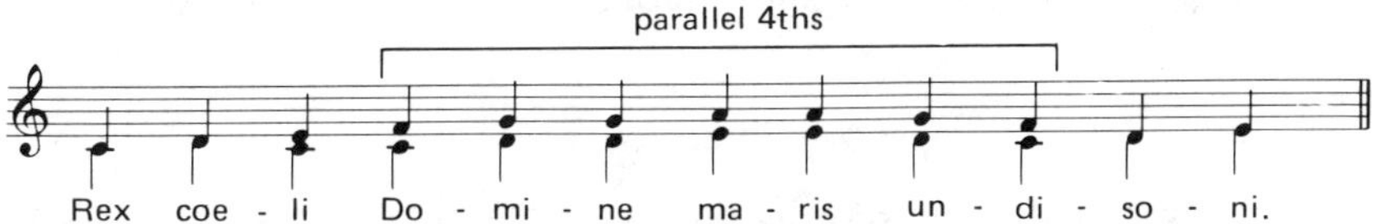

Suggested Listening: MM No. 6. Parallel organum

By the 11th century, independence of direction began to appear consistently in organum known as free organum. Here, although parts still moved against each other at the same rhythmic rates, they exhibited oblique and contrary motion much of the time. (See below).

Suggested Listening: MM No. 7. Free organum

In the 12th century - particularly at the abbeys of St. Martial in Limoge, France and Santiago de Compostela in Northern Spain - a new form of organum appeared in which parts traveled at different rhythmic rates. Although the precise values of the notes were not fixed as they are today in ♪ or ♩. or ♪.. , it was clear that one line traveled in short note values while the other moved slowly in long note values. Because of the relationship of text to music (many short notes to one syllable of text) this kind of composition was known as melismatic organum. (See below.)

Suggested Listening: MM No. 8. Melismatic organum

The early development of organum represented an enormously important stride forward in the historical evolution of music. Like the invention of the wheel or the discovery of electricity, it set in motion the creative forces which would dominate the art for centuries to come. For the remainder of the Middle Ages, most musical refinements centered around the efforts of musicians to be ever more precise in the rhythmic notation of music, and ever more aware of how any given line might interact with another, or two others, or three others, etc.

The Ars Antiqua.

The years from around 1150 A.D. to 1300 A.D. saw further developments in organum. In particular, they saw the growth of new musical forms and the institution of notational practices which allowed rhythmic values to be expressed in proportional, measured notes. During this era, the musical center of Europe was Paris, especially the Cathedral of Notre Dame. The era is generally known as the Ars Antiqua (Old Art).

From a political point of view, the Ars Antiqua coincided with the age of the Crusades. In England, King Henry II reigned and vied with Thomas Beckett for absolute secular and sacred power; in France, Louis IX ruled from 1226 to 1270; and the philosophical destiny of all Europe was being shaped by such men as St. Francis of Assisi, Roger Bacon, and St. Thomas Aquinas.

Notre Dame Organum. At the Cathedral of Notre Dame, composer Leoninus and his pupil Perotinus made the organum an ever more sophisticated musical form. The chants on which their compositions were based would be placed in a low vocal range, usually the tenor part. Then above it either one or two additional parts would be sung. In earlier centuries, these upper parts had not been notated with precise rhythms. Now they were, and the rhythms were based on the triple meter patterns of the Greek rhythmic modes which would flow along above the long held notes of the tenor chant. Occasionally, the tenor contained segments in modal rhythms as well. Such tenor sections were called "clausulae."

The textual style of the Notre Dame organum was melismatic, and the harmony generated by the integration of the various parts was rudimentary. The basic, most consonant intervals were octaves, fourths, and fifths which occurred, for the most part, on accented words. As time went on, thirds were employed more and more frequently, and eventually they came to be considered consonant rather than dissonant. Dissonances in the form of seconds and sevenths were used but restricted to weak, unaccented beats. In later centuries, there would be much stricter rules for the use of dissonance than there were in the Ars Antiqua.

From time to time, instruments were employed in organum. They could double the voice parts (thus adding volume to the sound and helping the singers to stay on pitch), or they could replace vocal lines altogether. In general, however, the organum was not an instrumental form. It was conceived for and performed predominantly by the human voice.

Suggested Listening: MM No. 9 Perotin 3-part organum

The Conductus. Organum was not the only musical form of the Ars Antiqua. The conductus, by contrast, was a syllabic setting of a text in a composition usually scored for three parts. Here, unlike the organum where the tenor was written in long, held notes, each voice would move in one of the rhythmic modes. Another major difference between conductus and organum was that in the conductus the tenor part was not a chant passed down through the centuries, but an originally composed melody. Otherwise, the conductus and organum expressed the same general musical style.

Suggested Listening: MM No. 11. Arts Antiqua conductus

The Motet. By the end of the 13th century a new type of composition, the motet, replaced the organum and conductus as the most important form of polyphony. Motets originated when words (the French word for "word" is "mot") were placed in the vocal part of the clausula segment of an organum. Eventually, the motet was standardized as a three-part composition. The lowest part, the tenor, was a chant melody written with measured notes in one of the rhythmic modes. Above it, also in measured notation, were two additional parts (the motetus and triplum) which usually moved in note values faster than the tenor. Frequently, the tenor was played by an instrument while the motetus and triplum were sung. Generally, the upper two parts had different texts. Often one was sacred (Latin), the other secular (French), creating a composition of mixed flavors - instrumental and vocal, sacred and secular. The great motet composer of the late Ars Antiqua was Petrus de Cruce.

Sugggested Listening: MM No. 10. 13th century motet

Imitative Forms. Imitation was not an important Ars Antiqua device, but it did exist, and because it came to play such an important part in later history, Ars Antiqua imitation is worth noting. There were two main imitative forms. The first was the rota which was exactly like a modern-day canon or round. The second was the rondellus. In this latter form, the parts would exchange material with each other so that every voice would eventually do what the others did but in a different order. Voice no. 1, for example, would sing "e-a-t," voice no. 2 "a-t-e," and voice no. 3 "t-e-a." The combination of all three voices would fit both vertically and horizontally like the words of a crossword puzzle (see below).

Voice no. 1	e	a	t
Voice no. 2	a	t	e
Voice no. 3	t	e	a

The Ars Nova

From 1300 A.D. to around 1400 A.D. polyphony continued to develop, particularly in the use of more and more intricate rhythmic patterns. The period was known as the Ars Nova (New Art), and it was centered primarily in France and Italy. Politically, the Ars Nova occurred against a volatile background. The Church became fragmented to the point where two papacies existed, one in Rome and one in Avignon (from 1378-1418). The Black Plague scourged Europe from 1348 to 1350, and the Hundred Years War between England and France (1337-1453) dominated European politics. However, it was not a time of total barbarism. The arts did flourish in many of the European courts and cities, and some of the greatest minds of medieval Europe began a cultural awakening which would blossom into the Renaissance of the 15th and 16th centuries. Petrarch, Dante, Boccaccio, Chaucer, and the great Florentine painter Giotto all signaled the end of the Middle Ages and pointed the way to a new secular humanism.

The Ars Nova in France. The motet continued as the dominant French polyphonic form but developed in complexity through a technique known as isorhythm. Here, a rhythmic pattern called the "talea," much longer and more complex than the old rhythmic modes, was established by the composer. Against it was pitted a melodic pattern, the "color," usually of a different length. Thus, the two patterns would overlap and interweave within one and the same line (see below).

The isorhythmic voice of a motet was usually the tenor against which two or three additional parts were composed. But the principle of isorhythm extended beyond the motet to settings of the Mass and even to the writing of secular polyphonic forms like the ballade, the rondeau and the virelai. The greatest exponent of the technique of isorhythm was Guillaume de Machaut (1305-77) who also wrote one of the earliest 4-part settings of the Mass Ordinary.

Suggested Listening: MM No. 13. Machaut Agnus Dei

The techniques of Machaut were by no means the only ones which made the Ars Nova a "new art." Perhaps even more important was the growing sophistication of rhythm. The most complete view of 14th century developments in rhythm came from the French composer and theorist Philippe de Vitry (1290-1361) whose treatise entitled "Ars Nova" gave the era its name.

De Vitry began his theory with the acknowledgement of an underlying pulse against which various proportional rhythms might occur. The note value often associated with the pulse was the "breve" (▰). The breve could be divided either into "tempus perfectum" (3 equal parts, each equal to a note called a semi-breve, ◆) or "tempus imperfectum" (2 equal parts, each equal to a semibreve). The semibreve could then be divided further into either "major prolation" (3 equal parts, each represented by the minima, ♩) or "minor prolation" (2 equal parts represented in minima). De Vitry went on to give the various combinations of tempus and prolation which, for the first time, theoretically acknowledged the use of duple meter and simple subdivision. Once this was done, rhythm could be vastly more complex than the old rhythmic modes.

In modern terms, de Vitry's breve was like the modern measure. His tempus perfectum was like triple meter, his tempus imperfectum like duple meter. His major prolation was like compound pulse division, his minor prolation like simple division. For each of his terms he used a metric symbol which indicated the pattern of the composition. These were akin to modern-day meter signatures, and some of them are used to this day. (See below.)

Tempus	Prolation	Proportions	Symbol	Modern equal
Perfect	Major	▬ = ♦ ♦ ♦ ♦ = ♪ ♪ ♪	☉	$\frac{9}{8}$ meter
Perfect	Minor	▬ = ♦ ♦ ♦ ♦ = ♪ ♪	○	$\frac{3}{4}$ meter
Imperfect	Major	▬ = ♦ ♦ ♦ = ♪ ♪ ♪	◖	$\frac{6}{8}$ meter
Imperfect	Minor	▬ = ♦ ♦ ♦ = ♪ ♪	C	$\frac{2}{4}$ meter

The Ars Nova in Italy. Although the Italian tradition of 14th century music is extensive, it was neither as complex nor as influential as French music. Generally, the Italian style was rhythmically simpler. It avoided the cantus firmus technique (where the tenor contained a chant around which the other parts were written) and used less complex textures than the 4-part writing of Machaut.

The most important Italian forms were secular: the madrigal, the caccia (an early form of canon), and the ballata (which resembled the French virelai). The leading Italian composer of the period was Francesco Landini (1325-97), an organist blind from birth who wrote both organ and vocal works. The most common scalar cadential pattern of the era (7-6-1) bears his name. (see below.)

Suggested Listening: MM No. 14. Landini ballata

The 7-6-1 cadence was not limited to Italy. Neither was 4-part writing or the technique of isorhythm wholly restricted to France. Eventually, all the devices of the 14th century gained universal acceptance and were employed throughout Europe. Gradually, they began to transform the style of medieval music into a new era, the Renaissance.

Instruments of the Middle Ages.

Though vocal music provided the overwhelming percentage of the medieval output, instruments did exist and were used extensively both to double vocal lines and to provide dance music in small ensembles called consorts. The principal instruments were from the string family (vielles and rebecs, bowed forerunners of the violin); the harp family (lute and psaltery); the wind family (recorders of various sizes, horns and trumpets); and the organ family (portable and stationary varieties powered by air). Percussion instruments such as bells, drums, and cymbals were also in use.

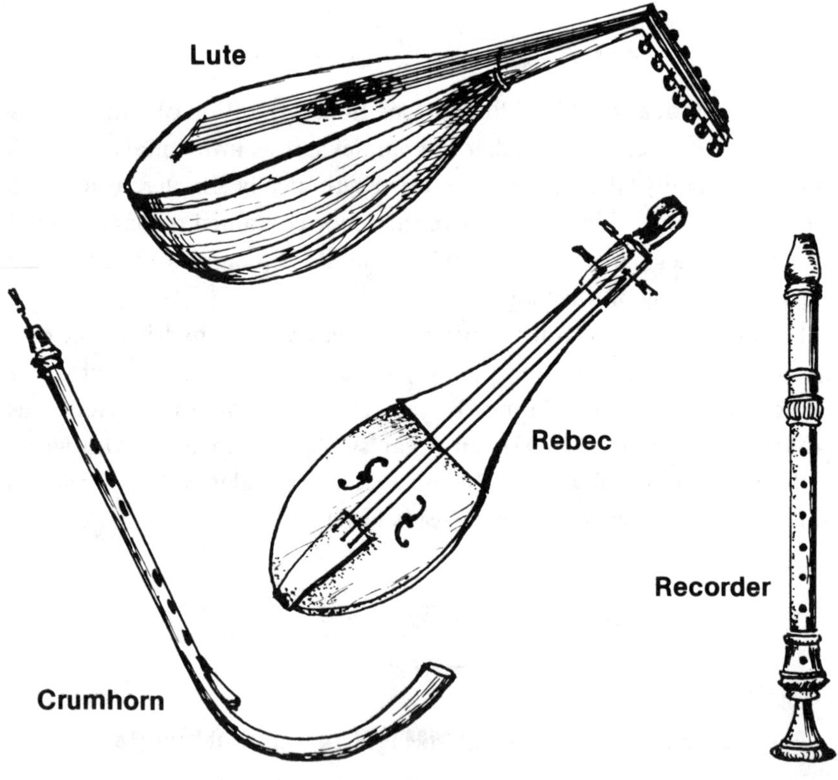

The most important kind of purely instrumental composition was dance music. Dances like the ductia, saltarello, and estampie were particularly favored. They paved the way for the great instrumental advances which were to come in the ensuing centuries.

Suggested Listening: MM No. 12. 13th century estampie

The Development of Notation.

When the Middle Ages began, music was notated in only the crudest, most imprecise ways. By the time the era had come to an end, pitches and rhythms were represented in clear, sophisticated terms, and not many new developments were needed to reach the level of modern notation. By the end of the 17th century, almost all of today's notational devices were in use.

Neumatic Notation. The earliest chant was indicated by inflection symbols called neumes written above the chant text. They represented only crude melodic direction and no rhythm at all.

A L L E L U I A

Near the end of the first millenium (950-1000 A.D.), a horizontal line representing the pitch F was added above the text, thus giving the neumes a bit more precise meaning.

A L L E L U I A

By the 11th century, a 4-line staff was in common use. From then to around 1200 A.D. there was much experimentation with the number of lines in the staff. By the 13th century most of Europe had settled on the 5-line staff we know today, and many of the medieval scribes were indicating what note each line represented (E or C or G, for example) by placing that letter at the beginning of the line. These letters eventually became our modern clef signs.

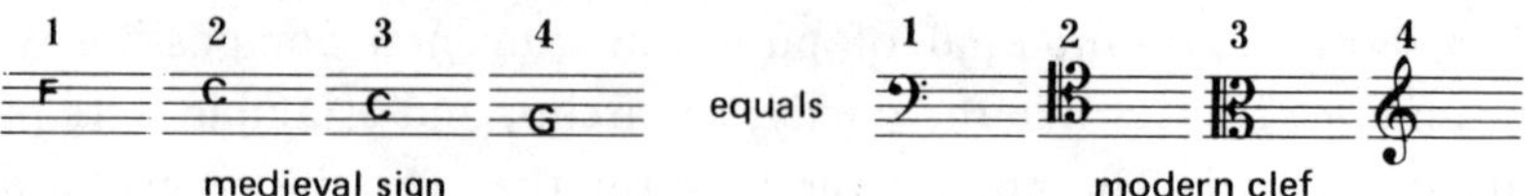

The advantage of different clefs was, of course, the avoidance of ledger lines. If one was writing a soprano part, for example, it would be good to have the note C low on the staff because sopranos sing almost all of their notes well above C. The same principle held true for all the ranges.

Modal Notation. Having solved the problem of representing pitches accurately, the next task for musicians became the precise notation of rhythm. By 1100 or so, a system of notation had arisen called modal notation (because it was based on the rhythmic modes). It used three basic note types - the longa (⌐), the breve (◄), and the semibreve (♦) - which could represent all the modal patterns. (See below.)

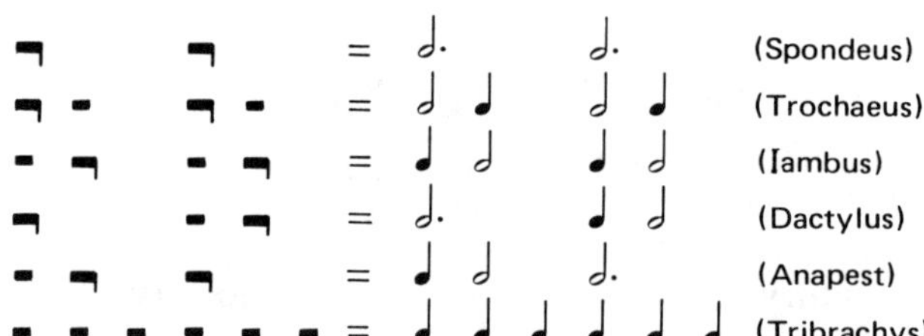

Modal notes could also be combined in groupings called ligatures which stood for various rhythmic patterns (all of them based on the rhythmic modes).

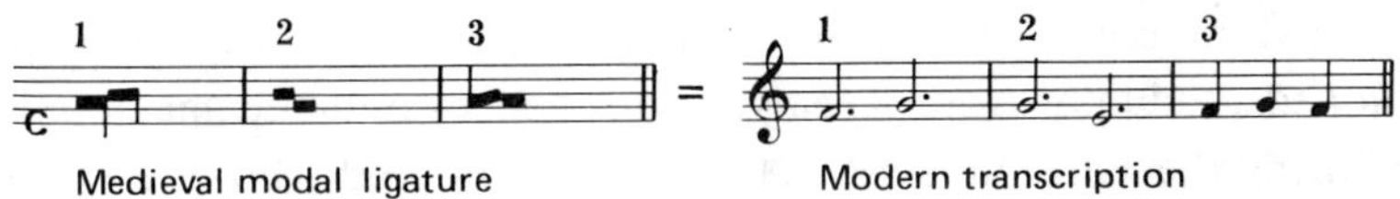

Around 1280 A.D. Franco of Cologne wrote the first comprehensive treatise on proportional note values, the "Ars Cantus Mensurabilis" (the art of measured music). He standardized the value of notes, ligatures, rests, etc. in a system which survived well into the 16th century. His system of note values appears below.

Modern Notation. Following Franco's work, the next great notational innovations came as a result of the "Ars Nova" treatise of Philippe de Vitry (discussed above). Though de Vitry did not change the actual writing of pitches and note values, his acknowledgement of duple meter and use of metric symbols was incorporated into the Franconian system.

The Franconian system used darkly colored notes for which it sometimes bears the name "black-note notation." At the end of the Middle Ages and during the era of the Renaissance (1400-1600), however, some black notes were replaced with open white ones. This combination of white and black notes formed the basis of the modern system of proportional values we use today. The chart below indicates the Renaissance version of Franconian notation and the modern-day refinements of the Renaissance system.

	maxima	longa	breve	semibreve	minima	semiminima	fusa	semifusa
Renaissance	◻	◻	◻	◇	♩	♦	♪	𝅘𝅥𝅯
Modern	not used	not used	double whole note	whole note	half note	quarter note	eighth note	sixteenth note

The use of bar lines, meter signatures, ties, dots, and double dots developed gradually from Renaissance practices and became standardized during the Baroque era (1600-1750). By the mid-18th century composers were commonly adding dynamic markings, tempo indications, and other written performance instructions to their music. In essence, the entire notational process was just about that of today. As for large scores which contained the parts of many instruments playing together, the practice of the 16th century Renaissance was to print only part books separately. The disadvantage of not being able to follow the entirety of a polyphonic composition, however, soon reversed this trend. By the end of the 17th century, part books were abandoned in favor of the full score. Today a conductor (who must follow all the parts at once) reads a full score while each separate performer reads from sheets that contain only his or her part (since that is all for which he or she is responsible).

CHAPTER ELEVEN:

THE RENAISSANCE (1400-1600)

The Renaissance - that is, the two hundred years from 1400 to 1600 - was a time of monumental change in Europe. The Eastern Roman Empire fell in 1453, and in the same year the Hundred Years War came to an end. In 1517 Martin Luther broke from the Catholic Church to begin the Protestant Reformation. From 1545 to 1563 the Catholic Council of Trent met to plan their counter-reformation. In 1588 the English defeated the Spanish Armada and rose to prominence as Europe's most powerful nation.

Throughout the entire era a great wave of exploration flowed from Europe. Columbus, Magellan, Balboa, Cortez, Pizarro, Cooke, Drake and many others sailed to distant lands which they claimed for their various European monarch patrons, thus setting in motion an age of colonialism and empire-building that would dominate world events into the 20th century. Invention and scientific investigation abounded, and with them came a greater interest in and awareness of the secular world.

Leonardo da Vinci, Kepler, Copernicus, Galileo and a host of others began to temper the medieval concern for the hereafter with a humanistic concern for the here and now. It was not that the world of religion was abandoned but that it became less overwhelmingly dominant. In all aspects of living - politics, art, science, theology, philosophy - making life understandable and workable was now as important as preparing for the kingdom of heaven after death. Indeed, many thought of the new secular humanism as another kind of service to God, another kind of preparation.

The new forces at work in Europe touched music no less than the other aspects of life, making the Renaissance a time of great musical activity and profound musical growth. The entire era can be viewed in two parts: the 15th century in which new musical styles and forces emerged, and the 16th century in which those forces were developed on a largely regional basis in the nations of Europe.

The 15th Century.

The music of the early 15th century took its direction from England and the Burgundy region of France. Toward the end of the century, musical activity shifted to Flanders where a style of composition known as the "Franco-Flemish school" arose.

Burgundian Music. The music of Burgundy was both 3-part and 4-part. It tended to have its melodic interest in the top voice (as opposed to the tenor), and it employed the interval of the third with great frequency, often in long series of first inversion triads. In keeping with the new secular spirit of the age, Burgundian composers at times used secular melodies instead of chant as the musical basis of their writing. The chief sacred Burgundian forms were the mass and the motet. In England the carol became a popular 2-part form. The dominant secular form continued to be the chanson, in particular the rondeau, a song in ABaAabAB form. The greatest Burgundian composers were Guillame Dufay (1400-1474) and Gilles Binchois (1400-1460) on the continent and John Dunstable (1370-1453) in England.

Suggested Listening: **MM No. 15. Dufay Kyrie**
MM No. 16. Binchois rondeau

Franco-Flemish Music. The two great hallmarks of the Franco-Flemish composers were a consistent use of 4-part texture and the development of all the techniques of imitative counterpoint. Their music was still modal, still triadic in chord construction, but the Landini cadence was used less often, replaced by the modern V-I or IV-I cadence. This made Franco-Flemish works sound closer to the 20th century concept of music than to the medieval concept. The mass and motet continued to be the most common Franco-Flemish sacred forms even though secular tunes were employed at times as the melodic basis of religious works. The chanson or lied (as it was called in Germany) continued to be the most common secular form. The great masters of the Franco-Flemish school were Johannes Ockeghem (1430-1495), Heinrich Isaac (1450-1517), Jacob Obrecht (1450-1505), and, perhaps the greatest of all, Josquin des Prez (1450-1521).

Suggested Listening: **MM No. 17. Ockeghem Sanctus**
MM No. 18. Obrecht motet
MM No. 19. Josquin motet

The 16th Century.

Few eras in human history have contained as much dramatic changes as the 16th century in Europe. The work of Kepler, Copernicus, and Galileo which proved that the earth was indeed not the center of life but merely one of nine rotating planets had a profound effect on people. It caused them to rethink man's place in the universe and helped to usher in an era of secular humanism and scientific thought which is still with us today. As if that were not enough, the political balance of Europe was shifting northward to England. With the defeat of the Spanish Armada in 1588, Britain took her place at the head of the governmental table, ruling an empire which would stand strong for the next three hundred years. Finally, the unquestioned supremacy of the Catholic Church was challenged when in 1517 the priest Martin Luther led his Protestant followers into open defiance of established tradition and into a new rival religious order. The reaction of the Church was to hold an eighteen-year discussion, the Council of Trent (1545-1563), which sought to stop the Protestant hemorrhage and reattract people to the old faith.

For each of these trends music played a dynamic role. The growth of secularism led to an increase in secular vocal music and a significant development of instrumental music as well. The rise of Protestanism demanded its own kind of worship music, and Catholic reassertions were in no small way dependent on the use of music in the Catholic service to lead people back to the fold. Musically, the century can be understood best by seeing music as part of an overall pattern of dynamic change.

Protestant Music. Martin Luther was himself a musician of considerable ability, and he was insistent that there be certain differences between Protestant and Catholic music. The most important of these was that chant would no longer provide the basis of his sacred compositions. Chant was foreign to the people, he argued. It was old and sung in Latin by choirs removed from the general congregation. He wanted the congregation to be involved. Therefore, everyone was to sing, and the language of the text would be German, the people's vernacular. The tunes would thus be accessible, the settings basic enough for any average congregation to perform.

The result was a new type of hymn called a chorale. These were simple 4-part settings of German sacred texts whose melodies were easy to learn and enjoyable to sing. The tunes were drawn from a variety of sources: simplified chants, secular German songs, and originally composed melodies. Luther himself wrote many chorale tunes, the best known perhaps "Ein feste Burg ist unser Gott" ("A mighty fortress is our God"). It was not so much in Luther's time that the chorale achieved great musical stature. Rather it was during the Baroque era (1600-1750) when composers like Johann Sebastian Bach would use chorale melodies as the underpinning for many great sacred works in much the same way that the chant had been used as the tenor line in sacred Catholic works.

Besides the German chorale, other Protestant music arose in other regions of Europe. In France the Huguenot churches set various psalm texts to simple melodies which were later made into more elaborate 4-part works. In England the anthem became a popular musical form in Anglican worship services. The anthem, unlike the chorale, was a complex vocal form, extended in time with both chordal and contrapuntal sections scored for combinations of chorus and solo voice. It was far more like a Protestant version of the motet than the German chorale.

Some of the names associated with Renaissance Protestant vocal music were Martin Luther and Michael Praetorius (1571-1621) in Germany, Claude LeJeune (1528-1600) in France, and William Byrd (1542-1623) and Thomas Tallis (1505-1585) in England. The Protestant composers who wrote in England did so somewhat later than those in Germany due to the fact that England remained a Catholic country until 1534 when King Henry VIII broke with the Church for political rather than religious reasons. (He wanted to remarry in the face of Catholic doctrine which forbids both divorce and polygomy.) It was not until the second half of the century that the new Anglican church and her musicians were able to produce a body of worship service and worship music.

Suggested Listening: **HMS, Vol. IV, side 2, band 4**
                                 (English church music)
                                 HMS, Vol. IV, side 3, band 1
                                 (Praetorius choral)

Catholic Music. The shock of the Protestant revolt ran deep to the heart of the Catholic Church, and one of the ways in which the Church leaders hoped to stem the tide was through music. Throughout the Catholic world, great composers were commissioned to write works of such exceeding beauty that no soul could resist remaining faithful to the Church. The result was a body of 16th century music unparalleled in Church history.

The mass and motet continued as the predominant Church musical forms. The texture of these works continued to be highly polyphonic (4, 5, and sometimes up to 8 parts). The style continued to be a contrapuntal and highly imitative. Triads were the basis of chordal structure and dissonances were carefully treated (usually confined to specific places such as passing tones or neighbor notes). What changed was the exclusive use of chant as the melodic basis of a work. Originally composed melodies and even secular tunes adapted to the Church liturgy were freely used. In Venice, even instruments, formerly banned in worship singing, were used as an accompaniment to the voices. This practice arose at the Cathedral of San Marco where the presence of two choir lofts allowed for either two full choirs or one vocal and one instrumental group to combine forces. The result was a rash of "double choir" music for voice as well as instruments.

The names associated with 16th century sacred vocal music include: Orlandus Lassus (1532-1594) from the Franco-Flemish region of Northern Europe; Jacob Handl (1550-1591) and Hans Leo Hassler (1564-1612) from Germany; Cristobal Morales (1500-1553) and Tomás Luiz de Victoria (1549-1611) from Spain; Byrd and Tallis in England; Andrea (1490-1562) and Giovanni Gabrieli (1557-1612), the uncle and nephew duo who wrote for the Cathedral of San Marco in Venice; and Pierluigi da Palestrina (1525-1594), the greatest of all Church composers who wrote in Rome for the Papal Chapel.

Suggested Listening: **MM No. 23. Lassus motet**
MM No. 24. Palestrina Agnus Dei
MM No. 25. Byrd motet

Secular Vocal Music. The rise of secular thought and a host of new secular poetry led to an explosion of 16th century secular song. The frottola in Italy, the villancico in Spain, the chanson in France, the canzonet and ayre in England, the lied and quodlibet in Germany were all musical expressions of this trend. But by far the most important secular vocal form, one which abounded in Italy, France, and England, was the madrigal.

The madrigal was an Italian development, a polyphonic composition for 4 or 5 or 6 or more parts which used intricate counterpoint and a great deal of melodic imitation. The texts for madrigals ranged through every human emotion: love, death, war, praise of nature, friendship. Sometimes the mood of a madrigal was somber and sad with highly chromatic passages. Sometimes it was light, in fast tempos with dance-like rhythms and refrains that used syllables like "fa-la-la" which had no meaning. Each region developed its own madrigal style and its own group of madrigal composers.

In Italy the greatest madrigalists included Luca Marenzio (1553-1599); Carlo Gesualdo (1560-1613); Claudio Monteverdi (1567-1643), who would also emerge as a great Baroque figure in the next century; and Orlandus Lassus (known in Italy as Orlando di Lasso), the Franco-Flemish composer who was able to master the late Renaissance forms on an international scale. In France the great madrigalists included Thomas Crecquillon (d. 1557), Guillaume Costeley (1531-1606), and Claude de Sermisy (1490-1562). In England the madrigal was closely associated with the Court of Elizabeth I and the plays of William Shakespeare. The great English madrigalists included John Bennet (d. 1620), John Dowland (1562-1626), Thomas Weelkes (1575-1623), Thomas Morley (1557-1603), and Orlando Gibbons (1583-1625). It has even been suggested that Queen Elizabeth herself authored many madrigals under various assumed names.

Suggested Listening: **MM No. 20. Crecquillon chanson**
MM No. 27. Marenzio madrigal
MM No. 28. Bennet madrigal

Instrumental Music. Instrumental music had been a part of the Middle Ages and a somewhat larger part of the early Renaissance. It was not until the 16th century, however, that it came into its own as a separate musical force, a style of expression not just to enhance voices or accompany dances but to create sounds specifically for the instrumental flavor of them. Much instrumental music was borrowed from vocal forms. The instrumental canzona was an outgrowth of the vocal chanson; the ricercare was the counterpart of the polyphonic motet. But instrumental music also had its own forms, pairs of dances and sets of variations, for example. And in all these forms, instrumental music was written to sound not vocal but idiomatic. Fast scalar passages in keyboard music, large leaps in string music, thick blends of sound in music for wind ensembles all gave instrumental music a life of its own apart from the vocal world which had so dominated the art for 1500 years and more.

The major Renaissance instruments belonged to the bowed-string, plucked-string, wind, and keyboard familes. Combinations of instruments played together in small ensembles called consorts. The chief bowed instruments were the viols - ancestors of the modern violin family - which came in sizes ranging from small soprano instruments to large bass ones. The lute and, later, the guitar dominated the plucked-string world while the chief wind instruments continued to be recorders, horns, cornets, trombones, and trumpets. Besides great wind organs which were constructed all over Europe, two smaller keyboard instruments dominated the scene. They were the harpsichord (which had a mechanism to pluck the string when the key was pressed) and the clavichord (which had a tangent to strike the string when the key was pressed). It was the clavichord which would lead to the modern piano around the year 1700.

The composers most associated with Renaissance instrumental music included Paumann (d. 1473) and Hofhaimer (d. 1537) - keyboard composers of Germany; Claudio Merulo (d. 1604) and the Gabrielis who wrote both keyboard and wind music in Italy; Antonio Cabezón (d. 1566), the great lute composer of Spain; Jean Titelouze (d. 1633) who wrote organ music in France; and Farnaby (d. 1640) and Dowland in England whose keyboard music became classics of their age.

For all these composers and for many vocal composers as well, the growth in popularity of their work was in part due to the new techniques of printing and publication which could spread one's music across the continent and earn for it an international reputation. The publicists Petrucci in Italy, Attaingnant in France, and Yonge in England were particularly responsible for the dissemination of 16th century music.

Suggested Listening: **MM No. 22. Lute dances**
MM No. 21. Gabrieli canzona
MM No. 29. Farnaby variations

CHAPTER TWELVE:

THE BAROQUE ERA (1600-1750)

From the historical view the Baroque era (1600-1750) represented different things in different regions of Europe. In Spain there was a decline of power after the defeat of the Armada (1588). In France there was the consolidation of power under the absolute rule of King Louis XIII and Louis XIV. There was also the abuse of that power which set in motion the forces which would lead to the French Revolution. In Germany there was fragmentation, much of it caused by the Catholic/Protestant schism. It erupted in the Thirty Years War (1618-48) which left the region weak and disunited. In England there was a Civil War (1642-49) which for a time replaced the monarchy with a puritanical commonwealth. It was not until 1660 that the monarchy was restored. For Italy it was an era of local rule rather than unification. As a center of trade and exploration, Italy was a cultural leader, but a leader without a central government. In Rome the Pope was dominant. In the cities of Florence and Venice city governments were dominant. In other areas nobles like the Dukes of Ferrara and Mantua were dominant. And over all of these separate forces hovered the constant factors of colonialization, empire building, world trade and the domination of the globe by Europe.

Musically, the Baroque was a time for planting seeds and watching them ripen into harvests. Terms not yet heard before - terms like opera, oratorio, orchestra, concerto, piano, ballet, and sonata - were all to sprout and bear fruit. And they all had their roots in the end of the Renaissance; in Italy, in the city of Florence, where new things were about to happen.

Early Baroque Vocal Developments and Their Effects.

The vocal music at the end of the Renaissance was highly polyphonic and very contrapuntal. Madrigals in 4, 5, 6, or more parts were common. So were similar masses and motets. The result of all this polyphony on the text of these works was that words were difficult to understand, for while one part was singing one word, another part would be singing other words. Such is the price one pays for rhythmically independent polyphony. In Florence at the turn of the 16th century, however, it was a price which was no longer desirable.

There, a group of singers, composers, and cultured noblemen called "The Camerata" consciously tried to create music which on the one hand would preserve the beauty of Renaissance polyphony and on the other would allow for great clarity of text. They called their ideas "nuove musiche" (new music) and accomplished their goals by creating a new kind of song called monody.

Monody. Monody was one-part singing with all the contrapuntal and harmonic support relegated to an instrumental accompaniment. The lowest voice (bass line) was written below the melody and text. Below the bass line in a kind of numerical shorthand were figures which stood for the middle voices between the bass line and melody. A low string or wind instrument would play the bass line. So would the left hand of a keyboard instrument (organ or harpsichord). The right hand of the keyboard would improvise the "inner parts" of the accompaniment according to the figures while the solo voice sang the melody with clear, uncluttered, textual declamation. The bass part itself became known as a "basso continuo" or "thorough bass." The bass line-with-numbers became known as a "figured bass." The improvisation of the keyboard right hand became known as "realizing" a figured bass. All of these practices - clear textual singing, improvisation, figured bass, basso continuo line - remained constant throughout the entire Baroque era and had a great influence upon it.

Above is the beginning of a monody by Giulio Caccini (1560-1618) showing the basso continuo line with figures and the vocal line with text.

Suggested Listening: **MM No. 30. Caccini monody**

Opera. The clarity of text which the monody afforded allowed not only for poetry to be presented clearly, it also allowed dialogue and drama to be sung in understandable form. The result was the development of opera, a monumental step in the history of Western music. Opera was staged drama with characters, costumes, and scenery wherein dialogue was either entirely sung or mixed in combinations varying from actual speech to extended melody.

In early opera as in every form of musical theatre from the early Baroque through the 20th century, there were five styles of verbal delivery possible.

- Speech. Normal spoken prose with no regularity of stress or pulse.
- Metered speech. Spoken prose or poetry not sung but set to a recurrent pulse or meter.
- Recitative. Sung declamation principally on one tone, but in any event using few tones, syllabic text setting, and sparse instrumental accompaniment.
- Arioso. Declamation in a generally syllabic style but with more elaborate accompaniment and more melodic interest than the few notes of the recitative.
- Aria. Extended song with extensive accompaniment using any and all types of text setting from syllabic to highly melismatic in long, fully developed melodies.

Italian opera began in and around Florence, spread to Rome, then centered in Venice where the first public opera house opened in 1637. By the late 17th century, Naples had emerged as the most important center of production. Throughout the 1600's Italian opera developed both serious and comic genres. It also developed a style of extended aria which would influence all of European musical drama for over two centuries. The composers most noted for Baroque Italian opera include: Claudio Monteverdi (1567-1643), the madrigalist who revised his Renaissance style to write operas for the new theatre at Venice; Stefano Landi (1590-1655) and Luigi Rossi (1597-1653) who wrote serious operas for the Roman audiences; and Alessandro Scarlatti (1660-1725) whose late Baroque operas dominated the Neapolitan musical scene.

Among the more important contributions of the opera composers of the Italian Baroque were the development of the ABA aria form (the so-called "da capo" aria) and the use of the Italian overture. The da capo aria was emulated in every major musical center of Europe. The Italian overture (a fast-slow-fast, 3-part instrumental prelude to the opera) became the forerunner of the classical symphony of the 18th and 19th centuries.

Suggested Listening: **MM No. 31. Monteverdi "Orfeo"**

Opera in France did not really come into its own until the middle of the 17th century, and when it did, it was chiefly associated with one man, Jean-Baptiste Lully (1632-1687). Lully was a native Italian (Lulli was his given name) who came to France, ultimately to rise to musical power as the chief musician for the court of Louis XIV. As Louis's employee he had the unlimited resources and power of the King behind him. He also had access to the dramatic works of some of the greatest writers in human history, among them Racine, Corneille, and Moliere. In this environment Lully composed operas of the most opulent kind for which he added two new ingredients. They were the fully developed concept of an orchestra and the infusion of ballet into the musical drama. In addition to these two significant contributions, Lully also developed a distinctly French style to his writing. In time his French overture (a 3-part slow-fast-slow prelude to the opera/ballet) became a musical form equal to its Italian counterpart. The work of Lully was continued in the late French Baroque by Jean-Philippe Rameau (1683-1764) who not only wrote operas but was one of the most important music theorists of his day.

Suggested Listening: **MM No. 36. Lully overture**
                                  MM No. 41. Rameau opera

Opera in both England and Germany during the 17th century never reached the same level of development as it did in Italy and France. This was in large part due to the chaos within each nation: the Civil War and Restoration in England; the Thirty Years War in Germany. However, there was some degree of musical theatre in both countries. In England the leading composer was Henry Purcell (1658-1695) who wrote both opera and incidental music for plays and poetic epics. In Germany there were several composers who wrote for the theatre in Hamburg, the center of German opera. The name most associated with the Hamburg productions was Reinhard Keiser (1674-1739). Keiser composed operas in a style known as "singspiel" where spoken dialogue was often mixed with musical declamation.

Sacred Vocal Music. The dramatic style of the early monody was an acorn from which two oaks grew. Opera was the secular one. There was also a sacred harvest which drew upon the innovations of the monodic style. Here was born the cantata and the oratorio. Although the mass and motet still continued to be written for the Catholic worship service, neither contained the potential for the inclusion of drama or aria. Both the cantata and the oratorio did, and they became the chief Baroque sacred vocal forms.

Cantatas were multisectional religious works whose texts were usually taken from Biblical passages. They were scored for voices and instruments, at times for full orchestral accompaniments. Since the cantata texts were not usually part of the Catholic worship service, the cantata was associated largely with the Protestant movement, frequently a Protestant chorale melody forming the basis of each section of the composition. In general cantatas contained between five and ten sections of contrasting character. One section might be a fast movement for full choir and orchestra, another a slow setting for solo voice and keyboard accompaniment. Thus cantatas were extended works lasting fifteen to twenty minutes or more. The leading cantata composers of the 17th century were frequently German; Heinrich Schutz (1585-1672) and the organists, Buxtehude (1637-1707) and Pachelbel (1650-1706), are three examples. By far, however, the greatest cantatas of the era were written by the late Baroque German master Johann Sebastian Bach (1685-1750) who composed over three hundred of them, about half of which have survived.

Suggested Listening: **MM No. 33. Schutz cantata**
                                   MM No. 46,
                                   MM No. 48. Bach Cantata No. 4

Oratorio was a kind of religious opera without scenery, props, or costumes. Its texts were stories from the Bible (Solomon, Samson, etc.) set to music which could include anything from recitative to solo aria to full chorus. Accompaniments to oratorios were as varied as the vocal settings themselves, ranging from keyboard to full orchestra. The number of sections in the typical Baroque oratorio was much greater than in the cantata. At times oratorios could have 20, 30, even 40 segments. Consequently, they were much more extensive than cantatas, often running up to one or two hours in length. Special oratorios dealing with the story of the Trial, Crucifixtion, and Resurrection of Christ were called passions, and passions were extremely popular, especially during the Easter season. The earliest oratorios were written in Italy, and the most noted oratorio composer of the early Baroque was Giacomo Carissimi (1605-1674). Following Carissimi's work, oratorios were composed in France, Germany, and England as well. Many of the great composers of opera turned their hand at times to the production of oratorio. By the end of the Baroque era, the form had developed into one of the most important sacred musical idioms of both Protestant and Catholic worship. Its leading exponents were the two giants of the late Baroque, Johann Sebastian Bach and George Frideric Handel (1685-1759), particularly the latter.

<table>
<tr><td>Suggested Listening:</td><td>MM No. 32. Carissimi oratorio scene
MM No. 45. Handel oratorio chorus</td></tr>
</table>

The Development of Instruments.

Instruments had to some extent maintained a life of their own during the Middle Ages, but it was a pale and weak life in comparison to vocal music. During the Renaissance instrumental music began to grow in importance, but the predominant musical forces were still vocal ones. In the Baroque era, however, instrumental music achieved equality with vocal music both in the quantity of it and in the significance it would have for future centuries. By the end of the Baroque era, instrumental music would be as important if not more important than its vocal counterpart.

The growth of instrumental music from 1600 to 1750 was due to a variety of factors, among them opera, violin and organ manufacturing, the development of keyboard instruments, and developments in tuning.

Instrumental Outgrowths of Opera. Once the monody had developed into full dramatic presentations, instruments became indispensable to the performances. With the advent of the ballet and the development of the overture, however, instruments began to take on a life of their own. Ensembles and orchestras became more commonplace, and gradually the public demanded whole presentations of instrumental music quite divorced from the mostly vocal world. New orchestral forms arose, the most important of which was the concerto grosso.

The concerto grosso was a large scale work in three separate movements (fast-slow-fast). Here the full orchestra (called the "ripieno") would alternate with a solo instrument or small ensemble of two or three instruments (the "concertino"). It was characteristic of the concerto grosso that the main theme would return periodically throughout a given movement. For this reason the theme was often called a "ritornello" (return).

The concerto grosso first appeared in Italy in works where voices and instruments "played together" in a "concerted" style. By the mid-17th century, however, it was a wholly instrumental form. The names most associated with the Baroque concerto grosso included George Philipp Telemann (1681-1767), Antonio Vivaldi (1669-1741), and of course Bach and Handel who were associated with every facet of Baroque composition.

Suggested Listening: **MM No. 43. Handel concerto grosso**
Vivaldi. "The Seasons"
J.S. Bach. Brandenburg Concerto No. 1

Violin and Organ Manufacturing. It is hard to say in what direction the influence between instrument makers and composers flows. Do the composers write new things because the manufacturers place instruments on the market which are capable of greater technical achievements; or do the manufacturers make better instruments because composers write more demanding music? The truth probably lies in between. The influences are probably reciprocal.

In the case of the Baroque, organ building - especially in France and Germany - reached a zenith during the years between 1650 and 1750. One great cathedral after another commissioned the building of organs capable of great power and great virtuosity. Similarly, in the art of violin making, the Baroque produced instruments which even to this day are considered among the greatest achievements in human craftsmanship. The center of violin manufacturing was the city of Cremona in Italy, particularly in the shops of the Guarneri, Stradivari and Amati families.

To support these new instruments, whole bodies of music were written from 1600 onward. In the field of organ composition two general styles became prominent: improvisational music and music based on the Protestant chorale. Improvisational forms - toccatas, fantasias, ricercars, and preludes - were pieces which grew out of the figured bass tradition. They were frequently virtuostic in nature and were often altered by the player during performance. The written versions were thus only approximations of the actual sound. Chorale forms used chorale melodies as their musical basis, embellishing them to make larger instrumental idioms. The names associated with Baroque organ compositions include Frescobaldi (1583-1643), Pachelbel (1653-1706), Buxtehude (1637-1707), and J.S. Bach (1685-1750).

Suggested Listening: **MM No. 34. Frescobaldi ricercar**
MM No. 37. Pachelbel toccata
MM No. 46. Bach Chorale (Christ Lag)
MM No. 47. Bach. Christ Lag Chorale Prelude

The string music of the Baroque, inspired both by the orchestral sounds which arose from opera and by the manufacture of instruments of unprecedented quality, grew to significant proportions by the beginning of the 18th century. In general, pieces for strings were called "sonatas," a word taken from the Italian "sonare" which means "to be played" (as opposed to "cantare" which means "to be sung"). There were two major types of string sonatas: the sonata da chiesa (church sonata) and the sonata da camera (chamber sonata). The latter was a series of dances scored for strings; the former, a work in four movements of alternating character (slow-fast-slow-fast). Though some sonatas were written for solo instruments, or single instrument with keyboard accompaniment (violin and harpsichord, for example), often they were written for small ensembles. The most important ensemble work was called a trio sonata because it was written on three staves. The upper two staves were for two solo instruments (often two violins) while the lower staff was played by a 'cello and the left hand of a keyboard instrument (harpsichord being the most common). The figures below the 'cello part enabled the keyboard player to improvise a full accompaniment above the 'cello line. The names most frequently associated with Baroque string music are Torelli (1658-1709), Corelli (1653-1713), Vivaldi (1669-1741),

Telemann (1681-1767), and the ubiquitous J.S. Bach and G.F. Handel.

Suggested Listening: MM No. 39. Corelli trio sonata da chiesa

The Development of Keyboard Instruments. The harpsichord and clavichord continued in importance from the Renaissance to the Baroque era, the harpsichord particularly because of its use as an accompaniment in opera as well as instrumental music. To these two instruments was added the piano, developed by Bartolommeo Cristofori around the year 1700. The piano used a hammer to strike a string under great tension and could thus produce a significant dynamic range between piano and forte. The piano, of course, was destined to become the dominant instrument of the the next three hundred years. Instrumental forms for these keyboard instruments included the suite, the theme and variations, the sonata, and the fugue.

The suite was a series of contrasting dances consisting of an allemande (fast-duple), courante (fast-triple), sarabande (slow-triple), and gigue (fast 6/8). Often, additional dances (minuet, bouree, gavotte) were interpolated between sarabande and gigue. The theme and variation forms had many names (chaccone, passacaglia, ground), but all of them were based on a repeated melodic or harmonic pattern (usually in the bass part) with a series of changes going on above it. The keyboard sonata of the Baroque era was not the large form used by the string instruments. Rather it was a binary or rounded binary idiom of modest proportions. The fugue was, even more than a keyboard form, a contrapuntal procedure involving imitation in settings ranging from 2 to 4 or more parts. Fugues were written not only for keyboard instruments but any and all Baroque ensembles, and they continued to show the influence of imitative counterpoint right up to the 20th century.

The composers most associated with keyboard music during the Baroque era included Froberger (1616-1667), Purcell (1659-1695), Couperin (1668-1733), Domenico Scarlatti (1685-1757), and of course Bach and Handel.

Suggested Listening: MM No. 35. Froberger suite
MM No. 38. Purcell ground
MM No. 40. Couperin clavecin piece
MM No. 50. J.S. Bach fugue

Equal Tuning. The observations of Pythagoras had demonstrated some disturbing facts about the nature of intervallic relationships. Simply put, Pythagoras had shown that if one tunes octaves according to perfect mathematical ratios, fifths will be out of tune. If fifths are tuned perfectly, thirds will be out of tune. In short, if any given interval is tuned to mathematically perfect proportions, others will be out of proportion. For centuries instrument makers of fixed pitch instruments (organs, harpsichords, flutes, etc.) had wrestled unsuccessfully with this dilemma. Then, around 1700 a new tuning method was invented called equal temperament. Briefly, what it did was tune every octave perfectly and create twelve equally tuned (but mathematically compromised) half steps within the octave. Every interval except the octave was now out of tune with the natural order of things. However, the degree to which the intervals were compromised was so slight as to make the system aurally workable. For the first time every note was possible in every instrument of fixed pitch. So great was Bach's joy at this change of events that he wrote a set of twenty-four preludes and fugues (one set in each of the twelve major and twelve minor keys) for the klavier.'' Published in 1722, he called his work ''The Well-Tempered Klavier.'' It was followed by a second set of twenty-four in 1744, and from this time onward, the harmonic variety of instrumental music was as assured as its technical variety.

Giants of the Late Baroque.

There are times in viewing the history of music when it is wiser to speak of trends, forms, and styles than of specific men. But there are also times when the musical genius of certain figures is so great that to understand an era, one must speak first of the composers themselves. The late Baroque is such a time. It is not that the Machauts or Josquins or Monteverdis of past eras were not great musicians. They were. It is that Johann Sebastian Bach and George Frideric Handel simply towered above everything around them.

Bach (1685-1750) and Handel (1685-1759) worked at the same time as other great composers (Vivaldi, Telemann, Rameau, etc.), but no one of their age so summed up the Baroque era as did they. For that reason they are worthy of special consideration.

George Frideric Handel. Handel was born in the German city of Halle in 1685. His father grudgingly allowed him to study music with the local church musician Friedrich Zachow, but it was to the musical theatre that Handel eventually turned. In 1702 he enrolled at the University of Halle but left in 1703 to work in Hamburg, the city which was the center of German opera. In 1705 his first opera "Almira" was performed. From 1706 to 1710 Handel journeyed to Italy, the birthplace of opera. Studying in Venice, Naples, Rome, and Florence, he met many of the great Italian masters of the time, including Corelli, Alessandro and Domenico Scarlatti, and Agostino Steffani, an opera composer whose style greatly influenced him. In 1709 his opera "Agrippina" was enthusiastically received in Venice, and he became an operatic force of his own.

Handel returned to Germany in 1710 to accept an appointment as the Musical Director to the court of the Elector of Hanover. As such, Handel was required to remain at court in the service of the Elector. The lure of the British operatic scene, however, was too great, and Handel placed himself in a position of truancy by leaving the Elector and journeying to London. In 1714, to Handel's embarrassment, the Elector of Hanover succeeded to the throne of England as King George I. For a time there was an understandable tension between Handel and the King, but their differences were smoothed out and Handel became free to pursue a career in the musical theatre. For over fifteen years Handel wrote operas for the Royal Academy of Music, a company formed under the patronage of wealthy noblemen and entrepreneurs. When, in the 1730's, opera fell into popular disfavor and became unprofitable, he turned to the composition of oratorio and became an instant sensation once more. His opera, "Giulio Cesare" (1724), and oratorios, "The Messiah" (1742) and "Judas Maccabaeus" (1746), remain, among his other works, as monuments of their respective forms. In addition to these Handel also composed some of the greatest purely instrumental music of his time.

He had become a naturalized British subject in 1726 and was regarded as a national treasure. On his death in 1759 he was buried in Westminster Abbey with full public honors.

Handel was an internationalist, widely popular, known for his works in the musical theatre. Johann Sebastian Bach, by contrast, never wrote an opera, never traveled more than two hundred miles from the place of his birth, and never achieved a reputation as a great composer until nearly seventy-five years after his death.

Johann Sebastian Bach. Bach was born in Eisenbach in 1685. He came from a long line of musicians, receiving his early training from his father, brother, and, later, from the organist Pachelbel. But the bulk of his learning came as he would copy and recopy the scores of the master composers of his time, dissecting them as it were and absorbing the techniques of their creation.

His professional life was successful but no more so than many other musicians of similar circumstance. He served as an organist in Arnstadt (1703-1707) and Mulhausen (1707-1708); then as concertmaster of the chapel of the Duke of Weimar (1708-1717). At thirty-two he was appointed Music Director to the Prince of Cothen (1717-1723), and finally he became Cantor of the St. Thomas School and Musical Director of the St. Thomas Church in the City of Leipzig (1723-1750).

Bach was well-known locally as a keyboard and violin virtuoso, a Latin teacher, and a scholarly counterpoint master; but in comparison to both the quantity and quality of his output, his reputation as a composer was pale. In general Bach wrote what he was paid to write. As an organist he wrote works for the organ. As a court director he wrote secular instrumental works for the court. As a church cantor he wrote vocal music for the Lutheran service. It is therefore not surprising that he composed no operas. But he wrote everything else, and he wrote it on a higher level than anyone else of his era or, for that matter, anyone else in the history of music. He regarded himself as a musical servant and dedicated his output, as he described it, "to the glory of God."

That output was enormous. Cantatas, oratorios, passions, masses, Magnificats, motets for the church; keyboard works, concerti grossi, and all manner of chamber works for the secular instrumental world. Sadly, little of his music was published during his lifetime. His place in the history of music was due more to what was saved by his four sons (particularly Karl Philipp Emanuel who achieved great fame as a musician) or rediscovered later by composers like Mozart and Mendelssohn. In an effort to preserve his own work, Bach took to engraving it onto copper in the last years of his life, often working by candlelight late into the night. When he died and was buried with modest fanfare in Leipzig, he was nearly blind from his efforts.

Suggested Listening: MM No. 44. Handel. Excerpts from "Rinaldo"
Handel. "The Water Music"
Handel. "The Messiah"
Bach. "The Well-tempered Klavier" Volume I
Bach. The Brandenburg Concertos Nos. 1-6
Bach. "The Magnificant"
MM No. 49. Bach. Excerpts from "St. Matthew Passion"

Bach Organ. This organ was played by J.S. Bach at his town church. It now resides in the Museum of Arnstadt.

George Frideric Handel

Johann Sebastian Bach

Francois Couperin

COMPOSERS OF THE

Jean Philippe Rameau

Domenico Scarlatti

Henry Purcell

BAROQUE ERA

Arcangelo Corelli

Antonio Vivaldi

Georg Philipp Telemann

CHAPTER THIRTEEN:

THE CLASSICAL ERA (1750-1825)

Few years have impacted as dramatically on the life of modern man as did those between the death of J.S. Bach (1750) and the death of Beethoven (1827). For centuries Europe had been ruled by monarchies or by oligarchies of sacred or secular bent. That the common man might have the right to control his own fortune and shape his own destiny was a thought at once foreign and dangerous to the established order, an order which Europe had imposed not only on itself but around the globe to every corner of its colonial empires. Now things were changing. The scientific and humanistic awakening of the Renaissance had led Europe to conceive of new orders and to challenge accepted dogma. The torches of doubt and, indeed, rebellion kindled in the 16th century by men like Copernicus, Kepler, Luther, and Galileo had been passed in the 17th century to philosophers like Rousseau, Locke, and Immanuel Kant.

"Why are we destined to be ruled by kings?" they asked. "Where is it written that the child of a nobleman is any more fit to govern than the child of a carpenter?" "And if it is true that the new science proves the sun and not the earth to be at the center of the heavens, then what other old ideas are to be challenged?" "Are the poor destined to be poor? Are the weak destined to remain weak? Or does each of us have inalienable rights? Are we equal and free to pursue our lives as we ourselves ordain?"

In the spirit of such questions men like Newton prepared a new vision of the universe, and men like Robespierre, Jefferson, and Franklin prepared a new vision of society. The new order entered into battle with the old, and the results were conflicts like the American Revolution, the French Revolution, and the Napoleonic Wars.

In the world of music the pursuit of universal order and the expression of the rights of man were no less pronounced than in the halls of government and science. The classical age became almost obsessed with clarity of form and structure, and the personalities of the three greatest musicians of the era - Haydn, Mozart, and Beethoven - each reflected the growing spirit of the common man. The changes wrought by emerging philosophies had profound effects on the musical output of the times.

Secular music was now more important than sacred music, at least as far as quantity was concerned. Instrumental music was - except for developments in opera - the new dominant musical genre.

Transitions from the Baroque.

The change from the style of Bach to that of Mozart was not a sudden one, not nearly as dramatic as the changes which had accompanied the monody during the years between the Renaissance and Baroque eras. In fact, the transition from Baroque to Classical music is often given a name of its own, the Rococo era, an age which lasts from about 1725 to about 1775. During these years - years in which the Baroque was in full bloom - new currents were arising which would eventually become dominant and change the center of musical focus to another style, another region, and another set of composers.

Gradually the idioms of the Baroque (overtures, suites, concerti, fugues, etc.) were modified or replaced entirely. The strictly contrapuntal Baroque style merged with more chordal, more vertically-conceived styles. Works of multiple sections (like the sinfonia and French overture) began to expand to larger forms where each of the old sections became full, self-contained movements. The basso continuo and the improvisation which it inspired died out. Bass lines were written without figures below them. Accompaniments were not left to the imagination of keyboard improvisation. Rather they were notated precisely. Forms became clarified and standardized; phrases became more regular; the orchestra developed into a set group with its own literature; the piano gradually replaced the harpsichord as the dominant keyboard instrument.

The composers associated with these new currents included Karl Philipp Emanuel Bach (1714-1788), J.S. Bach's eldest and most famous son; Johann Stamitz (1717-1757) who wrote for the orchestra at Mannheim; and G.B. Sammartini (1701-1775) who developed the orchestra in Milan. By the time these men had concluded their careers, a new era was well underway, the era of Classicism.

Elements of Classicism.

The Baroque era had gotten its name from a style of highly ornamental architecture which seemed to fit the image of contrapuntal music. The term classicism referred to the aesthetic style of ancient Greece, simple and clear of line, coherent of form. It was this image that the music written between 1750 and 1825 projected most consistently, and it did so in a variety of ways.

Classical Phrase Structure. The phrases of Baroque music tended to be long and somewhat irregular. By contrast classical phrase structure was regular, often in 4-measure design; often in antecedent/consequent arrangement.

Formal Classical Architecture. Classical form was precise and almost universally followed, especially in the genres of the piano sonata, symphony, and concerto. At its most fully developed point, the standard forms of the era included the sonata allegro form, the ABA form, the theme and variations form, the minuet-trio (or scherzo-trio) form, and the rondo form. It became common to architect the separate movements of large three or four movement works with these various forms. Since this was done often in the solo sonata and piano sonata, the multimovemental plan became known as the sonata cycle. In a typical sonata, the cycle would be as follows:

- First movement: sonata allegro form - rapid tempo
- Second movement: ABA or variation form - slow tempo and contrasting key
- Third movement: minuet-trio form - variable tempo and contrasting key
- Fourth movement: rondo or sonata allegro form - rapid tempo - original key

This cycle was repeated over and over in each of the instrumental genres of the era: the piano sonata, the solo concerto, the symphony, and the chamber sonata.

Classical Instrumental Genres. With the emergence of the piano as a solo instrument, a host of new keyboard music appeared after 1750. By far the most important form of piano composition was the sonata, a three or four movement work following the established sonata cycle pattern. Each of the three giants of the era - Haydn, Mozart, and Beethoven - wrote piano sonatas, and it is the collection of Beethoven's thirty-two sonatas which survives as the ultimate expression of the form.

Suggested Listening: **Beethoven. Sonata Op. 2, No. 3**
                                  Beethoven. Sonata Op. 13
                                  (The "Pathetique")

The classical concerto developed into a large scale, multimovemental work in which one solo instrument (typically, piano, violin, or 'cello) was featured with an accompanying orchestra. Generally, classical concerti were in three movements (fast sonata allegro; slow lyrical ABA or variation; and fast sonata allegro or rondo). Usually, the fast movements ended with virtuostic solo sections called cadenzas.

Suggested Listening: **Beethoven. Piano Concerto No. 5**
                                  (The "Emperor")

The most dominant orchestral genre of the age was the symphony, generally a three or four movement work for full orchestra following the sonata cycle mold. For the most part the classical orchestra consisted of 2 flutes, 2 oboes, 2 clarinets, 2 bassoons, 2 or 3 French horns, 2 trumpets; sometimes a trombone; always tympani, violins, violas, 'cellos, and basses. Haydn wrote over 100 symphonies, Mozart 41, and Beethoven 9. These stand among the greatest orchestral works ever produced.

As a rule classical symphonies were meant to depict nothing of a literary or poetic nature - only the music itself. However, this was not always the case. Some of Mozart's symphonies have taken on names because they are associated with a place (The "Linz" Symphony) or a mood (The "Jupiter" Symphony) or an instrument (The "Posthorn" Symphony). Some of Haydn's symphonies are also associated with moods (The "Surprise" Symphony) or effects (The "Clock" Symphony). Beethoven at times made a conscious attempt to associate his symphonic music with literary or historic ideas (for example, the "Pastoral" and "Eroica" symphonies). This relating of music to literary ideas would become an important trend in the next century, the so-called Romantic Era.

Suggested Listening: **Haydn. Symphony No. 101**
                                  (The "Clock")
                                  Mozart. Symphony No. 40 in G minor
                                  Mozart. Symphony No. 41
                                  (The "Jupiter")
                                  Beethoven. Symphony No. 5 in C minor
                                  Beethoven. Symphony No. 6
                                  (The "Pastoral")

Chamber music became an extremely important classical genre. Most chamber works were written either in sonata cycle forms or in less well-defined structures bearing the name "divertimento" or "serenade." Chamber groups could vary from duo ensembles (like piano and violin, or piano and 'cello) to quartets, quintets, sextets, or even small orchestras. The most popular classical instrumental chamber group was the string quartet consisting of 2 violins, viola, and 'cello.

Suggested Listening: **Haydn. String Quartet Op. 76, No. 2**
Mozart. String Quartet K. 458
(The "Hunt")
Beethoven. Sonata Op. 69
for 'cello and piano
Beethoven. String Quartet Op. 95
(The "Serioso")

Classical Vocal Music. The vocal output of the classical era can be divided into two large camps: opera on the one hand and sacred music on the other. Of the two, opera was by far the more prevalent, by far the more influential, and clearly the wave of the future.

The major forces of classical opera came from Italy, France, and Germany. Each country had both comic and serious operatic types, and each had composers particularly associated with a given region or style. The two most outstanding opera composers of the time were Christoph Willibald von Gluck (1714-1787) and Wolfgang Amadeus Mozart (1756-1791). Gluck began his career by composing in the Italian style, a style of overly complex plots and showy displays of musical virtuosity. In 1762, with his opera "Orfeo ed Euridice," Gluck returned to the clear dramatic lines of the Greek drama which had begun the operatic movement of the early Baroque era. He moved to Paris where he continued to reform the world of opera with a higher quality of music and a higher quality of drama. Mozart was the master of all the prevailing styles. His "Marriage of Figaro" was the epitome of the Italian satiric comedy; his "Idomeneo" was a triumph for the serious Italian style. "The Magic Flute" was one of the great German singspiel operas, and "Don Giovanni" was a unique and original blend of both comic and serious elements. By comparison, even Beethoven was not as great an opera composer, though his one opera, "Fidelio," stands as one of the great works of the Classical era.

**Suggested Listening: Gluck. "Orfeo ed Euridice"
Mozart. "The Marriage of Figaro"
Mozart. "The Magic Flute"**

The output of Classical sacred vocal music, while not nearly as large as the Baroque output, contained works of great magnitude. The mass and oratorio continued as the dominant religious forms, and all of the leading Classical composers contributed to the sacred repertoire. Haydn's oratorio "The Creation," Mozart's fifteen masses (particularly his "Requiem Mass"), and Beethoven's great "Missa Solemnis," for example, all stand as monuments of the sacred form, not only for the Classical era, but for all of music history.

**Suggested Listening: Haydn. "The Creation"
Beethoven. "Missa Solemnis"
Mozart. "Requiem Mass"**

Haydn, Mozart, and Beethoven.

Just as it is impossible to discuss the Baroque without knowing Bach and Handel, it is impossible to understand the Classical era without understanding the three masters who stood astride it, dominating every aspect of its music. In both their creative work and the force of their personalities, they epitomized the times in which they lived.

Franz Josef Haydn. Haydn was born in 1732 in Rohrau, a small Austrian village near the Hungarian border. He began his musical training at the age of six from an uncle with whom he lived. At eight he became a choirboy at St. Stephen's Cathedral in Vienna, remaining there until his voice changed. He was dismissed and forced to earn his own living by doing odd jobs and teaching music. Meanwhile he studied on his own and eventually managed to take lessons from the famous Italian composer and singer Nicola Porpora. In 1758 he was appointed Musical Director to the Chapel of the Count von Morzin. He remained there until 1761 when he went into the service of the Esterházy family. The Royal House of Esterházy was one of the wealthiest and most artistically minded in all of Europe. Prince Paul Anton, and his brother Nicholas the Magnificent who succeeded him, had built a palace at their Hungarian estate which rivaled that of Versailles. Haydn rose to become the Director of Music for their court and for thirty years he enjoyed - albeit as a servant - a position of unparalleled support. The palace was isolated but an unending parade of visitors and occasional trips to Vienna allowed Haydn to remain in touch with the Classical mainstream.

Typically, a musical servant was not permitted to sell or give away compositions written in the service of the nobility, but after 1770 or so, Prince Nicholas allowed Haydn to publish his work. The introduction of Haydn to the outside world gradually turned him into an international celebrity. When Nicholas died in 1790, Haydn was permitted to go to London for two two years. When he returned it was to Vienna to his own house. Although he was still technically in the employ of the Esterhazy Court, he was - for all practical purposes - his own man until his death in 1809. Not with blood as in the American or French Revolutions, but through loyal service and the strength of his own genius, Haydn achieved his artistic independence and embodied the spirit of his age. Musically his output - still not yet totally accounted for - was enormous. Over 100 symphonies, 68 string quartets, 60 piano sonatas, over 20 operas, 4 oratorios, 14 masses, and numerous other works for voice and chamber group all rank Haydn as one of the greatest composers in the history of Western man.

Wolfgang Amadeus Mozart. Mozart was born into a musician's family in Salzburg, Austria in the year 1756. His father, Leopold, was Assistant Director to the Chapel of the Archbishop of Salzburg, a position of both influence and responsibility. Leopold Mozart was a respected composer and performer, but it was not long before he realized that in comparison to his son, his own gifts were indeed modest. Wolfgang Mozart is considered by many to be among the greatest child geniuses mankind has ever produced. By the age of three he had mastered the keyboard. By six he was composing music of considerable quality. He was a virtuoso instrumentalist on piano, organ, and violin by the age of seven. By the time he was fifteen he was internationally known, a celebrated performer and composer, and a master of every instrumental and vocal idiom, every national style.

Mozart continued to live - with the exception of occasional journeys to the major musical centers of Europe - at home in Salzburg until 1781. However, he was unhappy there. The lack of opportunities for a man of his genius and the flamboyance of his own independent personality were hardly compatible with the role of a servant-musician in the court of a local archbishop. Whether consciously or unconsciously, the spirit which said that a man might take his destiny into his own hands grew heavier upon Mozart. From 1777 to 1781 he traveled intermittently to Munich, Augsburg, Mannheim; and with each sojourn he sought a position worthy of his stature. But with each, for one reason or another, he found nothing but disappointment. In Paris, in July of 1778, disappointment became tragedy when his mother, who was accompanying him on the journey, took sick and died.

Mozart's life in Salzburg became increasingly unbearable to him. Finally, against the wishes of his father, Mozart resigned his post as concertmaster and organist to the Archbishop and left for Vienna, intent upon securing his fortune as a free, independent artist. For a musician, even one of Mozart's stature and genius, to renounce the patronage of the church and court system which had dominated European life for centuries was at once a brave and dangerous step. But whatever kind of step it was for Mozart's personal future, it marked a significant change for the role of the artist in society. Mozart, and by implication all artists, would now face the world as independent, equal citizens, not as servants who entered and left through the servant quarters and thought of themselves as lesser social beings than their lords.

Surprisingly Mozart did well in Vienna, at least for the first few years he was there. His youthful reputation preceded him. His contacts among the wealthy nobility were of great aid, and his works, especially the operas, were regularly performed. He was paid well and had all the pupils he could handle. He was the idol of Vienna and, contrary to the general image of him, successful in every way. However, he was a flawed personality, and that would eventually change everything. Whatever psychological properties produced his genius, they also produced a host of anxieties and behavioral fetishes. The most disasterous of these was his penchant for gambling, a neurosis only recently acknowledged for its severity. By the mid-1780's much of his wealth had been dissipated. His family (by now he was married with children) demanded financial attention. His anxieties worsened; his health deteriorated. He was reduced to begging friends and former friends for money. His fame waned. His opportunities shrank. There are no sadder letters in all the history of music than those of the Mozart of this time in which he pleaded for help, not only financial but spiritual.

Despite continuing to create some of the world's greatest music, Mozart's life decayed to the point of his death in 1791 at the age of only

35. His operas were living legends of social satire and musical genius. His symphonies were among the most profound ever written. His piano and chamber works were destined never to be forgotton. But in his own person, he was wracked and lost. How he died still remains a mystery. Suicide, murder at the hands of a rival or debtor, death by natural causes are all conjectured. Maybe it was a little of each. He was buried in a pauper's grave, unheralded, and mourned publicly only by family and a few friends.

Ludwig van Beethoven. Beethoven, the last of the three great Classical masters, was born in the city of Bonn in 1770. His father, a singer in the court chapel, encouraged him in his early studies, and at the age of 17, Beethoven journeyed to Vienna where he met and played the piano for Mozart who predicted a great future for him. Beethoven returned to Bonn but in 1792 once more traveled to Vienna, this time to study with the great Josef Haydn. (Haydn had heard the young Beethoven two years earlier in Bonn and had urged Beethoven's master, the Archbishop Elector of Cologne, to send the young man to Vienna.) Beethoven studied with Haydn for two years and then, when Haydn left for London, became the pupil of the noted composers Albrechtsberger and Salieri.

Beethoven was a brilliant pianist, an accomplished violinist, but to say that music came easily to him would be misleading. He was a driving perfectionist who revised his work over and over again. We know from the sketch books which survive that for many of his compositions there are far more pages of discarded ideas than there are of finished product. But if he was an unrelenting perfectionist, he was also doggedly persistent, and finish his works he did, to the point where they towered above anything written before or since. Many people feel that in the area of the symphony, piano sonata, and string quartet especially, his work will never be surpassed.

Beethoven's gifts catapulted him to a position of preeminence in Vienna. Supported by a generous nobility and doting public, he enjoyed a life of creative and financial independence which few, if any, musicians had ever known. He was, in fact, the living embodiment of Mozart's dream of the venerated artist, and had it not been for fate, his existence would certainly have been an enviable one. Fate, however, began to exert its influence in the form of a disease - probably present from birth - which began to become apparent around 1798. The disease was a growing, incurable deafness, destined to rob the young musician of precisely the sense he needed most in his work. By 1802 there was no doubt in the young Beethoven's mind what inevitable end lay in store. He left his apartments in Vienna and secluded himself in the village of Heiligenstadt. There he wrestled with himself, now deciding to end his life, now deciding to try to compose despite his affliction. "I must live almost alone, as one who has been banished," he wrote. "If I approach near to people a hot terror seizes me . . . God grant me but one day of pure joy - it is so long since real joy resounded in my heart."

In the end Beethoven resolved to rise above his handicap. The tremendous strength of his own will coupled with a great musical genius won out. He taught himself to work in the inner world of his mind rather than the external world of his senses, and he went on to write some of the greatest music ever heard. Much of that music carried with it the same spirit of triumph which abounded both in his personal life and in the revolutionary struggles of his times. His third symphony, for example, entitled the "Eroica" - originally dedicated to Napoleon Bonaparte - depicts the heroism of his age. His opera "Fidelio" is the battle and ultimate triumph of good over evil. The last movement of his Ninth Symphony is an orchestral and choral setting of the poet Schiller's "Ode to Joy" which extols the values of human brotherhood and love of God.

In the increasing use of literary references and in the increasing chromaticism of his music, Beethoven not only summed up the principles of Classicism but pointed the way to a new era. In the spirit of Monteverdi before him, he was an artist whose development bridged a span between two styles. In the case of Beethoven, it might be said that he created the new style, so great was the influence of both his person and his art. In the mastery of old forms and genres, he was a Classical composer without equal. In the invention of new forms, the embodiment of literature in music, and a growing use of chromatic harmony, he was the first major prophet of the 19th century age of Romanticism. By his death in 1827, that age was at hand.

CHAPTER FOURTEEN:

THE ROMANTIC ERA (1825-1900 and beyond)

In the 19th century Europe and the developed nations of the world which she had spawned at last entered the modern age, Technologically, the century produced the railroad, photography, electricity, the telephone, telegraph, steam engine - and with them the rise of modern industrialization. Politically, it was an age of nationalism, of countries forming for the first time and coming into an awareness of themselves as entities with special cultural and historical roots. Socially, it was a time in which the assertion of human rights and dignities became the watch - word. The freeing of slaves after the American Civil War, the abolition of child brutality in England, the cries of Karl Marx for socialistic equality were all expressions of the fervor for inherent human dignity. The 19th century was also an era of tremendous literary output, and, because transportation and communication made the spread of ideas so much more rapid, tremendous literary influence. The works of Dickens, Hugo, Twain, Emerson, Byron, Wordsworth, Schiller, Hegel, Schopenhauer, Nietzche, and many more filled the world with new concepts and fresh questions for tomorrow.

In music it was a time of trends - some compatible, some conflicting - but all affected by the political, scientific, and social contexts in which they occurred. The more important of these trends included the following: (a) an affinity with literature which was manifested in all musical genres; (b) the technical development of instruments and a greater emphasis on virtuostic performance; (c) the expression of nationalism in music; (d) the development of tonal chromaticism; (e) the persistent influence of Classicism; (f) the development of musicology; and (g) the view of the artist as a unique individual personality.

Romantic Trends

The Influence of Literature. Music containing no literary reference, no underlying story, no attempt to portray a pictorial image or special idea, is called ''absolute'' music. Music for which there are such references is called ''program'' music. The Classical era was an age of absolute music. In Beethoven there is the hint that programmatic tendencies are on the rise. During the Romantic era program music achieved much the dominant position. One can see this trend clearly in the development of the symphony. The Mozart G minor Symphony (No. 40) had no programmatic meaning. The Beethoven "Pastoral" (No. 6) contained musical descriptions of storms and peasant dances, scenes of nature which Beethoven wished the listener to think of as the music unfolded. The "Symphonie Fantastique" by the French Romantic composer Hector Berlioz (1803-1869) had an entire accompanying story involving the hallucinatory dreams of a young man attempting suicide in the wake of an unhappy love affair. All these symphonies were written within fifty years of each other, but there is a world of difference between Mozart's perspective and that of Berlioz.

Suggested Listening: Berlioz. "Symphonie Fantastique"

The Development of Instruments. The 19th century saw many innovations in the manufacture of instruments which directly affected the compositions of the era. The piano, for example, was given greater technical ability in a variety of ways. More pedals were added, enabling a wider range of effects. Keys were made to move faster, allowing for greater speeds of performance. The steel frame permitted strings to be placed under more tension, thus making for a wider dynamic range and more brilliant sound. Apart from the piano, orchestras were expanded to include not only more conventional instruments but new ones as well. The piccolo, English horn, contrabassoon, and bass clarinet, for example, all became ensemble regulars. Trumpets and French horns began to be constructed with valves which made it possible for more virtuostic playing. For all these changes, composers like Liszt and Chopin, Brahms and Strauss, Wagner, Debussy, Rimsky-Korsakov, and hosts of others wrote music of a more technically demanding nature. The works below exemplify this trend.

Suggested Listening: Chopin. B minor Scherzo for Piano
Rimsky-Korsakov. "Scheherazade"

Nationalism. As the modern nations of Europe began to emerge, feelings of national pride were intensified throughout every country, old and new. One of the vehicles for expressing that pride was music. By incorporating the indigenous folk melodies and rhythms of a nation into their compositions, by entitling music with the names of local places, by having their music depict local legends, composers gave specific cultural flavors to their work. Some of the more intensely nationalistic composers are listed below with the countries or regions they represented.

Germanic region:	Richard Wagner (1813-1883)
Poland:	Frederic Chopin (1810-1849)
Russia:	Alexander Borodin (1833-1887) Nicolai Rimsky-Korsakov (1844-1908)
Norway:	Edward Grieg (1843-1907)
Finland:	Jean Sibelius (1865-1957)
Czechoslovakia:	Bedřich Smetana (1824-1884) Anton Dvorak (1841-1904)
Spain:	Isaac Albeniz (1860-1909) Enrique Granados (1867-1916)

Suggested Listening: Smetana. "The Moldau"

The Moldau is a river running through the Czechoslovakian heartland, and in his composition Smetana attempts to portray its life beginning as a small stream and growing in breadth and power. The work is one of a series of six pieces depicting Smetana's region. The collection is entitled "Ma Vlast" ("My Homeland").

Chromaticism. The organization of tonality around the major-minor scale system (which had itself replaced the modal system of the Middle Ages and Renaissance) reached its purest expression in the music of the Classical era. During the 19th century, chord structures became more elaborate. Many melodies incorporated notes which were not part of the key in which a composition was written. The old tonal order was clearly changing. By the end of the century, composers like Debussy were using scales other than those of the major-minor system. Modulations were so frequent that many works hardly appeared to have recognizable tonal centers at all. Dissonances became more frequent and less strictly used. The way was being prepared for the dissolution of tonality and an entrance into the pitch systems of the 20th century. The work below provides a good example of this trend.

Suggested Listening: Mussorgsky. "Night on Bald Mountain"

Continuing Classical influences. The development of new trends did not mean that the Classical sense of tonality, appreciation of highly organized architecture, and use of genres like the sonata, symphony or string quartet disappeared. They did not. A great deal of important 19th century music continued to exhibit many elements of Classicism. In fact, from the 19th century onward, diverse styles continued to exist side by side, almost as if the tastes of both artist and audience had broadened to the point where diversity was not only tolerable but desirable. Indeed, by the start of the 20th century, musical diversity was music's most singular feature.

The continuing influences of Classicism during the 19th century can be found in many areas but perhaps none more clear than in the four symphonies of Johannes Brahms (1833-1897). Brahms knew the symphonies of his predecessors and was particularly influenced by the mighty architectural designs of Beethoven. That Brahms used the symphonic form at all is an indication of the effect of Classicism upon him. That he organized his symphonies in the 4-movement sonata cycle pattern is further indication of the presence of the 18th century in the 19th.

Suggested Listening: Brahms. Symphony No. 2 in D major

The Development of Musicology. Musicology, the systematic study of music, developed as a disciplined investigation during the Romantic age. Its leaders included Karl Friedrich Chrysander (1826-1901), Guido Adler (1855-1941), and Hugo Riemann (1849-1919) among many others. The new research they did and the scientific developments of their age (transportation, electronic communication, increased publishing capacities, for example) enabled both musician and scholar to see the heritage from which music had come. Once that heritage was revealed, music would never again be the same, for now no matter what new developments would occur, the old would always be there as a reminder, as an influence. That is one of the ironies of all of man's progress: that as his technology sweeps him into his future, it also allows him to face his past.

Artistic Individualization. What Mozart had tried to do, what Beethoven had succeeded in doing - the assertion of themselves as unique and independent artists - finally came to be the rule in the 19th century. Musicians, both composers and performers, negotiated their own financial and artistic terms. They did not write because they were commanded as servants of church or court but because they themselves wished to create and then to sell their creations to a public from whom there was a demand. The individualization of the artist was accompanied by an individualization of style and even a kind of compositional specialization. Chopin, for example, wrote almost exclusively for the piano; Wagner and Verdi almost exclusively for the operatic stage; Schubert predominantly for the voice. This is not to say that Romantic composers were not multifaceted. Many were. Brahms, Schumann, Debussy, Mendelssohn, to name just a few, wrote in nearly all the idioms. It is also not to say that past masters did not specialize. Handel was chiefly an opera and oratorio composer; Corelli chiefly an instrumental one. But a trend was in progress rendering the artist temperamentally, economically, and creatively an individual of his own making.

Romantic Vocal Music

There were four major aspects of 19th century vocal music: opera, sacred composition, the art song, and the use of voice in instrumental works.

Opera. It was in the 19th century that opera reached its greatest heights, and since it was such a dominant Romantic form, it clearly revealed all the trends of the age - particularly nationalism and chromaticism. Italian opera tended to be less innovative than other national styles. Plots avoided bizarre subject matter and concentrated on intensely emotional human relations. Chromaticism was less pronounced than in Germany. There was a concentration on melody and long arias.

German opera tended toward the use of regional folk legend, supernatural plots, and highly chromatic vocal lines. French opera tended toward the grand spectacle on the one hand and the poetically lyrical on the other. It was less nationalistic in its plots than German opera and generally less chromatic. In other areas - Russia, Czechoslovakia, and England predominantly - opera flourished and exhibited the general characteristics of its time. Some of the more noted operatic composers of the age are listed below.

Italy:	Gioacchino Rossini (1792-1868) Vincenzo Bellini (1801-1835) Gaetano Donizetti (1797-1848) Giuseppe Verdi (1813-1901) Giacomo Puccini (1858-1924)
Germany:	Carl Maria Von Weber (1786-1826) Heinrich Marschner (1795-1861) Richard Wagner (1813-1883) Richard Strauss (1864-1949)
France:	Giacomo Meyerbeer (1791-1864) Charles Gounod (1818-1893) Georges Bizet (1838-1875) Claude Debussy (1862-1918)
Russia:	Modest Mussorgsky (1839-1881) Nicolai Rimsky-Korsakov (1844-1908) Alexander Borodin (1833-1887)
England:	William Gilbert and Sir Arthur Sullivan (1842-1900)
Czechoslovakia:	Bedrich Smetana (1824-1884)

Suggested Listening: **Mussorgsky. "Boris Godunov"**
Gilbert and Sullivan. "The Mikado"
Bizet. "Carmen"

Of all the Romantic operatic figures it was Verdi in Italy and Wagner in Germany who dominated the development of the form. Verdi typified the characteristics of lyricism and the Romantic alliance with great literature. His style was less chromatic than Wagner's; his arias more flowing and more pervasive. He chose great dramatic texts, often using Shakespeare (e.g., *Othello* and *Falstaff*) as his librettist. Wagner typified the chromaticism and nationalism of his time. His orchestra was large; his tonality complex and not easily identified with a single key; his subjects (as in "Tristan und Isolde," "Siegfried," "Das Rheingold," etc.) were often stories of German or Nordic mythology. Together Wagner and Verdi exemplified all the major characteristics of Romantic opera.

Suggested Listening: **Verdi. "Othello"**
                             Wagner. "Das Rheingold"

The Art Song. Besides opera, the Romantic era also produced a great deal of literature for solo voice. Art songs, as they were called, were settings of some of the greatest poetry of the day. They became one of the most important genres of the 19th century. Chief among the composers of the art song were Franz Schubert (1797-1828), Robert Schumann (1810-1859), Johannes Brahms (1833-1897), and Hugo Wolf (1860-1903) from Germany; Claude Debussy (1862-1918) from France; Modest Mussorgsky (1839-1891) from Russia. The art song was often written in groups called cycles, and it used the piano as an integrated accompaniment. The acknowledged master of the art song was Franz Schubert who composed many cycles totalling over 600 songs - songs which set the standard for the entire century.

Suggested Listening: **Schubert. "Der Erlkonig"**
                             Schubert. "Heidenroslein"

Romantic Sacred Vocal Music. Compared to the Middle Ages, Renaissance, and Baroque eras, there was little sacred music written in the 19th century. However, the sacred forms did not altogether disappear. Rather, in the hands of the Romanticists, they took on the characteristics of the age - operatic vocal solos, large orchestras increased chromaticism. Oratorios, masses, requiem masses, Stabat Maters, and psalms were all composed. Among the leading sacred vocal figures of the era were Felix Mendelssohn (1809-1847), Johannes Brahms (1833-1897), Hector Berlioz (1803-1869), César Franck (1822-1890), and Gabriel Fauré (1845-1924), It is important to realize that although the quantity of sacred vocal music was small, its quality during the 19th century was quite high. The Brahms "Requiem," Verdi "Requiem," the St. Cecilia Mass of Gounod, the "Elijah" oratorio of Mendelssohn, for example, all rank among the greatest sacred compositions ever written.

Suggested Listening: Verdi. "Requiem"

The Use of Voice in Instrumental Works. Perhaps the most innovative kind of singing in Romantic compositions was the addition of vocal parts (solo and chorus) to works conceived primarily for orchestra. The use of voice in this way was perfect for the style of the times. On the one hand, it allowed for yet another instrument and tone color; on the other, it allowed for specific literary references. Beethoven, Liszt, Mahler, Berlioz, Debussy, and many others used this technique, but perhaps Gustav Mahler (1860-1911) is best known for it. In his Symphony No. 8, he uses full chorus, and his "Lied von der Erde" ("Song of the Earth") is in actuality a song cycle for solo voice and orchestra. His Symphony No. 4 ends with a solo soprano singing poetry about a child's view of heaven.

Suggested Listening: Mahler. Symphony No. 4, 4th movement

Romantic Instrumental Music

The instrumental music of the 19th century exhibited both old Classical traits and new Romantic ones. The symphony, concerto, and some forms of chamber music continued to be written, but to them were added genres like the piano character piece, the grand ballet, and the tone poem. These new forms were typically Romantic - programmatic, virtuostic, and at times both nationalistic and chromatic.

The Classical Style Symphony. The Classical 4-movement symphonic work using the forms of the sonata cycle was by no means universally composed in the 19th century. However, the Classical concept of the symphony did survive in the works of Franz Schubert (1797-1828), Felix Mendelssohn (1809-1847), Robert Schumann (1810-1856), and Johannes Brahms (1833-1897). For other Romantic composers - like Hector Berlioz (1803-1869), Anton Dvorak (1841-1904), Peter Ilich Tchaikowsky (1840-1893), and Jean Sibelius (1865-1957) - the symphonic form was freer, the number of movements more variable, the forms of each movement less strictly defined.

Suggested Listening: **Brahms. Symphony No. 4**
Mendelssohn. The "Italian" Symphony
Dvorak. The "New World" Symphony

The Concerto. The solo concerto continued to be an important form in the Romantic era, particularly for the piano and violin, and particularly because the genre could serve as a vehicle for the virtuosity so prized by the age. Brahms, Mendelssohn, Tchaikowsky, Schumann, Edward Grieg (1843-1907), Frederic Chopin (1810-1849), and Franz Liszt (1811-1886) all used the genre to produce works which remain monuments of the literature to this day.

Suggested Listening: **Brahms. Piano Concerto No. 2**
Tchaikowsky. Violin Concerto

19th Century Chamber Music. Chamber music in the Romantic era, while written to some extent, did not occupy a position of importance in any way comparable to its position in the Classical era. There were few composers beyond Beethoven who devoted much time to the chamber idiom. Those who did include Schubert, Mendelssohn, Schumann, Brahms, and Dvořák.

Suggested Listening: **Schubert. The "Trout" Quintet**

Romantic Ballet. Ballet emerged in the 19th century as an important instrumental and theatrical genre, especially during the second half of the century. Adam's "Giselle" (1841); Tchaikowsky's "Swan Lake" (1877), "Nutcracker" (1892), and "Sleeping Beauty" (1890); and Delibes's "Sylvia" (1876) are all works which not only dominated their own age but became staples of the 20th century repertoire, thus spurring a major modern movement in the ballet form. In addition to complete ballets like these, the Romantic era also incorporated many dance sections into the operas of the time. The dances from Borodin's opera "Prince Igor" are a typical example.

Suggested Listening: **Tchaikowsky. The "Nutcracker Suite"**

Romantic Piano Music. A tremendous amount of 19th century instrumental music was devoted to the piano since it was the perfect vehicle for Romantic tastes. With the improvement of the foot pedal system and the manufacture of faster keys and steel frames, the piano became a versatile instrument capable of a tremendous variety of effects. It lent itself to virtuosity; it could express literary concepts in poetic musical terms; it could encompass a tremendous tonal range; it was capable of intricate chromatic harmony. Sonatas of the Classical variety, dances, etudes (technically difficult studies used to build up performance virtuosity), and short, so-called "character" pieces which were often programmatic in nature were all written for the piano. Schubert, Schumann, Mendelssohn, Brahms, Chopin, and Liszt were the great masters of Romantic keyboard literature. Their works stand as monuments of the art and are played and replayed to this day.

Suggested Listening: **Chopin. Ballades Nos. 1-4**
Liszt. The "Mephisto Waltz"
Schumann. "Kinderscenen"

The Tone Poem. While the Classical symphony continued to exert some influence in the Romantic era, it was not the preeminent orchestral genre. That honor went to a kind of composition which came to be called a "tone poem" or "symphonic poem." The principal characteristic of this type of work was its highly programmatic nature. Tone poems appeared as overtures to concerts, incidental music to plays, expressions of nationalism, portrayals of stories in musical form, suites of dances, etc. They were almost never in the sonata cycle format, though it was not unusual to find them grouped together in an orchestral series with a larger title (as an art song might be grouped in a larger cycle).

Examples of single tone poems and tone poem groups abound in the Romantic literature. Mendelssohn ("Fingal's Cave" overture), Brahms ("Academic Festival" overture), and Tchaikowsky ("1812" overture) wrote single concert overtures. Debussy ("Nocturnes" for orchestra, "Prelude to the Afternoon of a Faun") and Richard Strauss ("Till Eulenspiegel's Merry Pranks," "Don Quixote," "Death and Transfiguration," "Thus Spake Zarathustra") were both famous for their short orchestral forms. Instrumental works such as Mussorgsky's "Night on Bald Mountain," Smetana's "The Moldau," and the "Danse Macabre" by the French composer Camille Saint-Saëns (1835-1921) were famous compositions of their time and have become favorites of the 20th century concert literature as well.

Suggested Listening: **Richard Strauss. "Till Eulenspiegel"**
Richard Strauss. "Thus Spake Zarathustra"
Mendelssohn. "A Midsummer Night's Dream" Overture

Felix Mendelssohn

Robert Schumann

COMPOSERS   OF   THE

Frederic Chopin

Franz Liszt

ROMANTIC   ERA

Hector Berlioz

Giuseppe Verdi

CHAPTER FIFTEEN:

THE TWENTIETH CENTURY

The 20th century is at once a time of vast change and vast contradiction - change and contradiction unprecedented in all human history. From the technological standpoint it begins in the era of the horse and buggy and ends with the exploration of outer space. From candlelight to lasers, from home remedy medications to radiation therapy, from simple grade school primers to computers with billions of pieces of data on microchips as small as a dot, the century explodes with progress and innovation more dramatic and more rapid than in all the preceding ages of history.

Socially and politically, it is a time of incredible contradictions, of opposites existing side-by-side in a world shrunk by high speed communication and transportation. The organization of the United Nations is established to promote world peace and yet the century is torn by almost constant warfare of the most terrible kind. Technology creates societies of enormous bounty while millions of people in underdeveloped nations live and die in squalor. The struggle for human rights becomes almost a moral obsession in some quarters while in others people are repressed by some of the most savage totalitarian states of human history. Scientific advances promise to improve and prolong life beyond man's wildest dreams at the very same time that they threaten nuclear and ecological extinction. It is almost as if the century is a crucible in which man must test his power and will to survive. If his mortality and humanity can control his technology and his irrationalities, he will live to join whatever cosmic brotherhood awaits. If not, by his own hand he will go the way of the dinosaur in one great burst of self-annihilation.

Musically, the century is as diverse as it can be. The development of musicology and technology thrust all the styles of the past and present into an aesthetic potpourri never experienced before by the artistic community. Tonality gives birth to different systems of tonal organization yet survives to live side-by-side with them. Movements like Impressionism, Expressionism, and Neoclassicism rise up, exert their influence, fade in prominence, but never completely leave the scene. The use of rhythm and melody are radically altered in some compositional styles, while in others, the conventions of the past are preserved. Romantic traits like nationalism and chromatic tonality persist in some composers, while others experiment with electronicism and computerization in the creation of new sounds. Media like the ballet, concerto, opera, chamber work, and solo work survive but are joined by genres as radical as music written by pure chance. Finally, the century is divided by a sharp schism between the "popular" and "serious" musical worlds, a schism deeper than any previously known.

The Breakdown of Tonality

The more extensive the chromaticism of the late 19th century became, the more difficult it was to feel that any given piece of music was in a particular key. With dissonance a constant occurrence and modulation from one tonal region to another a pervasive technique, the ear could no longer hear one note as a fixed center of activity. The concept of tonality organized around the major and minor scales which had begun in the Renaissance and dominated musical composition for three hundred years was now fading from the mainstream. Replacing it was a variety of organizational devices which used scales other than the major and minor ones and techniques designed specifically to avoid the feeling of a tonic.

Impressionism. In France composers like Claude Debussy (1862-1918) and Maurice Ravel (1875-1937) began to organize melodies and harmonies around the whole-tone and chromatic scales. These scales generated chords quite different from the triads of Bach and Mozart. They created dissonances whose treatment was less strict than in bygone eras and melodies whose architecture was new and sometimes startling.

But Debussy and Ravel were not wholly divorced from Romanticism. Their music was highly programmatic and closely allied with a group of French painters and poets known as Impressionists. These artists sought in their works not to represent photographically exact duplicates of reality but rather the moods or impressions created by objects and events. In the paintings of Monet, Manet, Degas, Seurat, and Renoir one saw sweeping pastels or splashes of color or multitudes of dots which captured an emotion rather than a clear image. So too, Debussy and Ravel tried to capture moods.

Of the two men Debussy was the more noted Impressionist. His sense of architecture and tonal organization rank him among the greatest com-

RENOIR

Girl with a Watering Can

posers of all times. Ravel was regarded as a great orchestrator, famous not only for his own works but for orchestrating the works of other composers as well. The influence of both men on the 20th century - Debussy for his tonal style, Ravel for his orchestrational techniques - cannot be ignored. In France alone composers like Erik Satie (1866-1925), Arthur Honegger (1892-1955), Francis Poulenc (1899-1963), and Darius Milhaud (1892-1974) owed their very compositional lives to the pioneering of Impressionism. And elsewhere composers like Manuel de Falla of Spain (1876-1946), Ottorino Respighi of Italy (1879-1936), Frederick Delius of England (1862-1934), and Charles Griffes of America (1884-1920) freely acknowledged their debt to the Impressionists. As Monteverdi and Beethoven had stood astride two eras, Debussy and the Impressionist school were an indispensible bridge between Romanticism and the 20th century.

Suggested Listening: **Debussy. "La Mer"**
Debussy. Nocturnes for Orchestra
Ravel. "Daphnis and Chloe" Suite

Polytonality. Impressionism was not the only bridge between the 19th and 20th centuries, nor was its system of tonal organization the only new system. As the style of key-centered tonality waned, a new style called polytonality arose. In music of this kind chords with different roots (C major and D major, for example) were combined to form new sonorities. Unusual dissonances were thus "accepted" into the composition where once they would have been either strictly treated or avoided altogether. The Frenchmen Milhaud and Honneger both used the techniques of polytonality in their compositions. In America the greatest proponent of the style was Aaron Copland (b. 1900)

Suggested Listening: **Copland. The "Appalachian Spring"**

Atonality. The music of Impressionism and polytonality still had vestiges of the chordal systems of Classical and Romantic music because they employed scales which used specific beginning and ending notes in the same way that major and minor scales use tonic notes. However, there was a branch of Romantic chromaticism which led to the complete avoidance of triadic chords and tonic notes. Such music made each note of the chromatic scale equal to the others in organizational importance. None was therefore capable of being the root of a chord, tonic of a key, or start of a scale. Because this music had no set tonal center, it generated no preestablished kind of chord. Melodies were motivically rather than tonally conceived. They were formed from combinations of intervals designed for the specific composition rather than from relationships which were part of a preexisting compositional theory.

Extreme Romantic chromaticism was especially popular in Germany, and it was not surprising that the "atonal" style, as it was called, developed there. In the works of Arnold Schönberg (1874-1951), Alban Berg (1885-1935), and Anton Webern (1883-1945) particularly, one can see the complete dissolution of tonality. The atonal style was especially adapted to expressing moods which suggested the eerie, mystical, dark, or subconscious. For a brief time it took on the name given to the art of its period, Expressionism.

Suggested Listening:　　**Schönberg. "Pierrot Lunaire"**
　　　　　　　　　　　　　　Schönberg. "Verklarte Nacht"

Serialism. Of the three German Expressionists it was Schönberg who emerged as the most dominant theorist and the most influential composer of the century. He reasoned that if it had been the practice of past eras to organize a series of tones so that one of them was the central or tonic note, it was just as possible to deliberately serialize the 12 notes of the octave to insure that none would be more important than the others. This Schönberg accomplished by ordering the 12 tones in such a way that no one of them was repeated until all of them were sounded. He also made sure that no consecutive group of 3 or 4 notes formed the outline of the triadic chords of times gone by. He called this arrangement a "tone row."

Example of a tone row

-237-

Once established the row could be transposed to begin on another tone, played in retrograde, inverted, or used in retrograde-inversion. Its first half might be combined with its second half; 3 or 4 note chords might be formed by playing any 3 or 4 adjacent notes of the row simultaneously.

Schönberg's principles became known as "serial music" or "dodecaphonic (12-tone) music," and they revolutionized the composition of the century. In time composers began to serialize not only the 12 tones of the octave but note values and dynamic markings as well, thus applying the techniques of tonal manipulation to the non-tonal aspects of music. (see below.)

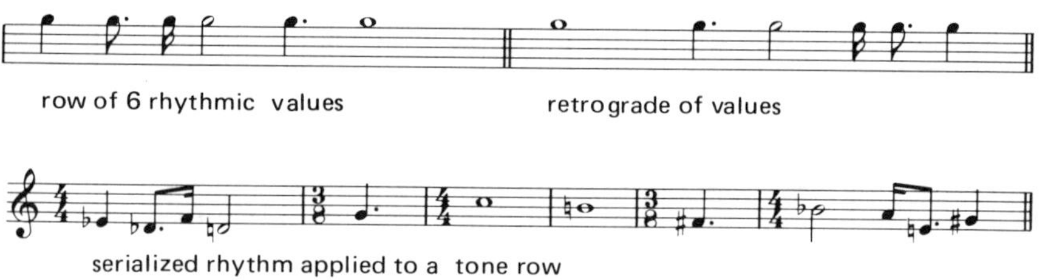

Suggested Listening: **Schönberg. "Variations for Orchestra"**
Webern. "Five Pieces for Orchestra"

Other New Trends of the 20th Century

The Artist-Audience Gap. Schönberg's principles were mathematical and cerebral, in much the same way that the isorhythms of Machaut and imitative techniques of Josquin were intellectualizations imposed upon the musical art. In studying Schonberg, or for that matter Machaut, Josquin, Bach, or Beethoven, it is important to understand that the mind of the composer is but half of his being. The other half is his heart, his desire to communicate deep feelings and messages. That Schönberg and his disciples were inspired by the logical systems of intellectual analysis was an influence of the technology of their times. They could no more have escaped those influences than any of us can escape the social, political, or scientific contexts in which we live.

For many 20th century listeners serialism seems remote, unpleasant, and uncommunicative. That may be. If that is your reaction, there is no arguing with it. But the fact that Schonberg, the most influential composer of his age, remains out of touch with the common man of his time may be a fault of the times rather than the man.

When Bach wrote his cantatas, they were heard and enjoyed by every church-goer in Leipzig. The hurdy-gurdy men of Vienna cranked out the arias of Mozart on the streets of the city at the same time they were being sung to the grand patrons of the opera house. What Chopin and Schumann were playing in the 19th century concert hall, the average man and woman could duplicate on their pianos at home. Not so with Schönberg. The common man of the 20th century does not listen to Schönberg's "Moses und Aaron" or "Pierrot Lunaire" or the "Variations for Orchestra." However, this gap between artist and audience - seen not only in Schonberg and his followers but in many of the painters, poets, playwrights, and novelists of the century - is, in fact, a normal outgrowth of the times. Change, when it occurs so rapidly in science, spurs equally rapid changes in art, in morality, in social behavior. The rate at which many 20th century artists experimented and grew was often far too fast for the average untutored audience.

Electronicism. During the second half of the 20th century, electronics began to dominate the compositional scene. New mechanical synthesizers could produce complex wave forms and strange sounds. Computers could be hooked up to the synthesizers, allowing sounds to be generated in ways no human composers or human performers could duplicate with conventional instruments.

Suggested Listening: **Selected works of Davidovsky, Babbitt, Bulent et al. on the "Columbia-Princeton Electronic Music Center" (Columbia LP MS 6566).**

Composers like Mario Davidovsky (b. 1934), Luciano Berio (b. 1925), Vladimir Ussachevsky (b. 1911), and Milton Babbitt (b. 1918) spurred tremendous compositional experimentation in electronics and computerization. They reached few in the general audience and were supported mostly by an academic community whose financial patronage did not have to be justified by receipts from the concert hall. Nor were the electronicists and serialists the only experimentors. Many composers of a more conservative bent still expressed the experimental atmosphere of the age by using strange instruments like water buffalo bells, police sirens, and even the sound of whales in their compositions. Most of the composers of the century used changing meters; simultaneous meters; leaping, disjunct melodies; and non-triadic harmonies as matters of commonplace writing. Some of the more radical composers used tape recorded sounds like breaking glass or screeching tires in their work, a technique called "musique concrete" by its French originator, Pierre Schaeffer (b. 1910).

Aleatory Music. Perhaps the most startling experiment of the age was the development of music written purely by chance. The technical name was "aleatory" music, and it gave an unprecedented freedom to the performer. Certain melodic or rhythmic fragments would be written out, for example. The performer(s) would then be free to play them in any order, at any speed, with any dynamic inflection. Sometimes the instructions to the performer were more specific; sometimes they were open-ended. There is even an aleatory composition for twelve radios, and another which calls for four minutes and thirty-three seconds of silence. Karlheinz Stockhausen (b. 1928) and John Cage (b. 1912) were among the leaders of the school of aleatory composition.

The apparently ridiculous trends of some 20th century works in music (and in other art forms such as "pop art" or "absurd theatre") are not as silly as they might at first appear, especially if one does not view them in the same way one views a Beethoven symphony. In Beethoven's Fifth Symphony the main theme opens with a motive and then a rest. The motive is sound; the rest, silence. John Cage's "4:33" (the work which consists of 4 minutes, 33 seconds of silence) is not a composition as such but a question. "We know," one can hear Cage saying, "that Beethoven's music uses sound and silence. We can then ask, how much sound is necessary for music? One note? Ten notes? Or perhaps no notes at all?"

This kind of experimental spirit, characteristic of the technological explosion of the century, is both understandable and inescapable. However, it does not represent the entirety of modern music. If the common man is not listening to serialism, electronicism, aleatory music, or atonality, he is certainly listening to something. That something largely involves two kinds of music: old forms from the past and a new, enlarged, highly commercialized world of so-called "popular music." These are the most accepted styles of the century.

Old Trends from Eras Past

Many modern composers have harkened back to the clarity of Classical forms and the sounds of modal tonality. They are the apostles of the so-called "neo-Classicism" and "neo-modality" of the 20th century. Examples of this kind of historical reverie can be seen in works like the "Octet for Winds" by Igor Stravinsky (1882-1971), the "Classical Symphony" by Sergei Prokofiev (1881-1953), and the string quartets of Paul Hindemith (1895-1963). It must be understood, however, that these compositions, while using some of the elements of ages past, are not duplicates of those ages. Rather, they are 20th century expressions of past techniques written in very 20th century terms, using 20th century elements alongside old ones. Such is the nature of a good deal of contemporary composition. It must also be understood that the composers associated with neo-Classicism in one work may be serialistic or atonal in another work. Such is the nature of many contemporary artists. A multiplicity of styles exists at one and the same time, often in one and the same person, sometimes in one and the same work.

Suggested Listening: Prokofiev. The "Classical" Symphony

Along with some of the tonal systems of the past, many former genres continued to inhabit the 20th century concert hall. Igor Stravinsky, for example, wrote some of the finest ballets of all time, spurring a great era in the history of the dance. Works like "The Rite of Spring," "The Firebird," and "Petrouchka," while at times controversial, nevertheless became monuments of the art.

Suggested Listening: Stravinsky. "The Rite of Spring"

Symphonists like Dmitri Shostakovich (1906-1975) in the Soviet Union and Ralph Vaughn-Williams (1872-1958) in England kept that genre vitally alive in the 20th century.

Suggested Listening: Shostakovich. Symphony No. 7

Sergei Rachmaninoff (1873-1943) of the Soviet Union and Samuel Barber (1910-1981) of the United States wrote some of the most stirring concertos in music history.

Suggested Listening: Rachmaninoff. Piano Concerto No. 2

Expressions of nationalism continued in abundance in the 20th century. Composers like Copland in America, Bela Bartok (1881-1945) in Hungary, Albert Ginastera (b. 1916) in Argentina, and many more from nations the world over have been intent on fusing native folk forms and melodies with their own creative genius.

Suggested Listening: Copland. "Hoedown" from "Rodeo"

Many works akin to the Romantic tone poem have also been a part of the modern scene. Hindemith's "Mathis der Mahler," Bartok's "Concerto for Orchestra," Schonberg's "Transfigured Night," and Stravinsky's "Pulcinella" are just a few examples.

Suggested Listening: Bartok. "Concerto for Orchestra"

The use of choral music within and outside the symphonic setting has carried over from the Romantic era to the 20th century. It can be seen in Stravinsky's "Symphony of Psalms," in the "Te Deum" of Benjamin Britten (1913-1976), and in the cantatas of Anton Webern to name just three of many examples.

Suggested Listening: Stravinsky. "Symphony of Psalms"

The opera has lost little of its zeal from the 19th century to the 20th, and it exists in every conceivable tonal style. Giacomo Puccini (1858-1924) wrote Italian Romantic opera; Debussy wrote French Impressionistic opera; Alban Berg wrote atonal Expressionistic opera; Benjamin Britten established his own style of English opera; while Stravinsky, Schonberg, Shostakovich, Gian-Carlo Menotti (b. 1911), and many more all contributed to the genre.

Suggested Listening: **Puccini. "La Boheme"**
Berg. "Wozzeck"
Britten. "Billy Budd"

In summation, the coexistence of different styles and genres within the century is so complex and so interwoven that it is difficult to establish which composer in which country is writing what kind of music. Besides, the world has been shrunk by technology and uprooted by war. Stravinsky, born in Czarist Russia, wrote ballets in Post-World War I Paris, then came to America to die as a naturalized citizen in Hollywood, California. He was neither completely Russian, nor Parisian, nor American. His music was at once Romantic, neo-Classical, atonal, and serial. He was typical of the century in complexity and diversity. Thus, perhaps it is best at least for this time period to simply list the most heralded composers and the region most associated with them.

France:	Debussy, Ravel, Milhaud, Poulenc
England:	Vaughn-Williams, Britten, William Walton (b. 1902)
Russia:	Shostakovich, Rachmaninoff, Stravinsky, Prokofiev, Dmitri Kabalevsky, Aram Khachaturian
Spain and South America:	Manuel de Falla, Ginastera, Heitor Villa-Lobos (1887-1959)
Austria and Germany:	Schonberg, Webern, Berg, Hindemith, Ernst Krenek (b. 1900), Carl Orff (b. 1895)
Central and Eastern Europe:	Leoš Janáček (1854-1923), Bartok, Zoltán Kodály (1882-1967)
Italy:	Ferruccio Busoni (1866-1924), Ottorino Respighi, Luciano Berio, Luigi Dallapiccola (b. 1904)
United States:	Aaron Copland, Charles Ives (1874-1954), George Gershwin (1898-1937), Leonard Bernstein (b. 1918), Walter Piston (1894-1976)

"Popular" Music

Finally, 20th century man is listening to a brand of music born entirely of the folk culture of the 19th century English dance hall and the traditions of America's slave and wilderness societies. It is referred to as "popular" music, and it has a history and tradition all its own.

Beginnings. From the country dances and folk songs of 19th century America, but especially from the African rhythms and melodies which nourished the music of colonial slave cultures, a kind of popular singing and playing tradition grew up in the United States in the 1800's. Following the American Civil War, after the slaves were freed, many traveling minstrel shows comprised of talented black performers toured the land. When the population centers began to shift from the countryside to the cities in the late 19th century, the minstrel shows no longer needed to move to attract paying customers. Instead, the music of the parlor piano and minstrel show could now be combined to form non-traveling variety productions which might remain permanently in the city.

Major metropolitan centers became the home of a new popular musical style called vaudeville. For the vaudeville circuit, a whole subculture of musical composition and publication gradually arose, the most noted example of which was the Broadway/Tin Pan Alley district of New York City.

Ragtime. During the last decade of the 1800's and the first ten years or so of the 1900's, another style emerged in the pop culture of the cities. It had its roots in the piano playing of the 19th century parlor, the lively dances of the folk cultures in the countryside, and the incessant syncopation of a rich, black musical tradition. It was called "ragtime," and its most important proponent was the black composer, Scott Joplin (1868-1917).

Suggested Listening: **Joplin. "Maple Leaf Rag"**
Joplin and many other early pop sources may be heard on the Folkways "History of Jazz" series (FJ 2801-2811) and Leonard Feather's "Encyclopedia of Jazz on Records" (MCA 2-4061-63).

The important aspect of the ragtime years is that they produced not only an aesthetic culture apart from that of "serious music" but a commercially successful one as well. The people of Tin Pan Alley who published Scott Joplin and the others of his era did not need the works of Debussy, Stravinsky, and Schonberg in order to survive. Indeed, they were surviving even better than the "serious" composers of Impressionism, Expressionism, and neo-Classicism.

It is also important to understand that the popular and serious musical worlds were not totally divorced. Stravinsky wrote a composition entitled "Ragtime" which used the syncopations and instrumental effects of the age. Similarly, Debussy used the black cakewalk dance as the form for one of his piano compositions. These early hybrids between two seemingly segregated musical worlds were harbingers of hybrids which would exist throughout the century. Ernst Krenek would write a jazz opera ("Johnny Spielt Auf"); George Gershwin would use the black jazz idiom for his stage work "Porgy and Bess;" Leonard Bernstein would combine both popular and serious elements in his musical "West Side Story;" pop groups like The Beatles and Emerson-Lake-and-Palmer would use the Romantic music of Mussorgsky and the Classical genre of the string quartet in some of their compositions.

The Jazz Age. During the 1920's new popular styles were born. "The blues" were sad compositions drawn from the laments of the black spirituals. "Dixieland" was an instrumental idiom of theme and variation. These styles comprised what is now known as the Jazz Age. The music of the age was partly modal, combining elements of the major-minor system with alterations to the 2nd, 3rd, 6th, and 7th scale steps. It also used a standardized instrumental ensemble which included voice, piano, drums, bass, clarinet, trumpet, trombone, and saxophone. But most of all, it borrowed from the two inescapable characteristics of black music: syncopation on the one hand and improvisation on the other. Not since the days of the Baroque figured bass had improvisation played so major a role in a musical genre. Improvisation and jazz now became inseparable.

Besides the advent of jazz styles, the 1920's saw two other great beginnings. The first was the development of music for the record, radio, and film industries which by the early 1930's were big businesses. The second was the emergence of the American musical theatre into a position of commercial and artistic prominence. The musical particularly - a kind of hybrid between Romantic opera, operetta, dance hall variety show, and vaudeville - was about to become one of the nation's most influential media.

The leading figures of the popular music of the Jazz Age were: for blues, "Ma" Rainey (1886-1939) and Bessie Smith (1895-1937); for Dixieland jazz, Louis Armstrong (1900-1971) and King Oliver (1885-1935); for the musical theatre, Richard Rodgers (1902-1982) and Jerome Kern (1885-1945).

Suggested Listening: **Armstrong/Oliver. "When The Saints Go Marching In"**
Smith. "Jailhouse Blues"
Kern. "Showboat"

1930-1950. Pop music in the 1930's and 1940's saw a shift to large bands with solo singers and featured instrumentalists. Benny Goodman, Woody Herman, Tommy and Jimmy Dorsey, Duke Ellington, Count Basie, Glen Miller, Paul Whiteman, Harry James, Guy Lombardo, and Stan Kenton were the most noted of the big band leaders. The vocalists who sang with them, many of whom later became musical idols on their own, included people like Peggy Lee, Helen O'Connell, Billy Holiday, Bing Crosby, Rudy Vallee, and Frank Sinatra. Their music was nicknamed "Swing."

In the musical theatre the most remarkable work of the age was Gershwin's "Porgy and Bess." The most celebrated authors of the day were Richard Rodgers and Oscar Hammerstein who collaborated on such hits as "Oklahoma," "Carousel," and "South Pacific."

Suggested Listening: **Benny Goodman. "Sing, Sing, Sing"**
Duke Ellington. "Take the A Train"
Gershwin. "Porgy and Bess"
Rodgers/Hammerstein. "South Pacific"

After the War. Following World War II, a financial dispute arose between the broadcast industry and the music publishing industry which led to the fragmentation of popular music into four distinct streams. (1) Jazz continued to develop as an improvised form, often achieving the status of fine art and often incorporating the dissonances of atonality and serialism. (2) The musical theatre reached a zenith in both quantity and quality which lasted until the early 1970's. (3) The Tin Pan Alley song continued to be written but in lesser amounts than in previous decades.

Suggested Listening: **For Jazz, Dave Brubeck's "Time Out" and Charlie Parker's "Byrd Symbols" For musicals, Lerner and Loewe's "My Fair Lady" For pop songs, Barbra Streisand's "Greatest Hits"**

The fourth pop stream of post-World War II America was called "rock and roll." It was a populist form refined by the technology and promoted by the marketing techniques of the industrialized city. A cross-pollination of blues, country music, folk styles and jazz, the new popular sound exploded onto the scene in the year 1954 with a song called "Rock Around the Clock." The song was used as the background for a film about juvenile delinquents in a New York City high school. That is particularly symbolic. The fact that the song received its exposure from a motion picture is an indication of the role which the mass media (film, radio, record, television) played in the commercialization of popular music. The fact that the film itself dealt with adolescent behavior is indicative of the market toward which popular music was primarily geared - the youth market, flushed with the affluence of the post-war world, able to spend billions on new products designed for it. Finally, the film was set in a large city, and it was the city (New York, Los Angeles, Detroit, and Nashville, primarily) which became the new marketplaces of the popular musical product.

For the most part the music of this era was of very poor artistic quality - not so much in terms of the recording and manufacturing technology which produced it - but in terms of the craft with which it was written and performed. Here and there, popular artists (especially those with the wisdom and integrity to seek the help of trained musicians) did produce fine works. However, most of them were unschooled musicians who had and still appear to have an attitude of defiant righteousness about them, an attitude which seeks to defend poor quality and musical ignorance.

Today's pop music achieves success not because its art is developed but because the power of mass media supports it and markets it largely to adolescents whose poor musical education leaves them susceptible to the worst influences of the craft. The financial success of popular artists and the industrialists who promote them seems sufficient to justify the continued existence of their abjectly poor product. The fact that such poor quality can live side by side with the great art of Stravinsky and his colleagues is yet another manifestation of the contradictions and diversity of the 20th century.

The two most influential pop entities of the post-World War II era were the American solo singer Elvis Presley and the British rock group The Beatles. Each, like the century which spawned them, produced works of both shoddy quality and true art. The Beatles, especially - with the help of their record producer and arranger, George Martin - wrote some of the most surprisingly sophisticated literature of the popular mainstream.

Suggested Listening: **The Beatles. "Abbey Road"**
Elvis Presley. "Elvis's Golden Records"

Final Thoughts

At this writing the 20th century is not yet done. What the last few years of it have in store does not look to be much different from what it already has produced. As the century draws to a close, the state of music does not look as robust as in centuries past. The giants of the age - Schönberg, Stravinsky, Bartok - are dead. The Coplands and Bernsteins are approaching the end of their lives, and it is difficult to see new musical geniuses rising to replace them. Rather, the direction of music seems to be one of technological experimentation guided as much by theorists of mathematical and electronic training as by musicians of traditional schooling. Whether or not this new generation - composers like Glass, Zinn, Corigliano, and others - achieves the glories of generations past is a matter which only history will decide.

On the popular scene, the work of The Beatles and other artists of genuine ability seems to have been overshadowed recently by music of a much inferior vintage. In the musical theatre, many new shows have been replaced with revivals from the past and with revues which harken back to the days of vaudeville.

Whatever the future holds, it seems certain that technology and the finances of mass culture will play enormous roles in it. It also seems likely that unless the serious composer makes more of an effort to reach the common man, and the common man makes more of an effort to educate himself to what is worthy in the art of music, the mediocrity of pop music and isolation of serious music will continue to grow. This is not a fitting end to the story of one of man's most glorious arts, nor a fitting tribute to the majesty of the Machauts and Josquins, Palestrinas and Bachs, Beethovens and Debussys who have given so much to mankind.

Further Reading.

1. Masterpieces of music before 1750. Carl Parish and John Ohl. (New York: Norton, 1951).

2. Source readings in music history. Oliver Strunk. (New York: Norton, 1950).

3. The notation of polyphonic music, 900-1600, 5th ed. Willi Apel. (Cambridge, Mass.: The Medieval Academy, 1961).

4. The history of music theory. Hugo Riemann. (Lincoln, Nebraska: Univ. of Nebraska Press, 1962).

5. The history of music, college outline, 4th ed. Hugh Miller. (New York: Barnes and Noble, 1972).

6. A history of Western music. rev. ed. Donald J. Grout. (New York: Norton, 1973).

7. Music in Western civilization. Paul Henry Lang. (New York: Norton, 1941).

8. History of music, 5th ed. Karl H. Worner. (New York: The Free Press, 1973).

9. All the years of American popular music. David Ewen. (Englewood Cliffs, New Jersey: Prentice-Hall, 1977).

10. Rhythm and harmony in the music of The Beatles, doctoral dissertation. Steven Porter. University Microfilms No. 79-13, 156. (Ann Arbor, Michigan: University Microfilms, 1979).

The sources above are listed not in the usual alphabetical order but in the order of the history of music from past to present. They will provide a rich supplement to all of Part III of this text, not only in terms of additional information, but for their bibliographies and discographies as well. However, remember as you read further that music is an aural art. The words written about it are meaningless until and unless you listen to the sound of music itself. It is my heartfelt recommendation that before you do any extensive reading - or at least while you do it - you exhaust the recordings in your local libraries which will make music a living, breathing entity for you.

David B. Zinn; composer-author-theoretician-pianist at his **Kurzweil 250.** The Kurzweil 250 computer music system represents the most advanced and versatile digital synthesizer available on the market today.

PART IV

INSTRUMENTS AND PERFORMANCE

CHAPTER SIXTEEN:

THE INSTRUMENTS OF MODERN MUSIC

The various instruments used to make music today fall into five categories: strings, winds, percussion instruments, electronic instruments, and the human voice. Within each category are several subdivisions which allow us to group families of instruments together conveniently. One of the best ways to learn more about music is to become familiar with instruments from both an intellectual and a practical point of view.

String Instruments

A string instrument is one which produces a sound by being bowed, plucked, or strummed. The most common string instruments are the violin, viola, 'cello, bass, harp, banjo, and guitar. These are by no means, however, the only string instruments. There is the koto of Japan, the mandolin and balalaika of Russia, the zither of the Middle East. Some strings have higher ranges (e.g., the violin); some, lower ones (the bass); and some cover wide ranges (the guitar). Each is capable of playing more than one note at a time, and some are capable of playing difficult polyphony, depending, of course, on the skill of the performer.

Wind Instruments

A wind instrument is defined as one which produces sounds by means of a vibrating column of air. There are several sub-categories of wind instruments, and sometimes it is not entirely clear why certain instruments belong to certain wind families.

Woodwinds. On the face of it, woodwinds ought to be those wind instruments made of wood, but unfortunately that is not quite true. The flute, for example, is a woodwind, and while at one time flutes were wooden, today they are decidedly metallic. A better definition of a woodwind comes from the way in which it changes pitches. Woodwinds are instruments with holes bored along a column. The air which vibrates inside the column is allowed to escape through one hole or another, and the pitch of the sound is determined by the choice of holes through which the air escapes. The most common woodwinds are the flute, oboe, clarinet, bassoon, English horn, saxophone, and recorder.

Many of the woodwinds are produced in families whose members cover a wide range of pitches. For example, there is a soprano saxophone, an alto sax, tenor sax, and baritone sax. Each - like the human voice ranges for which they are named - plays in a specific range. The recorder family has several members (soprano, alto, and tenor being the most common), and so does the clarinet family (which sports a very low bass clarinet).

Reeds. Reed instruments are wind instruments whose vibrating column of air is set into motion by the vibration of either a single or double reed system. The saxophone and clarinet are the most common single reeds, while the oboe, English horn, and bassoon are the most common double reeds. By contrast the flute and recorder are not reeds. The designation of woodwinds as either reeds or non-reeds is yet another of the many ways wind instruments may be classified.

Brasses. Brass instruments are grouped together not only because they are made of metal, but because they all change pitch by varying the length of tubing through which the air inside them flows. The most frequently encountered brass instruments are the trumpet, French horn, trombone, baritone horn, and tuba. Each is similarly constructed in that each has a mouthpiece through which the performer expels air, tubing through which the air travels, and a bell or flared opening out of which the air escapes. The length of the tubing is changed either by depressing keys (which open and shut valves that can block off sections of tubing) or by sliding one section of tubing into another. The trumpet, French horn, baritone horn, and tuba all use keys. The trombone uses the sliding mechanism.

Unusual Winds. Besides the woodwind, reed, and brass families, there are wind instruments which are not conveniently placed in any family. Whistles, for example, and harmonicas are both members of the wind family. So, for that matter, is the organ in which each pipe is a kind of whistle on a very large, complex scale.

Percussion Instruments

Percussion instruments are those which produce a sound by being struck or by having one instrumental part strike another. These instruments fall into two sub-divisions, those of definite pitch and those of indefinite pitch.

Percussion instruments of definite pitch. The most common of these instruments are the bells, chimes, vibraphone, glockenspeil, tuned tympani drums, xylophone, marimba, and celeste.

Percussion instruments of indefinite pitch. The most common of these are the snare drum, bass drum, wood blocks, triangle, tambourine, rasp, whip, gong, cymbals, tom-tom, claves, and castanets.

Electronic Instruments

Electronic instruments are those which produce sounds as a result of electric power. They may be conventional instruments like the guitar, bass, flute, xylophone, etc. which are electrified and amplified, or they may be wholly new instruments like synthesizers which generate complex wave forms and control all of the properties of sound (overtones, attack times, decay times, vibrato, reverberation, etc.) separately.

STRING INSTRUMENTS

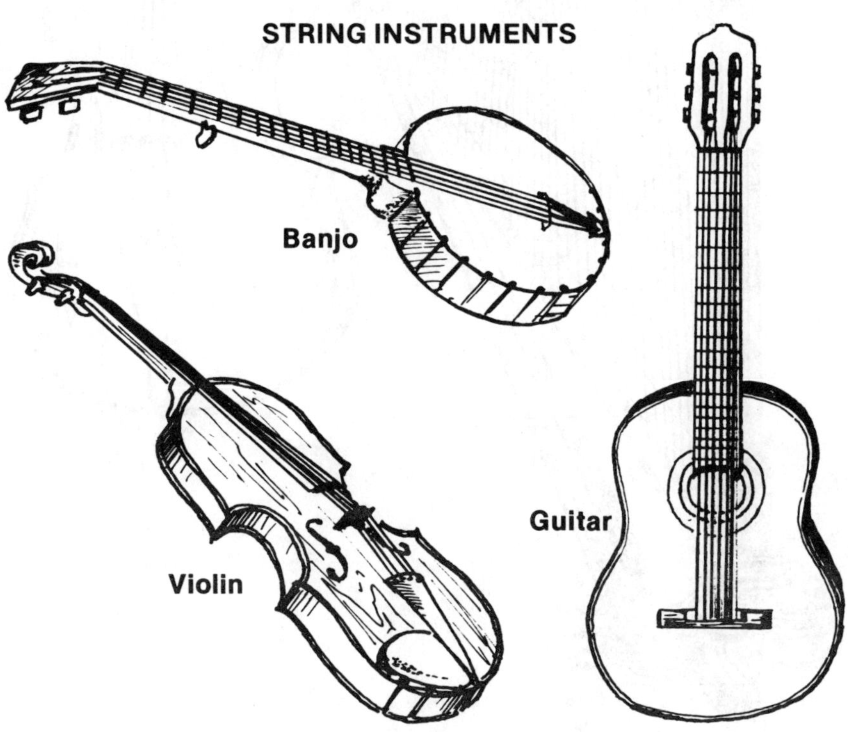

STRING INSTRUMENTS

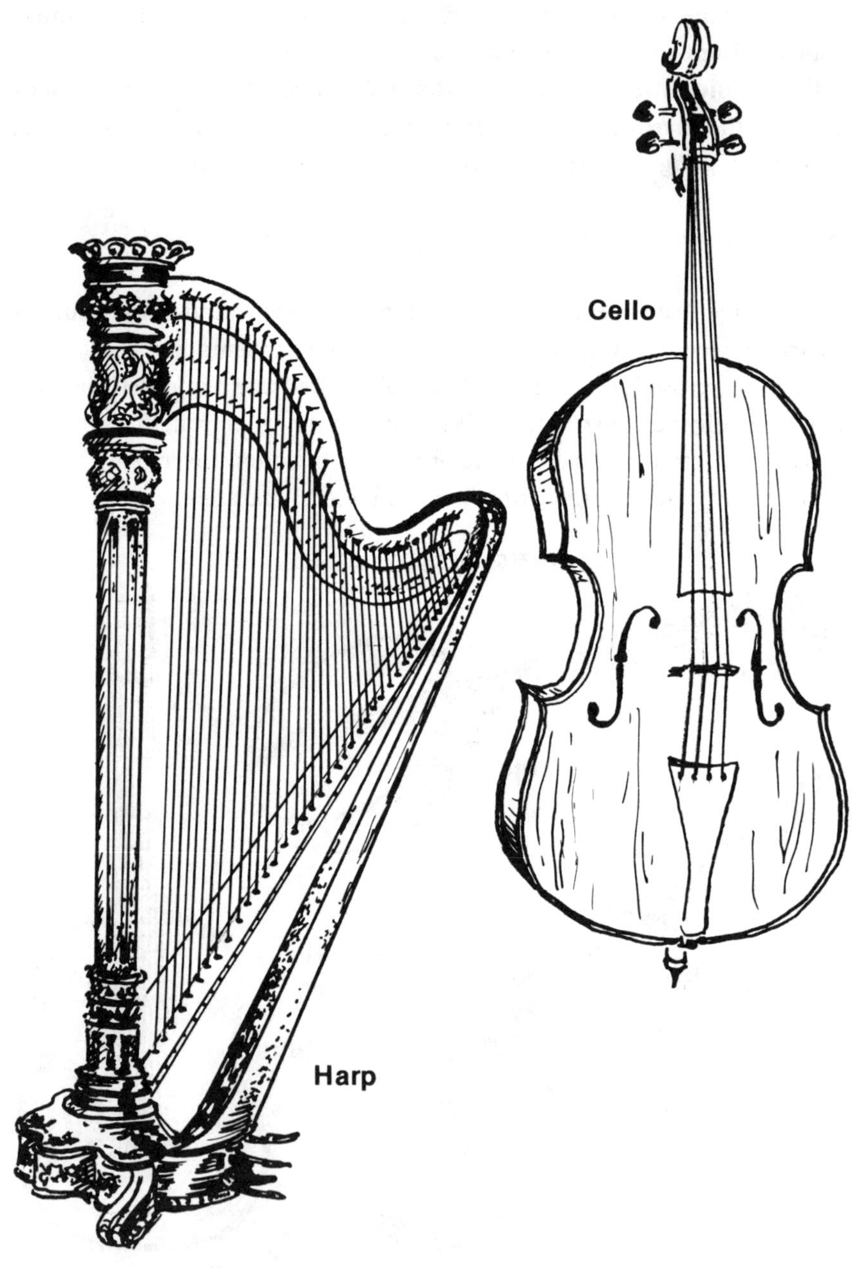

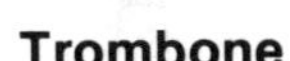
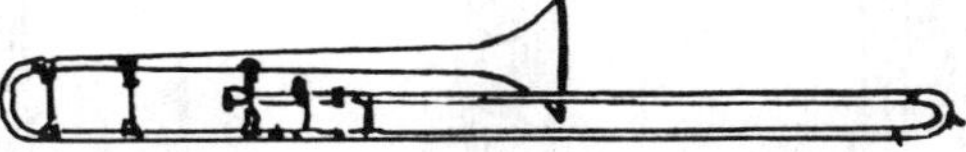

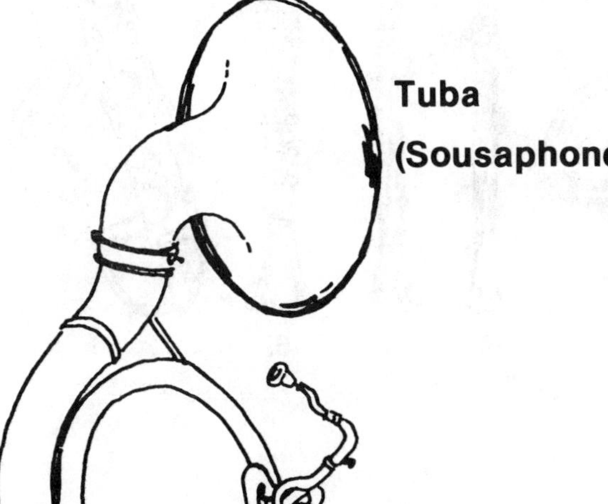

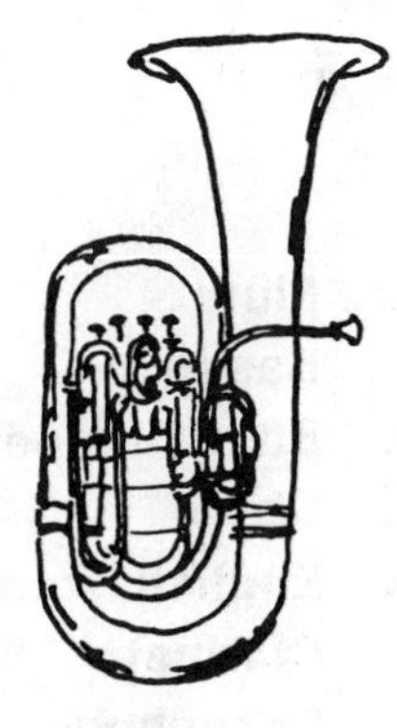

BRASS INSTRUMENTS

1. **Flute**
2. **Bassoon**
3. **Bass Clarinet**
4. **Oboe**
5. **English Horn**
6. **Clarinet**
7. **Saxophone**

WOODWIND INSTRUMENTS

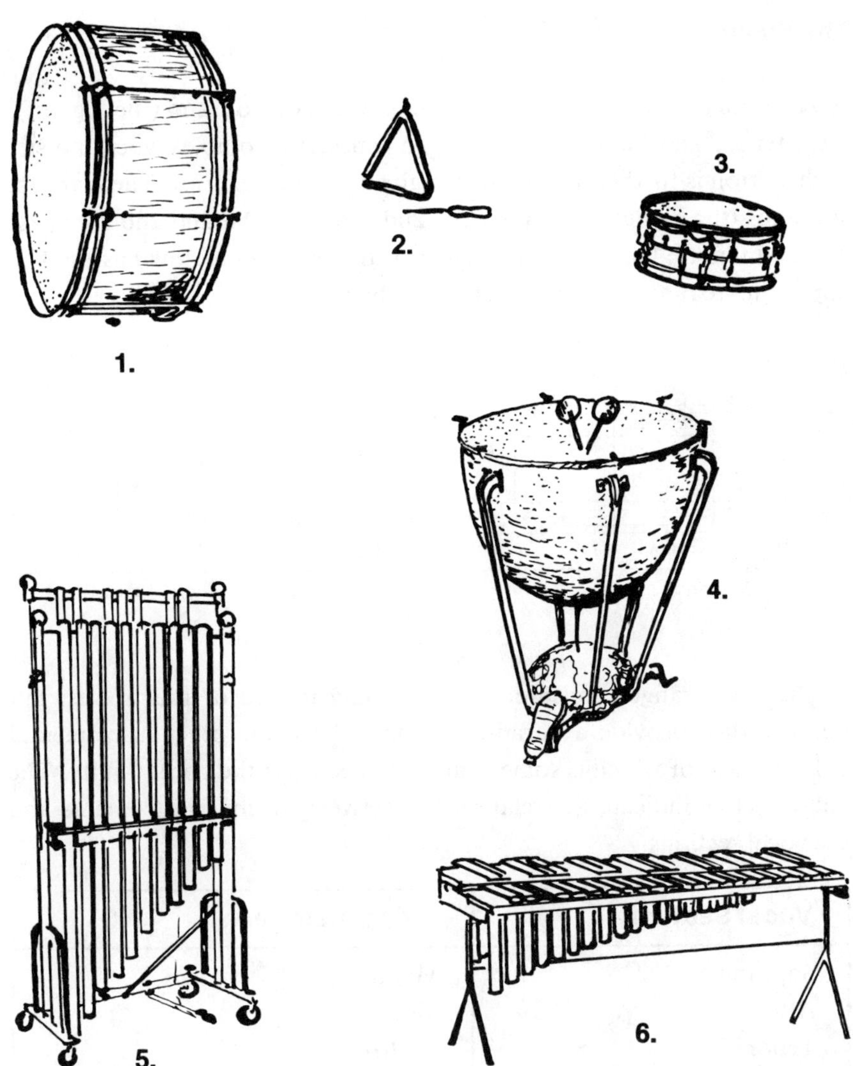

1. Bass Drum
2. Triangle
3. Snare Drum
4. Tympani
5. Chimes
6. Vibraphone

PERCUSSION INSTRUMENTS

The Voice

The human voice falls into four general ranges: soprano (the highest), alto, tenor, and bass (the lowest). In especially complex vocal music, each section is further divided into high and low categories. There are 1st sopranos (the highest sopranos) and 2nd sopranos; 1st and 2nd altos; 1st and 2nd tenors; baritones (the higher of the basses) and low basses. The approximate ranges for each section are below.

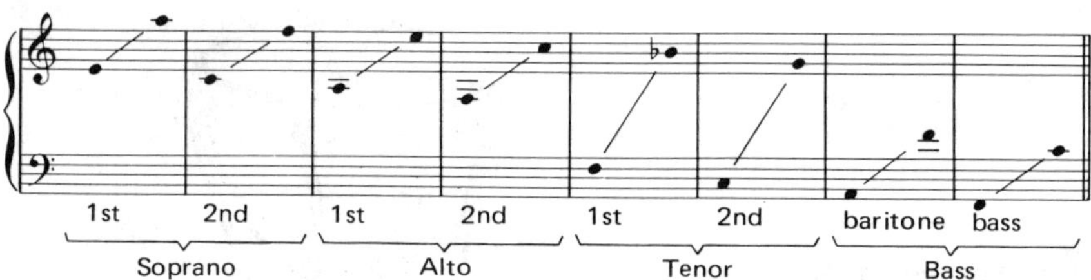

The vocal ranges are important not only in and of themselves, but because they provide a paradigm or model for the other instrumental groups, each of which is somewhat patterned after the vocal family. The charts below indicate the relationship between various instruments and the vocal sections.

Vocal Section	String Instrument
Soprano	violin
Alto	viola
Tenor	'cello
Bass	bass
Combined ranges	guitar, banjo, harp

Vocal Section	Woodwind Instrument
Soprano	flute, soprano sax
Alto	oboe, alto sax
Tenor	clarinet, English horn, tenor sax
Bass	bassoon, baritone sax, bass clarinet

Vocal Section	Brass Instrument
Soprano	trumpet
Alto	French horn
Tenor	trombone
Bass	tuba, baritone horn, bass trombone

Vocal Section	Percussion Instrument
Soprano	triangle, bells
Alto	chimes
Tenor	snare drum
Bass	bass drum, tympani
Combined ranges	xylophone

The Modern Orchestra

The analogy between the vocal sections of a choir and the various sections of the modern orchestra is a bit strained when dealing with the percussion section, but for the strings and winds it is a useful one. In fact, the language of orchestration frequently speaks of the "string choir" or "woodwind choir" or "brass choir" in referring to the various instrumental families. It is quite appropriate to think of the modern orchestra as a series of choirs: the woodwinds on top, the brasses next, and then the strings, with percussion instruments filling out effects. The following list illustrates this view.

Piccolo	(1st soprano)	
Flute	(2nd soprano)	
Oboe	(alto)	
English horn		Woodwinds
Clarinet	(tenors)	
Bass clarinet		
Bassoon	(basses)	

(Occasionally modern orchestras also use members of the saxophone family in their woodwind sections.)

XVI *The instruments of modern music*

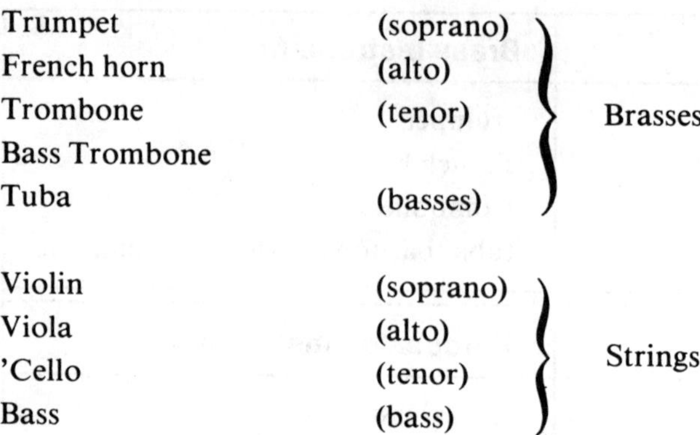

With the basic list above a good deal of orchestral music calls for harp, piano, and a whole host of percussion instruments of both definite and indefinite pitch.

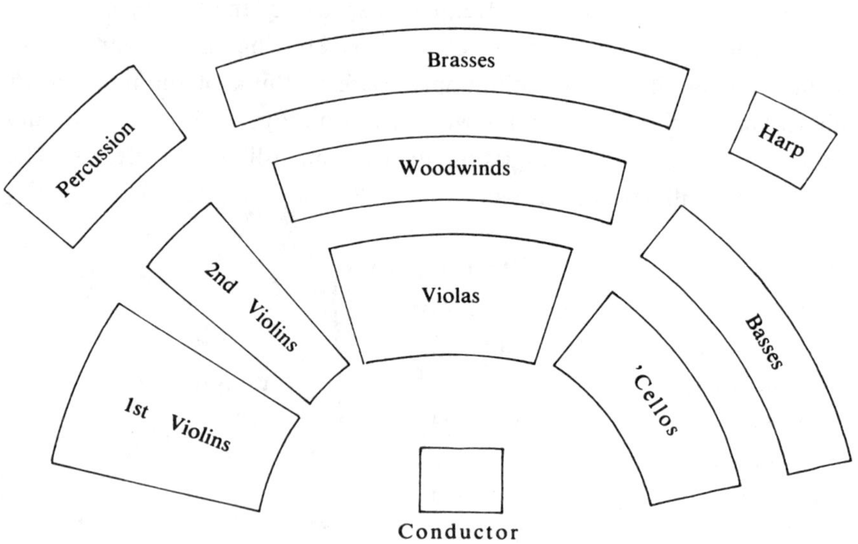

Keyboard Instruments

There are four principle keyboard instruments in modern-day use: the piano, the electric keyboard, the organ, and - to a lesser extent - the harpsichord. They all cover a wide range of pitches and are, of course, capable of playing single lines, chords, and complex polyphony. Technically, the piano is a percussion instrument since it produces its sound by having a felt-covered hammer strike a metal string. The electric piano does not employ this mechanism but rather uses electricity to activate oscillators which vibrate at the desired pitch. It is thus a purely electronic animal. The modern organ, while powered by electricity, nonetheless is a wind instrument whose sound is achieved by forcing air into and out of great stationary pipes. The harpsichord, used mostly in the performance of old music from the Renaissance or Baroque eras, is in fact a member of the string family because it produces its sound by having a mechanical jack pluck the metal strings stretched across its frame.

The Transposing Instrument

For some instruments it is an inconvenient but very real fact that the notes which are written are not the pitches which are sounded when the performer reads his part. This is not because the performer is playing incorrectly but because his instrument is simply not manufactured to reproduce the printed page exactly as it is printed.

The trumpet, for instance, is built in such a way that when none of its three valves is depressed, it will produce the note B♭. That in itself presents no complications. However, it has become customary in writing music that the note produced in such an "open position" is written as a "C." Thus what is "C" to a trumpet player is "B♭" to the ear of the audience. To get the trumpet player to play the "real C" (or so-called "concert C") one must write a "D." The trumpet, reading "D," will then produce a pitch one full tone below what he is reading. For a trumpet: written D = concert C.

Instruments whose "open positions" (no holes covered, no valves depressed, etc.) produce a note other than "concert C" are called transposing instruments. There are several of them in the common orchestra including the clarinet, English horn, trumpet, French horn, and

the entire saxophone family. As we have seen, the trumpet is pitched to
B♭. So is the clarinet; but other transposing instruments are pitched to
different notes. The alto sax, for example, is pitched to E♭; the French
horn to F; the piccolo sounds an octave higher than it is written (even
though it is pitched to C); the string bass sounds an octave lower than
written (though it is also pitched to C). In addition, not all the instruments of the orchestra read treble or bass clef. The viola is written in
alto clef; the trombone and 'cello on occasion must read not only bass
but tenor clef.

All of this business of transposing instruments and using many clefs
makes an orchestra score very difficult to read. In a composition in C
major, for example, where the violins will read treble clef and use the key
signature of C (no ♯'s or ♭'s), the trumpets will be reading the signature
of D major (2♯'s), the French horn will be using the signature of G major (1♯), the viola will be reading in alto clef, the piccolo notes will actually sound a full octave above what is written in the score, etc. Conductors and composers must be highly trained and highly skilled to handle these complexities, not only because they are in themselves difficult,
but even more because they all occur at the same time.

Suggested Listening: **Benjamin Britten. "Young Person's
Guide to the Orchestra"**

Performing

As much as books and records can mean to the study of music - and it
is a considerable amount - they cannot replace the experience of making
music. The next unit is designed to allow you to make music in each of
the major instrumental categories: string, wind, percussion, keyboard,
and voice. As you perform in each of these media, you will have to draw
on your ability to read treble and bass clef and to play simple rhythmic
patterns. To these skills you will add a rudimentary knowledge of each
instrument you play. The purpose here is not to demand any extensive
technical or musical proficiency but simply to give you some idea of what
it takes to make a musical sound. Should you discover a facility with any
of the performing you do, you may wish to expand your talent on your
own with performance method books (which are available in abundance)
or with a private instructor.

Making music is one of the great joys of human existence, and if as a result of your work in this text you feel you have the ability and interest to pursue that joy, then so much the better. However, for most people the next chapters are designed not to start you on a career or an avocation, but simply to give you a greater understanding - a first-hand understanding - of how music is made.

The specific media in which you will be working are guitar (string), tonette or recorder (wind), piano (keyboard), drum set (percussion), and singing (voice).

CHAPTER SEVENTEEN:

PLAYING THE GUITAR

The guitar, as almost everyone knows, has six strings stretched across its neck and body. They are tuned (from lowest to highest) to the pitches E, A, D, G, B, and E. Across the neck of the guitar are horizontal metal striations called frets. The crossing of strings and frets interact to make a grid fingerboard along the neck of the guitar. By depressing the strings on the spaces between the frets, the pitches of the strings are altered so that melodies and chords can be played. A diagram of the strings and the four frets furthest from the guitar's body appears below. The strings are numbered from 1 (the highest in pitch) to 6 (the lowest). The indication° above a string means that it is open or unstopped by a finger.

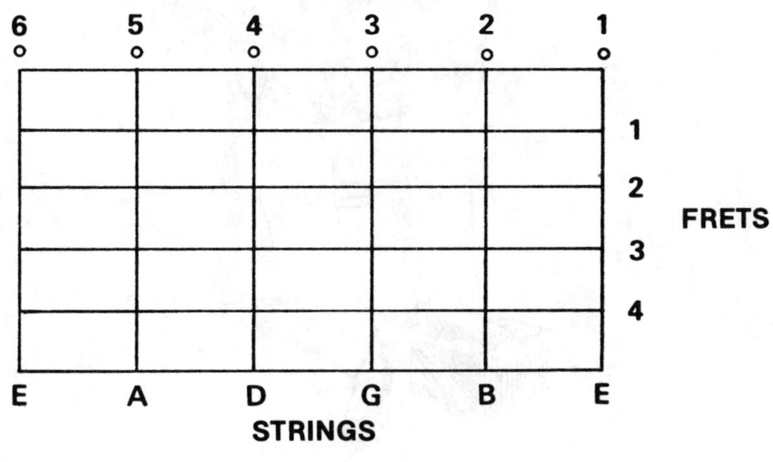

These open strings correspond to the following notes:

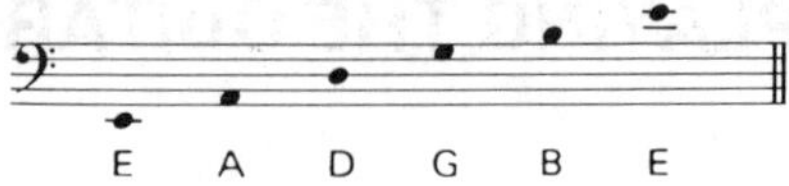

Though the guitarist reads the same pitches he plays (i.e., if he sees an F in his part, he plays a "real" or concert F), his part is written an octave higher than it sounds. Traditionally, guitar parts are written in treble clef. (See below.)

The guitar is held with the right hand in position to strum or pick (pluck) the strings while the left plays the fingerboard. The body of the guitar rests on the leg with the performer in a sitting position.

In this configuration, the fingerboard fits into the crook of the left hand between the thumb and first finger. The left thumb thus cannot depress the strings of the fingerboard. For this reason, guitar music indicates fingering on the fingerboard with the numbers 1-4 standing for the 2nd, 3rd, 4th finger, and pinky respectively.

For the purposes of this text, that fingering method is not useful, principally because later in our unit on the piano, the number 1 will be used to refer to the thumb. Therefore, for our study here, we will use the numbers 1-5 to indicate thumb-pinky in all the units on performance.

Below is the top of a fingerboard with all the chromatic tones and appropriate fingering indicated. This series of notes constitutes the "first position" of the guitar for each of the 6 strings (since in order to play any higher on any given string, the entire left hand would have to be shifted up the neck toward the body).

The idea is to press firmly on the strings with the tips of the left fingers so that the strings touch the fingerboard itself in the area between the frets. (Depressing the string directly onto the fret will produce a poor sound.) Your first task on the guitar is to play the chromatic scale from low E (open 6th string) to high G♯ (5th finger, 4th fret, 1st string). Try playing it both upward and downward.

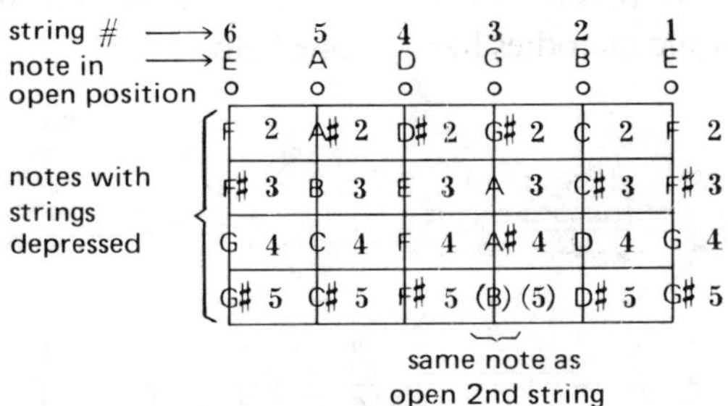

By selecting the correct notes of the chromatic scale, you can play the E major scale. Since so many of the strings are tuned to notes of the E major scale, this is a particularly good one with which to start. The correct fingering and note names for the E major scale are given below. Use the thumb of your right hand to pluck the appropriate string.

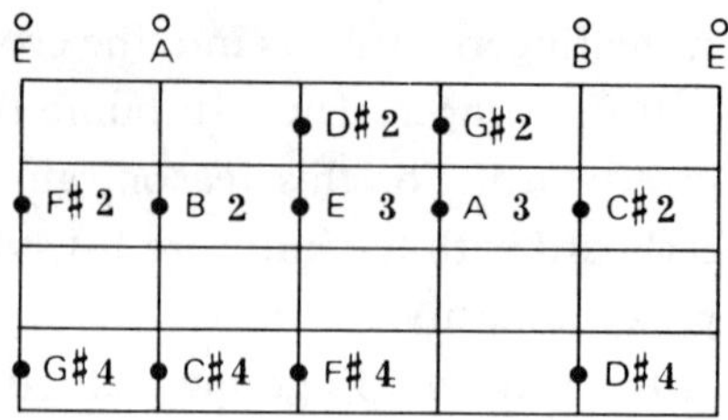

This pattern corresponds to the notes

which are actually written for the guitar one octave higher than sounded (see below).

When you develop some facility with this scale, you may try playing simple monophonic melodies like the one below.

In playing this melody, a left hand fingering is suggested above the staff. Hands, however, differ in size, and you may find your own finger-ing more suitable. Your right hand (thumb) should begin by plucking the 5th string, then move directly to the 4th string. From there, the strings you use will be the same as the ones you used for the notes of the E major scale.

The guitar is capable of playing chords as well as single line melodies. Below are the fingerboard charts for several chords in the key of E major. These chords will enable you to harmonize many melodies. In music which uses guitar chord accompaniments, the letter name of the chord (E, A B⁷, etc.) is often printed above the melody. By learning the position of the most frequently used chords, you can readily provide a guitar accompaniment to songs.

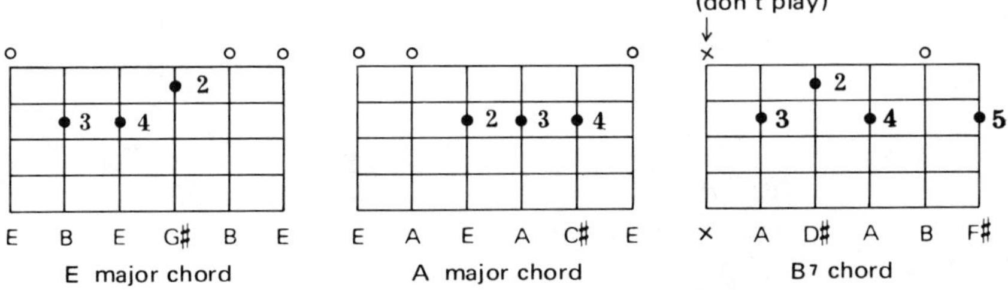

In addition to strumming the strings with the flesh edge of the right thumb (and occasionally the nail side of the right hand fingers), the right hand is capable of plucking (or "picking," as it is called) many different patterns on the strings. The right hand plucks the strings in the area where they cross the sounding hole of the body as the left hand works the fingerboard of the guitar neck. Below is a typical pick pattern.

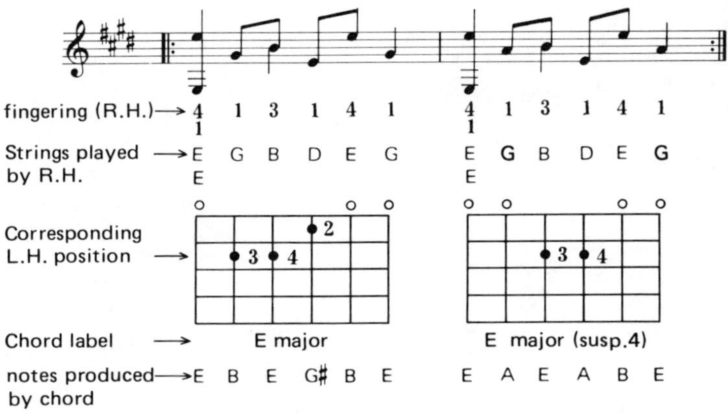

The scales and melodies, chords and picks above, hardly constitute a comprehensive guitar course. They won't make you a virtuoso or even a dedicated beginner. However, they will give you some idea of what it takes to make guitar music as opposed to listening to it. There are many beginning guitar methods you might try if you wish to continue. Your teacher, local music store, or a private guitar instructor can all help you with further study should you desire it.

CHAPTER EIGHTEEN:

PLAYING THE RECORDER (TONETTE)

The recorder is a simple, inexpensive but effective introduction to playing a wind instrument. It is a fairly small woodwind pitched to C and fingered using all five digits of both hands.

There is no reed in a recorder; it requires only that one blow into it to produce a sound. It is held upright with the following finger placement.

Left Hand	LH thumb on underside hole	1 o2 o o3 o4 x5 o2	**KEY** x = no hole-finger rest o = open hole • = closed hole
Right Hand	RH thumb on underside rest	1 o3 x o4 o5	

By stopping some holes with the fingers (indicated •) and leaving others open (indicated o), the recorder can produce all twelve tones of the octave (see below).

	C	D	E	F	G	A	B	C	D
L.H. (X not shown)									
R.H. (X not shown)									

	D♯ or E♭	F♯ or G♭	G♯ or A♭	A♯ or B♭	C♯ or D♭
L.H. (X not shown)					
R.H. (X not shown)					

Before playing any scales on the recorder, it is necessary to understand some things about correct breathing. As normal as breathing is to you, most people's breathing habits have changed since the sheltered days of infancy. In the relatively anxiety free environment of early life, babies generally breathe "diaphragmatically." that is, they relax their shoulders and torso while allowing their stomach muscles to do the work. Instead of gasping air high in the chest and forcing it down into the lungs, they work the diaphragm muscle band below the rib cage and in a relaxed movement draw the air downward. Conversely, the expulsion of air comes from a rising intensification of the diaphragm band rather than a tightening of the chest or clavicle (collar bone) region.

Anxiety produces clavicular breathing which is more shallow and less powerful than diaphragmatic breathing. You can see this in animals. Observe a dog or cat at rest. The shoulders hardly move. Instead there is a relaxed in-out motion of the abdominal musculature. The same animal in a state of fear or excitement will begin to pant. Breathing is more rapid, more tense, more shallow. Less air is taken in per breath; less lung capacity is used. Shoulders - sometimes the whole body - shake with the activity.

Breathing borne of tension is not conducive to good tone production either in playing a wind instrument or in singing. When the body is tense, the lung capacity is not fully used. Tone control, pitch accuracy, and tone quality suffer as a result. The first step in learning to play a wind instrument or in singing is to breathe in a relaxed, diaphragmatic way. A common exercise to relearn the diaphragmatic technique natural to infants is to lie on your back with your shoulders flush to the floor (or bed) and your arms (palms down) resting at your side. Place a book on your stomach and breathe in through your mouth in such a way that only the book rises. Keep your shoulders, throat, and arms relaxed. Exhale so that only the book falls. When you can do this without thought or effort, duplicate the process in a standing and sitting position. Finally, breathe this way when you take in and release air for singing or playing a wind instrument.

To do this, your posture must allow your diaphragm free play. When you sit, your back should neither hunch over nor be militarily rigid. Your feet should be firmly planted on the ground in front of you, and you should be about half way forward in your chair so that as you breathe, your ribs and torso can expand and contract easily.

In this position you will be able to release air into the recorder (or sing) with a smoothness and evenness which makes for a good tone. If you have really relaxed sufficiently, you will start to notice a natural pulsation or warbling of the tones you produce. This is called "vibrato," and for most musical situations it adds a maturity and warmth to the tone. It also has the additional benefit of helping to maintain the proper pitch. Vibrato can be increased or decreased by the experienced performer, and, like all things, too much vibrato will make the tone seem shaky, trembling, and thus unpleasant. Vibrato is best used in moderation and is only possible on notes of longer durational value. It occurs, again, as the result of relaxed tone production. Muscle strain, improper breathing, poor posture, and too much volume will all inhibit the development of vibrato. With all this in mind, try playing the melody below. Once it has been mastered, try the duet with another recorder player.

The phrase marks and commas above the staff indicate where to breathe. Breathe at the commas, not within the phrase markings.

CHAPTER NINETEEN:

PLAYING THE DRUM SET

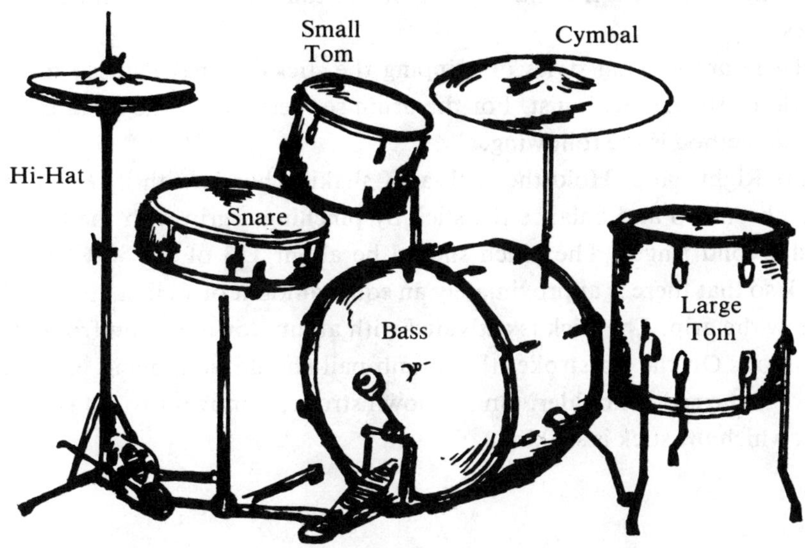

A drum set is a common sight, especially in environments where "popular" music is played. Though sets can be very elaborate, the basic ingredients include a bass drum, snare drum, riding tom-tom (attached to the bass drum frame), standing or "floor" tom-tom, suspended cymbal, and high-hat (a double cymbal worked by a foot pedal).

The four "skin" parts of the set each have different pitches and timbres. Ranked from lowest pitch to highest, they are: bass drum, floor tom-tom, riding tom-tom, and snare drum. The suspended cymbal can keep a steady beat ("ride" along, as the expression goes) or produce a great "crash" when struck hard. For those reasons it is often called a ride/crash cymbal. The high-hat may be struck either while it is closed (producing a metallic thud) or open (producing a cymbal's ring). Most of the additional parts of more complex drum sets are variations of the ingredients above. For example, some sets will have several suspended cymbals - cymbals just for riding or just for crashes. Some may have many floor or riding tom-toms. There may even be two bass drums. In addition, wood blocks, cow bells, and other "special effects" pieces can be attached to the frame of the bass drum and become a part of the drum set.

Playing a drum set requires the coordination of all four limbs (2 arms, 2 legs). It is thus difficult to start a unit on percussion by playing a full set. We will therefore begin with more simple things like hand coordination. Later, toward the end of the unit, we can try some four-limb exercises.

There are varying styles of gripping the sticks or mallets used in the world of the percussionist. For the drum set performer, the more traditional method is the following:

(a) Right hand. Hold the stick as if shaking hands with it. Keep the thumb on top and balance the stick by pinching a grip with the thumb and second finger. The pinch should be about 1/3 of the way up the stick so that there is approximately an equal amount of weight above and below the grip. The stick is activated with an up-down motion from this position. On the up stroke, the thumb nail should be moving in a line toward the right shoulder. On the down stroke, it moves toward the object which the stick is striking.

(b) Left hand. The left hand holds the stick by resting the shaft between thumb and first finger at the base of the thumb and pinching a grip at that spot. The left palm is turned upward so that it faces the performer. The top part of the stick rests between the third and fourth fingers, the latter being curled inward toward the palm to provide a ledge on which the stick can rest. The thumb pinch should occur about 1/3 of the way up the shaft, allowing the fourth finger rest to occur around the 2/3 mark, thus leaving the remaining 1/3 of the stick (the third containing the tip) to strike whatever on the drum set it is going to play. The stick is activated by rotating the wrist inward so that the thumb and palm end in a position facing downward. For the beginner, this motion is often awkward and takes getting used to.

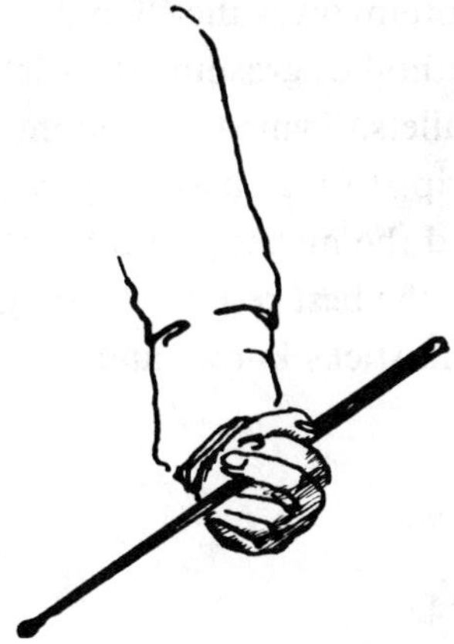

(c) When the sticks are held properly, the tips should meet at a right angle directly on the spot they strike. To do this the right hand will be closer to the body, the left extended out a little.

(d) In having the sticks strike the drum, care should be taken that the performer is at a convenient height from the drum head. Too high and the sticks will not contact the head when the wrists are rotated downward. Too low and the rotation will not allow the tips to strike properly.

(e) Finally, the place where the tips strike the head should be a little away from the center of the head as this is the spot which yields the best tone. Striking too close to the rim will give the head no chance to vibrate and make its characteristic sound.

Another hand position involves the "hand shake" grip for both right and left hands. This method of grasping the sticks is reserved for the percussionists who use mallets. Tympani, xylophone, vibraphone, etc. are all played using this grip. In recent years percussionists in rock groups have sometimes adopted the mallet group for their drum sets, though it probably does not yield the best results. A competent percussionist skilled with both mallets and sticks knows and uses both grips to maximum advantage.

Finally, before a percussionist plays his instrument, he usually tunes the skin parts of the drum set by tightening (or loosening) the pins which secure the skin to the frame. This is accomplished with the aid of a drum key. The tuning process both adjusts the pitch of the drum and regulates the tension of the drum head, assuring the proper action of sticks or mallets when they strike the head.

If the percussionist wishes to practice when drums are not available or when space is limited, a practice pad is often used. The pad's rubberized mat provides a fair approximation of the drum head, and it allows percussion practice with an ease and degree of quiet not otherwise available. In the classroom setting the practice pad is financially, logistically, and accoustically more desireable than having six or seven or ten drum sets going at one time. If the pad is used, the stick position, hand position, and body position should be the same as those used for the regular drum set.

Below are a series of two-limb exercises with which a new percussion student may begin.

This first exercise is a simple alternation of strokes. It should be worked on until the alternation is precise and even. Start at a slow speed and increase it gradually as the hands and wrists strengthen.

This exercise is also an alternate stroke exercise, one in which the note values get progressively smaller. It starts with 4 measures of alternating whole notes; then 4 measures of half notes; then 4 of quarters, eighths, triplets, and finally sixteenth notes. With each change of note value, the strokes alternate more rapidly. Try playing the exercise forward (from whole to sixteenth notes), then backward (from sixteenth to triplet, to eighth, to quarter, etc.) until reaching the whole note value once more. Remember that evenness, not speed, is the first goal of the percussionist. Speed comes with practice and time. Evenness is much the more important thing at this stage. If you can't get an even stroke or steady tempo, try using a metronome as you practice.

The next exercise is very familiar to percussionists. It is called a "paradiddle," and it introduces the idea of the repeated stroke along with the alternating stroke.

Again, the idea is to play slowly and evenly, gradually building up speed without sacrificing precision of execution.

After mastering the paradiddle, one can go on to more demanding repeated stroke exercises, all of which, when played at sufficient speeds, will produce drum rolls of various kinds.

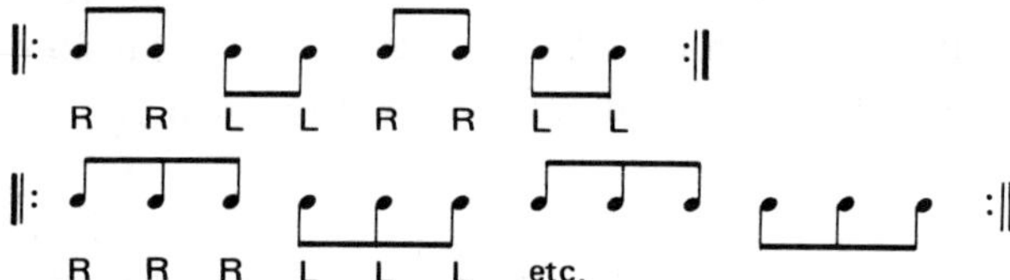

The two patterns above, when played at high speeds, will not require a separate wrist motion for each note. Rather, the drum sticks can be "bounced" two or three times per wrist motion. The "two bounce" pattern produces a double stroke roll (the so-called "mama-daddy" roll). The "three bounce" pattern produces a triple stroke roll. One can also press the stick tip into the drum head to produce a roll made up of many short strokes per wrist motion. This is the so-called "crush" roll.

Having gotten both hands to coordinate, the next step in playing a full drum set is coordinating the feet. The right foot is used to play the bass drum, the left to activate the high hat. Generally, percussionists keep the strong downbeat of each measure with the bass drum while the high hat fills in the weak afterbeats. In 4/4 time, for example, the right foot (bass drum) will play beats 1 and 3 while the left (high hat) plays beats 2 and 4. This alternation makes a good first exercise for the feet.

After your feet are accustomed to moving in coordinated patterns, you can try more complex rhythmic patterns. Two are suggested below.

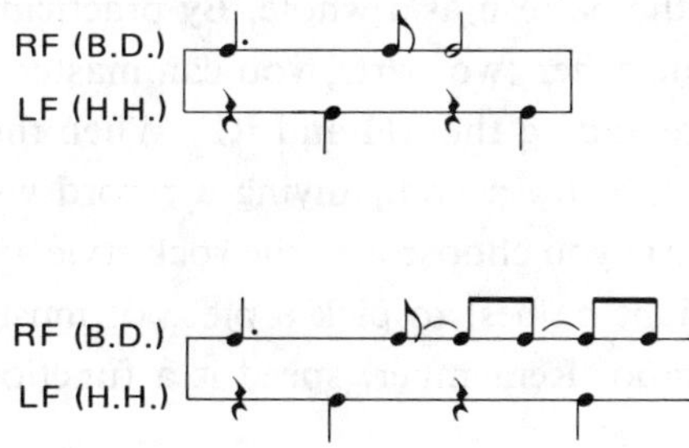

(In playing this syncopation, count 8 in your mind. The RF plays on 1 - 4 - 6 - 8; the LF on 3 and 7 as indicated below.

Finally, you are ready to try a 4-limb pattern. A common one, used frequently to keep a "rock beat" in popular music is written below. In mastering it, practice each limb separately, then combine them in various ways until you can get them all functioning in a smooth even pattern. As with all musical exercises, start slowly and work gradually up to a faster tempo.

This pattern has an interesting interaction between the RH and LF on the high hat. As the foot moves to release the high hat pedal, the cymbals open briefly (indicated in the RH part by an open note head), then close. The interplay of hand and foot produce a varied timbre which adds a new dimension to the pattern as a whole. By practicing the RH and LF together without the other two parts, you can master that aspect of the exercise first before adding the LH and RF. When the entire pattern is within your command, try accompanying a record with it. Be sure, of course, that the music you choose is in the rock style and in simple duple time. At first it might be best to pick a piece of music that moves in a somewhat slow tempo. Remember, speed is a function of practice and time.

CHAPTER TWENTY:

THE VOICE

Singing is the one musical act in which the performer himself is the instrument. For that reason alone it is probably the most delicate performance medium. As we have seen the human voice divides itself into approximately 8 ranges (soprano 1, soprano 2, alto 1, alto 2, tenor 1, tenor 2, baritone, and bass - going from highest to lowest). The first step in learning to sing is discovering which range is most natural for you.

This can be accomplished by singing through several scales with the aid of a piano. For women it is best to begin with middle C, matching the pitches downward and upward from C through the C major scale. Men can begin on the G below middle C and match pitches through the G major scale. With both sexes the easiest syllable for this initial evaluation is "lu." The "oo" sound naturally rounds the mouth, helps to lower the tongue, relax the soft palate, and eliminate the muscle tension which produces a poor tone.

For some people matching pitches may be difficult. Sometimes we call such people "tone deaf" and assume that they can't sing. Unless there is some physical or mental abnormality, however, that assumption is wrong. Singing, like talking, is a learned response which depends upon exposure to the sound, development of the musculature which produces it, and practice imitating it. With proper instruction and an atmosphere of encouragement, matching difficulties rarely persist.

If pitch matching is a problem, try any or all of the following: (1) change the pitch to another part of the range, one more compatible with the muscle development of the singer; (2) remove the singer from the presence of others so that embarrassment or peer pressure does not adversely affect tone production; (3) have the singer play the piano as he sings so that the vibrations of the piano can be felt (a technique used often in teaching the deaf); (4) have the singer match a voice rather than a piano, with his hands on the larynx of the person whose pitch he is trying to imitate; (5) have the singer practice with a flutophone (a children's instrument shaped like a trumpet but with a small piano keyboard instead of trumpet valves). By producing flutophone pitches which vibrate and resonate in the bone structure of the singer's head, the matching process is often made easier.

In testing out your range, you may notice a place near the upper notes where your voice seems to crack or lose control. This area is called the "break," and it occurs because at that point your body is shifting its place of resonance from thoracic cavity to nasal cavity. Just as a guitar body resonates sound through the open hole beneath the strings into the hollow area below, the human body resonates sound in the "open spaces" where our breath vibrates within us. Unlike the guitar, however, which has only one large resonating chamber, we have two areas of resonance, the chest and the head. Lower tones tend to resonate in the chest, higher ones in the head. The pitches which lie on the border between the two areas constitute the "vocal break." Your break may be mild or severe, high or low in relation to other singers. Those with severe breaks must work harder at controlling the area. Women with higher breaks are usually sopranos as opposed to altos. Men with higher breaks are usually tenors rather than basses.

As you test your range, use the same principles of diaphragmatic breathing, good posture, and muscle relaxation you learned in playing the tonette. The "lu" syllable will help you do this. It will also allow you to move more easily across your break and explore the pitches in your "head tone" area. Above all remember that tension is the enemy of good singing. The power you need should be generated by the diaphragm. The more relaxed the muscles of the throat, neck, soft palate, and shoulder line, the better the voice will sound. The voice, when everything is said and done, is not something you sing with, but something you sing through. Like any set of muscles, the singing mechanism will eventually strengthen and improve with proper use, and here the word "proper" means, above all else, without strain.

The "lu" sound is hardly the only one available to you. There are dozens of singing sounds comprised of consonances and vowels. Of the two, it is the vowels which sustain the singing tone while the consonants do the job of shaping and defining words.

Vowels can occur as single sounds or in combinations called dipthongs, as the chart below shows.

Single Vowel Sounds

1) oo (as in "zoo")
2) ah (as in "far")
3) uh (as in "run")
4) aw (as in "paw")
5) ee (as in "tree")
6) eh (as in "get")
7) ih (as in "with")
8) a (as in "cat")

Dipthongs

1) ah + ee = i (as in "try")
2) ah + oo = ow (as in "cow")
3) uh + oo = oh (as in "go")
4) aw + ee = oy (as in "boy")
5) eh + ee = a (as in "day")

Consonants also occur in two varieties, those on which pitches may be sustained (voiced consonants) and those which cut off the flow of air (unvoiced consonants). The list below illustrates.

Voiced consonants: L, M, N, R, V, Z
Unvoiced consonants: B, C, D, F, G, H, J, K, P, Q (QU), S, T, W, X

"S" can be sustained as a sound without a definite pitch;
"Y" is a vowel, often pronounced as a dipthong (ee + uh).

Like an athlete before a game, singers should warm up before they sing. Warm-ups serve both to prepare the musculature and to strengthen it. There are dozens of warm-up exercises used routinely by soloists and choruses. The one below is fairly common. It should start low in the range and progress upward by half steps until all the range is worked. With each half step the syllable is changed so that the voice loosens up, and has a chance to use various sounds. The syllables "may - mee - mah - moh - moo" are the most typical because they utilize most of the important vowel sounds.

XX The voice

Other warm-ups may include singing up and down full 8-note scales on various syllables ("lu" is a good one to start with) or singing through various chords ("ah" is a good syllable here because it opens the throat). (See below.)

As with the first exercise, these last two should begin low in the range and proceed upward by half steps.

The quality of your voice as you warm up and then sing is a matter somewhat apart from the actual exercises you do. If you sound breathy or rasping, if your tone is nasal or your volume constricted, the warm-ups themselves may not remedy the problem. Developing good tone quality is a longer and more complex study than the limitations of this introduction to singing permit. Besides the few problems mentioned above there are many more, each with a specific cause and set of remedies. For our purposes here, we can generalize a list of guidelines which will minimize poor quality and maximize good quality.

1. Breathe diaphragmatically.
2. Make sure your posture is good.
3. Relax the throat musculature as much as possible.
4. Keep the soft palate (the area at the rear and top of the mouth) gently arched to help open the throat.
5. Keep the tongue relaxed and low so that it doesn't ride up in the back of the mouth, thereby blocking the sound. (The position of the tongue and soft palate on a hum or "ah" or "oo" will help tone quality.)
6. Don't breathe in or sing out through the nose.

These principles will aid the development of a rounded tone; one which is not harsh or grating; one which is not muffled or constricted; one in which natural overtones and a natural vibrato will add maturity, warmth, and depth.

BREATHING MECHANISM

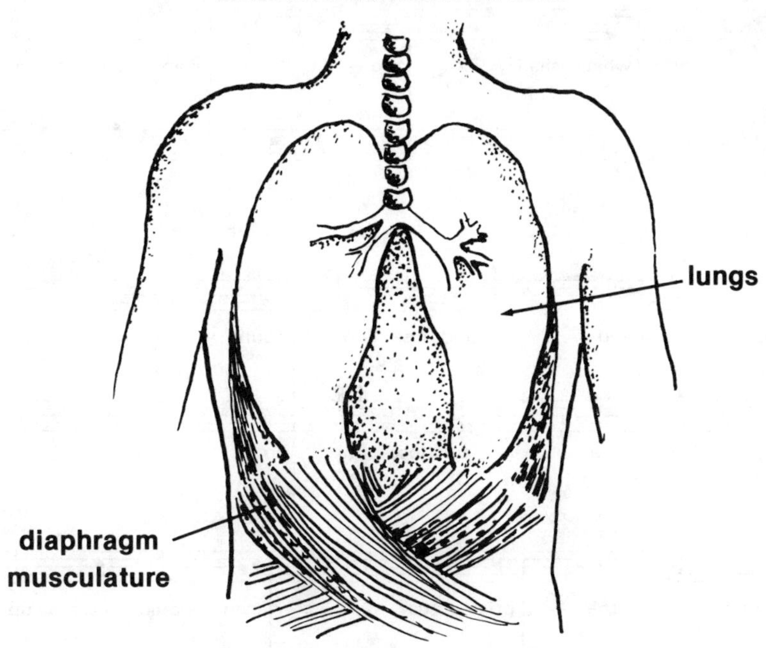

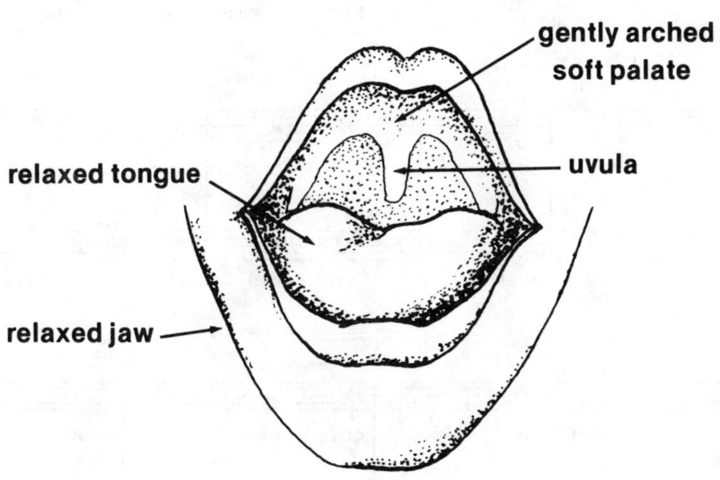

proper mouth position

Having worked a bit with your teacher on vocal technique, try the music below as a chorus. It is an excerpt of a setting of the words of Christ taken from the Testament according to Mark (8:36).

XX *The voice*

Slowly
mp
S A
T B
For what shall it pro - fit a man that he shall
For what shall it

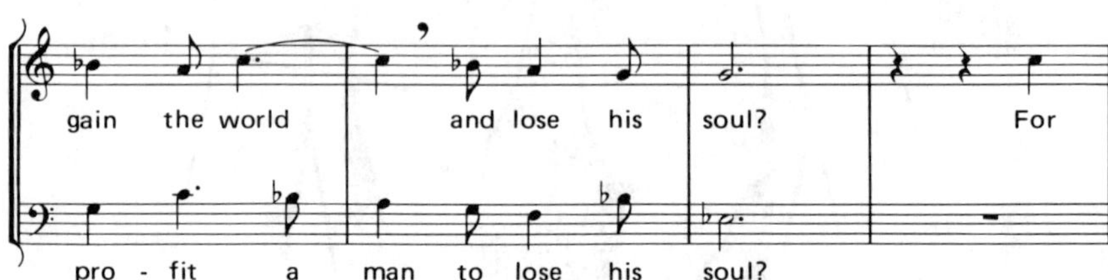

gain the world and lose his soul? For
pro - fit a man to lose his soul?

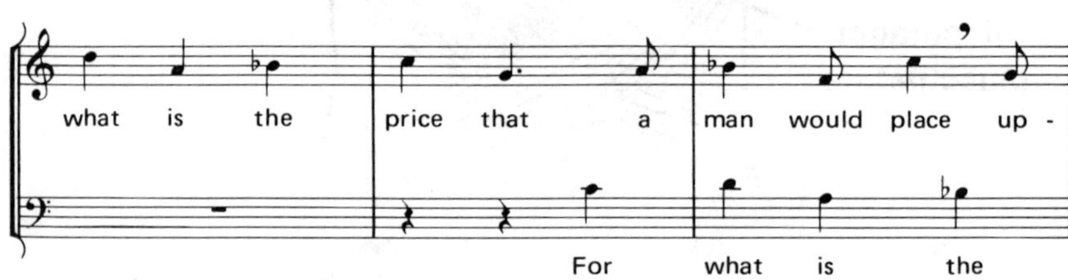

what is the price that a man would place up -
For what is the

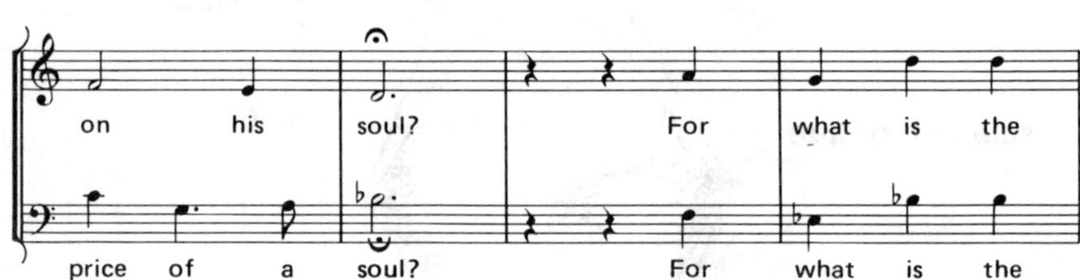

on his soul? For what is the
price of a soul? For what is the

price, what is the price of a soul?
price, what is the price of a soul?

You will probably need help learning the rhythm, and at first you may need a piano to stay on pitch. After a little rehearsal, however, you may have gotten enough into your system to sing without accompaniment (or "a cappella," as is called). That should provide a real sense of accomplishment.

CHAPTER TWENTY-ONE:

PLAYING THE PIANO

The piano is probably the most frequently encountered instrument of our times and, for the purposes of music education, the most important because it permits the convenient visualization of all harmonic and contrapuntal techniques. Invented in the early 1700's by an Italian named Christofori and refined considerably over the centuries, the modern piano is a steel and wood-framed keyboard instrument with 88 keys for the hands and 3 pedals used by the feet.

The piano keyboard ranges a little more than 7 octaves (its lowest note is A, its highest C) in the recurrent pattern below.

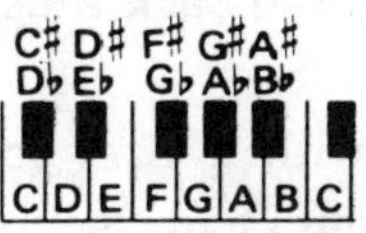

The note C is always to the lower left of the group of 2 black keys. F is to the lower left of the group of 3.

The three pedals of a piano produce a variety of effects. The pedal at the right is called the damper pedal. When depressed it moves the felt dampers inside the piano away from the strings, allowing the strings to vibrate and sustain the sound. The damper pedal is activated by the right foot. The left foot uses the so-called una chorda or "soft" pedal. When depressed this pedal shifts the entire keyboard and hammer mechanism slightly so that when the hammers strike the strings they are forced to produce a softer dynamic level. The una chorda pedal thus expands the dynamic range of the piano. The middle pedal, most often used by the left foot, is called the sostenuto pedal. It does what the damper pedal does (sustain sounds) but only for certain notes (usually low notes) while other notes are free to play normally and die away quickly.

In playing the piano the first thing you must do is position yourself correctly. Unlike the guitar or tonette, the piano takes up a good deal of space. Unless you address it properly, you will not be able to command that space. To begin with, the center of your body should be aligned with the center of the keyboard. You can use as a guide the alignment of your nose with middle C (the C directly in the middle of the keyboard). Next you must make sure that you are the proper height and distance from the keyboard. Adjustable piano seats are particularly useful here. If you don't have one, you will need a variety of chairs for the purpose.

Your sitting height should be such that when you hold your arms at a gentle right angle, your wrists are level with the keyboard rather than uncomfortably raised or lowered. This will allow your fingers to work without strain. Your distance from the keyboard should be such that your arms form about a 100° angle at the elbow. For a person of average height this usually means that the waist is a foot or so away from the piano. Next your feet should be positioned so that the right heel rests on the floor with the right toe on the damper pedal (without depressing it). The left foot is generally placed back toward the base of the chair and rested on the toes with heel raised. This foot position allows for leverage from side to side and forward to back which is needed to cover the large span of the keyboard.

Finally, you should sit with a firm (but not rigid) posture about halfway along the seat of your chair. Sitting all the way back in the seat restricts side to side movement. Sitting too far forward may cause you to lose your balance.

The positions described above are of course very general. Each person makes little adjustments of his own to fit individual needs, just as batters in a baseball game vary their stances and swings one from the other. The idea is to maximize comfort, movement, and balance.

Once the body is positioned correctly, it is time to position the hands on the keyboard. Most teachers agree that the hands should be cupped in a gentle "C" shape so that the fingers are curved and the palm elevated away from the keys. This allows the tips of the fingers to strike the keys. Playing with flat fingers restricts movement and contributes to many inaccuracies as the music unfolds.

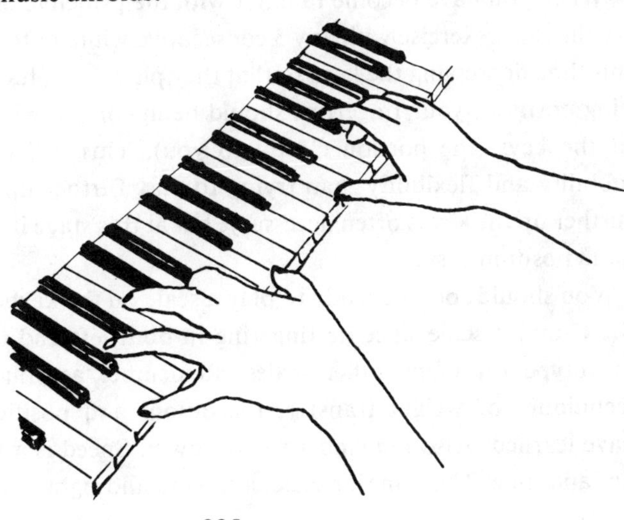

Your fingers should be kept relaxed except for the moment when they make contact with the key. Then, of course, they must be supported. In playing with a relaxed hand, it should be understood that power is generated by the arms, shoulders, and back of the pianist in most cases. Only rarely do the wrists and fingers themselves take on the responsibility of generating power. When the fingers are asked to do this to any degree, they will tense, become less fluid, and produce an awkward, clumsy style of playing.

To allow for fingers to tense and relax while the wrist, arm, and shoulder support the pianist's weight is by no means an easy thing. It requires practice and the mastery of a technique known as weight transfer. Here the weight of the hand and arm is shifted from one finger to the next as each strikes a note. This allows the non-working fingers to relax and ultimately allows the student to develop great flexibility, speed, and strength. To begin learning the principle of weight transfer, try placing your hand on a table, positioning it as if the table were a piano keyboard. Now support the weight of your arm on one finger while the others are relaxed. (This is not easy to do. You may have to work at it awhile.) Next, shift your weight to the next finger, relaxing the one you just left. Don't pick up your fingers or strike the table. Just shift the weight. Keep doing this until you have experienced the weight transfer on all five fingers of each hand. If you get tired, stop, rest, then continue. Discomfort is inevitable when developing muscle strength, but it need not be maximized and indeed may be a sign that your technique is wrong.

When you have become familiar with the principle of weight transfer, try the same exercise with any 5 consecutive white notes of the keyboard, this time depressing the keys so that they play the notes. In a good beginning position, your fingertips should be in contact with the end portion of the keys (the portion closest to you). This will allow you greater mobility and flexibility than trying to play further up the key. Playing further up the key is often necessary, but at this stage it is best to keep the hand position easy.

You should soon be ready to play a scale on the keyboard. We will use the C major scale since its fingering in both left and right hands is the prototype for many other scales. Remember as you play to use the techniques of weight transfer, relaxation, and positioning which you have learned. Also remember to go slowly. Speed is a function of practice and time. The C major scale, left hand and right, appears below.

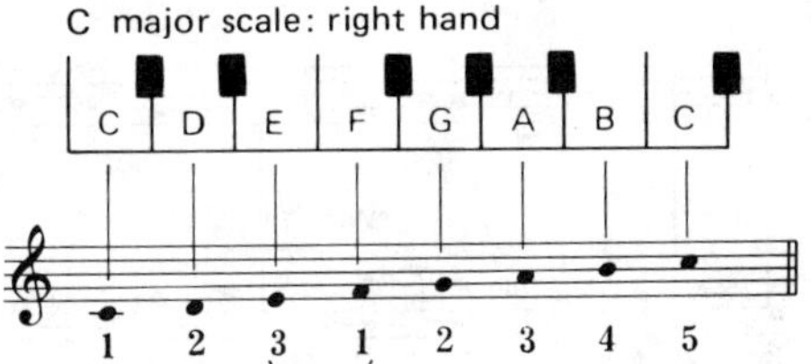

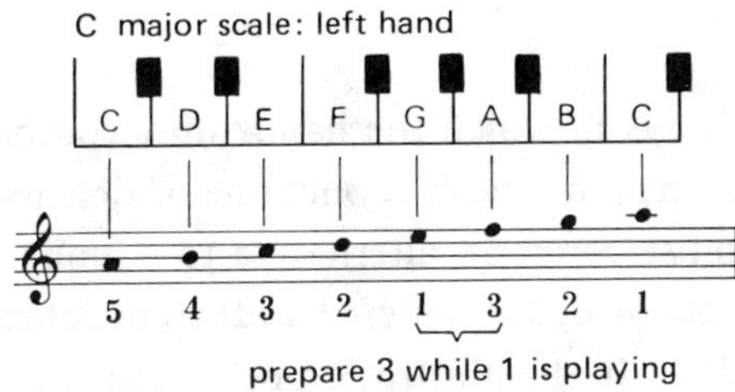

Practice the scales upward and downward, hands separately at first. When you have developed some smoothness, put the hands together at a slow, even, steady rate of speed. This fingering will work not only for C major but for D, E, G, and A major as well. Using it for scales other than C major will give you some experience with the black keys. When your hands have acquired some fluidity, you can try the duet used earlier for the tonette. Practice it slowly, hands separately first, then with hands together. The fingering for each hand is suggested for you. It has been worked out so that there is a minimum of "position switching" in both hands.

There are many ways in which the hands may combine pianistically. The single line counterpoint above is only one of dozens upon dozens of possibilities. The most common alternative to equally voiced counterpoint is for one hand (usually the left hand) to accompany the melody with a series of chords. In the illustration below, the melody remains the same in the right hand while the left fills in the sound with block chords. Again, fingerings are suggested for each of the hands.

Further Reading.

Musical instruments through the ages. Anthony Baines, ed. (Baltimore, Md.: Penguin, 1973). This book is a compilation of some of the most noted writing on instruments and their development through the ages. Its bibliography is extensive should more reading be required.

The **Harvard Dictionary of Music** will again provide you with articles on "electronic instruments" and "electronic music," topics which are not well covered by the Baines anthology above. Article bibliographies suggest further reading.

Finally, the approach to performance in Part IV of this text is meant to be cursory. There are many beginning methods for voice, recorder, drums, guitar, and piano on the market. These and private instruction will continue any interested student on the performance path. Your teacher or local music store can assist you in getting further instruction.

PART V

MUSIC IN SOCIETY

CHAPTER TWENTY-TWO:

THE MANY FACES OF MUSIC

A General View

The impact of music on today's society is considerably more extensive than one may at first imagine. There are, of course, the pop singers, orchestra conductors, and music teachers who come immediately to mind. However, there are also music therapists who work in medicine, theatrical lawyers who service the entertainment industries, recording engineers, accoustical architects, engravers, printers, manufacturers, producers, and secretaries - all of whom make their livelihoods because of music. Music is an integral part of many avenues of modern life.

In this final unit we will take a brief look at the way in which music interfaces with the rest of society so that you can see its full scope, and if you have a mind to do so, plan for your own personal role in the musical picture. We will start our investigation by looking at the general fields in which music is involved, and we will end it by following a piece of music through one particular field in some detail.

There are several areas in which music services modern society and offers a wide variety of career opportunities. These areas include: (1) education, (2) the world of the composer, (3) the world of performance, (4) the role of the conductor or musical director, (5) music in the mass media (including the recording and publishing industries), (6) instrument manufacture and repair, (7) the world of management and law, (8) music in the health field, and (9) music in the field of general science (including architecture, civic engineering, and aerospace technology).

Music and Education

The world of music education is vast and affords many opportunities on many levels. Teachers may specialize in academic classroom subjects, in performance, conducting, or composition. They may serve any age group from elementary school children to adults. They may work in schools, museums, or private studios. They may teach, supervise or administrate programs. Often in music education, one person wears many hats.

Classroom Subjects and Performance. Perhaps the broadest division one can make in music education is between the person who teaches a classroom subject and one who teaches a performance skill. The history of music, the theory of how it is put together, the art of composing or conducting it, the cataloging and research of it, the marketing and manufacturing of it - these are some of the broad areas of classroom music study. One may spend many years and earn many degrees becoming expert in these areas. For example, the college professor who teaches music history and music appreciation, or who supervises music research will probably have taken ten years to earn the graduate credentials for his job.

In opposition to the academic side of music is the performance side. Here music educators teach the art of making music. By and large these teachers specialize in a single area - piano or voice, clarinet or violin. Sometimes a gifted teacher will be able to teach all the brasses or all the strings. Academic degrees are certainly common among teachers of performance, but more important are the teachers' own skills as performers. In this area there is no substitute for firsthand knowledge.

Ages and Grade Levels. Usually, teachers specialize in a particular age in addition to a particular area. Generally, the ages of students coincide with the schools they attend: elementary, junior high, senior high, college, and graduate school. Elementary school teachers are often jacks-of-all-trades in music. They may teach a little voice, a little instrumental work, a little theoretical or historical material. On the secondary school level, specialization is more common. A high school music teacher will probably teach band alone or chorus alone, perhaps with a classroom assignment or two thrown in. On the college and graduate school level, specialization becomes the rule. One is hired specifically as a theory professor, or music historian, or an expert in piano performance. The older the age of the pupil, the more demanding the nature of the material and - as a rule - the more sophisticated the skills of the teacher.

Institutions and Private Studios. Most music educators are employed by an institution of learning - a school system or college. However, there are many teachers, especially performance teachers, who operate their own studios, usually right in their own homes. These teachers build up a private clientele, set their own rates of pay, select their own hours, and in every sense function as independent agents. By comparison, the institutional teacher is salaried and must conform to the various financial and educational idiosyncracies of his place of employment. Some teachers are able to function in both worlds, spending some time in the institutional setting and some in the private studio.

Supervisory Roles. Not in the private studio, of course, but in the institutional setting where there are apt to be many teachers and many music programs, it is necessary to have department chairpersons who supervise, administrate, and coordinate activities. These educators frequently teach, but the preponderance of their time is administrative. The music supervisor is not only a trained musician but a trained administrator as well. His creativity must extend beyond the making of music to the development of new programs, the wise use of personnel, and the search for the funding which will continue to expand his department.

Unusual Educational Roles. Though not actually teachers in the normal sense, there are some people whose work in music is so closely allied with education, it is convenient to mention them here. There is the music librarian who may work in a school, municipal, or government library and who is especially trained in the art of musical categorization and research. There is the museum curator who has received advanced degrees in musical iconography (the study of music through pictures) and organology (the study of music through implements) and who may acquire rare and valuable musical treasures, verify their authenticity, and instruct the public about them. Finally, there is the community or government expert. He may do things like planning cultural activities, reviewing research grant applications, working in agencies like the National Endowment for the Arts or working for various local, state, and federal Departments of Education. Many of these people operate in a context larger than the single classroom, studio or school. Some of them are in charge of directing policies with regard to the arts which impact on entire regions - even nations - by funding various cultural activities and establishing broad cultural patterns.

The World of the Composer

A composer is a person who creates new music either from material entirely his own or from some combination of original and previously conceived work (as in a composition which might use an old melody or

Gregorian chant as its musical basis). The twentieth century composer, as we have seen from our unit on history, may write in any or all of several styles and genres. The most common kinds of composition today are "serious" music, "popular" music, music for education, music for the electronic media, and music for the world of commercial marketing. Again, it is not unusual to find a single person wearing many compositional hats.

"Serious" Composition. The world of the concert hall is not as much in demand today as it once was, and when it is, public tastes generally run counter to the atonality, electronicism, seriality, and computerization of the serious 20th century composer. Beethoven is much more popular to the season ticket subscriber than Milton Babbitt. This has left the modern serious composer with a narrow audience and relegated much of his activity to academic, esoteric, or avant-garde environments.

"Pop" Composition. "Popular" music is one of the most demanded and lucrative forms of composition because its sales potential is enormous. It includes music for mass media and musical theatre; it serves locations from car radio to nightclub to dentist's office; it reaches into every crevice of modern life. The pop music composer has the opportunity to achieve great fame and fortune as well as high artistic merit. He may write for the stage, for a given singer, for a band, or for any medium which utilizes his brand of music. Many pop composers are trained musicians, but training is not a prerequisite in this field. Just as many pop composers are self-taught musicians who have picked up musical skills from the practical experience of the streets. The diversity of competence, craftsmanship, and education among pop composers is as extensive as the musical diversity of the 20th century.

Educational Composition. There is nothing new about educational composition. Bach wrote many works for children who grew up learning the art of music - and so did Beethoven, Schumann, Bartok and others. However, since the end of World War II, music education has grown enormously. It is now a huge business, and many composers specialize in writing books and music for the developing student. In working for this market, the educational composer must be at once a skilled craftsman and a knowledgeable teacher. That is not a combination frequently encountered, and music publishers are forever on the lookout for musicians who embody both qualities. Once considered more trivial than other forms of composition, educational works have steadily elevated the level of their art so that now many of them are recognized as compositions of the highest order. There seems little doubt that as education increases in importance and scope, this field is destined to grow rapidly.

Composition for Mass Media. The value of music as a background for film and television cannot be underestimated, and the composer who writes for these media is greatly in demand and very highly paid. In fact, media composers have included some of the greatest names of our time: Prokofiev, Copland, Bernstein, Thomson, Vaughn-Williams, Satie, to name just a few. The art of media composition requires the precise ability to capture moods and express emotions in exact calculations of time (often measured to the tenth of a second). Of great interest is the fact that media music often contains the dissonances and oddities rejected by the concert hall. A serial composition by Webern played in the abstract environment of the symphony auditorium may leave the audience cold and unsatisfied. However, the same music set as the background to a science fiction movie may not only find acceptance from the viewing audience but may be fundamental to the emotional impact of the celluloid product. The media composer is thus a finely trained craftsman who has mastered the additional requirements of the film and electronic worlds of the 20th century.

Commercial Composing. The marketing of products on radio and television many times requires music which has become known as the commercial "jingle." Here, in a 30 or 60 second time frame, the composer must create a mood, synchronize with video material, establish a relationship between product and music, and try to do it in such a way that the music instantly recalls product identification in the mind of the consumer. Most commercial jingles are at best only relatively successful, but some have been so skillfully crafted that they have become miniature classics of the media, not only selling the products for which they were written, but outliving them through the years. The commercial composer may free-lance out of his own studio, or may be on the staff of an advertising agency. His income is determined not only by the initial pay he receives but also by the amount his jingle is played. The residual payments for replays may, in a successful case, add up to thousands upon thousands of dollars. Commercial music can produce wealthy men.

Arranging. The composer creates original material. The arranger adapts the material created by others for his own special purposes. If a pop singer records a song, the marketplace may demand an instrumental version of that song with no words or voice. An instrumental arranger will convert the original material for the purpose. Similarly, arrangers may write for specific media, for educational consumption, or for specific people. One singer may prefer his or her own arrangement of a pre-existing work; one band or orchestra may wish to project a certain style of performance which only a special arrangement can provide.

Often arrangers are among the most skilled and creative musical craftsmen. Their work extends the beauty of the original material many times over. One has but to listen to the arrangements of people like Peter Matz, Dave Grusin, or George Martin to appreciate how gifted they are. In the case of educational arrangers, music previously unperformable by youngsters is made accessible to them, thereby exposing them to a cultural richness not otherwise available and giving them the joys and benefits of artistic expression.

Even though the arranger draws upon the material of others, he can be a valuable and brilliant creative force in his own right, and when he applies his powers to the popular and educational world, he can also be handsomely paid. No one becomes an arranger without first becoming a thoroughly trained and skilled musician. Arranging is thus one of the most precise and rewarding of modern musical careers.

The World of the Performer

There can be no music without people to make it, and being a performer requires years of training; an inborn talent; and usually great quantities of dedication, sacrifice, and luck. Even in the pop field where performance skills are often the least honed, very few musicians carve out careers of any great longevity. However, if talent and training, luck and perseverance all somehow combine, then performance can be nectar for the soul and the springboard for wealth, fame, power, and adulation. Without belaboring the obvious, below is a brief listing of the fields and genres in which musical performance may occur.

"Serious" and "Pop." It is not often that a performer will have a successful career in both popular and serious music. He will generally choose one world and specialize in one skill. A "classical" musician, for example, will play the oboe in a symphony orchestra; a "pop" musician will play tenor sax in a jazz band. Rarely will you find a musician who is expert in more than one thing. The skills needed to master a second instrument or second style are usually too great. So is the competition for jobs.

Having said that, however, it is not totally unheard of for performers to "double in brass," especially in the less musically sophisticated world of the "rock" musician where guitarists or pianists can also be lead singers. Occasionally, and this is extremely rare, you might find a great classical talent with a flair for the pop world. Pianist/conductor Andre Previn comes to mind, for example, as do several lesser known performers who will play a symphony concert on Saturday night and record a pop style television commercial Monday morning.

Soloist and Ensemblist. A performer may choose a career in which he performs alone or one in which he is a member of a larger group. Frequently, the performer does both. The best example of a solo performer, perhaps, is the concert pianist. The piano is an instrument capable of standing on its own, and it has a literature and history which supply enough material to last any soloist several lifetimes. For an oboist, a drummer, or a singer, solo work is less in demand. The oboist needs an orchestra, the drummer a band, the singer at least an accompanist in order to perform. The most usual ensembles are the orchestra, band, chorus, or small consort (such as the string quartet from the classical world or the jazz group from the pop world). Again, the performers who inhabit these groups may often wear many hats. The violinist in a symphony orchestra may well become the featured soloist in a recital or one of a smaller number of players in a chamber group. He may also teach or compose or conduct to augment his income and round out his life. Such is the nature of musical performance careers.

Performing Environments. The musician may use his performance skills in a wide variety of places either as a soloist or an ensemblist. The concert hall comes immediately to mind, but it is hardly the only potential location. Television, the film media, the record industry, the commercial studio, the nightclub, opera, musical theatre, church, school, and community group all require performers either on an intermittent or constant basis. In a few instances, performers can carve out a career by staying in one performing environment. The opera singer, for example, may never venture beyond the stage. However, in most cases, performers go where the work is, and that usually means a wide variety of jobs and environments. Some performers, in fact, relish the variety. In contrast to the many people who report to the same office at the same time to do the same job year after year, most performers are able to experience change and freshness as a regular part of their existence.

The Conductor or Director

For each of the ensembles mentioned above, in each separate environment, there is a conductor or musical director to keep the group together, make final creative or interpretive decisions, select concert material, choose performance personnel, and generally lead the group. It is hard to imagine how a large group could survive without a conductor, if for nothing else than to preserve rhythmic cohesion. If you doubt this, try asking an average class of students to clap after ten seconds have gone by. You will probably hear as many sounds as there are people in the class. Imagine how much more demanding it is for an orchestra or chorus of 50, 60, 70 or more people to stay together measure after measure, tempo change after tempo change, mood after mood.

But keeping time is only one of the conductor's duties. He must be the chief decision-maker for all musical matters, and many non-musical ones as well. He must know every note of every performer's part as well as the strengths and weaknesses of the people themselves. His is a constant act of juggling creative, administrative, and at times financial variables, some of which he has been trained to do, some of which he must intuit. Of all the people in the performing world, the conductor usually receives the most rigorous training. Only the cream of the musical crop succeeds as a musical director. Good ones are hard to find. Great ones are rarities in every generation.

Music in the Mass Media

The electronics revolution of the 20th century has created whole industries in which music is prominent, and dozens upon dozens of careers in each industry. Television, radio, motion pictures, the print media, and the electronics industry itself require experts who fuse musical skills with other talents - people besides the composers, arrangers, performers, and conductors who merely supply and perform the music. Below we shall briefly describe the more important mass media functions.

Media Music Editor. For every movie, television program, video commercial, and radio commercial there must be a skilled editor who takes the recorded product of composer or arranger and synchronizes it to voice and/or action. That is the job of the music editor.

Disc Jockey or Program Host. For the person who fuses a love of music with a career in communications, the program host acts a a middleman between artist and audience. Whether moderating opera broadcasts or spinning top-ten pop hits, this line of work can be lucrative as well as spiritually rewarding.

Station Program Personnel. Behind the host are a number of people who work to bring broadcast music to the listener. Station programmers decide what is to be played. Engineers of all kinds run the studio equipment, while other electronics experts service and maintain it. Producers and directors guide the programs from inception to execution, coordinating all phases of it. Writers may create various scripts for the programs. Sales staffs sell and market air time to sponsors who are interested in exposing their products to the audience through the program's advertisements. Batteries of secretaries and industry executives, equipment craftsmen and service personnel also work hidden from the microphone and camera to bring media music to the public at large. In all, stations across the world employ hundreds of thousands of workers - many of them simply to disseminate the art of music.

Critic. As the cost of records and concerts rise, as the quantity of musical events increases, it has become ever more necessary for people to rely on a critic to guide them in the purchase of the musical product. What recording is better? To what concert should I go? Which musical or opera is worth my time and money? The critic who addresses these questions should be a trained musician skilled also in the craft of journalism and endowed with integrity and a sense of wanting to educate the public. Unfortunately, these characteristics are all too rare, a sad but true reality of modern music.

Critics are people who control the careers of many artists. Their opinions influence the expenditure of billions. It is not comforting to know that many critics are ignorant of the craft they criticize and untrained to do what they do. Recently, a critic for one of the national networks said in an interview that training for his job was really not necessary. "It's all personal opinion," he expounded. Can you imagine the disasters which would occur if critics in the field of science, medicine, engineering, psychology, or space technology had the same attitude? The critic *must* be able to evaluate more than his own subjective reactions. By being expert in the craft of music, he can perform a much needed function. To the extent he is deficient, the audience suffers both spiritually and financially.

The Record Industry. It is impossible here to give a detailed description of how a record is made. That would probably take a book in itself. But we can go through the general stages of record making and see the key people involved. The record starts in a recording studio where performers, engineers, producers, and supporting staff combine to set the musical product down on tape. Generally, a professional quality tape will have many channels or tracks on it, each of which houses a separate phase of the total sound. For example, a chorus with piano accompaniment might use five tracks, one each for sopranos, altos, tenors, basses, and piano. More complex music may use many more tracks, and modern electronic technology is capable of having a track for every separate instrument, every effect.

The next step of the process is to mix all the tracks together for just the right blend, just the right balance. This mixing process involves the same studio personnel and is one of the things which makes a recording so different from a live performance. In the latter, the performers must blend and balance themselves. The conductor, of course, helps. He may cue the sopranos up or the altos down, but he does not have anything approaching the balancing capabilities of a modern electronic studio.

When the final mix is achieved, a master tape is prepared and sent to a record mastering house. Here highly skilled engineers using remarkably precise instruments transfer the sounds of the master tape to a metal record. This record is called a "mother stamper" and from it other stampers are made, each of which is capable of stamping the grooves, electronic impulses, and potential sounds of the mother onto the plastic discs which are commercially available. The process of mastering and manufacturing stampers and then stamping out the commercial copies involves several complex steps and may, in fact, occur in different industrial plants.

But the record is still not done. Labels must be made up and affixed to the record, record jackets must be printed, artwork prepared, record sleeves manufactured, and all of it brought together into the package you see at a record store. These steps require hosts of technicians, artists, and general staff to accomplish, and still the record is not in your hands.

Once manufactured, the recording must be distributed and marketed to the consumer. Countless people - truckers, advertising experts, retail sales personnel, accountants, secretaries - are employed in this final phase of the process. In all, the recording industry requires many tens of thousands of people and accounts for many billions of dollars. It is a major industry worldwide.

The Publishing Industry. At the end of this chapter, we will follow a piece of music as it travels from the composer's pen through the publishing industry to the consumer. For now it is necessary only to mention that music publishing, like the record industry, is an international business involving billions of dollars, hundreds of thousands of workers, and dozens upon dozens of skilled and semi-skilled jobs. It is one of the significant areas in which music interfaces with the rest of society.

Published music is used of course by the professional performer, but it is also a staple of the educational environment and an indispensible part of the world of scholarly research. In fact, the print media in music, art, literature, and science is the way in which mankind transfers his knowledge and history from one generation to generations greatly removed in time and distance. It is impossible to underestimate the value of music publishing. Without it we would never know the mind of a Beethoven or the legacy of a fundamental human expression. The people we shall meet later within the confines of the publishing world do more than earn a weekly salary. They help to maintain the record of man's artistic progress through the ages.

Instruments and Equipment

Before any performer picks up an instrument, someone must design and manufacture it, and during the years of its use, someone must maintain it and repair it when it becomes damaged. The technicians who design the violins and oboes, pianos and guitars; the craftsmen who make them; the stores and salesmen who market them constitute a tremendous industry. To these designers, manufacturers, and distributors we may add the battery of technicians who tune the pianos, restring the violins, fix the broken clarinet keys, or hone the oboe reeds. Often the maintenance and repair people provide several services. The piano tuner, for example, who keeps the instrument in playing shape is generally the one who adds a new part when an old one breaks or wears down.

The union of design, manufacture, and maintenance in a single person or shop is especially true in the new industry of electronic instrumentation. Synthesizers, music computers, electric keyboards, and all the accoutrements they require are often produced and maintained by the same company - sometimes by the same craftsman. Frequently, these men are also experts at demonstrating the capabilities of the products on which they work.

Ours is not the first time the history of music has witnessed an era of instrumental innovation. The violin makers of Cremona in the early Baroque, the technicians and inventors who masterminded the piano and added valves to the trumpet were all forerunners of the craftsmen at the center of the instrument industry today. As technology increases, it seems certain that this phase of the music world will also grow in both size and complexity.

Management and Law

Because the music industry involves so many people and so many questions about legalities and finances, a whole subsidiary industry has grown up around it. Contractors, managers, lawyers, and performing rights societies form the backbone of this attendant field, and we shall look at each briefly.

Contractors. You are an ad agency executive in charge of the Blooper Soap commercial. The music for it has been written and today you are going to Studio Z to observe the recording session. You are located in a large city with thousands of musicians capable of making the recording. Whom do you choose and how do you do so? Well, you probably don't. You probably are not a musician yourself, so you call a contractor. The contractor is a musician who knows all or most of the experienced professionals you might need. For a fee he will provide your musical crew. He wants good men since his own reputation rides on their performance. If they do a good job, you will hire him again. If not, it could be the beginning of bleak times for him. Contractors are powerful men who control the livelihoods of many of their colleagues. They are generally old-timers who rise through the ranks of the performers to positions which are coveted and lucrative.

Managers and Agents. Many performers find it impossible to keep tabs on the jobs available in an entire industry. Many are so popular that they are flooded with more offers than they could possibly handle. Whether to find work or select from a variety of offers, artists often turn to managers or agents. For a percentage of what their clients earn (usually 10-20%), managers comb the field, sift through the offers, rub elbows with the people who hire, and find the best opportunities. The management industry is large and powerful. Getting the right manager may often be the key to success for an otherwise talented but unemployed musician.

Entertainment Law. Just as lawyers will specialize in criminal justice or constitutional law, trial law, or tax law, they can specialize in the legal dealings which attend the music industry. Drawing up contracts, deciding on the legalities of copyrights and publishing, representing music companies or individuals in the field - these are just some of the things found in the world of entertainment law. The lawyer in this field need not be a trained musician, but familiarity with the art and business worlds is a more and more frequent characteristic of the best entertainment lawyers. Entertainment law is a growing area of specialization which beckons to the person at once interested in music and the legal profession.

Performing Rights Societies. As a composer or performer, you are often entitled to be paid for your labor not only at the initial performance but - if it is a performance on a film or record capable of being replayed - at every subsequent performance. There are agencies which monitor the broadcast and publishing industries. They make sure that the monies due those involved in the dissemination of music to the public are properly paid. The two largest such agencies are ASCAP (the American Society of Composers, Authors, and Publishers) and BMI (Broadcast Music, Inc.). These and other organizations like them earn a fee for seeing to it that any money which a piece of music earns is accurately distributed to its creators and producers according to whatever contractual arrangements have been established.

Music and the Field of Health

Since the days of ancient Greece we have theorized that music is beneficial to the soul. In the 20th century we have also discovered that it is beneficial to the body. Recreation therapy and music therapy, both now common medical practices, employ music in the treatment of disease.

The recreation therapist works with recovering or indigent patients, using various forms of recreation to add purpose and enjoyment to an otherwise limited and often painful existence. Music is a frequent part of the recreation plan. Whether using it as a background for exercises, as part of a doctor-patient performing ensemble, or simply as a listening pastime, physicians have seen improvements with music where there were none before. Recreation therapists are found in many hospitals and nursing homes, in geriatric and child care centers, in military hospitals, and hospitals for the emotionally and mentally disabled. How wonderful, how magical, that through his own genius and the genius of others, a Bach might speak across the centuries on a phonograph machine he never guessed would exist to bring a smile to the face of a sick child or joy to the heart of an old woman.

In music therapy the music has an even more direct bearing on the physiological treatment of the patient. We have found that it can be used to lower blood pressure in hypertensives who cannot or do not respond to medication; we have seen it soothe the violence of autistic children - children who used to be straight-jacketed and kept from destroying themselves with electric cattle prods. So promising has the field of music therapy become that many colleges and universities now offer both undergraduate and graduate degrees in it. If you have a love of music and a fascination with medicine, a career in music therapy might be enormously rewarding.

Music and Sound in General Science

Not really proper to the use of music per se, but certainly part of the interrelationship between music, sound, and science are the fields of accoustical engineering, noise pollution control, ultrasound diagnosis, and space exploration.

Accoustical Engineering. Concert halls, theatres, sound studios, auditorium facilities must all be designed and built by people aware of the scientific properties of sound in general and music in particular. The architects who plan these structures and the engineers who build them need a knowledge of tones and overtones, rhythm and dynamics, reverberation and absorption in order to provide an environment in which music can be conducted successfully to audience or microphone .

Noise Pollution. The effect of sound on the ecology of an environment is a recent study. The loudness of a construction jackhammer, the squeak of a subway train wheel as it rounds a bend, the sonic boom of a jet at a local airport, the decibel level of a rock concert - these are all germane to the civil engineers who are responsible for the safety and sanity of the public. In solving problems of noise pollution, a knowledge of sound and some knowledge of music is fundamental.

Ultrasound Diagnosis and Otorhinolaryngology. Sound is used today to diagnose internal conditions with great accuracy and greater safety than older X-ray procedures. Sound wave patterns aimed at and bounced back from localized body regions can locate tumors, aid in the delivery of babies, and provide valuable knowledge for the surgeon about to operate. Similarly, the treatment of ear disorders, whether they are simple ruptures of the tympanum or complex operations to remove otosclerotic bones, require medical personnel whose tests and treatment depend on the knowledge of sound.

Space Technology. The field of radio astronomy is now being used to observe the heavens and send messages to the depths of the galaxy. The pulsations of stars, sound emissions from the magnetic spheres of planets, and communications between the earth and the satellites launched to travel the interstellar void all depend upon the scientist's knowledge of sound waves. The Voyager spacecraft sent by America to drift beyond the solar system not only depends on sound to communicate with earth, but carries with it a golden record which bears instructions on how to play it, and which contains the sounds and pictures, the art and music of mankind. What a fitting way to travel among the stars, beyond the earth. Perhaps a thousand or a million or a billion years from now, our intergalactic phonograph album will be intercepted and deciphered by a life form searching as we do for meaning and companionship in the universe. And there for the inhabitants of another world to hear will be the sound of our dogs barking, our children laughing, our brooks running through the forest, and our music. I wonder what they will think of the Beethoven and Bach and folk songs and Beatle tunes we have sent them. I wonder if they will understand, if music will be as majestic and magical to them as it has been to us.

A Journey Through the Publishing Industry

Now that we have looked in a general way at the many fields in which music plays a role, let us go through one industry - the music publishing industry - to see in a bit more depth what is needed to bring a piece of music to the marketplace.

Our journey begins far from the publishers' offices in the studio of a composer. Driven by whatever drives the composer, he sits at his desk or piano staring at a blank piece of music paper. Let us assume he is a creature both of necessity and creativity. He may be a teacher or a conductor in addition to being a composer. He may be creating something he needs for a concert as well as fulfilling some artistic urge within. Let's endow him with some characteristics so that we can understand his work and its progress through the industry a bit better. Let's call him a high schools chorus director. He is writing an original composition for the group which will perform it some time during the year. He struggles with it, polishes it here, changes it there, sculpts it until finally it meets his satisfaction. Then he teaches it to his chorus and at last sings it before an audience.

After the concert someone walks up to him and says, "Gee, that thing you wrote for the chorus was really nice. You ought to have it published." The compliment passes into the haze of the evening, but the thought remains in our composer's mind. "There might be a market for it at that," he thinks. "After all, my kids enjoyed doing it. They learned it well enough, so it could work for any chorus of high school calibre or better. And the audience seemed to like it. Why not send it to a publisher?" Convinced of its quality and sure that it will have enough of a market to justify a publisher's time and expense, he decides to send it to a company which might be interested.

Carefully he copies it over. He may even pay a professional copyist to do the job. Many skilled copyists are employed by private artists as well as publishing companies to do this kind of work. When the music is ready, he may photocopy the manuscript (preferring not to send the original). He writes a covering letter to the publisher and sends it off through the mail.

When the work arrives at the publisher's office, it is probably opened by a secretary whose job, among others, is to screen the mail. She herself is not qualified or authorized to make a decision regarding the manuscript, so she sends it on to an editor. The editor is a trained musician, capable not only of seeing the musical merit of a work but also of evaluating the way in which it fits into the musical marketplace. He reads the cover letter and plays through the composition. It has merit, he thinks. Perhaps enough to publish. With thousands upon thousands of schools, each with dozens and dozens of singers, the company might be able to make money from the work. And it is a good work, one which will enhance the general repertoire. The editor knows that not many unsolicited manuscripts are good enough to deserve publication. Perhaps not even one of every hundred he receives. But this one is surely worth a second opinion.

The editor must now turn to others in the company for the final decision on whether or not to publish. A meeting is called with the editor, an educational publications coordinator, a productions coordinator, and a high level executive impowered to make yes-or-no decisions on publication. At the meeting many works are reviewed. Some are accepted, some rejected as the production schedule for the year is worked out. The company budget and its expectation of a return on its investment all point to a worthwhile risk. Yes, our composer's composition will be published.

The focus of attention now shifts to the production department where a production secretary types a letter of acceptance and contract for the composer. According to the contract, the composer will give up ownership of the work to the publisher in exchange for a percentage of whatever the work brings in. The production meeting has already fixed the price of each copy according to the length of the work and an estimate of what it will cost to produce. In this case, let's say the work will sell for one dollar per copy. The royalty to the composer will be 10% of the selling price or 10 cents for every copy sold. The remaining 90 cents will go to pay for the costs of production, distribution, promotion, and accounting. In a typical case the publisher's profit will be about the same as the composer's, around 10 to 15 cents per copy.

The composer receives the letter and contract and with great glee signs on the dotted line. As soon as the signed contract is returned and all is in legal order, the production department swings into action. Back goes the manuscript to the editor, or to an associate editor, who now screens it carefully for any mistakes in notation. Everything must be in proper form before the work can go on to be engraved and printed. Any mistakes not caught here will cost much more to correct later on, and mistakes never caught will become a part of the final printing to be repeated in every performance from publication onward. If the editor has any question, he may contact the composer. "In measure 43, in the alto part, did you want an E♭ there or was that an E♮?" When the editor is satisfied that all is well, the work - now bearing the legal copyright notice of the publisher - goes off to the engraver.

The engraver makes a single print-quality copy from the edited manuscript. He may do this by actually punching out the notes, staves, and symbols onto a copper plate as it has been done for centuries, but in modern times, this is not the usual method. Today a music typewriter or even a computerized music word processor does the basic work with far less time and expense. Once the basics of the notation are set down, a finisher will do the variables of a score by hand, variables which cannot be done by machine. The lengths of slurs or ties, the beams of certain figures are not exact and thus cannot be programmed for even the most sensitive equipment. Even today, there are certain elements of music typography which need the human touch.

When the engraver has completed setting the words and music, he makes a photocopy of his work and returns it to the production editor for proofreading. The editor makes his corrections and sends the photocopy on to the composer who adds any corrections of his own. After the first engraving is fully corrected, the final engraving is done and sent to the publisher.

Now the work goes to the art department so that a cover for it may be designed. Once the artists finish their work, the art and final engraving are sent to the printer. Since this is a choral work, it will probably be done in a process known as photo offset printing. Each page of art and music engraving is photographed and the photo plates then specially treated so that they can be placed onto huge presses which print out the thousands of copies ordered by the publisher. When the printing is done, the pages are properly cut and bound, usually with staples known in the trade as wire stitching. The printing and binding processes seen here are hardly the only ones used in the printing industry. All of the techniques available today from the old linotypes to ink jets to computerized lasers would be the subject of another book. For choral music the photo offset/wire stitch method is still the most common.

The composition once only in the mind of our composer is now arrayed by the thousands in the warehouse of a printer. From here on it is the job of the publisher to get those copies into the marketplace and eventually into the hands of a conductor and choir like the one which first performed the work. This is the primary job of the sales department. Sales personnel will travel through the country contacting the large music distributors in different regions, giving them all the information on the publisher's latest line of material, one item of which is our composition. If the salesmen have a recorded performance of the work, so much the better. Many distributors are not trained musicians and cannot at all envision how a work will sound by looking at a printed copy. A tape or record of a performance can greatly aid sales.

In addition to sending out salesmen, the sales department of the publishing company can also prepare advertisements to be placed in the trade journals which go to music educators and choral directors. Finally, the publisher can organize workshops and clinics which the directors may attend during vacation time. At these workshops, clinicians - known experts in the field - work with the directors to improve their skills, and of course expose them to the new line of music.

Hopefully, the ads and salesmen, workshops and clinics do the job. Orders now start to come in for the new work. They are received by an order department, processed and shipped throughout the country - perhaps throughout the world. Bills for the music are prepared by an accounting department, and when they are paid, according to the contract signed by the composer, the publisher writes out a royalty check for 10% of the total sales of the work.

If it is particularly successful, it will sell out its first printing and then go to the production department where it will be prepared for reprinting. Perhaps an error was not caught on the first run, perhaps the cover is to be changed, perhaps the price on the copy must be raised or lowered. Perhaps there will be no changes at all. Whatever is needed, the reprint department will do the job and send the corrected copy back to the printer for another round. So it will go until other new works arrive for the review of editor and staff.

There is more to the music publishing industry, of course, but we have seen a good bit of it. Think of all the facets of the industry - composer, copyist, general secretary, general editor, education coordinator, production coordinator, executive-in-charge, production secretary, production editor, engraver, finisher, art department personnel, printing and binding personnel, sales staff personnel, distributor, clinician, order department personnel, shipping department personnel, accounting department personnel, reprint department personnel - all employed in the process of making printed music available.

And this is but one of many industries providing a musical product, each of them needing far more than just a performer or a composer. For those of you with skills and interests in music, there is a world of career choices available so that you can fuse those skills with the various applications of music in society. Whether you do this as a career, a hobby, or a consumer, you will become part of a great and long heritage.

A Final Thought

As long as there has been man, there has been music, and there will probably always be the need for man to express himself in this way. It may be that such a need is fundamental to all intelligent life, and that when the Voyager spacecraft we talked of earlier makes contact with other beings, Beethoven will hold as much for them as he holds for us. If this is true, I wonder what their music is like and how much benefit we might derive if we could only hear it.

Further Reading

1. **Music educators journal,** October, 1982, Vol. 69, No. 2. (Reston, Virginia: Music Educators National Conference, 1982) This issue is devoted entirely to music and careers.

2. **Music business handbook and career guide,** 3rd ed. David Baskerville. (Denver, Colorado: The Sherwood Co., 1981)

3. **The business of music,** 4th ed. Sidney Shemel and M. William Karsilovsky. (Lakewood, N.J.: Billboard Books, 1979)

Index